Fred Harsley

Eadwine's Canterbury Psalter

Fred Harsley

Eadwine's Canterbury Psalter

ISBN/EAN: 9783337324827

Printed in Europe, USA, Canada, Australia, Japan

Cover: Foto ©Andreas Hilbeck / pixelio.de

More available books at **www.hansebooks.com**

Eadwine's Canterbury Psalter,

EDITED,

WITH INTRODUCTION AND NOTES,

FROM

THE MANUSCRIPT IN TRINITY COLLEGE, CAMBRIDGE,

BY

FRED HARSLEY, M.A.

Langton Fellow of The Owens College, Victoria University, Manchester.

PART II.

TEXT AND NOTES.

LONDON:

PUBLISHED FOR THE EARLY ENGLISH TEXT SOCIETY

BY N. TRÜBNER AND CO., 57 AND 59 LUDGATE HILL.

M DCCC LXXXIX.

TEMPORARY NOTICE.

An edition of 'Eadwine's Canterbury Psalter' (the name by which the Manuscript is popularly called in Cambridge) was undertaken about eighteen years ago by Dr. W. Aldis Wright when Librarian of Trinity College; but, through pressure of other literary work and increasing College duties, he was obliged, after having copied the English gloss, to put the work on one side for an indefinite period. Calling upon him last summer, he kindly offered to give me his copy as soon as I found an opportunity of editing. For this copy, for the loan of necessary books, and for other help given during the progress of the work, I owe him my grateful acknowledgments.

Dr. Wright's copy was again carefully collated with the Manuscript and the Latin text added before going to press. The Manuscript was a second time gone through for the erasures, which caused considerable difficulty: and for the footnotes in which these are given (as for the text too, in its present form) I am alone responsible. Finally the proofsheets were collated with the Manuscript to avoid any misreadings which might have been left in the copy; but my stay in Cambridge being a limited one, I only found time to correct the English, the final revision of the Latin being generously undertaken by Mr. James G. Frazer, Fellow of the College. For this timely aid I take this opportunity of expressing my great obligations. Prof. A. S. Napier and Prof. T. Northcote Toller were also kind enough to look at certain peculiar forms which occur in the text, and to the Librarians of Trinity College, especially to Mr. White, thanks are due for the ready way in which they placed the Manuscript at my disposal.

But my warmest thanks must be given to Prof. Skeat for his friendly and frequent assistance. Whenever I was in a difficulty it was always taken to him, and from the kindly way in which he explained my difficulties by reference to similar difficulties he had met with in his own work, I was not only always put on the right track, but learnt much besides.

At the moment of writing it is uncertain whether the 'Canticles' which are found at the end of the Manuscript will be ready for publication with the Psalter; but if not, they will be sent out a little later to be bound up with the present text.

I had intended writing a longer Preface with a full description of the Manuscript, etc., but finding all that would have to be repeated in my 'Introduction on the Lautlehre, Dialect, Date,' etc. (in preparation as Göttingen Inaugral Dissertation), it has, for the present, been left. The 'Introduction' will be published as Part I. With it too a full list of the Latin variants will be given.

F. HARSLEY.

BERLIN UNIVERSITY,
Christmas, 1888.

1.

Æði se were þe ne eode on ðere rede ꝉ þælhte arleasre
1. *Beatus vir qui non abiit in consilio impiorum*

7 on þan wege of þan sunfullan ne stod 7 on þan setele
et in via peccatorum non stetit et in cathedra

of þan quulmere ne set ac on æ of þan lauorde wes
pestilentiae non sedit 2. *Sed in lege domini fuit*

willa his 7 on æ his sceal smægan ꝉ þencean bi deige 7
voluntas eius et in lege eius meditabitur die ac

bi nihte 7 sceal beon al swea trecw þet is geset
nocte 3. *Et erit tanquam lignum quod plantatum est*

bi ða rynas of þa wæteras þet his wæstm ꝉ blæd
secus decursus aquarum Quod fructum suum

sceal giuan on his timan 7 his læf ne sceal tofallan 7
dabit in tempore suo et folium eius non decidet et

alle þa þing þa hit æure doth beoð sundfullede Na swa
omnia quaecunque fecerit prosperabuntur 4. *Non sic*

arleasa na swa ah swa þet dust þet se wind aworpet from of
impii non sic sed tanquam pulvis quem proicit ventus a

ansine eorþan Forðan ne arisaþ þa arlesan on dome
faciae terrae 5. *Ideo non resurgunt impii in iudicio*

ne þa firen- ꝉ synfullan on geþeahte ꝉ rede rihtwisra
neque peccatores in consilio iustorum

Forðan þe dryhten cneow weig þara soþfestra 7 siþfet
6. *Quoniam novit dominus viam iustorum et iter*

þara arleasra forwurþað
impiorum peribit

The verses in Ps. 1 numbered as in Stevenson; following Psalms as in the Vespasian Psalter.
1. 1. -ede ꝉ þæhte arleasre add. by Corrector on er. 2. æ (1st) on er. *his sceal* cov. by d. ink. 3. *rynas* cov. by d. ink. *þa*, fin. let. er. *wæstm ꝉ* prob. add. Er. bef. *his* (3rd). 4. *Na*, a from e. Er. bef. *arleasa. arleasa*, fin. let. er. *na* (2nd), *a* from e. *aworpet*, part. on er. 5. Er. aft. *arisaþ. ꝉ syn* wr. over the line and prob. add. *ꝉ rede rihtwisra* add. on er. 6. Er. bef. *cneow. cneow* in d. ink prob. add.

B

2.

Forhwan grymmetedon þeode 7 folc   smeagdon idelnesse
1. *Quare fremuerunt gentes et populi meditati sunt inania*

Et stoden eorðan cyninges 7 ealdermen becomen   tosomne
2. *Astiterunt reges terrae et principes convenerunt in unum*

ongean dryhten 7 ongean   criste   his   we tosliten
adversus dominum et adversus christum eius   3. Dirumpamus

heora bendas 7 aweorpan we heora   geoc from us   Se þe
vincula eorum et proiciamus a nobis iugum ipsorum   4. Qui

eardeð on heofenum ispeð ł hyscþ hio 7 drihten hyspeð ł holeð
habitat in caelis   irridebit   eos et dominus subsannabit

hie   þonne sprecð he to hem on his irre 7 on his wylme ł
eos   5. Tunc loquetur ad eos in ira sua et in furore suo

hatheortnysse he gedrefð heo   Ic soþlice heom geseted
        conturbabit eos   6. Ego autem constitutus sum

cining from him ofor syon his haligne dune   7 lerende
rex ab eo super syon montem sanctum eius   predicans

drihtnes bebod   drihten cweð to me min sunu eart
preceptum domini   7. Dominus dixit ad me filius meus es

ðu ic todæg þe acende   Gyrn to me 7 ic þe selle
tu ego hodie genui te   8. Postula a me et dabo tibi

þeode yrfeweardnesse þine 7 þine anwældnesse   eorðan
gentes haereditatem tuam et possessionem tuam terminos

gemerum   þu scęlt stieren hie on isenre gerde 7 swa swa
terrae   9.   Reges eos in virga ferrea et tanquam

tygelwyrhten fet þu heo gebrecest   7 nu kyniges
vas figuli confringes eos   10. Et nunc reges

ongeteð bioð gelærede ealle þa þe gedemað on eorðan
intelligite erudimini omnes qui iudicatis terram

þeowiæþ drihten on ege 7 geblissieð him mid fyrhto
11. *Servite domino in timore et exultate ei cum tremore*

gegrypað lare oððe stiernesse þiles hwonne yrhe drihten
12. *Apprehendite disciplinam ne quando irascatur dominus*

---

2. 1. -don on er. Er. bef. and aft. *folc.* Er. aft. *smeagdon*; -don on er.
2. *stoden* in pl. of er. Er. aft. 7. From *becomen* to *ongean* (2nd) prob. add. in
pl. of er. *dryhten, y* wr. over the line. *his* prps. add. 3. *we tosliten*
add. on er. 4. *ispeð ł hyscþ* add. *hyspeð ł* add. 5. *ł hatheortnysse*
add. by Cor. 8. *Gyrn* on er. Er. after *þeode. anwældnesse* smal. on er. Er.
of two lett. bef. *eorðan.* 9. *þu scęlt stieren* by Cor. on er. -*wyrhten, h* wr.
over the line. 10. *nu,* er. at end. 11. Er. aft. *on.* 12. Er. bef. *lare.*

7 ge forwyrðen of geweyge rihtum   Mydþe þe onberneð
et   pereatis   de   via   iusta   13. *Cum   exarserit*

in scortnesse hys yrres eadige bioþ ealle þæ þe getreowiað on
in   brevi   ira eius beati   omnes qui confidunt in

hine
eum

3.

drihten to hwi gemanifalde synt þa þe tregiað oððe swencað
2. *Domine quid multiplicati sunt qui   tribulant*

me manie on ariseð angean me   mánie cweðæt l seggeð
me multi insurgunt adversum me   3. *multi   dicunt*

saule minre nis nan hæle hire on gode hîre   þu soðlice
anime meae non est salus illi in deo eius   4. *Tu autem*

dryhten min onfeng ært 7 mine wulcor 7 mines hefdes up-
domine. susceptor meus es   gloria mea et exaltans caput

hebbende   Mine stefne to drihten ic cige l cleopede 7
meum   5. *Voce mea ad dominum   clamavi   et*

he me gehirde of his þære halgæn dune l munte   Ic
exaudivit me de   monte sancto suo   6. *Ego*

slep 7 swefne ic onfeng 7 ic aras forðæn þe drihten me
dormivi et sompnum coepi et resurrexi quoniam dominus sus-

onfeng   Ne ondrede ic me þusend folces me ymbsellendræ
cepit me   7. *Non   timebo   milia populi circundantis me*

ac arîs min drihten gedo me halne god min   Forðæn
exurge domine   salvum me fac deus meus   8. *Quoniam*

þu ofsloge l smite ealle wiðergiende me butan intyngan 7
tu   percussisti omnes adversantes michi sine causa

þæra synfulra teð þu abrutedest   Drihtnes is hęlo
dentes peccatorum contrivisti   9. *Domini est salus*

7 ofer   þin folc þin bletsung
et super populum tuum benedictio tua

4.

þanne ic gecigede ðe þu geherdest me god rihtwisnesse mi[n]re
2. *Cum invocarem te exaudisti me deus iustitiae meae*

-wyrðen, ð wr. over the line.   3. 3. seggeð, first g prob. from some
other let. hire on cov. by d. ink. gode hîre in p. ink.   5. MS.=cleowede.
6. slep, fin. let. (e?) er.   7. Er. aft. ac. arîs, fin. let. er. Two lett. er. aft.
halne.   8. Word (mines?) er. aft. ealle. abrutedest on er.   9. Two lett.
er. after is.   4. 2. þe er. aft. ic. -de ðe add. !

on geswince þu tobreddest me Miltse   me drihtæn 7 gehire
in tribulatione dilatasti   me Miserere michi domine et exaudi

mine gebed   Monna bearna hu lange swǽre ł heuie
orationem meam 3. *Filii hominum usque quo graves*

of heorten to hwon lufiað ge idelnesse 7 secað leasungæ
corde   ut quid diligitis vanitatem et queritis mendacium

Witoð þeðte   drihten gemiclædæ   his hæligne drihtæn
4. *Scitote quoniam magnificavit dominus sanctum suum dominus*

gehirde me þanne ic clypede to him   yrsyað   7 nellen
exaudivit me dum clamarem ad eum   5. *Irascimini et nolite*

ge sengien þa þe gecweðæþ on ewræn heortum 7 on ewrum
peccare   quae dicitis in cordibus vestris et in cubilibus

bedcliofum wesæþ onbryrdað ł reowsiað   Onseagæð
vestris   compungimini   6. *Sacrificate*

þa onsegdnesse ał geoffrieð offrunge of rihtwisnesse 7 gewenæþ on
sacrificium   iustitiae   et sperate in

drihten Monige cweðæþ hwilc ætæweð us gode   getacnod
domino Multi dicunt quis ostendit nobis bona 7. *signatum*

is ófer us drihten þet lioht þinnes onwlitan þu sealdest
est super nos lumen vultus tui domine Dedisti

blisse on herte minre   of tide hwætes wines 7 éles
laetitiam in corde meo 8. *a tempore frumenti vini et olei*

his hy send gemanifæld   on sibbe on þ selfe
sui multiplicati sunt 9. *In pace in id ipsum*

ic slæpe 7 réste   forþon þu drihcten synderlice
obdormiam et requiescam 10. *quoniam tu domine singulariter*

on hyhte þu gesettest me
in spe constituisti me

5.

Mine word drihten earum ænfoh ongiet mine cli-
2. *Verba mea auribus percipe domine intellige clamorem*

punge mine   begym stefne gebedes mines kyning
meum   3. *intende voci orationis meae rex*

3. From *hu* to *-nesse* on er. Er. bef. 7. Two lett. (ge ?) er. bef. *secað*.
4. *peðte* on er. *se* er bef. *drihten*? *his*, *s* cov. by d. ink; er. at end. *hæligne*
cov. by d. ink; *i* wr. over the line; let. er. betw. *g* and *n*. *cly-* on er. *him*
on er. 5. Er. bef. *yrsyað*. *nellen ge* cov. by d. ink. *onbryrdað ł reowsiað* by
Cor. 6. From *-dnesse* to *rihtwis-* on er. in p. ink. Er. bef. *cweðæþ*. *ætæweð us*
gode on. er. 7. *ófer*, false let. er. aft. *f*. 10. *drihcten*, *c* wr. over the line.
5. 2. *Mine*, *e* wr. over the line. Er. bef. *ongiet*; aft. it 'ł something' er.
mine (last) on er. 3. *begym stefne* on er.

min 7 min god   Forðæn drihten ic to þe gebidde
meus et deus meus   **4.** *Quoniam   aā te orabo domine*

on morgen 7 þu gehērst stefne mine   On mergen
mane   et   exaudies   vocem   meam   **5.** *Mane*

ic þe etstande 7 ic gesyo forðæn þu eart god na willende
astabo tibi   et videbo quoniam non deus volens iniqui-

unrihtwisnesse   Ne eardæþ neah þe awirged ne
tatem tu es   **6.** *Non habitabit iuxta te malignus neque*

þurþwuniæþ unsoðfestæn beforan þine eagum   þu
permanebunt iniusti   ante   oculos tuos   **7.**

hatest ł feoðest   drihten ealle þa þe wurceþ unrihtwisnesse
    Odisti   *domine omnes qui operantur iniquitatem*

þu forspillest þa þe sprecað leasunge wēre blode
perdes eos qui loquuntur mendacium Virum sanguinum

7 fakenfulne amanseð ł onscuniað drihten   Ic soðlice on
et dolosum   abhominabitur dominus   **8.** *Ego autem in*

manege þinre mildheortnesse ic ingonge drihten on þin
multitudine misericordiae tuae introibo domine in domum

hus ic gebidde to þinum halgan temple on þinum ege
tuam adorabo   ad templum sanctum tuum in timore tuo

geled me drihten on þine rihtwisnesse fore minum fiondum
9. *Deduc me domine in tua   iustitia propter inimicos meos*

gerece on þinre gesihðæ mine weg   Forðæn nis on
dirige in conspectu tuo viam meam   **10.** *Quoniam non est in*

hiræ muðe sodfestnesse 7 heortæ here ydel is   berien
ore eorum   veritas   cor eorum vanum est **11.** *Sepulchrum*

openende is heore hrache hioræ tungæn facenfulliche deoden
 patens est guttur eorum linguis suis   dolose   agebant

deme hi god Fræm hieræ geþohtum hie afeallæd efter
iudica illos deus   Decidant a cogitatibus suis   secundum

felefaldnesse arleasnesse heora adref hy forðæn hy gremeden
multitudinem impietatum eorum expelle eos quoniam exacerbaverunt

þe drihten   7 geblissigen ælle þa þe hyhteð on þe on
te domine **12.** *Et laetentur omnes qui sperant in te in*

---

4. Er. bef. *drihten. on morgen* on er.   5. *etstande, a* from some other
let. Er. aft. *god. na, a* from *o.*   6. Er. aft. *þe. -ed* on er.   Er. aft.
purþwuniæþ. 7. *hatest ł feoðest* on er. *ł onscuniað* add. by Cor. *drihten,
-ten* in pl. of er.   8. *in-* on er.?   Er. bef. *gebidde;* also fin. let. er.
9. *-wisnesse* on er.; *n* from *r*?   10. *heortæ,* fin. let. (n?) er.   11. *berien
openende* in d. ink. on er. 7 er. aft. *is. hi* one (or two?) fin. lett. er. From
efter to *hy* (1st) in pl. of er.   12. *geblissigen* on er.

ecnesse hyo fagniæð 7 þu on him eærdæst 7 hie wuldrieð on
aeternum exultabunt et inhabitabis in eis et gloriabuntur in

ðe ealle þæ þe lufiæd þīne nomæn   Forðæn þu
te omnes qui diligunt nomen tuum   13. *Quoniam tu*

drihten bletsæst þane rihtwisne drihten swa of scylde godes
domine benedices iustum domine ut scuto bone

  willen þines þu us gehelmedest
voluntatis tuae coronasti nos

6.

drihten on þinum yrre ne þrægæ þu me ne on þinum
2: *Domine ne in ira tua arguas me neque in furore*

wylme ne gegrip þu me   Miltsa me drihten forðæn
tuo corripias me   3. *Miserere michi domine quoniam*

ic eom seac ł untrum gehele me drihten forðæn þe gedrefede beoð
infirmus sum sana me domine quoniam conturbata

ł sinden eallæ mine bæn   7 min sæwle is swiðe gedrefed
sunt omnia ossa mea 4. *et anima mea turbata est valde*

7 þu drihten hu lange   beo gecyrred 7 genere mine
Et tu domine usque quo 5. *convertere et eripe animam*

sæwle halne me do fore þinre mildheortnesse Forðæn þe
meam salvum me fac propter misericordiam tuam 6. *Quoniam*

ne is on deaþe hwylc þe þines gemundige syo on helle
non est in morte qui memor sit tui in inferno

soðlice hwylc ondeteð þe Ic swanc on minre geomrunge
autem quis confitebitur tibi 7. *Laboravi in gemitu meo*

ic wessce þurh sindræ niehtæ min bed mid tearum strelum
lavabo per singulas noctes lectum meum lacrimis stratum

minum ic wete gedrefed is min eægæ for þinum yrrum
meum rigabo 8. *Turbatus est prae ira oculus meus*

7 ic eælddige betweoh eallum minum fiondum gewītæð
inveteravi inter omnes inimicos meos 9. *Discedite*

from me eælle þæ þe unriht wirchað forþæn þe drihten
a me omnes qui operamini iniquitatem quoniam exaudivit

geherde   stæfne   weopes   mines   gehyrde   drihten
dominus   vocem   fletus   mei   10. *exaudivit dominus*

    bene   mine 7   drihten   bene   mine   underfeng
deprecationem   meam   dominus   orationem   meam   assumpsit

    gescæmie   7 sien gedrefede   eælle   mine fiend   syon gecerred
11. *Erubescant   et   conturbentur omnes   inimici   mei   avertantur*

on hinder 7   scamie   swiðe   hredlice
retrorsum   et   erubescant   valde   velociter

7.

    Min drihten   god   on þe   ic gehopede   gefriolsa ł alys me 7
2. *Domine   deus   meus   in   te   speravi   libera   me*

genere me   from   eællum   ehtendum   me · 7 genere   me
            ab   omnibus   persequentibus   me   et   eripe   me

    þyles   hwonne gegripæð   swæ se lec   mine   saule   þanne
3. *Ne   quando   rapiat   ut   leo   animam meam   dum*

nis se þe   alise   ne   þe hælne gedo   Min drihten god
non est   qui   redimat neque qui salvum faciat   4. *Domine deus meus*

gif ic þis dyde   7   gif is   unryhtwisnesse on   handen   mine
si   feci istud   si   est   iniquitas   in   manibus   meis

    Gif   ic ageald   geldendum   me   yfela   ic ahreose be gewyrhtum
5. *Si   reddidi   retribuentibus   michi mala   decidam   merito*

fram   fiondum   minum   on   idel   Fulfylgæt   fynd
ab   inimicis   meis   inanis   6. *Persequatur   inimicus*

minre saule   7   gegripæ   hie   7   fortredeæþ   min   lif
animam   meam   et   comprehendat   eam   et   conculcet   in   terra

on eorðæn 7   min wuldor   on   dúste   gelede he   Aris
vitam   meam   et   gloriam   meam in pulverem deducat   7. *Exurge*

drihten   on erra   þinum 7   upaheue on ende   fyonde   þinre
domine   in   ira   tua   et   exaltare in finibus inimicorum tuorum

Aris   drihten   god   min   on   bebode   þet   þu bebude
Exurge   domine   deus   meus   in   precepto   quod   mandasti

    7 gesomnunge ł motstowe   þinra folcæ ymbselleð þe 7   for
8. *et   synagoga*   *populorum circundabit te Et propter*

9. *-erde* on er. *weopes mines, es* in both cases add. by Cor., the fore-parts
of the words being in p. ink.   10. *gehyrde* on er. in d. ink.   From *drihten*
to *underfeng* in another hand in p. ink.   11. From *syon* to *hinder* prob.
by Cor. in pl. of er.   7. 2. *-hopede* on er. prob. by Cor.   *ł alys* wr. over the
line by Cor.?   3. *hwonne* on er.   *þanne* on er.   *se þe* part. on er.   *ne* on er.
hælne, ne prob. on er.   4. *þis, i* on er. of another let.   5. *-wyrht- r* from *w.*
6. *Fulfylgæt* on er.   Er. aft. *fynd. hie* er. aft. 7 (1st).   *-pæ,* fin. let. (þ?) er.
7 er. bef. *hie.   for-* prps. pref. by Cor. Er. bef. *min* (2nd).   *on* on er.   Er.
aft. *dúste. gelede he* on er.   7. Er. bef. *drihten* (2nd).   *min.* on er.
8. *gesomnunge ł motstowe* on er.   *ymbselleð* in pl. of er.   Er. aft. *for.*

þas on heachnesse agen gechere drichten dem
hanc in altum regredere **9.** *domine iudica*

folcæ dem me drihten Efter minre soðfestnesse 7
populos iudica me domine Secundum iustitiam meam et

efter minræ unscyldinesse handum minum ofer me
secundum innocentiam manuum mearum super me

᾿ bio geendod þæ heteniþæs þæræ fyranfulræ 7 gereche
10. *Consummetur nequitia peccatorum et dirige*

þane rihtwisen smægende heortan 7 lendan ł lundlagan god
iustum scrutans corda et renes deus

rihtwis fultum min fram drihtne se hale
Iustum **11.** *adiutorium meum a domino qui salvos*

deþ rihtwise heorten god deme rihtwis strang 7
facit rectos corde **12.** *Deus iudex iustus fortis et*

langmodi cwistþu eorseð þurh sendrie dages bute
longanimis nunquid irascetur per singulos dies **13.** *nisi*

ge gecherren sweord his ascæcð ł cwahte bogen
convertamini gladium suum vibrabit Arcum

his he aþenede 7 gýrede hine 7 on him gérede fatu
suum tetendit et paravit illum **14.** *et in ipso paravit vasa*

deaþes flana his byrnendum gefremede eællengæ
mortis sagittas suas ardentibus effecit **15.** *Ecce*

he geæcnað unryhtwisnesse he onfeng sar 7 he cende
parturit iniustitiam concepit dolorem et peperiit

unrihcwisnesse Seað openede 7 adealf hine 7 onhreas
iniquitatem **16.** *Lacum aperuit et effodit eum et incidit*

on seað þone he wrohte bið gecyrred sar his on
in foveam quam fecit **17.** *Convertetur dolor eius in*

heauode his 7 on hnolle his unrihtwisnesse his astah
capite eius et in verticem eius iniquitas eius descendit

ic andette drihtene efter his rihtwisnesse 7 ic singe
18. *Confitebor domino secundum iustitiam eius et psallam*

drihtnes namen þæs hihstæn.
nomini domini altissimi

---

9. *dem,* fin. let. er. Er. bef. and aft. *folcæ. dem,* fin. let. er. *unscyldi-nesse* part. on er. 10. *bio,* fin. let. er. *-dod,* fin. let. er. 7 *lendan* ł *lund-lagan* by Cor. in pl. of er. *-wis,* fin. *ne* er. 12. *cwistþu* on er. Er. aft. *eorseð*; the scribe was prob. going to write ' ł something.' 13. *-æcð* ł on er. *gýr-,* ᵹ on er. 15. *unryht-,* y from *i*; ł from *c* by p. ink. 17. *unriht-,* ł from *c* by p. ink. 18. *-ette,* second *t* wr. over the line. *-tene,* fin. let. (s?) er. *rihtwisnesse* on er. *þæs, s* on er. of *m* ?

8.

Drichten god ure hu wunderlich is name þin on
2. *Domine dominus noster quam admirabile est nomen tuum in*

ealre eorðen Forþon upahauen is gemyclung ł merð þin
universa terra Quoniam elevata est magnificentia tua

ofer heofones of muðe childra 7 sukendre þu fulfremedest
super caelos 3. *ex ore infantium et lactentium perfecisti*

lof Fore fiondum þinum þet þu towerpe feond 7
laudem Propter inimicos tuos ut destruas inimicum et

gescyldend Forþan ic geseo heofenes weorc fingre þinra
defensorem 4. *Quoniam videbo caelos opera digitorum tuorum*

monan 7 steorren þa þu gestaðelodest hwet is
lunam et stellas quas tu fundasti 5. *Quid est*

se mæn þ gemendig ert his oþþe mcnnes sunu forðæn þ
homo quod memor es eius aut filius hominis quoniam

þu neosast hine þu wanedest hine litle læs from eanglan
visitas eum 6. *Minuisti eum paulo minus ab angelis*

of wuldor 7 arweorðunge þu gehelmedest hine 7 gesettes
gloria et honore coronasti eum 7. *et constituisti*

hine ofer wiorc handæ þinræ Eælle þing þu underþiedest
eum super opera manuum tuarum 8. *Omnia subiecisti*

under fotum his sceap 7 oxæn eællæ 7 ufonon þ neat
sub pedibus eius oves et boves universa insuper et pecora

feldes heofæne fuglæs 7 sefysces þa þurchgangeð
campi 9. *Volucres caeli et pisces maris qui perambulant*

stiga sæs Drichten godd ure hu wundorlic
semitas maris 10. *Domine dominus noster quam admirabile*

is þin nomæ on eælre eorðæn
est nomen tuum in universa terra

9.

Ic ondette þe drihten on eællre minre heortæn ic cyþe ł secge
2. *Confitebor tibi domine in toto corde meo narrabo*

---

8. 2. -*myc*-, orig. -*muc*-. 5. -*mendig, e* from ⸔ by p. ink. *ert his* in p. ink.
Er. aft. *þu. neosast* in p. ink on er. 6. *þu wanedest hine* in p. ink on er.;
hine cov. by d. ink. *litle* cov. by d. ink on er. *læs* on er. by Cor. *eanglan*
cov. by d. ink on er. -*helmedest* on er.; *hine* from *him.* 7. *7* er. before
hine; e on er. Er. bef. *ofer.* MS. = *þinræ handæ,* but marked for tranpos.
8. *þing* in p. ink on er. Er. bef. *fotum.* 7 er. bef. *eællæ.* 7 *ufonon þ* in p.
ink. 9. *heofæne,* final *e* prob. add. by Cor. Er. bef. *þa.* From *þa* to *sæs* in
p. ink in pl. of er. 10. *Drichten godd ure* in p. ink on er. 9. 2. Er. aft. *Ic.*

eælle wundre þine   Ic blissige 7 ic gefagenie on þe 7 singe
omnia mirabilia tua   3. *Laetabor et exultabo in te et psallam*

þinum þæm hihstæn namæn   On gecyrringe mine fiend
nomini tuo altissimæ   4. *In convertendo inimicum meum*

on bęclincg l hinder   hy geuntrumiað 7 forweorþeð from
retrorsum   *infirmabuntur et perient a*

þinre onsine l sihthe   Forðæn þe þu geworhtes minne
facie tua   5. *Quoniam fecisti iudicium*

dom 7 minne intingæn þu sits ouer heæhsętle l þrimsetle
meum et causam meam sedes super thronum

þu þe demest euennesse l enlicnesse   þu ðreadest l ciddest
qui iudicas aequitatem   6. *Increpasti*

þiode 7 forwarð se arlease 7 hioræ nomæn þu adilgodes on
gentes et periit impius nomen eorum delesti in

ecnesse 7 on worold worulde   fiend getyorodon
aeternum et in seculum seculi   7. *Inimici defecerunt*

of sweorde on ende 7 hiræ ceæstræ þu towurpe l bræce
framea in finem et civitates eorum destruxisti

hieræ gemind forweorþ mid hlydne   7 drihten on
Periit memoria eorum cum sonitu   8. *et dominus in*

æcnesse þurhwuneð he geærwæde on þæm dome his setle
aeternum permanet Paravit in iudicio sedem suam

7 he demeð eorðæn ymbhwyrft on efennysse
9. *et ipse iudicabit orbem terrae in aequitate*

he demeð folc mid ryhtwisnesse 7 geworðen is
Iudicabit populos cum iustitia 10. *et factus est*

drihten scyld l rotsung l frofer þearfana fultumend on
dominus refugium pauperum Adiutor in

gehyþelicnessum l on gerecvm 7 on eærfoðnesse l swince
opportunitatibus in tribulatione

Er. bef. *wundre.* Er. bef. *þine,* wh. is on er.   3. -*sige* on er.; *g* from *e.* *ic gefagenie* on er. *ic* er. aft. 7.   4. *On ge-* in p. ink in pl. of er.; -*inge* in p. ink on er. *gcuntrumiað 7 forweorþeð* in p. ink. *l sihthe* add.l in p. ink. 5. *ouer* in p. ink prob. on er. *l þrimsetle* add. on the marg. in p. ink. -*est, l* in p. ink on er. *euennesse* in p. ink.   6. From *ðreadest* to *arlease* in p. ink in pl. of er.   7. Er. bef. *fiend.* From *getyorodon* to *on* in p. ink on er. *hiræ* part. on er. *l bræce* add. in p. ink ; the *a* of the *æ* from *e. mid hlydne* in p. ink. 8. From 7 to *þurhwuneð* in p. ink. in pl. of er. -*de* add. in p. ink.   9. *he, e* from *i. ymbhwyrft,* let. (e l) er. aft. *b*; two fin. lett. (es l) er. *on efennysse* in p. ink under an er. From *demeð* to *ryhtwisnesse* in p. ink in pl. of er. 10. From *geworðen* to *þearfana* in p. ink in pl. of er ; *l rotsung* wr. over the line. 7 er. bef. *ful-*. *l on gerecvm* add. by Cor. *l swince* in p. ink prob. add.

7 wenen ł hyhten on þe ealle þa þe cuðen ł cniewen
11. *et sperent in te omnes qui noverunt*

þinne nomæn Forðæn ne forletst þu secende þe drihten
nomen tuum Quoniam non derelinques querentes te domine

singæþ drihtne ðe eærdæþ on syon ł on besceawodnesse
12. *psallite domino qui habitat in syon*

Secgæþ ł bodieð betweoxe þyode wundora his forðæn
Annuntiate inter gentes mirabilia eius 13. *quoniam*

secende hieræ blod he is gemyndi 7 nis ofergitende
requirens sanguinem eorum memoratus est et non est oblitus

þeærfne gebede geMiltse me drihten 7 gesioh
orationem pauperum 14. *Miserere michi domine et vide*

eædmodnesse mine fram fyondum minum þu þe ahefst
humilitatem meam de inimicis meis 15. *qui exaltas*

me of gatum deofles ł deoðes þ ic bodige ælle lofe
me de portis mortis ut annuntiem omnes laudationes

þine on gatum dohter syon Ic blissige ł winsumie on þinre
tuas in portis filiae syon 16. *Exultabo in salutari*

helo onfestnode sint þiodæ on forwyrde þæ hie geworhten on
tuo infixae sunt gentes in interitu quem fecerunt in

gegrinum þissum þæ hie digledon gegripen is hieræ
laqueo isto quem occultaverunt comprehensus est pes

fot drihtnes domes bið oncneæwen on worcum
eorum 17. *Cognoscitur dominus iudicia faciens in operibus*

hiere hændæ gegripen is se synfullæ gewirfede ł
manuum suarum comprehensus est peccator 18. *Conver-*

gecherred bioð þæ senfullan into helle eælle ðioda
tantur peccatores in infernum omnes gentes

þæ bioþ ofergitende drihten Forðæn na on ende
quae obliviscuntur dominum 19. *Quoniam non in finem*

ofergetelnis þeærfena geþild þeærfæna ne forwyrð on ende
oblivio erit pauperum patientia pauperum non peribit in finem

---

11. From *wenen* to *cniewen* in p. ink in pl. of er. Er. (þe ł) aft. *Forðæn*,
From *forletst* to *drihten* in p. ink in pl. of er. 12. ðe on er. ł *bodieð
betweoxe þyode* in p. ink in pl. of er. *wundora*, o dotted. 13. Er. bef. *sec-*.
-fne, fin. let. (s ł) er. *-ede*, fin. let. er. 14. Word (mine ł) er. aft. *-nesse. mine
fram* on er. *minum* on er. 15. Er. bef. *ahefst*. From *ahefst* to *deoðes* prob. in
pl. of er. 16. *-wyrde*, d from ð. Er. aft. *his* (2nd). *digledon* on er. 7 er. bef.
gegripen. Er. bef. *is*. 17. *on worcum* in p. ink on er. Er. bef. *gegripen*.
Er. (his ł) bef. *is. se synfullæ* on er. 18. *sen-*, s from some other let. on er.
Let. er. immed. aft. *into*. 19. *na* on er. *ofergetelnis þærfena geþild* on er.

Aris drihten ne   swiþie ł framie mon beoð gedemed
20. *Exurge domine non   prevaleat   homo iudicentur*

þiode on þinre gesihþe   Gesete þu drihten æs lædend
*gentes in conspectu tuo   **21.** Constitue domine legislatorem*

ofer hie þet þiodæ wytæn þeð   hyo men sint
super eos ut sciant gentes quoniam homines sunt

To hwæn drihten gewito þu fyor þu forsyhst ob hiræ
22. *Ut quid domine recessisti longe despicis   in*

gehyþnesse ł on gerecvm on eærfodnesse   þonne ofermodgeð
*opportunitatibus in tribulatione **23.** Dum superbit*

se arlease bioð onæled þarfa   hy biþ gegrypæne   on
impius   incenditur   pauper comprehenduntur   in

hiræ geþohtum þam ðe hy þohton   Forðæn bið gehered
*cogitationibus suis quas cogitant **24.** Quoniam laudatur*

se synfulle on gewilnunge his sæule 7 se þe unrihte deð
peccator in desideriis animae suae ut   qui iniqua gerit

he byð gebletsod   gremedæ drihcten se synfullæ   efter
*benedicetur **25.** Irritavit dominum peccator secundum*

micelnesse ł mænigfeldnisse his yrres ne onsecð   Ne
*multitudinem   irae suae non inquiret **26.** Non*

is god on gesihðe his his wégæs bioð besmitene on ęghwylce
est deus in conspectu eius   polluuntur viae eius   in   omni

tyde bioð afyrred domæs þine of ansyne his ælre
tempore Auferuntur iudicia tua a facie eius omnium

feonde his   he wælt   he cwæð sodliche on
*inimicorum suorum dominabitur **27.** Dixit   enim in*

heorten his ic ne beom astired on gecynde into gecyonde
corde suo non movebor de generatione in generatione

buton yfele   þæs muð of wyrgnisse 7 biternesse full
*sine malo **28.** Cuius os maledictione et amaritudine plenum*

is 7 of facne Vnder tungen his geswinc 7 sar   he siteð
*est et dolo Sub lingua eius labor et dolor   **29.** sedet*

---

20. *Aris*, fin. let. er. Er. (se ?) bef. *mon*. *beoð gedemed þiode* on er. prob.
by Cor.   21. Er. aft. *drihten*. *æs lædend* prob. by Cor. in pl. of er. *þeð*
hyo prob. by Cor. on er.   22. *gewito*, fin. let. (n ?) er. Er. betw. *þu* and
fyor. ·*yhst* on er. *t on gerecvm* add. by Cor.   23.´From *þonne* to *hy*
(1st) on er. prob. by the p. hand. *þam ðe hy* in pl. of er.   24. Er. bef.
gewil-. Er. bef. *his* ; *s* from *r* and fin. let. er. From *se þe* to end of v. in pl.
of er.   25. *gremedæ drihcten* on er. *synfullæ*, n on er. and fin. let. er.
Er. aft. *efter*. *onsecð*, *on-* on er. and fin. let. er.   26. Er. aft. *is*. *on* on er.
Er. betw. *his* and *his*. *-oð* (2nd) on er. From *þine* to *his* (1st) on er.
27. *beom*, *o* wr. over the line. *gecynde* ; *gecyonde*, *y* prob. on er. in both cases.
28. *wyrg-*, *g* prob. from some other let.

on searwum   mid   welegum   on   digelnesse   þeð   he ofslea
in   insidiis   cum   divitibus   in   occultis   ut   interficiat

unscyldigne   Eagan his   on þærfen   beseoð   he syrwð
innocentem   30. Oculi eius   in pauperem respiciunt insidiatur

on digelnisse   swa swa   leo   on   incleofe   his   he syrwð   þ
in   occulto   sicut   leo   in   cubili   suo   Insidiatur ut

he grīpe ðearfen gegripen   þearfen þanne he hine fram atyht hine
rapiat pauperem rapere   pauperem dum   attrahit   eum

on grene   his   genyþrað hine he onheldeð hine 7 gehreoseð
31. in laqueo suo humiliabit eum inclinabit   se et   cadet

þonne he wealdeð þam ðearfen   he cwæð soðlice on
dum   dominabitur   pauperi   32. Dixit   enim   in

heorten his ofergeten is god he acyrde ansyne hise þiles
corde   suo   oblitus est deus   avertit   faciem   suam   ne

he geseo oðð on ende   Aris drihten god min 7
videat   usque in finem   33. Exurge domine deus meus et

sy upahauen hand þin ne ofergit þu þærfene on ende
exaltetur   manus tua ne obliviscaris pauperum in finem

Fore hwet bismrade se arlease drihtne cweð soðlice on
34. Propter quid irritavit   impius   dominum dixit enim   in

his heortæn ne secð I myngeð god   þu gesyhst   þeð
corde suo non   requiret   deus   35. Vides   quoniam

þu geswinc 7 sar besceawest þ ðu selle hy on handum
tu laborem et dolorem consideras ut tradas eos in manibus

þinum þe soðlice læfed is þearfene steopcilde þu bist
tuis tibi enim derelictus est pauper pupillo tu eris

fultumiende þu forbrytest þes firenfullæs eærm 7
adiutor   36. Conteris   brachium peccatoris   et

awyrgedes bið soht scild his ne onfunden bioð
maligni requiretur delictum eius nec invenietur   37.

drihten rixæþ on ecnesse 7 on worldæ worlde þiodæ
Regnabit dominus in aeternum et in seculum seculi perib-

forweorðæþ of his eorþæn   Gewillnung I gyrnigge
itis gentes de terra eius   38.   Desiderium

---

29. *mid, d* prob. from *ð.*   30. Er. bef. *ðearfen.*   32. *an-, a* prob. from *o.*
34. *se arlease* on er. *-tne, t* wr. over the line. *secð, ð* from *e?*   35. From
gesyhst to *besceawest* in pl. of er.   From *þ* to *steopcilde* prob. in pl. of er.
-cilde, orig. = *-cildum?*   36. *þu forbrytest* prps. on er.   *awyrgedes, y* from *i;*
-des on er.   From *bið* to end of v. in pl. of er.   37. *worlde* add. by Cor.?
38. *I gyrnigge* add.?

þeærfenæ gyehirde drihten gewilnunge ł gyrnenga heortan
pauperum *exaudivit dominus* *desideria* *cordis*

heore gehirde þin eæræ To demene steopcilde 7
eorum *exaudivit* *auris tua* **39.** *Iudicare* *pupillo* *et*

eadmodum ꝥte na geteohige ł togesette ofer þet gemiclien
humili *ut non* *apponat* *ultra* *magnificare*

hiue mon ofer eorðæn
se *homo* *super terram*

10.

on drihten ic getryowe hu cweþe ge minre sæule
2. *In domino* *confido* *quomodo* *dicitis* *animae* *meae*

aleor ł flygan ouer dune swæ se spearwe Forðæn þe
transmigra *in montem sicut* *passer* **3.** *Quoniam*

ællungæ þæ firenfullæn æþeniæþ heræ bogæn gæærwiæþ
ecce *peccatores* *tetenderunt* *arcum* *paraverunt*

hieræ flane on cocere þette hie scotien on þisternesse þæ rihtæn
sagittas suas in pharetra ut *sagittent in* *obscuro* *rectos*

heortæn Forðon þæ ðe þu fulfremodost hie tebrecon
corde **4.** *Quoniam quae* *perfecisti* *destruxerunt*

eællungæ se soðfestæn wet dydo he drihten on his þæm
iustus *autem* *quid* *fecit* **5.** *Dominus in* *templo*

hælgæn temple drihten on heofone setle his egæn his on
sancto suo *dominus in* *caelo* *sedes eius* *Oculi* *eius in*

þarfena beseoð bræwes hise ahsiað mænne sunu ł bearn
pauperem respiciunt palpebrae eius interrogant *filios hominus*

Drihten axæþ þæ soþfestæn 7 þæ ærleæsæn soþlice þa þe
6. *Dominus interrogat* *iustum* *et* *impium* *qui autem*

lufigæþ unrihtnesse he fioþ ł hatað his sæwle He rinþ
· *diligit iniquitatem* *odit* *animam suam* **7.** *Pluit*

ofer ðæ firen- ł senfullæn gegrine swæ fires sweflðrosm 7 gæst
super *peccatores* *laqueos* *ignis sulphur et spiritus*

---

38. Er. bef. *gyehirde*; *y* from *i*; *e* er. betw. *r* and *d* ł *drihten* on er. *gyrnenga heortan heore* in pl. of er.; *y* from *e*. Er. (he ł) bef. *gehirde*; -*de* on er. 39. From -*mene* to *togesette* in pl. of er.; *geteohige*, second *g* from *e*. Er. aft. *þet*. 7 er. bef. *gemic*-. 10. 2. *ic getryowe* part. cov. by d. ink. Er. aft. *sæule*. From *aleor* to *dune* on er. Most of the words in the neighbourhood cov. by d. ink. 3. *heræ*, *e* from *i*. *flane* in p. ink on er. *cocere* in p. ink on er. 4. *ðe* wr. over the line, marked to follow *þæ*. Er. aft. *se*. *wet* prps. from *þet*; er. aft. it. *dydo*, fin. let. prob. er. 5. Er. aft. *on* (2nd). *heofone setle his* on er.; -*fo*- wr. over the line. Er. hef. and aft. *egæn*. From *on* to *ahsiað* on er. *mænne*, fin. let. (s ł) er. 6. *þa* orig. *þæ*. *hatað* on er. 7. *He*, *e* from some other let. on er. ł *sen*- wr. over the line. Er. bef. *gegrine*. -*ðrosm* 7 in p. ink.

ysta ł storm dæl ceolos here   Forðon þe ryhtwis
procellarum pars calicis eorum   **8.** *Quoniam iustus*

drihten 7 rihtwisnesse he lufode efennesse gesioþ his onsiene
dominus et iustitiam dilexit aequitatem videt vultus

ł andwlite
eius

11.

   hælne me do drihten forðon þe ateorede se hæli forðon
2. *Salvum me fac domine quoniam defecit sanctus quoniam*

gewænede sint soþfestnesse from mænnæ beærnum   Idelnesse
diminutae sunt veritates a filiis hominum   **3.** *Vana*

hy spræcan anre gewylc to nehstan his welere facne on
locuti sunt unusquisque ad proximum suum labia dolosa in

heorten 7 of heorten hyo sprecon yfele   Drihten forspille
corde et corde locuti sunt mala **4.** *Disperdat dominus*

eælle inwiddæn ł facne weleræs 7 þæ yfelⱬweþenden tungæn
universa labia dolosa et li-nguam maliloquam

þæ cweþæþ ure tungæn   we micliæþ ure weleræs from
5. *Qui dixerunt linguam nostram magnificabimus labia nostra a*

us sint hwilc is ure drihten   For yrmþe
nobis sunt quis noster est dominus   **6.** *Propter miseriam*

unspedigra ł wedlum 7 giomrungum þeærfnæ drihten cweþ nu ic
inopum et gemitum pauperum nunc exurgam dicit

arise   Ic asette ofer help ł halwendnesse mine getreowfullice
dominus Ponam super salutare meum fiducialiter

ic do on ðæms   sprece drih[t]nes sprecha sysra seolfor
agam in eo   **7.** *Eloquia domini eloquia casta argentum*

on fyre amered eorðen aclensod seoforfaldlice   þu
igne examinatum terrae purgatum septuplum   **8.** *Tu*

drihten geheældest us 7 beweardest us fram cnyorisse ðisre on
domine servabis nos et custodies nos a generatione hac in

<hr>

From *ysta* to *here* in p. ink.   8. From *ryhtwis* to *efennesse* on er.; *riht-*
wisnesse, *n* from some other let.   11. 2. *ateorede* on er. by Cor. *hæli*,
i on er; er. aft. the word.   3. From *anre* to *yfele* in pl. of er.   4. *ł facne*
wr. over the line.   5. Er. aft. *tungæn*. 7 er. bef. *ure*.   6. *yrmþe*, *e* from
some other let. *unspedigra ł* add on er.? 7 er. bef. *ł*. Er. aft. *-ungum*.
þeærfnæ pl. ov. *nunc* but marked for transposition to *pauperum*. From *Ic* (2nd)
to *ðæm* in pl. of er. and prob. orig. in the p. ink; part. cov. by d. ink; *ł* wr.
over the line.   7. This v. on er.   8. Er. aft. *drihten*. Er. aft. 7. From
beweardest to *ðisre* in pl. of er. prob. by Cor. *on* on er.

ecnesse   On ymbhwyrfte þæ ærleæsæ gængæð   efter
aeternum   9. *In circuitu impii ambulant secundum*

þinre heahnesse þu gemonigfyldes monnæ beærn
altitudinem tuam multiplicasti filios hominum

12.

hu lange drihten ofergietst þu me on ende oþ hwet
Usque quo domine oblivisceris me in finem quousque

acyrrest ðu onsine þine fram me   hu longe sette ic
avertis faciem tuam a me   2. *Quam diu ponam*

geþeæhtunge on mine sæule on minre heortæn sær þurh
consilium in animam meam dolorem in corde meo per

dæg   Oþ wænne bið upahafen min fyond ofer me
diem   3. *Usque quo exaltabitur inimicus meus super me*

min drihten god lócæ on me 7 gehire me Onliht
4. *respice et exaudi me domine deus meus Illumina*

mine eægæn þiles nefre ic aslæpæ on deæþe þeð
oculos meos ne umquam obdormiam in mortem 5. *Ne*

nefre ne cweðe min fiond ic magude ł swiþige ongean
quando dicat inimicus meus prevalui adversus

him þæ þe me eærfoþigæþ ł swencað hie hyhtaþ ł blyssieð gif
eum Qui tribulant me exultabunt si

ic bio onstyred ic soþlice on þine mildheortnesse
motus fuero 6. *ego autem in tua misericordia*

gehyhte Min heortæ winsumaþ ł blisseð on þine helo
sperabo Exultabit cor meum in salutari tuo

ic singe drihtne se me selde góde 7 ic singe þinum nomæn
cantabo domino qui bona tribuit michi et psallam nomini tuo

þæm hihstæn
altissime

13.

cwæð se unwise ł unsnotræ on herte his nis god hy gewemmede
Dixit insipiens in corde suo non est deus corrupti

ecnesse by Cor.   9. *heahnesse* on er.   12. Er. bef. *ofergietst* ; *-st* prob. on er. *me on* prob. on er. *hwet acyrrest* on er. Several words in the neighbourhood cov. by d. ink.   2. *hu, h* from something else. Er. bef. *sette. on* (2nd) prob. on er. *sær*, er. at end. *þurh dæg* on er.; *d* from *ð*.   3. *wænne bið upahafen* on er.; *f* on er. of some other let. From *me* to *drihten* (v. 4) in pl. of er.   4. From *lócæ* to *me* (2nd) in pl. of er. *Onliht mine* on er. *eægæn* on er. Er. aft. *þiles. aslæpæ*, let. er. immed. at end.   5. *þeð nefre* on er. *ic magude* on er. *-gean* on er. *-igæþ, g* wr. over the line. *ł swencað* prob. add. *ł blyssieð* prps. add.   6. *-hyhte* on er. *-ð* on er. *selde, de* on er. Er. aft. *nomæn*.   13. *unwise ł* prob. add. From *on* to *-lice* in pl. of er.

synt 7 onscunigenlice hie sint ł byoð gewordene on hieræ willæn
sunt et abominabiles   facti sunt   in voluntatibus suis

Nis se þe do   god   nis se oðð on ænne   Drihten
Non est qui faciat bonum non est   usque ad unum   2. Dominus

of heofone gelocede ofer mannæ beærn þet he gesio gif is
de caelo prospexit super filios hominum ut videat si est

ongetende ł understandende oþþe secende gode   Eælle
          intelligens   aut requirens deum   3. Omnes

fram ahyldæþ somed 7 on unnytenesse sindon gewordene nis
declinaverunt simul   inutiles   facti   sunt   non est

se þe do   god   ne is oðð to æne   Openende is byrgen
qui faciat bonum non est usque ad unum Sepulchrum patens est

ciolæn ł hracen hioræ tungæn heore facenfullice hy deodon átter
        guttur eorum linguis suis   dolose   agebant venenum

nedrana under welerum heore   þæræ muð of awargednesse
aspidum sub labiis eorum   Quorum os   maledictione

7 of biternesse ful is 7 hiræ fet hræþe ł snelle to
et amaritudine plenum est   veloces pedes eorum   ad

ægiotænæ ł to scedende blod   Forbrytednesse 7 ungeselignes
effundendum   sanguinem   Contricio et infelicitas

on hieræ wegum 7 sibbe weg hie ne oncneowon   Ne is
in viis eorum et viam pacis non cognoverunt Non est

godes ege beforen hieræ eægum   hie ne oncnewon eælle þa þe
timor dei ante oculos eorum   4. nonne cognoscent omnes qui

wircæþ unrihtnesse þa þe forswelgæþ min folc swæ méte
operantur iniquitatem Qui devorant plebem meam sicut escam

hlafes   gode hie ne gecygden ðær hie forhtodon þer
panis 5. deum non invocaverunt illic trepidaverunt timore ubi

ne nes næn ege   Forðon god on cneowrisse rihtwisne
non erat timor 6. Quoniam deus in generatione justa

is geþeahtunge wedlon ðu gedrefdest forðan god hihte his is
est consilium inopis confudisti quoniam deus spes eius est

---

se (3rd) on er. Er. bef. *œnne.* 2. From *on-* to *-dende* on er. *secende,*
nde prob. add. *gode, e* prob. add. 3. *fram a-* prob. add. *oðð* on er.
Openende, -ende add. on er.? ł *hracen* add.? From *heore* to *deodon* in pl. of
er. *nedrana* on er. *of awargednesse* on er. by Cor. *of* (2nd) prob. add.
ful is in pl. of er. *hiræ* er. aft. *is.* ł *snelle* prob. add. ł *to scedende*
prob. add. Er. bef. *blod.* *Forbrytednesse* on er. prob. by Cor. *beforen*
on er. of *on?* Er. aft. *eægum.* 4. *þa* orig.= *þæ* (twice). *hlafes* prob. add.;
er. aft. it. 5. *gode* on er. *ðær* on er. *nes* on er. 6. *his* er. aft. *on.*
From *wedlon* to *is* in pl. of er.

C

hwilc seleð of syon   helo israehelæ þanne acyrreð drihten
7. *Quis dabit ex* [*s*]*ion salutare israel   dum   avertit dominus*

  heftnieþ   his folces Iacob blissæþ 7 gehyht ysrahel
captivitatem plebis suae Laetetur iacob et exultet israhel

14.

Drihten wylc   eærdæþ   on þinre gesele ł eardungstowe ł teld
Domine quis habitabit in   tabernaculo tuo

opðæ wylc   resteþ   on þinre hælgæn dune ł munte   Se
aut   quis requiescet in   monte sancto tuo   2. *Qui*

  ingeþ butæn wemme 7 wyrcþ rihtwisnesse   Se þe
ingreditur sine   macula et operatur iustitiam   3. *Qui*

spryceþ soþfestnesse on his heortæn 7 ne deþ inwyd ł facn on
loquitur veritatem in   corde suo   et non egit   dolum   in

his tungæn Ne dyde his niextæn   yfel 7 edwit ł hosp ne
lingua sua Nec fecit proximo suo malum et obprobrium   non

anfeng ongean his niextæn   To   næhte   biþ geled
accepit adversus proximum suum   4. *Ad nichilum deductus est*

on his gesihþe se æwyrgedæ soðlice þæ þe drihten ondredæþ
in conspectu eius   malignus   timentes autem dominum

he hīg gemuclað Se þe sweræþ his niextæn 7 hiene ne beswicð
magnificat   Qui   iurat proximo suo et   non decipit eum

       7 his fioh   ne seleþ to westme oðð to hýre 7
5. *qui pecuniam suam non dedit   ad usuram   et*

his læc ne onfehþ ofer ðone unscyldygen Se þe þæs deþ ne
munera super innocentem non accepit Qui facit haec non

bið he astyred ł gedrefed on ecnesse
  commovebitur   in aeternum

15.

geheald me dryhten forðon on þe ic gewene ł hihte   ic cwiþe
Conserva me domine quoniam in te   speravi   2. *dixi*

7. *seleð*, *ð* prob. from *n* by Cor. *on* er. bef. *ysrahel.* *ysrahel*, fin. *e* er.
14. Er. bef. *gesele.* *eardungstowe* on er. ł *munte* add. by Cor. 2. *ingeþ* cov.
by d. ink; *i* on er. Er. aft. 7. *rihtwisnesse* on er. 3. ł *facn* add. *dyde*
on er. Er. aft. *his.* *edwit* ł *hosp* on er. *anfeng, a* from *o*; *n* from *h* and *g*
on er. *ongean his* on er. 4. *geled* er. (of two lett.?) at end. *-edæ, e* wr.
over the line. *gemuclað* prps. add. Er. aft. *his.* 5. *hýre, re* wr. over the
line. *astyred* by Cor. on er.; *y* from *i.* 15. ł *hihte* wr. over the line.

min drihten god þu eært forðæn minræ góde þu na
domino deus meus es tu quoniam bonorum meorum non

beðærft　　　　þæ hælgæn þe on his eorðæn beoð hie wundriæþ
indiges　　3.　Sanctis qui in terra sunt eius mirificabit

eælle　mines wyllæn betwion hie　　　Gemonigfealdode sint
omnes voluntates meas inter illos　　4. Multiplicate sunt

soþlice hire untrumnesse efter þon þe hie efston　　　Ic
enim infirmitates eorum postea acceleraverunt Non

ne gesomnige hieræ gemetinga ł sommunge of blodum
congregabo conventicula eorum de sanguinibus

ne ic ne bio gemindig hioræ nómæn þurh mine weleræs
nec memor ero nominum illorum per labia mea

　　drihten del minre erfeweardnesse 7 calices mines þu
5. Dominus pars haereditatis meae et calicis mei tu

eært þe me gesettest ł agefe yrfeweærdnesse mine　　Rapes
es qui restituisti michi haereditatem meam　6. Funes

me gefeollon on bryhtum 7 soþlice yrfewardnes min bryhte
ceciderunt michi in praeclaris et enim haereditas mea preclara

is me　　　　Ic bletsie drihten þe me salde andgyt
est michi　　7. Benedicam dominum qui michi tribuit intellectum

ofer þ 7　oðð　　nyhte begripen me lendene mine
insuper et usque ad noctem increpaverunt me renes mei

　　Drihten ic foresceawode on minre gesihþe simle forðæn
8. Providebam dominum in conspectu meo semper quoniam

to ðæm swiðran he is me þ ic astyred ne beo　　for þis
a dextris est michi nec commovear　9. Propter hoc

gelustfullede min heorte 7 gefagenede tunge mine ofer þ 7
delectatum est cor meum et exultavit lingua mea insuper et

min flesc rest on hyhte　　Forðon þu ne forletest
caro mea requiescit in spe　10. Quoniam non derelinques

mine sæwle on helle ne þu ne selest þinne hæligne to gesionne
animam meam in inferno nec dabis sanctum tuum videre

gegrip ł brosnunge　　Cuþe þu 'me dydest liues wegæs 7
corruptionem　11. Notas michi fecisti vias vitae

---

2. þu (2nd), u prob. on er.　na, orig. næ.　on er. aft. na ?　beðærft on er.　3.
his on er.　Er. bef. eorðæn.　beoð prob. on er.　betwion, n from h.　4. efston
prob. add.　gemetinga ł somnunge in pl. of er.　Er. bef. blodum.　bio, fin. m
er. ?　nómæn, ō in pl. of er. let.　5. From erfe- to mines by Cor. in pl. of er. ?
-ettest ł agefe prob. by Cor.　mine on er.　7. begripen me lendene in pl. of er.
8. foresceawode in p. ink.　From swiðran to beo in pl. of er.; beo, e from i.　9.
-fullede, fin. e in pl. of er. lett.　gefagenede tunge in pl. of er.　ofer on er.　hyhte,
y from i.　10. þinne, e on er. and n (2nd) prob. from u by d. ink.　-igne on er.

þu me gefillest of blisse mid andwliten þine gelustfulnesse on
adimplebis me laetitia cum vultu tuo delectationes in

þine swiþræn oþõe on ende
dextera tua usque in finem

16.

gehyr drihten mine ryhtwisnesse begem ł beheæld mine
Exaudi domine iustitiam meam intende deprecationi

bene mid Earum onfoh min gebed na on welerum
meae Auribus percipe orationem meam non in labiis

facenfulle of andwlitum þinum minne dom yppæþ mine
dolosis 2. *de vultu tuo iudicium meum prodeat oculi*

egæn gesioþ efennesse þu afandudest mine heortæn 7
mei videant aequitatem 3. *Probasti cor meum et*

þu neosodest me on niehte mid fire ameredest þu me ł streddest
visitasti nocte igne me examinasti

7 ne is gemet on me unrihtwisnesse þeõ ne sprece
et non est inventa in me iniquitas 4. *Ut non loquatur*

min muþ mænnæ weorcum for wordum þinræ weleræ ic
os meum opera hominum propter verba labiorum tuorum ego

gehyold heærde wegas Fulfreme mine stepæs on þinum
custodivi vias duras 5. *Perfice gressus meos in semitis*

stigum þet ne sien astyred swaõu mine Ic clipie
tuis ut non moveantur vestigia mea 6. *Ego clamavi*

forõon þu me gehierdest god onhyld þine eæræn to me 7
quoniam exaudisti me deus inclina aurem tuam michi et

gehiere mine word gewunderlyc þine mildheortnesse þe
exaudi verba mea 7. *Mirifica misericordias tuas qui*

hæle gedest hyhtende on õe fram wiõerstondende
salvos facis sperantes in te 8. *a resistentibus*

þinre swiþren geheæld me drihten swæ þærœ sione eages under
dexterae tuae Custodi me domine ut pupillam oculi sub

11. From *mid* to *-nesse* in p. ink prob. in pl. of er. *ende*, init. let. *h* er.?
16. *-wisnesse* on er. *mid* in p. ink. *na* in p. ink on er. *welerum facenfulle*
in p. ink on er. 2. From *of* to *þinum* in p. ink on er. 3. *-andudest* on er.
neos-, *e* from *i*. *gemet*, fin. lett. er. 7 er. bef. *on*. *-wis-* wr. over the line.
4. Er. aft. *muþ*. Er. aft. *for*. Er. bef. *ic*. *-yold* on er.? 5. Er. bef. *ne*.
astyred, fin. let. er. Er. aft. *mine*. 6. *-dest* on er. *onhyld*, *y* from *i* and
fin. let. er. 7. *gewunderlyc*, *ge* on er.; *-erlyc* in pl. of er. *þine*, *e* prob.
in pl. of er. *-st* prob. on er. *hyhtende on õe* in pl. of er. 8. First two
words part. cov. by d. ink. Er. aft. *þinre*. *swiþren*, *n* add. *sione cayes* in pl.
of er.

þinræ fiþræ   scæde gescylde me   fræm onsiene ærleæsræ
umbra alarum tuarum protege me **9.**   *a   facie impiorum*

þæ me swencton   Mine fiend   mine sæulæ   ymseældon
qui me afflixerunt Inimici   mei   animam meam circundederunt

fetnisse ł rysl heore bio betiendon ł belucon ł ymbelicton muþ
10.   *adipem   suum   concluserunt   os*

heore   sprec   on ofermodinesse ł on oferhydo   utæwurþonde
eorum loculum est   in superbiam **11.** *Proicientes*

me nu   ymbseældon me on eorðæn   hie   æsettæn hiræ eægæn
me nunc circundederunt me   oculos   suos statuerunt declinare

to aheldene   hye onfengon me swæ   gære lyo to þere
in   terram **12.** *Susceperunt me sicut leo paratus ad*

hlowe ł reaflace 7 swæ swæ þere leon hwelp eærdiæude bioð on
predam   et   sicut   catulus leonis   habitans   in

gehildum ł holum   Aris   drihten forecum hie 7 forwyrf
abditis **13.** *Exurge domine   preveni eos et subverte*

hie 7 genere ł alys   mine sæwle   fræm þæm eærleæsæ
eos   eripe   animam meam   ab   impio

sword ł meche   minræ fiondæ of þinre hændæ Drihten
frameam **14.** *inimicorum de manu tua Domine*

fræm feawum of eorðan   todief hie 7 underga hy on life
a   paucis a   terra dispertire eos et subplanta eos in vita

heore   Of þinum behyddum   gefylled   is hieræ wambe
ipsorum De   absconditis tuis   adimpletus est venter eorum

hy synt gefellede of fetnesse ł of swinisse ł fulnisse 7 hy lyfdon
saturati sunt   porcina   et reliquerunt

þæ ðer ofer weron hire lytlingum ł cyldum   Ic soþlice
quae superfuerunt   parvulis suis **15.** *Ego autem*

mid soþfestnesse ablice ł oðiwe on þinre gesihþe ic bio gefylled
cum iustitia   apparebo   in conspectu tuo   satiabor

þonne geswotoloð bið þin wuldor
dum manifestabitur gloria tua

---

9. Er. aft. *þæ*. Er. bef. and aft. *swencton*. *fiend, e* from *i* by orig. scribe. Er. aft. *-don*. 10. *fetnisse ł rysl* on er. From *ł be- to -nesse* prob. in pl. of er. *of* er. bef. *on* (1st). 11. Er. (hie?) bef. *æt-*; *-de* add. Er. bef. *ymb-*. 7 er. bef. *on*. *aheldene* on er. 12. Er. bef. and aft. *gære*. *hlowe, w* prob. from *þ*. *ł reaflace* add. *hwelp,* two fin. lett. er. *-ænde,* let. er. betw. *æ* and *n*; prob. orig. *eærdiæþ*; *-nde bioð* by Cor. 13. *forwyrf,* fin. let. (e?) er. *sword* on er. 14. From *feawum* to *heore* in pl. of er. *behyddum* on er. Er. aft. *is*. From *wambe* to *þæ* in pl. of er. *ł* (last) wr. over the line. 15. *ablice ł oðiwe* on er. *geswotoloð* on er.; *man* er. betw. *ge-* and *-sw-*.

17.

ic lufie ðe drihten mine megne   drihten þu eært
2. *Diligam te domine virtus mea*   3. *dominus firma-*

min trymnes 7 mín gescyld ł gehyht 7 min friolsend ł alysend min
mentum meum et refugium meum Et liberator meus deus

god min gefylstend ł fultumend 7 ic gehihte on hiene Min
meus adjutor meus et sperabo in eum Protector

scildend 7 horn hæle minne fultumend ł gefelstend min
meus et cornu salutis meae adiutor meus

heriende ic gecige drihten 7 fræm minum fiondum ic bio
4. *laudans invocabo dominum et ab inimicis meis salvus*

hæl   me ymbseældon deæþes geomrung 7 þæ burnan
ero 5. *Circumdederunt me gemitus mortis et torrentes*

unrihtwisnesse me gedrefdon   helle sær hie me
iniquitatis conturbaverunt me 6. *Dolores inferni circum-*

ymbsealdon 7 me forecomon deæþæs gegryno 7 on geswince
dederunt me prevenerunt me laquei mortis et 7. *in tri-*

ł eærfoþnesse minre ic gecigede drihten 7 to gode mine
bulatione mea invocavi dominum et ad deum meum

ic cleopode 7 he gehierde mine stemne of his þæn hælgæn
clamavi Et exaudivit de templo sancto suo vocem

temple 7 mine clipunge on his gesihþe ingeode on his
meam et clamor meus in conspectu eius introivit in aures

eæræn   And astyred is eorþe 7 forhtæde ł beuede 7
eius 8. *Et commota est et contremuit terra et*

grundwealles ł dunæ gestæþelungæ siondon gedrefede 7 onstyrede
fundamenta montium conturbata sunt et commota

forþon þe god him is yrre   Astagh smic ł réc on
sunt quoniam iratus est eis deus 9. *Ascendit fumus in*

his yrre 7 fir byrneþ of his onsiene Onheledæ sient gledæ
ira eius et ignis a facie eius exardescit Carbones succensi sunt

17. 3. *ł alysend* wr. over the line. *gefylstend* prob. on er. *gehihte* prob. on
er. Er. aft. *scildend. horn hæle* prob. in pl. of er. 7 er. bef. *minne. ł gefelstend* wr. over the line in p. ink. Er. aft. *min.* 4. *ic gecige* oů er. Er. bef.
fræm. 5. Er. bef. *me. deæpes geomrung* on er. *burnan unrihtwisnesse* on
er.; *n* of -*nesse* from some other let. 6. 7 (2nd) has a line drawn through
— for er.ł The Latin *et in tri-* is also on er. in d. ink. 7. *gehierde, d* from
e and *e* add. 7 er. bef. *ingeode*; *o* on er. (of þ ł) and *de* add. 8. *And, A*
from *o* by d. ink. -*æde, d* from *e* and *e* add. 7 *grundwealles* prob. add.
9. *Astagh* on er. Er. bef *on.* Er. bef. *fir. of* on er.

from him 7   he onhyldeþ heofonæs 7 adun astah 7 dimnesse
ab   eo et   10. inclinavit   caelos   et descendit et caligo

under his fotum   7 he æstag ofer cheruphin 7 he fleah
sub pedibus eius 11. Et ascendit super cherubin et volavit

7 he fleah ofer windæ heanesse ł fiþræs   7   he gesette
volavit super pennas ventorum   12. Et   posuit

þystro his digelnesse on ymbhwyrfte his eardungstowe
tenebras latibulum suum in circuitu eius tabernaculum eius

ðeosterfull weter on genipum ł wolon lyfte   legrescas
tenebrosa aqua in nubibus aeris   13. Pre fulgorae

on his gesihþe nipu ł wolon   færdon hegle ł yft 7 fyres
in conspectu eius nubes transierunt grando et carbones

gleden   7 denede ł þunerode of heofonæ drihten 7
ignis   14. Et   intonuit   de caelo dominus et

se heahesta gef ł selde his stemne   he sende flane his
altissimus dedit vocem suam   15. Misit sagittas

ł strelæ 7 he hi tostencte legte ł legrescas he gemonigfældæ 7
suas et dissipavit eos   fulgora   multiplicavit et

gedrefede hie   7 stywdon ł ataudon wetræ wyllæs 7
conturbavit eos   16. Et apparuerunt   fontes aquarum et

awrigene synt grundweallas ymbhwyrftes eorðan Drihten from
revelata sunt fundamenta   orbis   terrae Ab increpatione

þinræ prægunge of onepþgunge gæstes yrres ðines   he asende
tua domine ab inspiratione spiritus irae tuae 17. Misit

of heahnesse 7 me onfeng 7   me genæm   of   manege
de summo et accepit me et adsumpsit me de   multitudine

wetere   he generede me of fyondum mine ðam strengestum
aquarum 18. Eripuit me de inimicis meis fortissimis

7 fram ðyssum þe hateden me forþæm þe hi strængode weron
et ab his qui oderunt me quoniam confortati sunt

---

10. *adun astah* on er. in another hand. *dimnesse* prob. in another hand. *under* on er. Er. aft. *his.*   11. *æstag* part. on er. *fleah* on er. (twice). *ł* er. aft. *windæ.*   12. *gesette*, first *ł* wr. over the line. *digelnesse on ymb-* prob. add. Er. aft. *-hwyrfte. eardungstowe ðeosterfull* on er.   13. *legrescas* on er.; er. aft. it. Er. aft. *wolon. -don* on er. *hegle, g* from some other let. by orig. scribe. *-en* on er.   14. *denede ł þunerode* prob. in pl. of er. *-onæ,* fin. *s* er. *drihten* 7 *se heahesta* on er. Er. aft. *gef. selde, d* from some other let. and *e* on er.   15. *sende,* fin. let. prob. er. *flane* prob. add. Er. aft. *ł. tostencte,* fin. *te* prob. on er. *legrescas* prob. on er. *gemonigfældæ, ge-* wr. over the line and fin. let. er. Er. aft. this word. *-de* prob. in pl. of er. let.   16. *ataudon* on er. *wyllæs* er. (læs?) betw. *l* and *ł.* From -*læs* to *eorðan* by Cor. *of onepþgunge* on er. Er. aft. *yrres. ðines* part. on er.   17. *he asende of heahnesse* on er. Er. aft. *of* (2nd). *wetere* on er.   18. *he* on er. From *fyondum* to *me* (1st) in pl. of er.

ofer me   hy Me forecomon on dæge minre geswincednesse
super me   **19.** *Prevenerunt me in die afflictionis meae*

7 drihten is geworden scyldend min   7 he geledde me
et factus est dominus protector meus   **20.** *et eduxit me*

on tobredednesse halne he me dyde forðæn þe he wolde me
in latitudinem salvum me fecit quoniam voluit me

  7 me geeædleænyde ꝉ ageald drihten efter minre riht-
21. *Et   retribuit michi   dominus secundum iustitiam*

wisnesse 7   efter   unscyldinesse minre   hændæ me
meam   et secundum innocentiam manuum mearum re-

geedleænæde ꝉ ageald   Forðæn ic geheold wegas drihtnes
tribuit michi   **22.** *Quia   custodivi vias domini*

ne arleaslice ic dyde fram gódvm minum   Forþæn eællæ
nec impie gessi a deo meo   **23.** *Quoniam omnia*

his domæs on minre gesigþe sint æure 7 his rihtwisnesse
iudicia eius in conspectu meo sunt semper et iustitiam eius

ic ne anedde from me   7 Ic bio unwemme beforæn him
non reppuli a me **24.** *Et ero immaculatus coram eo*

7 ic me geheælde from minre unrihtwisnesse   7 drihten
si observavero me ab iniquitate mea   **25.** *Et retribuit*

me edleænæþ efter minre rihtwisnesse 7 efter on-
michi dominus secundum iustitiam meam et secundum in-

scyþenesse ꝉ unscyldgunge minre hændæ on his eægnæ
nocentiam   manuum mearum in conspectu

gesilþe   Mid hælgum hælig þu bist 7 mid were
oculorum eius   **26.** *Cum sancto sanctus eris et cum viro*

unscyldigum unscyldig ðu beost   7 mid gecorene gecoren
innocente innocens eris **(27.)** *et cum electo electus*

þu beost 7 mid ferhwyrfedum þu beost forhwyrwed   Forðan
eris et cum perverso subverteris   **28.** *Quoniam*

þu folc eadmod hal dest 7 eagan ofermodre þu geni-
tu populum humilem salvum facies et oculos superborum humi-

---

19. *geswinced-*, *-ed* wr. over the line. *min* on er.   20. 7 *he* on er. *me* on
er. From *tobred-* to next *me* on er. Er. aft. last *he.*   21. *-yde* on er. ꝉ
ageald prob. add. *rihtwis-* on er. *unscyldinesse,* first fonr lett. cov. by d.
ink ; rest of word on er. *-de* on er. ꝉ *ageald* prob. add.   22. *þe* er. aft.
Forðæn. *-eold* on er. From *ne* to *minum* in pl. of er.   23. *æure* by Cor. ;
init. let. (h ?) er. *rihtwisnesse* on er. *anedde* on er.   24. *bio,* fin. let. prob.
er.   25. *rihtwisnesse* on er. Er. aft. *efter.* ꝉ *unscyldgunge* add.   26.
Er. aft. *Mid.* *were* on er. From *-ldigum* to *beost* prob. in pl. of er.   (27.)
From 7 to *gecoren* prob. in pl. of er.   28. From *Forðan* to *-arust* in pl. of er.
ꝉ *ædmedest* add.

ðarast ł ædmedest   Forþon þu onlyhtes   mine blecernæ
  liabis   **29.** *Quoniam tu illuminas   lucernam*

ł leohtfet min drihten god   onlyhte   swartunge ł þistro minc
  meam   domine deus meus   inlumina   tenebras   meas

    Forðæn fræm þe ic beo genered fræm costungum 7 on
30. *Quoniam a te eripiar a temptatione et in*

minum gode ic ofergange þone weæll   Min god unbesmiten
  deo meo   transgrediar   murum   **31.** *Deus meus inpulluta*

his weg drihtnes gesprecæ of fyre   amered   he is scildend
  via eius   eloquia domini   igne   examinata   protector est

eælræ þæræ þe on hine gehopan   Forðæn hwylc god is
  omnium   sperantium in se   **32.** *Quoniam quis deus*

butæn   drihten oþþe hwylc god butæn urum   gode
  preter   dominum   aut   quis   deus preter   deum   nostrum

    god   se begyerde me of megne 7 gesette unwemne
33. *Deus qui   precinxit   me   virtute   et posuit inmaculatam*

minne weig   Se fulfremed mine   fet swæ swæ
  viam meam   **34.** *Qui perficit   pedes   meos   tanquam*

þæs heortes 7 ofer heahnesse he gesette me   Se þe lereþ minæ
  cervi   et super excelsa   statuit   me **35.** *Qui docet manus*

hændæ to gefiohte 7 he gesette swa swa erenne ł cyperene bogæn
  meas ad prelium et posuit   ut   arcum aereum

minum eærmum   7 þu seældæs me gescildnesse þinre
  brachia mea   **36.** *Et dedisti   michi protectionem salutis*

helo 7 þin swiþre me onfeng 7   lar þin hyo me lerde
tuae et dextera tua suscepit me et disciplina tua ipsa me docuit

þu gebreddæst mine stepæs under me 7 ne sindon geuntromode
37. *Dilatasti   gressus meos subtus me et non sunt   infirmata*

mine swæþu   ic fylge ł ehte minum fiondum 7 ic ge-
  vestigia mea   **38.** *Persequur   inimicos meos   et compre-*

grype hie 7 ic ne gecirræ oðð hye geteorieð   ic swenco
hendam illos et non convertar donec   deficiant   **39.** *adfligam*

---

30. Er. aft. *fræm* (2nd). *ofergange* on er. 31. *unbesmiten*, fin. e er. ł *weg*,
fin. -*æs* er. ł *of* wr. over the line. -*hopan* by Cor. in pl. of er. ; '*ł* something'
er. aft. this word. 33. *se* on er. *begyerde, y* from *ł* by d. ink and a fin. let.
er. 34. *Se* on er. -*med*, fin. *e* er. An er. under *heortes. heahnesse he* on er.
35. *he* on er. *gesette*, fin. let. er. ł *swa swa* add. *ł cyperene* add. 36. Er.
bef. and aft. 7 (3rd). Er. aft. *lar. hyo* on er. -*de* in pl. of er. 37. -*dæst, d*
wr. over the line and *t* add. by Cor. *under* on er. 38. Er. bef. *ic. ł ehte* add.
Er. (hie ?) aft. *ic.* 7 er. bef. *hie.* 7 *ic* add. *gecirræ, ge-* prob. pref. by Cor. ;
fin. let. er. ; orig. prob. *acirræ-. oðð hye geteorieð* by Cor. in pl. of er.

hye ne hye ne magen standen hie gefeællæþ under minum fotum
illos nec potuerunt stare Cadent subtus pedes meos

 and megne þu me begierdes to gefiohte þu underwyrtwæledæst
40. *et precinxisti me virtute ad bellum Subplantasti*

eælle onarisende on me under me 7 minum fyondum
omnes insurgentes in me subtus me **41.** *et inimicorum meorum*

þu me seældest bæcc 7 hatiende me þu forspildest hie
dedisti michi dorsum et odientes me disperdidisti **42.** *Clam-*

clypodon Ɨ cigden nes se hæle gedyde to drihtne ne
averunt nec erat qui salvos faceret ad dominum nec

he hie ne geherde 7 ic hie gewænige swæ þet dust
exaudivit eos **43.** *Et comminuam illos ut pulverem*

from onsine þes windes 7 swæ þæt fen Ɨ līm þæræ stræte ic hie
ante faciem venti ut lutum platearum delebo

adylge þu Generest Ɨ alysest me of folcæ wiþercwedolnesse Ɨ
eos **44.** *Eripies me de contradictionibus*

wiðersacum þu gesetst me on þiode heæfod þet folc
populi constitues me in caput gentium **45.** *Populus*

þe ic ne oncneow me þeowæde from eæræne gehlyste Ɨ hiernesse
quem non cognovi servivit michi abauditu auris

me gehlyste fremdæn beærn me syndon liogende
obaudivit michi **46.** *Filii alieni mentiti sunt michi*

fremdæn beærn synt eældigende 7 hy haltodon from hieræ
filii alieni inveterati sunt et claudicaverunt a semitis

siðfatum Dryhten liofæþ 7 min god is gebletsot 7
suis **47.** *Vivit dominus et benedictus deus meus et*

sy upæhafen god helo min god þu ðe me selest
exaltetur deus salutis meae **48.** *Deus qui das vindictam*

---

39. From *swence* to *standen* in pl. of er. by Cor. *under* on er. *minum* cov.
by d. ink. 40. *and, a* from *o.* Er. bef. *gefiohte.* From *on-* to *under* in pl.
of er. by Cor. 41. Er. aft. 7. *-est, t* prob. add. by Cor. Er. aft. this word.
From *bæcc* to *me* in pl. of er. Er. aft. *þu.* *-est, t* prob. add. by Cor. 42.
clypodon t add. *cig-* cov. by d. ink ; *-den* prob. add. on er. *nes* cov. by d.
ink. *se* in d. ink, with er. aft. it. Er. bef. *to. geherde, -de* by Cor. on er.
43. *-ige, g* from *e.* 7 er. bef. *swœ. fen t* add. *stræte* on er. 44. *þu* prob.
pref. by Cor. *-est* (1st), *-st* prob. add. by Cor. *t alysest* add. by Cor. ; misplaced in MS., but marked to follow *Generest. t widersacum* add. *gesetst, st*
add. on er. 45. *þe,* fin. *t* er. ? *ic* prob. add., a second *ic* being er. aft. it.
-de add. on er. *-hlyste t* add. *gehlyste* (2nd) by Cor. on er. 46. Er.
(*þæ* ?) bef. *fremdæn* (twice). *-igende, g* from *e. hy haltodon* by Cor. on er.
siðfatum in pl. of er. by Cor. 47. 7 *sy* add. in pl. of er. *-afen, a* from *e*
by Cor. ; *n* add. on er. *min,* fin. let. er. 48. *ðe* add. over the line.

wrece 7 underðeodest   folc   under me Drihten is min friolsend
michi et subdidisti   populos   sub   me   Liberator   meus

ł alysend of ðeodum   yrsiendum   7 fram onarisendum on
dominus de gentibus   iracundis   49. *et ab insurgentibus in*

me þu upahefst me 7 fram were unrihtwisum þu generest me
me   exaltabis   me   a   viro   iniquo.   eripies   me

Forþon   on folce drihten ic þe ondette   7 on þinum nomæn
50. *Propter ea confitebor tibi in populis domine et   nomini   tuo*

sealm   ic þe singe   Gemycligende   helo   his kyninges 7
psalmum   dicam   51. *Magnificans   salutare   regis ipsius et*

doende his cristes mildhertnesse dauide 7 sæde   his oððe on
faciens   misericordiam christo suo   dauid et semini eius usque in

worolde
saeculum

18.

heofones   seægæþ ł bodieð   godes   wuldor   7   weorc
2. *Celi   enarrant   gloriam dei   et   opera*

his hæudæ   cyþæþ ł bodiað trvmnesse ł staðel ł fesnesse
manuum eius   annuntiat   firmamentum

Se deig of þem   dege belceð   word   7   seo nieht þere nieht
3. *Dies   diei   eructuat verbum et   nox   nocti*

gecyþeð ł bycneþ ingehygð ł wit ł wisdom   Ne sindon
indicat   scientiam   4. *Non   sunt*

gespreca   ne   word   þæræ   ne bioþ gehired hieræ stemnæ
loquele   neque sermones quorum non audientur   voces eorum

On   eælræ   eorðæn   utgeode   sweg   heore 7 on endes
5. *In   omnem   terram   exivit   sonus eorum et in   fines*

ymbwyrftes eorðan word heora   On sunnæn he gesette
orbis   terrae   verba eorum   6. *In   sole   posuit*

his geteldunge ł ærdunge 7 he   swæ   se brydgumæ forþ-
tabernaculum suum   et ipse tanquam   sponsus   pro-

-derðeodest add. on er.   Er. bef. *folc* wh. has fin. *e* er.   *me* add. on er.
From *ł* to end of v. added in pl. of er.   49. From begin. of v. to *generest* add.
in pl. of er.; *-riht-, t* wr. over the line.   50. Er. aft. *on* (1st).   *sealm* add. in
pl. of er.   51. *dauide* on er. by Cor.   *sæde his oððe* on er. by Cor.   18. 2.
heofones add. ?   *ł bodieð* add.   Er. bef. *cyþæþ*.   *ł bodiað* add. part. on er.
trv-, v from *y*.   *ł staðel* add. by Cor.   *ł fesnesse* by Cor. in pl. of er.   3. *Se
deig* by Cor. in pl. of er.   *belceð* add., prob. part. on er.   From 7 to *gecyþeð* by
Cor. on er.   From *bycneþ* to *wisdom* add. in pl. of er.   4. *gespreca, a* orig.
æ ?; fin. let. prob. er.   Er. aft. *ne*.   Er. immed. bef. *þæræ*.   *gehired*, fin. let.
er. ?   5. *utgeode* add. on er.   From *heorc* to *heora* add. in pl. of er.   6. *he
gesette* add. on er.   *-teldunge* add. on er.   *ł ærdunge* add.

gongende of his brydbure ł gyftbure he winsumæde ł blitsode
cedens   de   thalamo suo   Exultavit

swæ swæ etenæs   weg to iernenne   from heofones hihþo
ut   gigans   ad currendam viam   7. a   summo caelo

utgang   his   7 edryne ł gencyr   his   oððe to beahnesse his
egressio eius et·   occursus   eius usque ad summum eius

nis se ðe hine behyde fram hetan his   Drihtnes ęe
nec est qui se abscondat a calore eius   8. Lex domini

ungripendlic is to gecierrenne saule cyþnes ł witnesse drihtnes
inreprehensibilis   convertens   animas   testimonium   domini

getrewful wisdom geærwiende litlingum ł childvm   Drihtnes
fidele   sapientiam   prestans   parvulis   9. Iustitiae

ryhtwisnesse ryhta geblissiende heortæn   bebod   drihtnes
domini   recte   laetificantes   corda   preceptum   domini

bryht onlyhtende eægæn   Drihtnes hælgæ ęge
lucidum inluminans oculos   10. Timor domini sanctus

þurhwunæþ æworoldæ worlde godes domas soþe gerihtwisede
permanet in seculum seculi iudicia domini vera iustificata

on hy sylfe   Gegyrnendlice ofer   gold   7 swiðe dior-
in semet ipsa   11. Desiderabilia super aurum et   lapidem

wiorðne stæn   7 swetræn ofer hunig 7 biebreæd ł hvnicamb
preciosum multum et dulciora super mel et   favum

witodlice 7 ðeow ðin gehylt hy on geheordnesse ł to
12. Nam et servus tuus custodiet ea in   custod-

bewitena ða edleæn micel   hwylc ongitt gyltes ł scyldes
iendo   illa retributio multa   13. Delicta quis intelligit

from minum dieglum geclensæ me dryhten   7 from
ab   occultis   meis   munda   me domine   14. et   ab

fremdum âra þinum þeowe Gif min hy ne bioþ weæooldænd
alienis parce servo tuo Si mei non fuerint dominati

---

bure ł gyft- add. -bure (2nd) cov. by d. ink. ł blitsode by Cor. wr. over
the line. Er. bef. and aft. weg. 7. From utgang to gencyr add. in pl. of
er. From oððe to end of v. add. in pl. of er. 8. Drihtnes, e er. betw. ł and n.
-lic add. From saule to wisdom add. in pl. of er. -de add. on er. litlingum
ł childvm add. prob. in pl. of er. 9. ryhtwisnesse, ryhta add. in pl. of er.
to er. bef. geblissiende; -de add. on er. (of ne ł). bebod add. on er. Er. aft.
drihtnes. bryht onlyhtende add. in pl. of er. 10. Er. bef. hælgæ. -riht- on
er. Er. bef. on. hy, y on er. sylfe, e in pl. of er. 11. -gyrnendlice add.
on er. swiðe add. on er.; 7 er. aft. it. -ne on er. stæn, two fin. lett. (es ł) er. ;
er. aft. this word. hunig, two fin. lett. (es ł) er. ł hvnicamb by Cor. in pl. of
er. 12. From witodlice to on by Cor. in pl. of er. edleæn, a fin. er. prob.
made. 13. ongitt gyltes on er. ł scyldes add. 14. 7 on er. Er. (þæm ł)
aft. from. fremdum, -em- on er. min, fin. c er.

þonne ic bio ungewemmed 7 ic beo clensod from scylde ꞇ gyltum
tunc   inmaculatus ero   et   emundabor   a   delicto

ðam mestan   7 bioþ þette gelicieð sprecæ mines
maximo   15. Et erunt ut complaceant eloquia oris

muþes 7 smeæwung ꞇ gemind minre heortæn ou þinre gesihþe
mei et   meditatio   cordis mei   in conspectu tuo

simle Drihten gefelstend min 7 alysend min
semper Domine adiutor   meus et redemptor meus

19.

Gehére þe drihten on dege þinre geswencnesse gescyldc þe
2. *Exaudiat te dominus in die   tribulationis   protegat te*

nomæ iæcobes godes   he ASende þe fultum of hælgum
nomen dei iacob   3. Mittat tibi auxilium de sancto

7 of syon ꞇ heahnesse he behealde þe   he Gemyndig sie
et de   Syon   tueatur te   4. Memor sit

eælre þinre onseigdnesse 7 þin offrung ꞇ onseigdnesse fett sie
omnis sacrificii tui   et   holocaustum tuum   pinguefiat

Selle þe drihten efter þinre heortæn. 7 eæl þin
5. *Tribuat tibi dominus secundum cor tuum et omne con-*

gepeæht he getrymme   We blissiæþ on þinre helo 7 on
silium tuum confirmet   6. Laetabimur in salutari tuo et in

drihtnes namæn ures godes we beoð gemiclode   drihten
nomine domini dei nostri magnificabimur   7. Impleat

gefylle eællæ þinæ benæ ꞇ gyrnenga nu ic oncneow forþæn
dominus omnes petitiones tuas nunc cognovi quoniam

halne gedeþ drihten kyning ꞇ criest his gehereþ hine of
salvum faciet dominus christum suum et exaudiet illum de

his hælegæ heofone on his miehte ꞇ anweldum helo his swyþre
celo sancto suo in   potentatibus   salus dextera eius

þa ꞇ hy on wenum ꞇ rynum 7 hy on horsum we soþlicc on
8. *Hi in   curribus et hi in equis nos autem in*

7 ic beo on er. ðam mestan on er.   15. Er. bef. geliceð; -ð on er.
sprecæ, init. ge- er.   19. 3. he pref. later. Er. aft. fultum. hælgum, -um
on er. ꞇ heahnesse he behealde on er.   4. he pref. later. Er. aft. sie.
-gdnesse (2nd), g from d; d from some other let.; er. betw. d and n.   5. þe
on er. eæl, a fin. er. made. þin, fin. e er. gepeæht, er. at end (unge?). -me
on er.   6. namæn, a on er. ures, r from some other let.; let. er. betw. r
and e; orig.= usses? beoð gemic- on er.   7. gefylle, fin. let. er. gyrnenga
wr. over the line. oncneow=orig. oncneawe? Er. aft. forþæn. MS. halue
not halne; a orig. æ. drihten on er. 7 er. bef. his; s in pl. of er. gehereþ,
i er. betw. h and e; of er. aft. this word. hine on er. hælegæ, fin. let. (n?)
er. Er. bef. on.   8. þa, orig.= þæ. ꞇ hy wr. over the line. From on (1st)
to horsum add. in pl. of er.

drihtnes nomæn ures godes beoð gemiclyde   hi   synt
nomine domini dei nostri magnificabimur   **9.** *Ipsi obligati*

gewriðene 7 gefeollen we soþlice ærysæþ 7 ryhte
sunt   et ceciderunt nos   vero resurreximus et erecti

bioþ gewordene   drihten gedo þone kyning hælne 7
sumus   **10.** *Domine   salvum fac regem   et*

gehiere us on degge on ðam þe we gecygen ꝉ clipien þe
exaudi nos in   die   in   qua   invocaverimus   te

20.

Drihten on þinum megne se kyning blissæþ 7 ofer hæle
2. *Domine in   virtute tua   laetabitur rex   et super salutare*

þine wyusumæde ꝉ blissade swiþe ꝉ ðearle   Gewil-
*tuum   exultavit   vehementer   **3.***

nunge ꝉ gyrninge his sæwle þu him seældest 7 fram wyllæn
Desiderium   anime eius   tribuisti ei   et   voluntate

his welere ꝉ lippe þu hine ne becyredest ꝉ bepehtes   Forðæn
*labiorum eius   non fraudasti eum   **4.** Quoniam*

þu forecome hine on þinre bletsunge swetnesse þu settest on
prevenisti   eum in   benedictione   dulcedinis   posuisti   in

his heæfode helm ꝉ coruna of þæm diorweorþestæn stænum
capite eius   coronam   de   lapide pretioso

Lyf he bed fram þe 7 þu seældest him langnisse dage
5. *Vitam petiit   a   te et   tribuisti   ei longitudinem dierum*

on worold aworlde   Micel is his wuldor on þinre helo
*in saeculum saeculi   **6.** Magna est gloria eius in   salutari tuo*

wuldor 7 micelne wlite ðu asetst ofer him   Forðon
*gloriam et magnum decorem inpones super eum   **7.** Quoniam*

þu hine selest on bletsunge on world aworlde þu hine geblissæst
dabis eum   in benedictione in seculum saeculi   laetificabis eum

on gefeæn myd þinre onsine ꝉ andwlitan   Forþæn þe se kyning
*in gaudio cum   vultu tuo   **8.** Quoniam   rex*

---

nomæn, o from some other let. *beoð, e* wr. over the line. *-de* on er.   9.
-wriðene on er.   *-feollen* on er. ; *o* from something else ?   10. From *degge* to
end of v. in pl. of er.   20. 2. *hæle þine* on er.   *-de* (1st) prob. on er.
ꝉ *blissade* prob. add. *swiþe* ꝉ add. by Cor.   3. *-est, t* (twice) prob. by Cor.
Er. aft. *fram. welere* ꝉ *lippe* in pl. of er. ꝉ *bepehtes* add. by Cor.   4. *-come
hine* on er. *þinre* underlined in MS. *helm* ꝉ add. by Cor.   5. *Lyf,* fin. *-es*
cr. *fram þe 7 þu* on er. *him langnisse* on er.   6. Er. aft. *wuldor* (1st).
asetst, a- on er. ; *-st* on er.

geweneþ ł hyhteð on drihten 7 on þes hihstæn mildheortnesse
sperabit in domino et in misericordia altissimi

he ne biþ onwended ł astyred bio gemet þin hand eællum
non commovebitur 9. *Invenictur manus tua omnibus*

þinum fyondum þin swiþræ geméte eælle þa þe fiogæþ ł hatedon
inimicis tuis dextera tua inveniat omnes qui te oderunt

þu hie gesetst swæ swa fyrðolle fyres on tyde þinre onsine
10. *Pones eos ut clibanum ignis in tempore vultus*

ł andwlite dryhten on his yrre gedrefþ hie 7 fyr hie forswylgþ
tui dominus in ira sua conturbabit eos et devorabit eos ignis

hieræ westm of eorþæn þu forspildest 7 hieræ sed from
11. *Fructum eorum de terra perdes et semen eorum a*

mannæ beærnum Forðæn hie ahyldon on þe yfela
filiis hominum 12. *Quoniam declinaverunt in te mala*

hy þohton geþeæhtunge ł gerun þeð na hy ne miehton
cogitaverunt consilium quod non potuerunt

gestathelien Forðæn þu hie asetst niþer ł adune on lafum
stabilire 13. *Quoniam pones eos deorsum in reliquiis*

þinum ðu gærwest andwliten heore upahefe drihten on
tuis preparabis vultum illorum 14. *Exaltare domine in*

megne þine we singeð 7 dremað þine megne
virtute tua cantabimus et psallemus virtutes tuas

21.

God god min loce on me forwæn forlete þu me fyor
2. *Deus deus meus respice in me quare me dereliquisti longe*

fram hele minra Word minræ ægyltæ min god
a salute mea Verba delictorum meorum 3. *deus meus*

ic cige þurh deg ne þu gehierest 7 on nyht 7 na to
clamabo per diem nec exaudies et nocte et non ad

unsnyternesse ł unwisdóme minre þu soþlice on hælgæn
insipientiam michi 4. *Tu autem in sancto*

8. Er. aft. *biþ.* 9. *bio,* fin. let. er. *gemet,* two fin. lett. er. *þin,* fin. let. er. *hand,* fin. let. er. ; *a* orig.=*œ. þa* orig.=*þœ.* 10. -*st* on er. *swa* on er. -*ðolle fyres* on er. Er. aft. *on* (1st). Er. bef. *fyr.* 11. *of* on er. *mannæ, a* from something else. 12. Er. aft. *Forðœn. ahyldon, a-* on er. 7 er. bef. *on.* Er. aft. *þohton. na, a* from e. *gestathelien,* part. on er. 13. -*st* on er. From *on* to end of v. in pl. of er. 14. From *up-* to *on* in pl. of er. From *þine* to *dremað* in pl. of er. *þine* (2nd), *e* on er. 21. 2. *min* in p. ink on er. *fyor fram hele* on er. 3. *ne þu* in pl. of er. Er. bef. *gehierest* ; -*est* on er. *on nyht* 7 *na to* on er. ł *unwisdóme* prps. add. 4. er. aft. *on.*

eardest lof israele ł haligen   on þe hyhton ł hopedon
habitas laus   israel   **5.** *in te   speraverunt*

ure federæs on þe hy gehopeden 7 þu hie alysdest   To
patres nostri   speraverunt   et   liberasti eos   **6.** *Ad*

þe hie clipoden 7 hale   hy gewordene   synt   on þe
te   clamaverunt et   salvi   facti   sunt   in   te

hie hopodon ł gehihton 7 ne syndon gescende   Ic Soþlice
speraverunt   et non   sunt   confusi   **7.** *Ego autem*

eom wyrm 7 na mann   ædwît ł hosp   manne 7 aworpednysse
sum vermis et non homo   obprobrium hominum et   abjectio

folces   Eælle þa þe me gesægen hyrpæden ł anscunedon me
plebis   **8.** *Omnes qui   videbant me   aspernabantur   me*

hy sprecen mid welleron ł lippen 7 weagedon ł rysedon heofod
locuti sunt   labiis   et   moverunt   caput

        he gehyhte ł hopade on drihten he hine generæþ ł alyseþ
9.   *Speravit   in domino   eripiet eum*

halne he gedeþ hine fordan he wile hine   Forðæn þu
salvum faciet   eum quoniam   vult eum   **10.** *Quoniam tu*

eært þe me fram âtuge of innoðe hope ł hyht min fram
es qui abstraxisti me de ventre   spes   mea ab

breostwelmum ł tyten moder minre   on ðe aworpen ic eom
uberibus   matris meae   **11.** *In te iactatus   sum*

of ingerife of innoðe moder minre god min eart þu   Ne
ex utero de ventre matris meae deus meus es tu   **12.** *Ne*

gewit þu from me forþon geswinc ł eærfoþu gehende ł neæh
discesseris a me quoniam   tribulatio   proxima

is 7   nis   se fultomie   Ymbseældon   me
est et   non est qui   adiuvet   **13.** *Circundederunt   me*

monegu ceolfæs feœrræs fætte me forsetnoden   hy
vituli multi   tauri pingues   obsederunt me   **14.**

---

eardest prob. added.   From *israele* to *haligen* on er.   5. From *on* to *hope-don* on er.   *hy gehopeden* on er.   *alysdest* on er.   6. -*oden* on er.   *hale*, orig.= *hæle*.   *hy* on er.   -*ene*, fin. *e* prps. add. by Cor.   *hopodon ł* on er.   7. Er. aft. *na.*   *mann* orig.= *mann.*   Er. bef. *ædwît ł*, which is on er.   Er. aft. *hosp.*   From *manne* to *folces* on er.   8. -*sægen* in pl. of er.   -*den ł anscune-don me* on er.   From *mid* to end of v. on er.   9. *he gehyhte* on er.   *ł hopade* prob. by two Cors.; first wrote *hopað* and second made *ð* into *d* and add. *e.*   *ł alyseþ* on er.   From *he* to *he* on er.   10. *fram âtuge* on er.   Er. aft. *of.*   From *innoðe* to end of v. on er.   11. From begin. of v. to *moder* on er.   *min eart þu* by Cor.   12. *gewit þu* on er.   *geswinc* on er.   *gehende* on er.   *is* on er.   Er. bef. *7.*   Er. bef. and aft. *se.* -*ie* on er.   13. Er. aft. *ceolfœs.*   *forsetnoden,'r* and first *n* prob. on er.

atyndon ł upenedon on me hioræ muþ swa swa lye gripende
Aperuerunt   in me   os   suum   . sicut   leo   rapiens

7 grymetgende   swæ swæ wætær agotene siondon 7
et   rugiens   **15.** *sicut   aqua   effusa   sunt · et*

tostencede beoð eælle mine ban 7 min heorte his geworden
dispersa   sunt omnia ossa mea Et   factum est cor meum

swæ swæ meltende wex on middum mines innoþes   Astiðude
tanquam cera liquescens in   medio   ventris mei   **16.** *Exaruit*

swæ swæ tigle megen min 7 mine tungæ ætfylgþ ł togecleouode
velut   testa virtus mea et lingua mea   adhesit

minum gómum   7   on   deæþes dusze he geledden me
faucibus meis   et.   in   pulverem mortis deduxerunt   me

       Forþæn ymbseældon me monigæ hundæs geþeaht ł réd
17. *Quoniam circundederunt me   canes multi   concilium*

awargedre ofsetnode me   Hie dulfun mine hænde 7
malignantium   obsedit   me   Foderunt   manus meas   et

mine fet   7 ærimeden ł tealdon eælle mine bæn hi
pedes meos   **18.**   *dinumeraverunt   omnia ossa mea Ipsi*

soþlice bescæwodon 7 behyoldon me   hy todeldon
vero   consideraverunt et conspexerunt me   **19.** *diviserunt*

him hregle mine 7 ofer min hregl ł wed hie sendon hlyht
sibi vestimenta mea et super   vestem meam   miserunt sortem

þu soþlice dryhten ne   dó þinne fultum fior   fræm me
20. *Tu autem domine ne longe facias auxilium tuum   a   me*

to minum gescyldnesse beseoh ł locæ   Genere fram sworde
ad defensionem meam   aspice   · **21.** *Erue   a   framea*

mine sæwlæ   7   mine annesse of þes hundes hændæ
animam meam   et   de manu canis unicam meam

Gefriolsæ me of þes leon muþe 7 from horne þes anhornede
22. *Libera me de   ore leonis et   a cornibus unicornuorum*

minre eæþmodnesse   Ic cyþe þinum nomon minum broþrum
humilitatem meam   **23.** *Narrabo nomen tuum   fratribus meis*

---

14. *ł upenedon* on er. *swa* (1st), orig.=*swæ*? *swa* (2nd) on er. Er. aft.
gripende. -etyende, er. betw. *t* and *g*.   15. *agotene*, a- on er. Er. bef.
siondon. ban, orig.=*bæn. mines, -es* on er.   16. *Astiðude* by Cor. on er.
swæ (2nd) by Cor. on er.   *tigle megen min* in pl. of er.   *ł togecleouode* add.
by Cor.   17. Er. aft. *Forþæn*. Er. aft. *hundæs*. *geþeaht ł réd awargedre* in
pl. of er. *ofsetnode*, er. of one (or two ?) lett. at end.   18. *7* on er.   *ł tealdon*
by Cor. on er.   *behyoldon* on er. Er. bef. *me*.   19. *-ldon*, o on er.   *him* on
er. *mine* on er.   20. *-nesse* on er.   21. *fram sworde* on er.   22. *horne
þes anhornede* by Cor. on er.   23. *cyþe* on er.   7 er. bef. *minum*.

D

on midre circeæn ic þe herige   ge þe ondredæþ drihten
in medio aecclesiae laudabo te **24.** *Qui timetis dominum*

heriæþ   hine   cæll   iæcobes sed   gemycliæþ hine
laudate eum universum semen iacob   magnificate eum

   hine ondredæ eæl itræhelæ sed   forþæn he ne forhygede
25. *Timeat eum omne semen israel quoniam   non sprevit*

7 ne   forseah bene   ðeaifna 7 he ne acyrde onsyne his
neque despexit precem pauperum neque avertit faciem suam

from me 7 þonne ic cleopode to him he me gehirde   Myd
a me et dum clamarem ad eum   exaudivit me   **26.** *Apud*

þe min   lof   on þere miclæn ciercæn dryhten mine gehát
te laus michi in   ecclesia magna   vota mea domino

ic ægilde befoiæn ðam ondredendum hine   þeærfæn etæþ
reddam coram   timentibus   eum   **27.** *Edent pauperes*

7 bioþ gefillede 7 herigað drihten þa ðe   secað hine
et saturabuntur et laudabunt dominum qui requirunt eum

hioræ heortæ lifæþ on world æworlde   hie gemuneð 7
Vivet cor eorum in seculum seculi   **28.** *reminiscentur et*

beoð gecyrrede to drihtne eællæ eorþæn endes 7 gebiddæþ
convertentur ad dominum universi fines terrae Et adorabunt

on gesyhðe his ealle eþeles þeoda   forðan þe drihtnes
in conspectu eius omnes patriae gentium **29.** *quoniam domini*

is riche 7 he waldeþ ðeode   hie eton
est regnum et ipse dominabitur gentium **30.** *Manducaverunt*

7 gebædon éalle welie eorðen on gesyhðe his   falleð
et adoraverunt omnes divites terrae in conspectu eius procident

eælle þe niðæræstigæþ on eorðen   Ond min sæwl
universi qui descendunt in terram **31.** *Et anima mea*

hym libbe 7 min sed him þewæþ   Bið cypæd t bodad
ipsi vivet et semen meum serviet illi **32.** *Adnuntiabitur*

drihtne þæ towerdæ cneowrisse 7 heofonæs cyþæþ t bodiað
domino   generatio ventura et   adnuntiabunt caeli

---

24. *ge þe* on er. *eæll*, fin. let. er.   25. *hine, e* on er.   *ondrcdæ*, fin. let.
(þ?) er. *isræhelæ*, orig. = *iræhelæ* ; *s* being from *i* and *i* pref. From *he* (1st)
to *onsyne* in pl. of er. by Cor. Er. aft. *his*. *þonne ic cleopode* on er. by Cor.
gehirde, de on er. by Cor.   26. *gehát*, orig. = *gehǽt*?   27. From *herigað*
to *hine* by Cor. in pl. of er.   28. *-neð* on er. From 7 to *drihtne* by Cor. in
pl. of er. Er. bef. *eorþæn*. *hie* er. aft. 7. *on gesyhðe his* by Cor. on er.
ealle eþeles þeoda by Cor. in pl. of er.   29. All by Cor. in pl. of er. 30. Er.
aft. *eton*. Er. aft. 7. From *gebædon* to *falleð* by Cor. in pl. of er. ; *falleð*, er.
betw. *l* and *l*. *n'ðær*, prps. pref. by Cor.   31. *hym* on er.   32. *cypæd*,
d on er. *towe. dæ*, fin. let. er. *t bodiað* by Cor. on er.

rihtwisnesse   his   folcæ   þæ   geboren   bið   þet   geworhte
iustitiam   *eius*   *populo*   *qui*   *nascetur*   *quem*   *fecit*

drihten
dominus

22.

drihten   me   gerecht   7   nawuht   me   wane   bið   on
Dominus   *regit*   *me*   *et*   *nichil*   *michi*   *deerit*   **2.** *in*

þæræ   stowe   fósternoðes   ðer   he   me   gestæþelede   Ofer   weteræs
loco   *pascue*   *ibi*   *me   collocavit*   *Super   aquam*

gereordunge   he   gefedde   me   sæwle   mine   he   gecyrde
refectionis   *educavit*   *me*   **3.** *animam   meam*   *convertit*

He ledde me   ofer   siðfet ł stige rihtwisnesse   for   his   nomæn
Deduxit me super   semitam   iustitiae   propter nomen suum

Witotlice   7   gef   ic   gange   on   myddæn   deæþes   sceaduwe   ne
4.   *Nam   etsi   ambulem   in   medio   umbre   mortis   non*

ondræde ic   yfæle   forþæn   þu   myd   me   bist ł ært   þin   gierd   7
timebo   mala   quoniam   tu   mecum   es   Virga tua   et

stef   þin   hy   me   frefredon   þu gæærwodest beod
baculus tuus ipsa me consolata sunt   **5.** *Parasti in conspectú*

on minre gesihþe   ongean   þa   þe   eærfoþigæþ ł swencton   me
meo mensam   adversus   eos   qui   tribulant   me

þu onbryddæs ł mestest   min   heæfod   on   ele   7   þin   dryncefæt
Inpinguasti   in   oleo caput meum et   poculum tuum

drungniende   hu   bryht ł mere   is   7   þin   mildheortnesse
inebrians   quam   preclarum   est   **6.** *Et   misericordia tua*

me efterfylgend   eællum   dægum   mines   lifes   þet   ic   eærdige   on
subsequitur me   omnibus   diebus   vitae meæe   Ut   inhabitem   in

drihtnes   huse   on   langnesse   minræ   dægæ
domo domini   in   longitudine   dierum

þæ, fin. let. prob. er.   **22.** *gerecht, ht* on er.   *na-,* orig. *næ-.   wane
bið* by Cor. on er.   **2.** *fosternoðes* by Cor. on er.   *gestæþelede, þ* from *e* ł;
-ede prob. by Cor. on er.   From *-ordunge* to *me* by Cor. on er.   **3.** *mine
he gecyrde* by Cor. on er.   *He ledde me* by Cor. on er.   From *siðfet* to
-nesse by Cor. on er.   *nomæn, o* from something else.   **4.** From *Witotlice* to
gange by Cor. on er.   *sceaduwe* by Cor. on er.   *ne ondræde ic* by Cor. on er.
yfæle, e prob. add. by Cor.   *ł ært* prob. add. by Cor.   From *þin* (2nd) to *fre-*
fredon in pl. of er. by Cor.   **5.** *-wodest, t* prob. add. by Cor.   *ongean þa þe*
in pl. of er. by Cor.   *ł swencton me* add. by Cor.   *ł mestest* add. by Cor.   *þin,*
fin. *ne* er. ł   *-fæt* by Cor. on er.   *is* in d. ink.   **6.** *-fylgend,* fin. *e* er.   *lang-*
nesse by Cor. on er.

23.

Drihtnes is sio eorþe 7 gefelledness hire ymbwyrft eorðena 7
Domini est terra et plenitudo eius orbis terrarum et

ælle þa ðe eærdiæþ on hieræ　　he ofer ses gegrund-
universi qui habitant in ea 2. *Ipse super maria fun-*

wallede hye ꝥ gestæþolædæ 7 ofer streæmæs he geærwode hie
davit eam et super flumina preparavit illam

hwylc æstigæþ on drihtnes dune opðæ wylc stent on his þere
3. *Quis ascendit in montem domini aut qui stabit in loco*

ælgæn stowe　　þæ underiende hændæ 7 þæ clenæ heortæn
sancto eius 4. *Innocens manibus et mundo corde*

se þe na onfeng on ydelnesse his sæwlæ ne ne swor on facne
qui non accepit in vano animam suam nec iuravit in dolo

his niehxtæn　　þes onfehþ bletsunge from drihtne 7
proximo suo 5. *Hic accipiet benedictionem a domino et*

mildheortnesse fram gode hæle his　　þios is cnyowris
misericordiam a deo salutari suo 6. *Haec est generatio*

secændra drihten secændre onsiene iæcobes godes
querentium dominum requirentium faciem dei iacob

Geopeniæþ gæto eowre eældormonne 7 upæhebbæþ þæ ece-
7. *Tollite portas principes vestras et elevamini porte*

lecæn gæto 7 ingeþ se wuldorfestæ kyning　　hwilc is
aeternales et introibit rex gloriae 8. *Quis est*

þes wuldorfestæ kyning drihten his mihtig 7 stræng drihtæn
iste rex gloriae dominus fortis et potens dominus

is stræng on gefiohte　　Geopeniæþ gæto eowres eældor-
potens in prelio 9. *Tollite portas principes*

monnes ond upæhebbæþ ðæ ecelecæn gæto 7 ingeþ se wuldor-
vestras et elevamini porte aeternales et introibit rex

festæ kyning　　hwilc is þes wuldorfestæ kyning drihten
gloriae 10. *Quis est iste rex glorie dominus*

of meigne he is kyning on wuldre
virtutum ipse est rex gloriae

·

---

23. *gefelledness* on er. 7 *ælle þa ðe* in pl. of er. *-iæþ, i* wr. over the line.
2. *is* er. aft. *he.* *gegrundwallede hye ꝥ* in pl. of er. prps. by Cor. *hie, e* on
er. 4. *underiende* by Cor. on er. *clenæ,* fin. let. er.; the *e*-part of the *œ*
in d. ink. *þe,* orig.=*þæ.* *na, a* from some other let. (e ?). *swor on facne his*
in pl. of er. prob. by Cor. A second *facne* er. aft. *facne.* Er. aft. *his.* 5. *fram
gode hæle his* by Cor. on er. 6. *þios, o* dotted. *cnyowris,* fin. *n* er. Er.
aft. this word. *-dra* on er. *-dre* on er. of *-ne* ? 7. *eowre,* fin. *s* er. *·monne*
fin. *s* er. 9. *·monnes, es* in d. ink on er. ?

24.

To þe drihten ic upahof   mine sæwle   min god on þe
Ad te domine   levavi   animam meam   **2.** *deus meus in te*

ic getreowe ic ne scæmige   7 na bysmrien me mine
confido   non erubescam   **3.** *Neque irrideant me inimici*

fiend 7 soþlice ealle   þa ðe anbidigeð drihtne na hy beoð gescynde
mei etenim universi qui te exspectant domine non   confundentur

Sien gescynde þa unrihtwisan doende idelu þine wegæs drihten
4. *Confundantur   iniqui   facientes vana vias tuas domine*

gedo me cuþe 7 þine stygæ ł siþfatu gelere me   Gerece me
notas fac michi et   semitas tuas   edoce me   **5.** *Dirige me*

on þine soþfestnesse 7 lere me forðon þu eært god   mín helend
in   veritate tua   et doce me quia tu es deus salutaris meus

7 ðe ic ærefne ł þyldgode æle deg   gemune   miltsunga
et te   sustinui   tota die   **6.** *Reminiscere miserationum*

þinre drihten 7 þinre mildheortnesse þe of worlde sindon
tuarum domine et   misericordiae tuae quae a saeculo sunt

Ægyltæs iuguðhades minre 7   nitenesse minre ne gemune ðu
7. *Delicta iuventutis meae et ignorantiae meae ne memineris*

drihten efter   micle mildheortnesse þinre gemyndig byo ðu
domine secundum magnam misericordiam   tuam   memor esto

min god   for   þinre godnesse drihten   swete 7 rihtwis
mei deus Propter bonitatem tuam domine   **8.** *dulcis et rectus*

drihtæn fore þissum æ he sette ðam agiltendum on wege
dominus Propter hoc legem statuit delinquentibus in via

he gerecþ bilewite ł eæþmoden on his dome he lereþ þam softon
9. *diriget   mites   in iudicio docebit mansuetos*

his wegæs   Eælle drihtnes wegæs myldheortnesse 7
vias suas **10.** *Universe vie domini misericordia   et*

---

24. 2. *on þe ic getreowe* by Cor. on er.   3. *7 na* on er. in d. ink.   *me* in
d. ink. *ealle þa* by Cor. on er.   *anbidigeð, a* from *o* by Cor.; *-igeð* by Cor.
on er.   From *drihtne* to *gescynde* by Cor. in pl. of er.   4. Er. aft. *gescynde.*
þa, orig. *= þæ.*   *-wisan* by Cor. on er.   *doende idelu* by Cor. in pl. of er.   *ł*
siþfatu prob. add. by Cor.   5. Er. aft. *god.*   7 *ðe* by Cor. on er.   *æle* by
Cor. on er. *deg,* fin. let. er.   6. From *gemune* to *þinre* (1st) by Cor. in pl.
of er. *þe of* by Cor. on er.   7. From *iuguðhaðes* to *micle* by Cor. on er.
gemyndig byo ðu by Cor. on er.   *min* cov. by d. ink.   *drihten* by Cor. on er.
8. *swete* by Cor. on er.   *þissum,* first *s* wr. over the line.   Er. aft. this word.
æ he by Cor. in pl. of er.   *sette,* init. *ge* er.; also fin. let. er.   From *ðam* to
wege by Cor. in pl. of er.   9. From *he* to *bilewitz* by Cor. in pl. of er. 7 er.
bef. *he* (2nd). *þam softon* by Cor. on er.   10. *Eælle,* fin. *s* er.

soþfestnesse   ðam   secendum   gecyþnesse   his 7 gewitnesse his
veritas   requirentibus   testamentum   eius et   testimonia eius

    For   þinun nomæn   dryhten þu gemildsast minum synnum
11. *Propter   nomen   tuum   domine   propitiaberis   peccato meo*

soþlice hiræ is manigfeald   hwylc   is   se mæn   se him
copiosum est enim   12. Quis   est   homo   qui timeat

drihten ondrede æ ł ewe he him gesette on wege þam he gecyst
dominum   legem   statuit ei   in via quam   elegit

   his sæwle on gode biþ wunigende 7 his sed yrfeweærdnesse
13. *Anima eius in bonis   demorabitur et semen eius   haereditate*

ægende eorðæu   trymnesse   is dryhten ðam ondred-
possidebit terram   14. Firmamentum est dominus   timen-

endum hine   cyþnesse   his   þ   heo sie geswutelad   heom
tibus eum et testamentum ipsius ut   manifestetur   illis

    Min eægæn   symle   to   drihtne forþæn þe he oferswyþeþ
15. *Oculi   mei   semper   ad   dominum quoniam ipse   evell-*

ł utaluceð of gegrynum   mine fet   Locæ ł syoh on me 7
et   de   laqueo   pedes meos   16. Respice   in me et

myltsæ me forþæn   anlic 7 þearfe ic heom   Eærfoþnesse
miserere mei quoniam unicus et pauper sum ego   17. Tribulationes

minre heortæn tobredde siendon of niedþeærfum mine genere me
cordis mei   dilatatae   sunt   de necessitatibus meis   eripe   me

    Gesioh mine eæþmodnesse 7 gewin ł swinc min   7   forlet
18. *Vide   humilitatem meam et   laborem   meum et dimitte*

ealle synne mine   locæ ł beseoh on mine fiend   forðæn
omnia peccata mea   19. Respice   inimicos meos quoniam

hy gemonifeældode syndon 7 fioung ł hatunge unryhtæ hy hatedon
multiplicati   sunt   et   odio   iniquo   oderunt

me   Geheæld   saule   mine 7 genere me drihten na ic be
me   20. Custodi animam meam et   eripe   me domine non con-

onscynd forðan ic gecleopode þe   þæ unscyldie 7 þæ rihtwise
fundar quoniam invocavi   te   21. Innocentes et   recti

Er. aft. *soþfestnesse.* *ðam secendum* by Cor. on er.   11. *þu gemildsast* by
Cor. on er.   12. *æ ł* add. by Cor. *gesette,* part. on er.   7 er. bef. *on,* wh. is
on er.   *þam he* on er.   13. *ægende,* accent doubtful,   *on* er. bef. *eorðæn.*
14. From *ðam* to *hine* by Cor. in pl. of er.   Er. bef. *his.*   *geswutelad* on er.
with er. aft. it.   16. *ł syoh* add. by Cor.   *anlic* on er.   *þearfe,* fin. let. er. ł
17. *niedþeærfum,* let. er. betw. *d* and *þ.*   18. *Gesioh, h* on er. of some other
let.   From *gewin* to *mine* by Cor. in pl. of er.   19. *fiend,* fin. *e* er. *ł hat-*
unge by Cor. on er.   *un-* on er.   *-y hatedon me* by Cor. on er.   20. From
saule to end of v. by Cor. on er.   21. *-die* on er.   Er. at end of *riht·*; *-wise*
add. by Cor.

me etfyolæþ ꝺ togeþeoddon forþæn ic forbær þe drihten
adheserunt michi *quoniam* *sustinui* *te* *domine*

Ælys me ysræhelæ god of eællum minum angsumnesse
22. *Redime me deus israel ex omnibus angustiis meis*

25.

Dem me drihten forþan þe ic on mynre unscyldignesse
Iudica me domine quoniam ego in innocentia mea

ic ingange 7 on ᐟ drihten hopiende na ic untrumie
ingressus sum et in domino sperans non infirmabor

Gecosta ꝺ afanda me drihten 7 costa me bern edren mine 7
2. *Proba me domine et tempta me ure renes meos et*

heortan mine Forðæn þæ þin myldheortnesse is beforæn
cor meum **3.** *Quoniam misericordia tua ante oculos*

minum eægæn 7 ic gelicode on þiure soþfestnesse Ic ne sæt
meos est et complacui in veritate tua · **4.** *Non sedi*

on ydelnesse gemotstowe 7 myd þæm unrihtberendum ꝺ dondum
in concilio vanitatis et cum iniqua gerentibus

ic in ne gængæ Ic fiode ꝺ hatude gesomninge awyrgedra
non introibo **5.** *Odivi congregationem malignorum*

7 myd þæm ærleæsum ic ne sitte Ic ðwea mine
et cum impiis non sedebo **6.** *Lavabo inter*

hænde betwyoh ðæm unscyldige ic ymbgonge wifod þin
innocentes manus meas et circuibo altare tuum

drihten þet ic gehiere stemne þines lofes 7 þet ic
domine **7.** *Ut audiam vocem laudis tuae ut*

secge ꝺ cyþe eælle þine wundoru drihten ic lufude
enarrem universa mirabilia tua **8.** *Domine dilexi*

wlite þines huses 7 stowe eærdungæ þines wuldres
decorem domus tuae et locum habitationis gloriae tuae

Ne forspil þu myd þæm ærleæsum mine sæwle 7 myd werœ
9. *Ne perdas cum impiis animam meam et cum viris*

ꝺ *togeþeoddon* add. by Cor. *forbær* on er. 22. Er. bef. *angsumnesse.*
25. -*ldignesse ic ingange* by Cor. on er. *hopiende na ic untrumie* by Cor. in
pl. of er. 2. ꝺ *afanda* add. by Cor. ? *costa me bern* by Cor. on er. 3. 7
ic gelicode by Cor. on er. 4. *sæt* on er. ꝺ *dondum* wr. over the line. 5.
ꝺ *hatude* add. by Cor. *gesomninge* by Cor. on er. *awyrgedra* by Cor. on er.
6. *Ic ðwea* by Cor. on er. *unscyldige* by Cor. on er. *wifod þin* by Cor. on er.;
wifod, a fin. let. rubbed out while wet. 7. *wuudoru*, u add. by Cor. 8.
-*ude* by Cor. on er. Er. aft. *stowe*. 9. *þu* on er. Er. aft. *myd* (2nd).

blodum min lyf   on þæræ hondum siendon
sanguinum vitam meam 10. *in quorum manibus iniquitates*

unryhtnesse hioræ swyþræ gefylled is læcum ɫ medsceattum
 sunt *Dextera eorum repleta est*   *muneribus*

 Ic soþlice on mynre unscyldinesse ic ingeode æles me
11. *ego autem in innocentia mea ingressus sum redime me*

7 myltsæ me   fot soþlice min stod on rihtum wege on
et miserere mei 12. *Pes enim meus stetit in via recta in*

cyrceæn ic bletsie drihten
aecclesiis benedicam dominum

26.

Drithen is min onlihtnesse 7 mine helæ ᚹone ic me ondrede
Dominus illuminatio mea et salus mea quem timebo

Drihten is scyldon mines lifes for ᚹæn ic forhtie Midþy
Dominus defensor vitae mee a quo trepidabo 2. *Dum*

genealæcaᚹ ofer me scepᚹende þet hie eton flesc mine þa ᚹe
adpropiant super me nocentes ut edant carnes meas qui

swencat me fynd mine   sint geuntromode 7 gefeælleᚹ
tribulant me inimici mei ipsi infirmati sunt et ceciderunt

 Gif stondæþ ongean me weredu na ondredcᚹ heorte min
3. *Si consistant adversum me castra non timebit cor meum*

gif ærisæþ on me gefioht on þisum ic gchyhte ɫ gewene
si exsurgat in me prelium in hoc ego   sperabo

 Anes ic bæd fram drihtne þæs ic sece ɫ gegyrnde þet
4. *Unam petii a domino hanc requiram ut*

ic on dryhtnes huse eærdie eælle dægæs mines lifes þet
inhabitem in domo domini omnibus diebus vitae meae Ut

ic gesio mines drihtnes willæn 7 ic sie gescylded from his
videam voluntatem domini et protegar a templo

hulgæn temple forᚹæn þe me gehidde on his geteldunge
sancto eius 5. Quoniam abscondit me in tabernaculo suo

---

10. Er. aft. *hiorœ.* 11. *on* on er. *unscyldinesse ic ingeode* by Cor. on
cr. *æles, e* from *i* by Cor. and fin. let. er. 12. From *fot* to *stod* by Cor. on
er.   26. A fresh hand (in p. ink) begins here. It ends with the last
v. of Psalm 77. *Drithen* by Cor. 2. *genealœcaᚹ* by Cor. *scepᚹende* by
Cor. *þa ᚹe* cov. by d. ink by Cor. From *swencat* to *mine* by Cor., *fynd* being
on er. 3. *hie* er. aft. *Gif.* *ongean* by Cor. ; er. of two lett. betw. *n* and *g.*
weredu na ondredeᚹ by Cor. on er. *min* by Cor. on er. Er. bef. *gif* (2nd).
þisum, þi- cov. by d. ink. *gehyhte ɫ* by Cor. 4. *-æd* in d. ink on er. *fram*
cov. by d. ink. *-tne* cov. by d. ink. *ɫ gegyrnde* ins. by Cor. *þe* er. aft. *his.*
temple by Cor.

on dege þæræ yflæ gescilde me on gedygelnesse geteældunge his
in die malorum protexit me in abscondito tabernaculi sui

on þæn stænæ he upæhof me   Nu ðonne soðlice upæhefþ mīn
6. *in petra exaltavit me   Nunc autem exaltavit caput*

hæfod ofer fiend mine ic ymbgonge 7 ic offrige on his
meum super inimicos meos circuibo et immolabo in taber-

geteældunge onsægdnesse lofes ł dremes ic singe 7 seælm
naculo eius hostiam iubilationis cantabo et psalmum

ic cwiðe drihtne   Gehier drihten mine stemne þæ
dicam domino '   **7.** *Exaudi domine vocem meam qua*

ic chige ł clypie to þe mildsæ me 7 ongehiere me   þe
clamavi ad te miserere mei et exaudi me **8.** *Tibi*

sægde min heorte ic sohte ðine andwlitan ł onsine ðine
dixit cor meum quesivi vultum tuum vultum tuum

dryhten ic sece   Ne acyrre ðu þine onsiene from me 7
domine requiram **9.** *Ne avertas faciem tuam a me et*

ne hyld ł becyrre ðu on eorre þeowe þine Gefylstend min
ne declines in ira a servo tuo Adiutor meus

þu beo ne forlet þu me ne forSioh þu me god mine
esto ne derelinquas me neque despicias me deus salutaris

hęlo   Forðæn feder mīn 7 moder min hy forleton me
meus **10.** *Quoniam pater meus et mater mea dereliquerunt me*

drihten soðlice anfeng me   Æwe me gesette •
dominus autem assumpsit me **11.** *Legem michi constitue*

drihten on wege ðinum 7 gerece me on stigæ ł on siðfæte rihtæ
domine in via tua et dirige me in semita recta

for fiondum minum   Ne sele þu me on Sæwlæ
propter inimicos meos **12.** *Ne tradideris me in animas*

ehtendræ me forðæn onrison on me cyþras ł gewiten
persequentium me quoniam insurrexerunt in me testes

unrihtwise 7 leasfyrhte is unryhtwisnes him   Ic geliefe
iniqui et mentita est iniquitas sibi 13. *Credo*

drihtnes god to gesionne on liuiendræ eorðæn   ic onbide
videre bona domini in terra viventium 14. *exspecta*

drihtnes 7 ic werlice do 7 si gestrængod þin heorte 7 geanbida
dominum et viriliter age et confortetur cor tuum et sustine
drihten
dominum

27.

To þe drihten ic clipode min god ne swiga þu from me 7
1. *Ad te domine clamavi deus meus ne sileas a me et*

ic bîo gelic þæm niþerstigendum on seþe   Gehire
ero similis descendentibus in lacum 2. Exaudi

stemne mines gebedes midþie ic togebidde 7 ðonne
vocem deprecationis meae dum oro ad te et dum

ic uphebbe mine hænde to þinum hælgæn temple Na
extollo manus meas ad templum sanctum tuum 3. Ne

somod þu selle me mid synfullum 7 mid þæm wircendum
simul tradas me cum peccatoribus et cum operantibus

unrihtnesse ne forspil ðu me Mid þysum þe her sprecæð sibbe
iniquitatem ne perdas me Cum his qui loquuntur pacem

mid hirum nixtum soðlice yfel sint on hioræ heortæn
cum proximo suo mala autem sunt in cordibus eorum

Sele hem efter hioræ weorce 7 efter hiore niþbete
4. *Da illis secundum opera eorum et secundum nequitiam*

hioræ gecneorþnisse ł tilengæ geedleænæ hem Agield hioræ
studiorum ipsorum retribue illis Redde retri-

edleænængæ hem   forðon þe hie ne ongeæton drihtnes
butionem eorum ipsis 5. quoniam non intellexerunt in opera

weorc 7 on his worce his honde hie ne sceæwodon Tobrec
domini et in opera manuum eius non considerant Desirue

hie ne þu hie ne getimbre gebletsæd drihten forðon þe
illos nec aedificabis eos 6. benedictus dominus quoniam

Er. bef. *unrihtwise; -wise* by Cor. From *leasfyrhte* to *him* by Cor. on er.
13. *Ic* cov. by d. ink. 14. *-bide* cov. by d. ink. 7 *geanbida drihten* by
Cor.   27. 1. *To* by Cor. *-ode* by Cor. on er. *ne swiga þu* by Cor. *seþe*
cov. by d. ink.   2. From 7 to *uphebbe* by Cor. *mine* part. cov. by d. ink.
Er. aft. *þinum.* 3. From *Na* to *selle* by Cor. Er. bef. and aft. *mid.* *syn-*
by Cor. *ðu, -u* by Cor. on er. 4. *hem, e* from *i.* *gecneorþnisse t* add. by
Cor. *hem* (2nd), *e* from *i.* *hem* (3rd), *e* from *i.* 5. *honde,* the *e* made by
d. ink. 6. *sæd, d* in d. ink prob. add. by Cor. *þe he* in d, ink.

he gehierde stemne mines gebedes Drihten is min
exaudivit vocem deprecationis mee 7. *Dominus adiutor*

fultum 7 min scyldend 7 on hine gehyhte ꝉ geweneþ min heorte
meus et protector meus et in ipso speravit cor meum

7 gefultumod ic eom 7 blostmæt ꝉ bleow min flesc 7 of minum
et adiutus sum Et refloruit caro mea et ex voluntate

willum ic ondette him Drihtnes strengðo his folce 7
mea confitebor illi 8. *Dominus fortitudo plebis suae et*

gescyld crist hiorä helo is Gedo hæl þin
protector salutarium christi sui est 9 *Salvum fac populum*

folc drihten 7 gebletsæ þine hyrfeweærdnesse 7 gerece hie 7
tuum domine et benedic haereditati tuae et rege eos et

genim ꝉ ahefe hie oþþe on world ꝉ on ecnisse
extolle illos usque in aeternum

28.

gebringað drihtne godes beærn gebrengæð drihtne weþræs ꝉ
Afferte domino filii dei afferte domino filios

romma beærn Gebrengæð drihtne wuldor 7 arwurðunge
arietum 2. *Afferte domino gloriam et honorem*

gebrengæð drihten wundor his næmon Gebiddæþ drihten on
afferte domino gloriam nomini eius Adorate dominum in

his hæligre hælla drihtnes stem ofer weteru 7 godes
aula sancta eius 3. *vox domini super aquas deus*

megenþrym ontyneþ ꝉ onswegde drihten ofor monigo weteru
maiestatis intonuit dominus super aquas multas

Drihtnes stem on megene drihtnes stem on micelnessæ
4. *Vox domini in virtute vox domini in magnificentia*

Drihtnes stem gebrecende þone cedorbeæm 7 drihten ge-
5. *Vox domini confringentis cedros et confringet do-*

briceð cederas of libani 7 forgnideð hie swæ swæ þet sceælf
minus cedros libani 6. *et comminuet eas tanquam vitulum*

þe er. aft. *he. gehierde* cov. by d. ink. 7. Er. aft. *fultum. gehyhte* ꝉ
add. by Cor. 7 cov. by d. ink ; an er. aft. it. *gefultumod* cov. by d. ink. *ic
eom* in d. ink by Cor. *blostmæt* part. cov. by d. ink. ꝉ *bleow* add. in d. ink.
8. *his* from *þis*? 9. ꝉ *ahefe* add. by Cor. ꝉ *on ecnisse* by Cor. 28. *gebringað* by Cor. *weþræs, s* by Cor. ꝉ *romma* by Cor. 2. *Geb-* cov. by Cor.
7 *arwurðunge* by Cor. on er. *gebrengæð, ge-* part. cov. by d. ink. *hæligre* by
Cor. -*lla* by Cor. 3. *weteru, -u* by Cor. ꝉ *onswegde* by Cor. *weteru, -u*
by Cor. 5. *cederas of libani* by Cor. 6. 7 *forgnideð* by Cor. Er. bef.
and aft. *hie. swæ* (1st) part. cov. by d. ink.

on libani 7 leofne swæ swæ beærn ænhyrnedes diores
libani   et dilectus sicut filios unicornuorum

Drihten stem tosceaddendis leg þæm fire stefn drihtnes
7. *Vox domini intercidentis flammam ignis* **8.** *vox domini*

hrysiendis on westen 7 astyred drihten onwendeþ westen
concutientis solitudinem et commovebit dominus desertum

gefeællende Drihtnes stem gecerwiende þæ heortes 7 to ônwreonne
cades **9.** *Vox domini preparantis cervos et revelabit*

þiccettu ł hioræ den 7 on his temple eælle cweþæþ wuldor
condensa et in templo eius omnes dicent gloriam

Drihtæn flod oneærdæþ 7 onsitt drihten kining on
10. *Dominus diluvium inhabitat et sedebit dominus rex in*

eccnesse Drihtnes megen his folce seleoð 7 gebletsæð
aeternum **11.** *Dominus virtutem populo suo dabit et benedicet*

folc hys on sibbe
populum suum in pace

29.

Ic ahebbe þe drihten forðæn þu me onfenge ne þu na to-
2. *Exaltabo te domine quoniam suscepisti me nec delect-*

breddest mine fiend ofer me Min drihten god to þe ic
asti inimicos meos super me **3.** *Domine deus meus cla-*

chige ł cleopode 7 þu me gehældest drihten þu widtihx from
mavi ad te et sanasti me **4.** *domine abstraxisti ab*

helwarum mine sæwle 7 þu me geheldest from þæm niþersti-
inferis animam meam salvasti me a descenden-

gendum on þone Seæþ Singæð drihtne his hælgum 7
tibus in lacum **5.** *Psallite domino sancti eius et*

ondettæþ mid geminde his hælignisse Forðæn eorre biþ
confitemini memoriae sanctitatis eius **6.** *Quoniam ira*

on ebylgnesse his 7 lyf on his willæn On ðon efen bið
in indignatione eius et vita in voluntate eius Ad vesperum dem-

---

From *on* to *leofne* by Cor. on˙er., the 7 being merely cov. in d. ink. Er. bef. *ænhyrnedes*; the *es* by Cor. on er. *diores, es* by Cor. on er. **7.** *tosceaddendis leg* by Cor. on er. **8.** *stefn* by Cor. on er. *hrysiendis* by Cor. on er. *westen* by Cor. on er. Er. aft. 7. *astyred* by Cor. on er. 7 er. bef. *drihten.* **9.** *þiccettu ł* by Cor. **10.** *flod* by Cor. Er. bef. *oneærdæþ.* *onsitt*, let. (d) er. betw. *n* and *s.* **11.** *hys* by Cor. **29. 2.** *Ic ahebbe þe* by Cor. *ne þu na to-* by Cor. *-dest, t* add. by Cor. **3.** *ł cleopode* add. by Cor. *·est* by Cor. on er. **4.** *helwarum* by Cor.; er. aft. it. *-dest, d* wr. over the line. **5.** Er. bef. *his* (1st). *hælignisse* cov. in d. ink by Cor.

wuniende wóóp 7 to þæm uhtlicum ł dægred blis   Ic
orabitur fletus et ad   matutinum   letitia   7. Ego

soðlice cwęð on minre genihtsumnisse þet ic me ne onwende ł astyred
autem dixi in mea habundantia   non   movebor

on ecnesse   drihten on þinum goðæn willæn þu geærwedest
in aeternum   8. Domine in bona voluntate tua   prestitisti

minum wlite þin megen þu æwirfdes þine onsine fram me 7
decori meo virtutem avertisti faciem tuam   a   me et

ic geworden eom gedrefed   drihten to þe ic cliepie 7 to
factus sum   conturbatus   9. Ad te domine clamabo et ad

minum godum 7 ic bio biddende   hwylc netnesse on minum
deum meum   deprecabor   10. quae utilitas in sanguine

blode þonne ic niðærstige on gegripnesse ł onbrosnunga Is þes
meo dum descendo in   corruptionem   Nun-

wén þet ic þe ondette þe dust opðe bodaþ soþfæstnisse þine
quid confitebitur tibi pulvis aut annuntiabit veritatem tuam.

Drihten gehierde 7 is miltsigende me drihten is geworden
11. *Audivit dominus et misertus est michi dominus factus est*

ge min fultumend ł gefylstend   ðu gecirdest   minne heof
adiutor meus   12. Convertisti planctum meum

on gefeæn me þu tostlite ł -curfe mine sęc ł hæran 7 me be-
in gaudium michi conscidisti   saccum meum et pre-

gierdest me on blisse   þ ic singe þe wuldor min 7 ic ne
cinxisti me laetitia 13. ut cantem tibi gloria mea et non

síe ł ne beo onbryrd Min drihten god on ecnesse ic ondette þe
conpungar   Domine deus meus in æternum confitebor tibi

30.

On þe drihten ic gewene ł hyhte þet ic ne sie gescynd on
2. *In te domine   speravi   non confundar   in*

ecnesse on þinre soþfestnesse gefriolsæ ł alys me ⁊ nere me
aeternum in tua iustitia libera me et eripe me

Onhyld þin eære to me ⁊ þu hredlice ł efest nere me
3. *Inclina ad me aurem tuam accelera ut eripias me*

Beó þu me on gode gescyldend ⁊ on stowe rotnisse oþþet
Esto michi in deum protectorem et in locum refugii ut

þu me hæle gedó Forðæn mine trimnesse ⁊ min
salvum me facias 4. *Quoniam firmamentum meum et refu-*

gescyld west þu ⁊ for þinum nomæn mín lættþeow þu bist
gium meum es tu et propter nomen tuum dux michi eris

⁊ þu me afeddest ⁊ læddest þu me of gryne þissum þa
et enutries me 5. *Et educes me de laqueo isto quem*

me gedieledon forðon þu art gescyldend min drihten
occultaverunt michi quoniam tu es protector meus domine

on þine hænde ic etfeste ł ic bebeode þe mine gæst þu me
6. *in manus tuas commendo spiritum meum Rede-*

alisdest drihten god on soðfestnesse þu fiodes ł hatudest
misti me domine deus veritatis 7. *odisti*

þæ beweardgende idelnesse ofer þæ emettgæn ł unnytlice Ic soðlice
observantes vanitatem super vacue Ego autem

on drihten hyhte ic winsumie ł fægenie ⁊ blissiæ on þine
in domino sperabo 8. *exultabor et laetabor in tua*

mildheortnessæ Forðæn þu gelocedes ł sawe eæþmodnesse mine ⁊
misericordia Quia respexisti humilitatem meam

hele me gedydest of minum niedþeærfnessvm ł nedum sæwle
salvam fecisti de necessitatibus animam

mine ne ðu na beluce me on fiondæs hændum þu gesettest
meam 9. *nec conclusisti me in manus inimici Statuisti*

mine fęt on stowe rumre ł widgilre miltsæ me drihten
in loco spatioso pedes meos 10. *miserere michi domine*

From ł to me (2nd) by Cor. on er. ? 3. *Onhyld*, fin. let. (e ?) er. ł *efest*
add. by Cor. *nere me* by Cor. on er. From *Beó* to *gode* by Cor. on er. *ge-*
pref. by Cor. *rotnisse* by Cor. wr. above an er. Er. aft. *rotnisse.* 4. *lætt-*
þeow part. cov. by d. ink. 5, *læddest þu* cov. by d. ink. *of gryne* by Cor.
on er. *þissum*, er. betw. *s* and *s*. Er. aft. *þissum. gedieledon*, let. er. aft.
second *e*. *þu art gescyldend* by Cor. *min* by Cor. on er. 6. *etfeste*, last *e*
in d. ink. *þe* by Cor. *-e·t, t* prob. add. by Cor. 7. ł *hatudest* add. by Cor.
beweardgende by Cor. on er. ł *unnytlice* add. over the line by Cor. *hyhte* by
Cor. 8. *ic winsumie* part. cov. by d. ink. ł *fægcnie* (or *fægnie* ?) by Cor.
ł *sawe* by Cor. ; er. aft. it. *mine* by Cor. ł *nedum* add. by Cor. 9. From
ne to *on* (1st) by Cor. *-dæs, s* in d. ink. *-est, t* prob. add. by Cor. *rumre,*
prob. cov. by d. ink by Cor. ł *widgilre* by Cor. 10. *miltsæ*, let. (m ?) at
end er.

forþon ic iem geeærfoþod Gedrefed is min egæ for irre
quoniam tribulor Conturbatus est in ira oculus meus

sæul mîn 7 innoð min Forðæn þe teorode min lyf on
anima mea et venter meus 11. *Quoniam defecit in dolore vita*

særæ 7 mine geær on giomrungum Geuntrumæd is on þeærflicnisse
mea et anni mei in gemitibus Infirmata est in paupertate

mægen min 7 bæn mine gedrefede synt Ofer eællæ
virtus mea et ossa mea conturbata sunt 12. *Super omnes*

mine fiend geworden ic eom hosp neahgeburum minum
inimicos meos factus sum obprobrium vicinis meis

to swiðe 7 ege cuþum minum ða þe me gesiowon ute hie flugon
nimium et timor notis meis Qui videbant me foras fugiebant

from me 7 ic gefeol swæ swæ dead fram heortæn 7 ic eom
a me 13. *excidi tanquam mortuus a corde et factus*

geworden swæ swæ þet forlore fęt Forðæn ic gehierda
sum sicut vas perditum 14. *Quoniam audivi*

tale manigra ymbeærdiendra On him ða hy
vituperationem multorum circumhabitantium In eo dum con-

gesomnodon eælle Somed ongean me þet hie onfeangen mine
gregarentur omnes simul adversum me ut acciperent animam

. sæwle hy geþeahtiende sindon Ic soðlice on þe gewene ł
meam consiliati sunt 15. *Ego vero in te sper-*

hyhte drihten ic cweð þu eært min god on þinum hændum
avi domine dixi tu es deus meus 16. *in manibus tuis*

sint mine tidæ Gefriolsæ ł alyse me 7 genere me of minræ fiondæ
tempora mea Libera me et eripe me de manibus inimi-

hændum 7 from me ehtendum Onlihtæ þine onsiene
corum meorum et a persequentibus me 17. *Inlumina faciem tuam*

ofer þinne þiow 7 gedo me hælne on þinre mildheortnesse
super servum tuum et salvum me fac in tua misericordia

---

min, fin. e er. egœ, fin. n er. Er. aft. sœul. min (3rd) by Cor.; er. immed.
bef. it. 11. teorode by Cor. Er. aft. gœr. -licnesse by Cor. Er. aft. it.
mœgen by Cor. min, fin. e er., also an er. bef. the word. mine by Cor. synt
by Cor. 12. geworden ic eom hosp by Cor. on er. From neah- to ege by
Cor.; h on er. of g. minum (2nd) by Cor. on er. ða, a altered from some other
let. -owon by Cor. part. on er. -ugon by Cor. on er. 13. gefeul by Cor.
swœ dead by Cor. on er., also an er. aft. it. fram by Cor. on er. -lore prob. by
Cor. on er. 14. -da by Cor. on er.; orig. = gehiere? manigra on er., also
er. bef. and aft. it. ymbeœrdiendra, fin. e of ymb- er.; also one let. er. bef. the
first e, and -ra by Cor. on er. (of e?). ða hy by Cor. on er. -on by Cor. on
er. (of e?). ongean by Cor. feangen by Cor. part. on er. 15. ł hyhte by
Cor. cweð, fin. let. (e?) er.

drihten þet ic ne sie gescynd forðon   ic þe chide Sceæmigen
18. *domine*   *non confundar*   *quoniam invocavi te Erubescant*

ærleæsum 7 Sien geledde on   helle   dumbe Sien geworðen
impii et deducantur in infernum   **19.** *muta*   *efficiantur*

weleras facenfulle þe   sprecað ongen ryhtwisne unrihtwisnesse
labia dolosa   *quae loquuntur adversus iustum*   *iniquitatem*

on ofermodnisse 7 forsewennisse   hu   micel is þin menigo
in superbia et contemptu   **20.** *Quam magna multitudo*

þinre swetnesse drihten   þe   ondredendum þæ þu behiddest
dulcedinis tuae domine quam   *abscondisti timentibus te*

7 þu hie fulfremedest on þe gewenende i hyhte on gesihþe   mænnæ
et perfecisti eam   *sperantibus in te*   *in conspectu filiorum*

beærnæ   ðu gehyddest hie on dygelnesse þinre onsienc
hominum   **21.** *Abscondes eos in abditu vultus tui*

from gedrefnesse   mænnæ ðu hie ge[s]cildest on þinre
a conturbatione hominum   *Proteges eos*   *in taber-*

eærdungstowe from þæm wiðercweðelum tungum   Gebletsod
naculo tuo a contradictione linguarum   **22.** *Benedictus*

drihten forðæn   wuldrede his his mildheortnesse on ymbstan-
dominus quoniam mirificavit   *misericordiam suam in civitate*

dendræ þære ceæstre   Ic soðlice cweð on minre firhte
circumstantiae   **23.** *Ego autem dixi in pavore meo*

ic eom aworpen from onsine þinræ eægænæ Forþon þu gehierdes
proiectus sum a vultu oculorum tuorum Ideo exaudisti

stemne   minre bene   þonne ic clepedo to þe   drihtæn
vocem deprecationis meae dum clamarem ad te   **24.** *Diligite*

lufiæþ   eællc his hælge forðon hi secæð soðfestnesse 7 drihten
dominum omnes sancti eius quoniam veritatem requiret dominus et

edlenæð þam þe geinehtsumnesse doþ ofermodinesse
retribuet his qui habundanter faciunt superbiam

---

18. *chide, d* from *e*? *þœ* er. aft. *Sceæmigen.*   19. *-ðen, n* add. by Cor.; er. aft. this word. *weleras facenfulle þe* by Cor. on er. *-að*, by Cor. on er. *ongen ryhtwisne*, by Cor. on er. *-wisnesse* by Cor. on er.; *s* (1st) wr. over the line. *on ofermodnisse* by Cor. partly on er. *forsewennisse* by Cor. on er.   20. *-dest* (1st), *t* in d. ink prob. add. by Cor. *-dest* (2nd) *t* in d. ink over the line prob. add. by Cor. *t hyhte* by Cor.   21. *-ddest, t* in d. ink prob. add. by Cor. *dygel-* by Cor. on er. *-ldest, st* prob. add. by Cor. *-stowe* by Cor. *from*, MS. = *fron.*   22. *Gebletsod* blotted by d. ink betw. *s* and *o.* *drede* by Cor. on er. MS. = *-stand-*?   23. *cweð*, fin. e er. *on* in d. ink. Let. er. bef. *onsine. þonne* by Cor. on er. *clepedo, e* from *i* in both cases; *-do* prob. by Cor.   24. 7 er. bef. *edlenæð. þam, am* by Cor. on er. MS. = *-ineht-.* Er. aft. *doþ. -modinesse* by Cor.

doþ wẻrlice   7 sie gestronged eowre heortæn   eælle þæ
25. *Viriliter agite   et   confortetur   cor vestrum   omnes qui*
geweneþ hyhten on drihten
 speratis   in domino

31.

Ædige   þara   þe forgefene sint hioræ unrihtwisnesse 7   ðara
1. *Beati quorum   remisse   sunt   iniquitates   et quorum*

þe bewrigene synt   synna   Eadig wer þæm þe na ne
 tecta   sunt peccata   **2.** *Beatus vir   cui   non*

ætwiteð dryhten   his synnæ 7 ne nis on muðe his facn
imputavit dominus   peccatum   nec es: in   ore eius dolus

Forþæn ic swigie 7   eælle mine bæn eældiæþ   midþy þonne
3. *Quoniam tacui   inveteraverunt omnia ossa mea   dum*

ic clipie to ðe ælce ĩ allan deige   Forðæn deges 7 niehtes
clamarem   tota   die   **4.** *Quoniam die ac nocte*

gehefogod is ofer me þin hænd 7 ic eom gewyrfed on geriwo ĩ on
 gravata est super me manus tua   conversus sum   in erum-

angnisse mine þonne bið tobrocen hrycgban   Mine egyltæs
 pna   mea dum confringitur spina **5.** *Delictum meum*

ic dide þe oncnæwe 7 mine unsoðfestnesse ic ne oferwreah Ic cweð
cognitum tibi feci et iniustitias meas   non operui Dixi

þet ic sege ĩ bodige ongean ĩ wiþ me 7 mine unsoþfestnesse drihten
 pronuntiabo   adversum   me   iniustitias meas domino

7 þu forlete arleasnesse minre heortæn   For þisum gebiddæþ
et tu remisisti impietatem cordis mei **6.** *Pro hac   orabit*

cælle hælige to þe on   tide gehyþelicre ðeah hweþre Soðlice
ad te omnis sanctus in tempore oportuno   verum   tam-

þonne on flode wẹtra monigræ to him na togeneælecæþ
 en in diluvio aquarum multarum ad eum non adproximabunt

---

25. 7 *sie* in d. ink.   *hyhten on* by Cor. on er.   **31.** 1. *Ædige* by Cor. *þara*
þe by Cor. on er.   *for-* cov. by d. ink ; *-gefene* by Cor. on er. ? *-twisnesse*
part. cov. by Cor.; orig. = *unrihtnesse*?   From *ðara* to *synna* by Cor. in pl. of
er.   2. *þæm, m* by Cor.   From *na* to *dryhten* by Cor. in pl. of er.   From 7
to *muðe* by Cor. on er.   *his* part. cov. by d. ink.   *facn* by Cor. on er.   3.
swigie part. cov. by d. ink.   *þonne* by Cor.   From *to* to *allan* by Cor.   *deige,*
-ige by Cor.   4. *þin,* fin. *e* er.   *hænd,* fin. let. (æ ?) er.   *t on angnisse* add.
by Cor.   From *mine* to *-ban* by Cor. in pl. of er. ; the *c* of *hrycgban* wr. over
the line.   5. Er. bef. *oncnæwe.*   *oferwreah* by Cor. on er.   *cweð,* fin. let.
(e ?) er.   *t bodige ongean t* add. by Cor., the *g* of *bodige* prob. from *e.*   *arleas-*
nesse on er. ; the first *a* orig. prob. *œ.*   6. Er. aft. *tide.*   *gehyþelicre*
ðeahhwcþre by Cor. in pl. of er.   *-ne on flode* by Cor. on er.   Er. aft. *wẹtra.*

þu eært   min   frofr   fram ofðriccednisse þc ymbsealde
7. *Tu   es   michi refugium   a   pressura   quae circumdedit*

me   blis   min alyse me fram ymbsellendum   Ondgiet
me exultatio mea redime me a   circundantibus me   **8.** *Intellectum*

ic þe selle 7 ic þe lære on þisum wegc þe þu iu ongangest
dabo tibi et instruam te in   via hac   qua   ingredieris

ic getrymme ofer þe eagan mine   nellen ge beon swa hors
firmabo super te oculos meos   **9.** *Nolite   fieri sicut equus*

‾ mul on þæm nis nenig ontgiet   On þæm bridle 7 on
mulus in quibus non est intellectus In   freno   et

þ¢re walde ceocan heoræ gewryð ł gebind þa na togcnealecað
chamo   maxillas eorum   constringe qui non adproximant

to þe   Monigo ł fela swîpo ł swingella þæræ firenfulræ ł
ad te **10.**   *Multa   flagella   pecca-*

synfulra hihtende soþlice on drihtcn mildheortnis ymbselð utan
torum sperantes autem in domino   misericordia   circumdabit

· we blissiæð on drihtne 7 fægniað rihtwise 7 eælle wuldriæd
11. *Laetamini in domino et exultate   iusti   et gloriamini omnes*

on rihtre heortæn
recti corde

32.

gefeinigað ryhtwise on drihtne ryh[t]wise gerist somodhering
1. *Gaudete   iusti   in domino rectos   decet conlaudatio*

Ondettæþ   drihtne on eærpungum 7 on psalterum tyen
2. *Confitemini domino in   cythara   in psalterio decem*

strenga singæþ him   Singæþ him niewne song and
cordarum psallite ei   **3.** *Cantate ei   canticum novum*

wel singæþ him on wyndreame ł on lofe   Forðæn þe
bene psallite ei in   iubilatione   **4.** *Quoniam*

riht is drihtnes word and eælla his weorc on lofe
rectus est sermo domini et   omnia opera eius in fide

---

7. *frofr* by Cor. on er.? From *þe* to *fram* by Cor. in pl. of er. Er. bef. *ymb-*. 8. *Ond-* part. cov. by d. ink. *lære* by Cor. on er. *þe þu in ongan-gest* wr. over an er. *eagan mine* by Cor. on er. 9. *nellen ge bcon swa* by Cor. on er. *walde* by Cor.? *ceocan* by Cor. on er. *-ryð* by Cor. on er. From *ł gebind* to *-lecoð* by Cor. prob. on er. 10. *ł swingella* and *ł synfulra* crowded in. *mildheortnis* by Cor. on er.? 11. *fægniað* on er. 32. The whole of the first v. by Cor.?; *gefeinigað*, first *ł* on er. of *g*. 2. *Ondettæþ* part. cov. by d. ink. *tyen strenga* by Cor. on er. Er. aft. *strenga*. 3. *and, a* prob. from *o*. From *on* (1st) to *lofe* by Cor. on er. 4. *and, a* from *o*. *eælla, a* in d. ink. *on lofe* by Cor. on er.

he lufæþ miltheortnesse 7 drihtnes dóm his mildheortnesse
5. *Diligit   misericordiam et   iudicium   misericordia*

drihtnes ful is eorþe   drihtenes wordes 7 heofonæs
domini plena est terra   **6.** *verbo domini   caeli*

Sient getrimede 7 on gaste his muðes eæll hioræ megen
firmati sunt   et   spiritu   oris eius omnis virtus eorum

Gesomniende swæ swæ on bytt wætere sæs gesettende on
7. *Congregans   sicut   in utrem aquas maris ponens   in*

goldhordum on niwolnesse ł grundas   drihten him ondrędæþ
thesauris   abyssos   **8.** *Timeat dominum*

eælle eorþe from him soðlice bid onwended
omnis terra ab ipso autem commoveantur universi

ond eælle þæ þe eærdigæþ on ymbhwirfte   Forþæn he
et omnes qui   habitant orbem   **9.** *Quoniam ipse*

cweð 7 gewordene sind he bebead and gesceæpene hy synd
dixit et   facta   sunt ipse mandavit et   creata sunt

Drihten tostencte geþeaht þiodæ he wyðcyst soðlice
10. *Dominus dissipat consilia gentium   reprobat   autem*

geþohtas þæræ þiodæ ł folca 7 wiðcostode þære geþoht aldra
cogitationes   populorum   et reprobat consilia   principum

geþeæht soþlice drihtnes wunæþ on ecnesse his heortæn
11. *Consilium vero   domini   manet in aeternum cogitationes*

geþoht on alraworld æworold   Eædig þiod þes ðę is
cordis eius in saeculum   saeculi   **12.** *Beata gens cuius est*

hioræ drihten god folc þem drihten gesceæs on
dominus deus eorum populus quem   elegit dominus   in

yrfeweardnis him   Drihten of hefonum gelocode 7 geseah
hereditatem sibi   **13.** *De caelo prospexit dominus et vidit*

eællæ monnæ beærn   be þere gearwunge his eardunge
omnes filios hominum   **14.** *de   preparato   habitaculo suo*

---

7. *swæ on bytt wætere sæs* by Cor. on er. *goldhordum, -um* by Cor. ł
grundas add. by Cor.   8. Er. aft. *on.*   9. Er. (þe?) aft. *Forþæn. gewor-*
dene by Cor. on er.   *he bebead* by Cor. on er.   *and, a* from *o*?   *hy synd* by
Cor.   10. *geþeaht* by Cor. on er.   *he wyðcyst* by Cor. on er.   *soðlice geþohtas*
by Cor. on er. *þiodæ* part. cov. by d. ink. ł *folca* add. by Cor. *geþoht*
aldra by Cor. on er.   11. *geþeæht, ł* cov. by d. ink. *soþlice drihtnes* by
Cor. on er. *wunæþ* part. cov. by d. ink. Er. aft. *geþoht.*   *on alr-* prob.
pref. by Cor.; *-world, l* cov. by d. ink.   12. *þiod, d* from ð.   *drihten* by
Cor. *on yrfeweardnis him,* by Cor. on er.   13. *gelocode,* er. bef. it; *ge-* and
-ode by Cor. on er. *geseah, h* in d. ink on er.

7 he locode   ofer   cælle   þe   eærdiæþ   on ymbhwirft   Se
respexit   super omnes qui   habitant orbem   15. *Qui*

hiwode   Sienderlice   hioræ   heortæn   þæ   angetæþ   on   ealle hioræ
finxit   singillatim   corda eorum   qui intelligit   in omnia opera

weorc   Ne biþ   se kiuing geheled   þurh   his micle
eorum   16. *Non   salvabitur rex   per   multam virtutem*

megen   ne   se   eten   ne   bið   geheled   on mycelnesse ł menigo
suam   nec   gigas   salvus   erit   in   multitudine

his streingþo   leæs   hors   to   hęlo   on geniehtsumnesse
fortitudinis suae   17. *Falsus equus ad salutem in   abundantia*

soðlice megenes   his   ne bioþ hal   in gesyhþe eagan drihtnes
autem   virtutis suae non erit salvus 18.   *Ecce   oculi domini*

ofer   andredende   hine   hyhtende soþlice   on mildheortnisse   his
super   timentes   eum   sperantes autem   in   misericordia   eius

þ he nerige fram deaðe saule hioræ 7 feąle hy on hungre
19. *ut   eripiat   a   morte animas eorum et alat eos   in fame.*

Soþlice   ure   sæule forbyrdigað ł geðolað drihten   forðon
20. *Anima autem nostra   sustinet   dominum quoniam*

gefylsta 7 gescildend   ure   he is   7 on him   blissiad
adiutor et   protector   noster   est   21. *et in ipso laetabitur*

heorte   ure   7 on noman halgum   his   we hyhtað   Drihtæn
cor   nostrum et in nomine sancto eius sperabimus   22. *Fiat*

Sie   þin mildheortnes ofer   us   swæ swæ we hyhton on þe
domine misericordia tua super nos   sicut   speravimus in te

33.

Ic bletsige   drihten   on   egwilc   tid   simle   his   lof on
2. *Benedicam dominum in   omni tempore semper laus eius in*

minum muðie   On   drihtne   biþ   hered   min   sawle
ore meo   3. *In   domino   laudabitur   anima   mea*

---

14. -*ode* by Cor. on er.   *ymbhwirft*, fin. *e* er.   15. *hiwode* by Cor. on er.
Er. both bef. and aft. *Sienderlice.   an*-, *a* from *o* by d. ink.   Er. aft. *angetæþ.
on ealle* by Cor.   16. *ł menigo* add. by Cor.   17. *leæs*, about two lett. er.
both immed. bef. and aft. this word.   Er. aft. *hęlo.   on* by Cor.   Er. aft. *soðlice.   hal*, orig.=*hæle?*   18. From *in gesyhþe* to *on* by Cor. on er.
mildheortnisse his by Cor.   19. From *þ* to *saule* by Cor. part. on er.   *hioræ*
part. cov. in d. ink.   7 *fede hy on* by Cor. on er.   *hungre* part. cov. by d. ink.
20. *Soþlice* by Cor. on er.   From *forbyrdigað* to *gefylsta* by Cor. part. on er.
7 *ge-* by Cor.; -*scildend* part. cov. by d. ink.   From *ure* to end of v. 21 by
Cor. part. on er.   22. Er. aft. *swæ* (1st).   *swæ we hyhton on* by Cor.   *þe*
part. cov. by d. ink.   33. 2. *Ic bletsige* in d. ink.   3. *hered*, let. er.
betw. *r* and *e*, also er. aft. the word; orig.=*heriende?*

hie geheren þæ geþwernesse ɫ bilewitan 7 blissiæn   geMi-
audiant   mansueti   et laetentur   4. Mag-

cliæþ drihtæn mid me 7 we upæhebbæn his nomæn eow
nificate dominum mecum et   exaltemus   nomen eius in in-

betwionum   Ic sohte   drihten 7 he me gehirde 7 of
vicem   5. Inquisivi dominum et   exaudivit me   et ex

eællum minum eærfoþnessum he me generede   Genealæcet
omnibus tribulationibus meis   eripuit me   6. Accedite

to him 7 hie bioþ onlihte 7 andwlitan eowre ne onsceæmiæþ
ad eum et inluminamini et   vultus   vestri non erubescent

ðes þeærfæ clipæde 7 drihten hiene gehyrde 7 of eællum
7. *Iste pauper clamavit et dominus exaudivit eum et ex omnibus*

his eærfoþnessum ɫ geswincum alysde hiene he alysde ɫ gefriolsæþ
tribulationibus eius   liberavit eum

drihten onsendeð his englon   ymbhwyrfte ɫ gænge hine
8. *Inmittet angelum dominus in   circuitu   timen-*

ondredende 7 he hie genereþ   Onbirgæþ 7 gesioþ   hu
tium eum et   eripiet eos   9. Gustate et videte quoniam

winsum drihten is eædig biþ Se wer þe gehyht on hine
suavis est dominus   beatus vir   qui sperat in eum

Ondredæþ drihten eælle his hælige forðæn nenigwyht
10.   *Timete dominum omnes sancti eius quoniam   nichil*

wana is ðam ondredendum hine   wælige beþorfton 7
deest   timentibus   eum   11. Divites eguerunt   et

hy hyngredon þa Soþlice secende drihten ne geteoriað eællum
esurierunt inquirentes autem dominum non deficient omni

godum   Cumæþ beærn gehieræþ me drihtnes   ege
bono   12. Venite filii audite me timorem domini

ic eow lere   hwilc is se mon se þe wile lif ond wilnæþ
docebo vos   13. Quis est homo qui vult vitam et cupit

---

gehe*ren*, -*eren* on er. of something else; this word orig. ending in *þ*. ɫ
bilewi'an in d. inl. *blissiæn, n* in d. ink (on er. of *þ* ?).   4. ge*Micliæþ, ge*
in d. ink prob. pref. by Cor., *M* being a capital; *M* part. cov. by d. ink. *eow*
betwionum part. cov. by d. ink,   5. *Ic* in d. ink. A second *ic* er. bef. *sohte*.
generede, fin. *e* prob. add. by Cor. and *d* prob. from *ð*.   6. *Genealæcet*
to *him* by Cor. part. on er.   *andwlitan eowre ne* by Cor,   *on-, o* prob. pref.
later in d. ink; fin. let. (*e* ?) er.; orig. prob. this *on-* was *ne*.   7. *clipæde, d*
from *ð* ?; *e* prob. add. by Cor. *gehyrde, d* from some other let. (*e*?) and fin. let.
er. ɫ *geswincum alysde* by Cor.; *ge-* on er. ? *he alysde ɫ* by Cor.   8.
-*hwyrfte ɫ* in d. ink. *gænge, n* cov. by d. ink.   9. *On-* prob. pref. by Cor.
gehyht on hine by Cor., but prob. only cov.   10. From *nenigwyht* to *hine*
by Cor.   11. *wælige beþorfton* by Cor. on er.   *hyngredon* by Cor. on er.
þa by Cor. Er. bef. *ne*. *geteoriað* by Cor, on er. -*um* (twice) by Cor.

gode dægæs tô gesionne   bewere þine tungæn from
videre dies bonos   **14.** *Cohibe* *linguam tuam* *a*

yfle 7 þine weleræs þet ·hie ne sprecen facen   Acer ł
malo et *labia tua* *ne loquantur* *dolum*   **15.** *De-*

gewit from yfle 7 do god sec sibbe and folgæ hiere
verte *a* *malo et fac bonum inquire pacem et sequere eam*

    Drihtnes eægæn ofer þæ Soþfestæn 7 his eæræn to hioræ
16. *Oculi domini* *super* *iustos* *et aures eius ad preces*

bene   Soðlice andwlita drihtnes ofor donde yfelu þet
eorum **17.** *Vultus* *autem* *domini* *super facientes mala ut*

he forspilde on eorðæn gemind hire   ðæ soðfestæn
perdat *de terra* *memoriam eorum*   **18.** *Clamaverunt*

clipiæþ 7 drihten hi gehireþ 7 of eællum eærfoþnessum
iusti *et dominus exaudivit eos et ex omnibus* *tribula-*

ł geswincum heora he aliesde hy   Neæh is drihten
tionibus *eorum* *liberavit eos*   **19.** *Iuxta est dominus*

þem þe geswencedre synt heortan 7 eaðmode on gaste he gehelþ
his qui *tribulato sunt corde et humiles spiritu salvabit*

    Monigæ eærfoðnesse þæræ soðfestræ 7 be þisum eællum
20. *Multe tribulationes* *iustorum* *et de* *his omnibus*

alyseþ hem drihten   ðrihten gehealdeþ ealle bæn
liberabit eos dominus **21.** *Dominus custodit omnia ossa*

heora an of ðam ne bið tobrocen   deaþ synfulra
eorum unum ex his non *conteretur*   **22.** *Mors peccatorum*

wyrst is 7 þa ðe hatedon ryhtwise he forlet   ðrihten
pessima est et qui oderunt iustum delinquent   **23.** *Redimet*

ælised sæwle þiowræ his 7 na forleateþ he ealle þæ
dominus animas servorum suorum et non derelinquet omnes qui

þe hyhtat on hine
sperant in eum

---

14. *facen* by Cor. on er.   15. *Acer ł gewit* by Cor. on er.   Er. aft. *god.*
sec, fin. let. (e ?) er.   17. From *andwlita* to *yfelu* by Cor. on er.   Er. bef.
gemind. hire by Cor.   18. *soðfestæn,* fin. let. er. *of, f* in d. ink.   Er. aft.
cællum. geswincum prob. by Cor.; *-um* on er.   *heora he* by Cor. *aliesde,* a-
and *-de* by Cor.; *d* from *t. hy* in d. ink on er.   19. From *þem* to *gaste* by
Cor. on er.   20. Er. aft. *eællum. alyseþ hem drihten* by Cor. on er.   21.
ðrihten, ð cov. by d. ink ; er. aft. this word. *gehealdeþ ealle* by Cor. part. on
er.   From *heora* to *to-* by Cor. part. on er.   22. From *deaþ* to *ryhtwise* by
Cor. on er.   23. Er. aft. *sæwle.* -*ræ, r* wr. over the line in d. ink. From
his to *ealle* by Cor. on er. From *þæ* to *hine* by Cor.

34.

Dem   drihten   deriende   me   oferwin   onwinnendes   me
Iudica   domine   nocentes   me   expugna   inpugnantes   me

Gegrip   wepn   7   Scild   7   æris   me   on   fultum
2. *Apprehende   arma   et   scutum   et   exurge in adiutorium michi*

Ægiot ut   sword   7   beluc   ꞁ   betiene   ongean   hy   þe   me
3. *Effunde frameam   et   conclude   adversus eos   qui   me*

eahtað   sege sæwle minre helo þin ic eom   Gescamigen
persequuntur dic anime meae salus tua ego sum   **4.** *Confundantur*

7   cirrede   ꞁ   wandien   mine   fiend   þæ   þe   secæþ   mine sæwle
et   revereantur   inimici mei   qui   querunt animam meam

Sien gewirfede ꞁ sin gecyrrede on becling ond scæmige þæ þe
Avertantur   retrorsum   et   erubescant   qui

me þencæþ   yfeles   Sin hie   swæ   þet dust beforæn
cogitant michi   mala   **5.** *Fiant tanquam   pulvis   ante*

onsine þes windes 7 drihtnes engel hie swencende   Sin
faciem   venti   et angelus domini   adfligens eos   **6.** *Fiant*

wegas   heora   þystro 7   stlidornis 7   angel   drihtnes · ehtende
vie   eorum   tenebre et lubricum et angelus domini   persequens

hie   Forðæn gifum hy hyddon me   forwirð grines
eos   **7.** *Quoniam gratis absconderunt michi interitum laquei*

heora on idel hy hyspton   mine sawle   Cumo hem
sui   vane exprobraverunt animam meam   **8.** *Veniat illis*

grin   þet hi ne gecnawaþ 7 gegripennis þare þæ   hie
laqueus quem   ignorant   et   captio   quam   occult-

gedigledon   gegripæ   hy on grino hie gefælled on þet selfe
averunt   adprehendat eos in laqueum   incidant   in id ipsum

Soðlice   min   sæwle blissode on   drihtne   lustfulleð
9. *Anima   autem   mea   exultabit in   domino   et delectabitur*

---

34. *Dem* by Cor. on er. From *deriende* to end of v. by Cor. part. on er.
2. Er. bef. *wepn*. Er. bef. *Scild*. 3. *ut* by Cor.; er. aft. it. *sword* by Cor.;
er. bef. and aft. it. -*luc* ꞁ *be*- add. by Cor. *ongean hy* by Cor. part. on er.
eahtað by Cor. on er. *sege* by Cor.; er. bef. it. *minre* by Cor. on er. *þin ic
eom* by Cor. part. on er. 4. *Gescamigen* by Cor. on er. ꞁ *wandien* prob.
add. by Cor. ꞁ *sin gecyrrede* by Cor. over the line. 5. *Sin*, let. (e?) er. betw. *i*
and *n*. *swencende* by Cor. on er. 6. This v. by Cor. (except *Sin*) on er. 7.
From *gifum* to *hyspton* by Cor. part. on er. (except *forwirð* wh. is cov. by d. ink).
8. *Cumo*, fin. *n* er. *hem*, *e* from *i* by Cor. *grin*, init. lett. (ge?) er.; also fin. *o*
er. *þet* part. cov. by d. ink; fin. let. (or lett.) er. *hi* cov. by d. ink. From
ne to *gegripennis* by Cor. part. on er. Er. (of hie n-?) bef. *gegripæ*; *geg-* in
d. ink; a fin. let. (or lett.) er. *grino*, *g* cov. by d. ink; init. *ge-* er. 9. Er.
aft. *sæwle*. *þy* er. bef. *blissode*. *blissode on drihtne* by Cor. part. on er.
-*fulleð* cov. by d. ink.

ofer   his helo   Eælle mine bǽn cweþæð drihten hwilc
super salutare eius   **10.** *Omnia ossa mea dicent domine quis*

gelic þe nerigende unspedigne of hænde strengran his
similis tibi eripiens   inopem   de manu fortioris eius

wedlæn Ɫ elþeodigne 7 þeærfæn from him reafiendum
egenum   et pauperem a   rapientibus eum

Ærisende cyþras unryhtwise þa ic nyste hy acsodon
11. *Exsurgentes testes iniqui quae ignorabam interrogabant*

me 7   aguldon me yfelu for gode 7 stedignisse sawle
me et **12.** *retribuebant michi mala pro bonis et sterilitatem anime*

minre   Ic soðlice þonne me unyþgiende weron
meae **13.** *Ego autem dum michi molesti essent*

ic scrydde me of heron 7 ic eæðmodde on festenum mine
induebam me cilicio et humiliabam in ieiunio animam

sæwle 7 min gebed on bosm minum si gecirred   Swæ suæ
meam et oratio mea in sinu meo convertetur **14.** *Sicut*

niextæn 7 swæ urne broþur swæ ic licode swa swa
proximum et sicut fratrem nostrum ita conplacebam tanquam

heofendæ geunrotsod swæ ic geeæðmedde   Ongean
lugens et contristatus ita humiliabar **15.** *Adversum*

me hy blissodon 7 tosomne becomen 7 hy gegæderedon on me
me laetati sunt et convenerunt et congregaverunt in me

swipæn Ɫ swyngla 7 hy nyston   Tolysede sind ne
flagella   et ignoraverunt **16.** *Dissoluti sunt nec*

hy abryrde sind hy fandedon   bismeredon hie of hleahtre
compuncti sunt temptaverunt me et deriserunt   derisu

hy gristbitedon on me toþum heora   Drihten hwonne
striderunt in me dentibus suis **17.** *Domine quando*

forelocæst þu þet þu gesette mine sæwle from hioræ yflum
respicies   restitue   animam meam a   malefactis

---

10. Words er. bef. and aft. *gelic.* -*ende, d* on er. *unspedigne* by Cor. on er. Er. aft. *hænde. -ran* by Cor.; *ꞃ* on er. Er. aft. *his. Ɫ elþeodigne* add. by Cor. Er. aft. *7. reafiendum* by Cor. on er. **11.** Er. aft. *Ærisende.* From *cyþras* to end of v. by Cor. in pl. of er. **12.** From *me* to end of v. by Cor. in pl. of er.; *sawle, ꞃ* from *u.* **13.** Er. aft. *soðlice. scrydde* by Cor. on er.; *y* er. aft. *c.* Er. aft. *ic. eaðmodde* from *eæðmode* (or -*mede*?). *bosm minum si* by Cor. on er. **14.** *suæ* by Cor. on er. -*ode* prob. by Cor. on er.; er. aft. it. *swa swa* in d. ink. Er. aft. -*dæ.* Er. aft. *ic.* -*de* prob. by Cor. on er. **15.** *Ongean* by Cor. on er. -*odon* prob. by Cor. on er. *tosomne* prob. by Cor. -*en, n* on er. *hy gegæderedon* prob. by Cor. on er. Er. bef. *swipæn. 7 hy nyston* by Cor. on er. **16.** From *ne* to *fandedon* by Cor. on er.; er. aft. the last word. -*eredon* by Cor.; er. aft. it. From *of* to *on* by Cor. part. on er. *heora* prob. by Cor.

dędum ꝺ from ænnesse þæræ leonæ   Ic þe andette
eorum et   a   leonibus unicam meam   **18.** *Confitebor tibi*

drihten on halgresomuinga micelre on folce hefigum ic þe herige
domine in   aecclesia   magna in populo gravi   laudabo te

    þet na bysmerigen on me þa þe wiþærweardiað me un-
19. *Ut non insultent in me qui   adversantur michi in-*

rihtlice þa hatedon me   ꝺ bycnedon mid egum
iquae qui oderunt me gratis et anꭓuebant   oculis

    Forðæn þe me witodlice gesibsumlice he spręcon ꝺ ofer
20. *Quoniam michi quidem   pacifice   loquebantur et super*

yrre facenfullice hy þohten   hie geᴐreddon on me heoræ
*iram dolose   cogitabant   **21.** Dilataverunt in me os*

muð hie cwedon eulæ eule hie gesæwæn úræ eægæn
suum   dixerunt euge euge   viderunt   oculi nostri

    þu geseæwe drihten ne swiga þu drihten ne gewit þu fram me
22. *vidisti   domine ne sileas domine ne discedas a me*

    Aris drihten ꝺ beheæld minne dóm min drihten god
23. *Exurge domine et intende iudicium meum deus meus et dominus*

min intingæn min   Dem me drihten efter
*meus in causam meam   **24.** Iudica me domine secundum*

þinre mildheortnesse min drihten god þet na bismerien
misericordiam tuam domine deus meus ut non insultent

on me mine fiend   ne ne cwedæn on hioræ heortæn
*in me inimici mei   **25.** nec dicant in cordibus suis*

eala t wellawel ure sæwle ne cwedæn we besencton hyne
euge euge animae nostrae nec dicant obsorbuimus eum

    Scæmien ꝺ arweorþien ætgedere þa ðe þanciað yfelum
26. *Erubescant et revereantur simul qui gratulantur malis*

minum Sin gescrydde forwandunge ꝺ arweorþunge þe mætu
meis induantur pudore et reverentia qui maligna

---

18. From *hal-* to *hefigum* by Cor. on er.   19. *þet, þ* cov. by d. ink ; two fin.
lett. (*te*?) er.   *na, a* from *e* by Cor.   *bysmerigen* by Cor. on er.   Er. aft. *me,*
this er. being the gloss of *inimici mei,* wh. is dotted.   From *þa þe* to *egum* by
Cor. on er.   20. Er. aft. *ofer. facenfullice hy* on er.   21. *heoræ, e* from
i ; *o* wr. over the line.   22. *-en* prob. by Cor.   *ne swiga þu* by Cor. on er.
gewit by Cor. on er.   *fram* by Cor.   23. *Aris,* fin. *e* er.   ꝺ er. bef. *min* (2nd)
wh. has about two fin. lett. er.   *min* (3rd) in d. ink.   24. *Dem,* fin. *e* er.   *na*
bismerien by Cor. on er.   25. *ne ne* in d. ink with er. bef.   *-dæn* (twice), *n* in
d. ink on er. of another let. (*þ*?).   *eala t wellawe‍l* by Cor.; orig. *ealla,* but
second *l* er.   *we* from *þe*? *besencton hyne* by Cor. on er.   26. From *arweor-*
þien to *minum* by Cor. on er.   *Sin, e* er. betw. *i* and *n.*   From *gescrydde* to
me by Cor. on er.

specaþ　ongean　me　　　　　Fægnien 7 blissiæþ þa þe þæ þe
loquuntur adversum me　　**27.** *Exultent et laetentur qui*

willæþ　ryhtwisnisse　min　7 cweþen symle Síe gemiclod drihten
volunt　iustitiam　meam et dicant semper magnificetur dominus

þa ðe　willað　sybbe　þeowes　his　　　　7 eac　tunge min
qui　volunt　pacem　servi　eius　　**28.** *Sed et lingua mea*

smeægendæ　þine ryhtwisnesse ęlce dei　þin　lof
meditabitur　iustitiam tuam　tota die laudem tuam

<h2 style="text-align:center">35.</h2>

　　Cwæð se unrihtwise þet he forlet ł agylte on him Selfum
2. *Dixit　iniustus　ut　delinquat　in　semetipso*

ne　is　ęge　beforæn his eægum　　Forðæn facenfullic
non est timor dei　ante　oculos eius　**3.** *Quoniam　dolose*

de dide on gesiehðe his þette he gemette unrihtwisnesse his
egit　in conspectu eius　ut　inveniret　iniquitatem suam

7 hatunge　　　　Word　his　muðes　unrihtwisnesse 7 facn
et　odium　　**4.** *Verba　oris eius　iniquitas　et dolus*

he nolde　ongetan　þ　he . węl dede　　　　unrihtwysnisse
noluit　intelligere　ut　bene ageret　　**5.** *iniquitatem*

he smeade　on his bedcliofum he Etstod eælle wegæs ne god
meditatus est in　cubili suo　Astitit　omni　vie　non bone

hetenið ł yfelnisse soðlice　na he hatode　　　　Drihten　on
malitiam　autem non　odivit　　**6.** *Domine　in*

hefonum　þin mildheortnes　7　þin soðfestnes　oþþet　to
caelo　misericordia tua　et　veritas tua　usque　ad

wolcn ł genipum　　　þin soþfestnes swæ swæ godes dún
nubes　　**7.** *Iustitia tua　sicut　montes*

ł muntas　7　þine domæs　deopnis ł niowelnesse felafæald
dei　et　iudicia tua　abyssus　multa

27. *Fægnien* by Cor. on er.　*þa þe* by Cor. (over *qui*) ; he did not notice the *þæ þe* (of the p. hand) which, with *willaþ*, is w. over *volunt*. Hence the gloss of *qui* is repeated.　From *ryht-* to *symle* by Cor. on er.　Er. aft. *symle*. *-od* prob. by Cor. on er.　From *drihten* to end of v. by Cor. on er.　28. From 7 to *min* by Cor. on er.　*ryhtwisnesse* by Cor. on er. ; er. aft. it.　*dei þin lof* prob. by Cor.　35. 2. *Cwæð se un-* by Cor.　*-rihtwise* on er.　ł *agylte* add. by Cor.　*ne* by Cor. on er.　Er. aft. *is.　be-* by Cor.　3. From *facen-* to *on* by Cor.　*his* by Cor.　*-wisnesse* by Cor. on er.　*hatunge* on er.　4. From *-wis-nesse* to *dede* by Cor. in pl. of er.　5. *-wysnisse* by Cor. on er.　*he, e* from *i* on er.　*-de* by Cor. on er.　*-fum*, lett. er. betw. *f* and *u*.　*he* (2nd) pref. later. Er. aft. *ne.　ł yfelnisse* add. by Cor.　*na* by Cor.　*hatode* by Cor. on er.　6. *to* by Cor.　ł *genipum* add. by Cor.　7. *swæ* (1st) by Cor.　ł *muntas* add. by Cor.　Er. aft. *domæs.　deopnis* ł by Cor. on er.　*niow-* cov. by d. ink. *felafæald* add. by Cor.

Men 7 niteno þu hæle gedest drihten   swa swa
Homines et iumenta salvos facies domine   8. *quemadmodum*

þu gemonigfeældeæst þine mildheortnesse god Mænnæ beærn
   multiplicasti   misericordias tuas deus Filii autem

soðlice on geScildnisse þinræ fiþræ hyhtat ł gewenæþ
hominum in protectione alarum tuarum   sperabunt

   ondruncniende 7 of genyhtsumnisse þines huses 7 of burnan
9. *inebriabuntur   ab   ubertate   domus tuae et torrente*

þines willæn þu drencæst hy   Forþæn mit þe is
voluntatis tuae potabis   eos   10. *Quoniam apud te est*

lifes wielle ond on þinum liohte we gesioþ lioht   Aspread
fons vitae et in lumine tuo videbimus lumen   11. *Pre-*

ł þene þine mildheortnesse þe witendum   þine soðfestnesse
tende misericordiam tuam scientibus te et iustitiam tuam

þam þe rihte heortæn sindon   Ne   cume   me   fot
his qui recto sunt   corde   12. *Non veniat michi pes*

ofermodinesse 7 hand synfulra ne styrige me   ðer
   superbie et manus peccatorum non moveat me   13. *Ibi*

hie gefiollon eælle þæ þe wircæþ unrihtwisnessc hi sint utacnyssed
   ceciderunt omnes qui operantur iniquitatem   expulsi sunt

þ hie ne mæhton stondon
nec potuerunt stare

36.

Nelle þu þe onscuniæn betwioh þæm awyrgendan ne onhyred
Noli   emulari   inter   malignantes   neque emulatus

þu beo ða dondan unrihtnesse   Forðæn swæ swæ heg
fueris facientes iniquitatem 2. *Quoniam tanquam foenum*

hreadlice hy adrigiað 7 swa swa blæda ł leæf wyrta raðe
velociter arescent et sicut   holera herbarum cito

hreosað ł feælleþ   Gewene ł hyht on drihten 7 do godnesse
   cadent   3.   *Spera   in domino et fac bonitatem*

7 þu eærdest on eorðæn 7 þu bist fed on his welum
et   inhabita   terram   et   pasceris   in   divitiis eius

Gelustfullæ on drihtæn 7 he þe seleþ bene þinre
4. *Delectare   in   domino   et   dabit tibi   petitionem   cordis*

heortæn   Awrioh drihtne þinne weg 7 gewene ł hyht
tui   5. *Revela   domino   viam tuam et   spera*

on hine ond he deð   7 he ðe ledeþ swæ swæ þet lioht
in eum   et   ipse faciet 6. *Et   educet   tamquam   lumen*

þinre soðfestenesse 7 ðinne dom swæ swæ middeig
iustitiam tuam   et   iudicium tuum   sicut   meridiem

Beo ðu drihtne underþied 7 halsa hine na onhyre
7. *Subditus esto domino   et obsecra   eum   ne emulatus*

ðu hine þe bið gesunfullod on wæge his on men dondum
fueris eum qui   prosperatur   in   via   sua in homine faciente

unrihtwisnesse   Ablin from yrræ 7 forlet hatheor[t]nesse
iniquitatem   8. *Desine ab   ira et derelinque   furorem*

na anhyre ðu þ nearolice þu do   Forðæn þæ þe heteniþ
ne emuleris ut nequiter facias   9. *Quoniam qui nequiter*

doþ beoð geteorode þa ðe. soþlice geanbidiað drihten hie
agunt exterminabuntur   qui   vero   expectant dominum ipsi

yrfeweærdnesse   agon   eorðæn   lytel fæc nugyt 7
hereditate   possidebunt terram   10. *Pusillum   adhuc   et*

ne bið synful 7 secest his Stowe na þu gemetest
non erit peccator et   queris locum   eius   nec   invenies

þa geþwæran soþlice agun eorðan 7 gelustfulliað on
11. *Mansueti   autem possidebunt terram et delectabuntur in*

manigfealdnisse sibbe   begimþ þe synfulla riht 7
multitudine   pacis   12. *Observabit   peccator   iustum et*

grimetað ofer hine toþum his   drihten soþlice
fremet   super eum dentibus suis   13. *dominus   autem*

Er. aft. *fed.* 4. *-læ*, fin. let. (þł) er.   5. *Awrioh*, let. (nł) er. betw. *A* and *w*.
Er. bef. *drihtne.   weg* in d. ink.   ł *hyht* in d. ink.   Er. of two lett. aft. *he.*
6. *swæ* (2nd) in d. ink.   *on* er. bef. *middeig* ; er. of about two lett. betw. *d* and *d*.
7. *Beo ðu* cov. by d. ink.   *halsa*, let. er. betw. *l* and *s*.   From *halsa* to *dondum*
by Cor. on er. *-wisnesse* prob. add. by Cor. ; first *s* wr. over the line. 8. From
hat- to end of v. by Cor. on er.   9. *Forðæn* part. cov. by d. ink.   From *doþ*
to *drihten* by Cor. on er.   *agon*, orig. *ægon* ; er. aft. it.   10. *lytel fæc nugyt*
by Cor. on er.   Er. bef. 7.   Er. aft. *bið.   synful* by Cor. on er.   *secest, -st* by
Cor. prob. on er.   Er. aft. *Stowe.   na, a* by Cor. from some other let.   *þu* by
Cor. on er.   *gemetest, ge-* prob. pref. by Cor. ; *st* on er.   11. From *þa* to
eorðan by Cor. on er.   Er. aft. 7.   *gel-* part. cov. by d. ink ; *-iað* prob. by Cor.
on er.   Er. bef. *on.   manigfealdnisse* by Cor. on er.   12. *begimþ þe synfulla*
by Cor. on er.   From 7 to *toþum* by Cor. on er.   Er. aft. *his.*   13. From
soþlice to end of v. (except þ) by Cor. on er.

onhyscð   him   forðan þe   he forsceawað   þ   cumeð   dęg   his
irridebit   eum   quoniam   prospicit   quod   veniet   dies   eius

Sweord   of sceaðe   atugon   þæ   synfullan   æþenedon   hioræ
14. *Gladium   evaginaverunt   peccatores   tetenderunt   arcum*

bogæn   þet hi   æwiorpen unmagan 7   wedlen 1 þearfan   þ   hy cwelmen
suum   ut   deiciant   inopem   et   pauperem   ut trucident

ryhtwise   on   hiortæn   hioræ   sweord   ongeþ   on   heoræ
rectos   corde   15. Gladius eorum   intret   in   cor

heortæn   ond   hioræ   bogæ   bið   gebrocen   Selre 1 betere
ipsorum   et   arcus   eorum   conteratur   16.   Melius

is   medmicel   þam   rihtwisan   ofer   welan   synna   manige
est   modicum   iusto   super   divitias peccatorum multas

Forðæn   earmas   synfulra   beoð   tobrocene   getrimeð   soþlice
17. *Quoniam brachia peccatorum   conterentur   confirmat autem*

rihtwise   drihten   Can   drihten   wegas   onwemmendra
iustos   dominus   18. Novit dominus   vias   immaculatorum

7 hiræ   yrfæweærdnis   on   ecnesse bið   Ne bioþ gescende
et   haereditas eorum   in   eternum erit   19. Non confundentur

on þere yflen tyde 7 on   þæm hingriendum dægum   bioð gefillede
in   tempore malo et in   diebis famis   saturabuntur

forðæn   synfullæn   forwiorþæþ   Fynd   soþlice   drihtnes sona
20. *quoniam peccatores   peribunt   Inimici autem   domini   mox*

gearweorþode   7 upahafene   beoð   getcoriend   swa   swa   smic
honorati   et   exaltari   fuerint   deficientes   ut   fumus

he geteorað   borgað   se synfulla 7   ne 1 agylt bið ælised
deficient   21. Mutuatur   peccator   et non   solvet

se   rihtwise   soþlice   ofearmað   7   alenð   Forðæn
iustus   autem   miseretur   et commodat   22. Quoniam

hine bletsiende   agun   eorðan   yfelcweþelginde soþlice hine
benedicentes eum possidebunt terram   maledicentes   autem illum

forworðaþ   From   drihtne   stæpas   monnæs   beoþ   gerihte
disperient   23.   A   domino   gressus   hominis   dirigentur

7 wæg his he wilnæþ swiþe   þonne hreoseþ se rihtwisa
et viam eius cupiet nimis ` **24.** *Cum ceciderit iustus*

na hi biѕ gedrefed forѕon dryhten trymeѕ hand his
non conturbabitur quia dominus firmat manum eius

Ic wes giongre 7 ic eældode 7 ic ne seæh ryhtwisne
25. *Iunior fui et senui et non vidi iustum*

forlætenne na sæd his þarfende hlæfe   Elce deie
derelictum nec semen eius egens pane **26.** *Tota die*

he miltseoþ 7 lænþ 7 his sed on bletsunge biþ
miseretur et commodat et semen eius in benedictione erit

Onheld from yfle 7 do god 7 onwune ꞇ eærdæ on world `
27. *Declina a malo et fac bonum et inhabita in seculum*

æworld Forѕæn drihten lufæþ dóm 7 na forlætæþ
seculi **28.** *Quoniam dominus amat iudicium et non derelinquet*

his hælgæn on ecnesse hy bioþ gehældene unryhtwise soþlice
sanctos suos in aeternum conservabuntur Iniusti autem

beoѕ gewitnode 7 sæd ærleæsræ forweorþeþ ryhtwise
punientur et semen impiorum peribit **29.** *Iusti*

soþlice yrfeweærdeiesse ægon eorѕæn 7 oneærdæþ on
vero haereditate possidebunt terram et inhabitabunt in

world aworlde ofer hy Muѕ ryhtwises smeaѕ ꞇ gemyneþ
seculum seculi super eam **30.** *Os iusti meditabitur*

wisdom 7 his tunge spricþ dóm Godes æ his
sapientiam et lingua eius loquetur iudicium **31.** *Lex dei eius*

on his heortæn ond ne bioþ underwirtwælede ꞇ plantade
in corde ipsius et non supplantabuntur

his stepæs beosceawaþ þe synfulla ryhtwisne 7 secþ
gressus eius **32.** *Considerat peccator iustum et querit*

hine tóforspillan Soþlice drihten ne forlet hiene
perdere eum **33.** *Dominus autem non derelinquet eum*

on his hondum ne hine ne geniѕræþ midþy him biѕ demend
in manibus eius nec damnabit eum cum iudicabitur illi

---

24. The whole of the v. by Cor. in pl. of er. 25. -re7 ins. by Cor. ꞁ From
ryht- to *sæd* prob. by Cor. in pl. of er. 26. *miltseoþ* prob. by Cor. on er.
lænþ on er. 27. *Onheld, e* from *i* prob. by Cor. ; fin. *e* er. ; *ge* er. aft. this word.
on-, fin. let. (d ꞏ) er. ; *-wune* ꞇ prob. add. later by Cor., ꞇ being wr. over the line.
28. *Forѕæn, -æn* cov. by d. ink, the *s*-part of the *æ* not cov. *na forlætæþ* prob.
by Cor. on er. Er. aft. *his.* From *un-* to *sæd* by Cor. on er. Er. bef. *ær-.*
29. *ryhtwise soþlice* by Cor. on er. Er. bef. *yrfe-.* on er. bef. *eorѕæn. hy, y*
by Cor. in pl. of two or three other er. lett. 30. From *ryht-* to *wisdom* by
Cor. on er. Er. bef. and aft. *his.* 31. *Godes, s* cov. by d. ink. æ *his* part.
cov. by d. ink ; *his* orig. = *hiorœ* ꞇ ꞇ *plantade* by Cor. 32. From *beo-* to
-wisne by Cor. on er. *-lan* by Cor. on er. (of *lænne* ?) 33. *demend,* fin. *e* er.

GeOnbide drihten 7 geheæld his wegæs 7 he upahefeð
34. *Expecta dominum et custodi vias eius et exaltabit*

þe þ þu oneærdige eorðæn þonne forweorþað synfulle þu gesihst
te ut inhabites terram cum pereunt peccatores videbis

Ic geseæh arleasne ofergeuferudne 7 upahafenne ofer
35. *Vidi impium superexaltatum et elevatum super*

cedertrowes Ic ferde ł ofereode 7 on gesyhðe
cedros libani 36. *Transivi et ecce*

he næs ł na wes ic sohte hine 7 ne is gemet his stow
non erat quesivi eum et non est inventus locus eius

Gehcæld soðfestnesse 7 gesioh efennisse forðæn Sient
37. *Custodi veritatem et vide aequitatem quoniam sunt*

forletnesse ł laue mon geSibsumum Soðlice þæ
reliquiae homini pacifico 38. *Iniusti*

unryhtwise forwiorþeþ somod lafa ærleæsræ forwiorþeþ
autem disperient simul reliquiae impiorum peribunt

Soðlice helo þæræ soþfestræ to drihtne is 7 hioræ gescild
39. *Salus autem iustorum a domino est et protector eorum*

is on tide eærfoðnesse 7 gefylsteþ hy drihten 7
est in tempore tribulationis 40. *Et adiuvabit eos dominus et*

alyseð hi 7 genereð hy from synfullum 7 hale gedeþ
liberavit eos et eripiet eos a peccatoribus et salvos faciet

hy forþæn gewenæþ ł hihton on hine
eos quoniam speraverunt in eum

37.

Dryhten ne on eorre þinum þu ðreage me na on
2. *Domine ne in ira tua arguas me neque in*

hatheortnesse þinre þu nyrewe me Forðæn þine strele
furore tuo corripias me 3. *Quoniam sagittae*

---

34. *GeOnbide, Ge-* and *-e* by Cor.; *d* from ð. *-ien* prob. by Cor. (in pl. of orig. *-enes* ?). Er. aft. *he.* *upahefeð, a* wr. over the line; ð by Cor. Er. bef. þ. Let. (or lett.) er. immed. aft. þ. *þu on-* by Cor.; *-ige* by Cor. on er. From *þonne* to end of v. by Cor. on er. 35. From *arleasne* to end of v. by Cor. on er. 36. From 7 to *hine* by Cor. in pl. of er. *gemet,* fin. *-ed* prob. er. 37. *efennisse* by Cor. on er. *ł laue* prob. add. by Cor. *mon,* fin. lett. (*-næ* ?) er. *geSibsumum, ge-* prob. pref. by Cor.; *-mum* on er. 38. *-ryhtwise* by Cor. on er. *somod, d* on er. *lafa* by Cor. on er. 39. *to* on er. 40. From begin. of v. to *alyseð* by Cor. on er. Er. aft. *from.* *syn-* by Cor. on er. (of *firen* ?). *hale gedeþ hy* by Cor. on er. *ł hihton* prps. add. by Cor.; er. of two lett. (*hi* ?) betw. *i* and *h.* 37. 2. From *on* (1st) to end of v. prob. by Cor. on er.

ł flane on me . sint gefestnode 7 þu getrimedest þin hænd
tuae infixe sunt michi et confirmasti super me

ofer me Na is hælpe on flæsce mina of andwlitan
manum tuam 4. *Nec est sanitas in carne mea a vultu*

eorres þines 7 ne is sibbe banum minum of ansine minræ
irae tuae et non est pax ossibus meis a facie peccatorum

Sinnæ Forþæn mine unrihtnesse oferseton min
meorum 5. *Quoniam iniquitates meae superposuerunt caput*

heæfod swa swa byrþe hefige gehefogode sindon ofer me
meum sicut onus gravae gravatae sunt super me

rotodon 7 wyrsodon dolswaðo mine of ansyne
6. *Conputruerunt et deterioraverunt cicatrices meae a facie*

unwisdomes mines Of yrmþum geswenced ic eom 7
insipientiae meae 7. *Miseriis aflictus sum et*

gedrefed oþ on ende alla dæg geunrotsod ic ineode
turbatus sum usque in finem tota die contristatus ingrediebar

Forþæn þe sæwl min gefylled is bysmrungum 7 na is
8. *Quoniam anima mea completa est inlusionibus et non est*

hælpe on minum flescum gebyed ic am 7 geeæðmed
sanitas in carne mea 9. *Incurvatus sum et humiliatus*

ic am agehwar ic grymetede of geomrunga heortæn minre
sum usquequaque rugiebam a gemitu cordis mei

7 beforan þe is æl gewilnung min 7 geomrung min
10. *et ante te est omne desiderium meum et gemitus meus*

fram þe ne is behid Min heortæn gedrefed is
a te non est absconditus 11. *Cor meum conturbatum est*

on me 7 forlet me strengo min 7 lioht minræ egænæ
in me et deseruit me fortitudo mea et lumen oculorum meorum

minre ne is mid me Mine frend 7 mine nixtan
non est mecum 12. *Amici mei et proximi mei*

---

3. *ł flane* add. by Cor. *-dest, ł* prob. add. by Cor. *þin hænd*, fin. let. (e ?) er. in both words. 4. From the *a* (of *Na*) to *þines* by Cor. on er. From *sibbe* to *an-* by Cor. ? 6. From *rotodon* to end of v. by Cor. in pl. of er. ; except *mine* wh. is only cov. by the d. ink. 7. *geswenced ic eom* 7 by Cor. on er. Er. aft. *-fed.* From *oþ* to end of v. by Cor. on er. 8. Er. (of *min* ?) bef. *sæwl.* From *min* to *hælpe* by Cor. in pl. of er. 9. *gebyed ic am* by Cor. ; er. betw. *y* and *e.* Er. aft. 7. *-med*, two fin. lett. er. From *ic am* to *geomrunga* by Cor. on er. *minre* by Cor. on er. 10. From 7 to *gewilnung* by Cor. on er. 7 *geomrung min* by Cor. on er. Er. aft. *is. behid*, two fin. lett. er. ? 11. *forlet me* by Cor. on er. *min* 7 prob. by Cor. *minre* cov. by d. ink. 12. *Mine, e* by Cor. on er. *frend* in d. ink.

ongen me geneælecton 7 stodon 7 mine þæ niextæn
adversum me adpropiaverunt et steterunt et   proximi mei

fer stodon   7 nyd dydon þa þe sohton
a longe steterunt   13. Et vim faciebant qui querebant

mine sæwle 7 þæ sohton yfel me hye sprecen
animam meam et qui inquirebant mala michi locuti sunt

idelnesse 7 facne elce dei hye smeæiden   Ic soðlice
vanitatem et dolos tota die meditabantur   14. Ego autem

swæ swæ deæf na ic geherde 7 swæ swa dumb Se ne
velud surdus non audiebam et sicut mutus qui non

ontyende his muð   Ond ic eom geworden swæ swæ
aperuit os suum 15. Et   factus sum   ut

mon ne gehierende 7 ne hębbende on his muðe on geþræorspreca
homo non audiens et non habens in ore suo   increpationes

Forðæn on þe drihten ic hyhte ic cweð þu gehirsþ drihten
16. *Quoniam in te domine speravi dixi tu exaudies domine*

god min   Forðæn sæde t̄ cwiþe þyles ahwonne
deus meus 17. Quia   dixi   ne aliquando

hyspen on me mine fiend 7 þonne weron astyrede fet mine
insultent in me inimici mei et dum   conmoventur pedes mei

on me fela hy sprecen   Forðæn ic to swingellum
in me magna locuti sunt   18. Quoniam ego ad   flagella

gearo ic eom 7 sær min ongean me is simle   Forðæn
paratus sum et dolor meus ante me est semper 19. Quoniam

unrihtwisnesse mine ic cyþe 7 ic þynce for sinne
iniquitatem meam ego pronuntio et cogitabo pro peccato

---

ongen in d. ink. *gene-* in d. ink, the *ne* being only part. cov. Er. bef. and aft. last 7. *fer, -er* in d. ink (on er. ?). 13. 7 on er. *nyd* prob. by Cor. on er. Er. aft. *þa þe. sohton* part. cov. by d. ink. Er. aft. *þæ. sohton* (2nd) part. cov. by d. ink. *me* prob. from something else. Er. aft. *sprecen. facne* in d. ink. *hye* part. cov. by d. ink. *smeæiden* prob. from *smeægende* by Cor. 14. *swæ* (2nd) in d. ink on er. *na* by Cor. on er. *geherde* prob. from *gehere* by Cor. *swa* in d. ink. *on-* part. cov. by d. ink ; *-ende* prob. by Cor. (on er. ?). 15. *swæ* (2nd) by Cor. on er. *-ende* (1st) by Cor. in pl. of er. *hębbende* part. cov. by d. ink. *his, -is* in d. ink, prps. on er. *-præor-*, the *e*-part of the *-æ-* and the *-or-* in d. ink on er. ; *-spreca* in d. ink. 16. *on* in d. ink. Er. aft. *drihten. hyhte* by Cor. on er. *cweð* part. cov. by d. ink ; fin. *e* er. *þu* cov. by d. ink. 17. *sæde t̄* by Cor. *cwiþe þyles* part. cov. by d. ink. *ahwonne hyspen* by Cor. on er. *þonne weron astyrede* by Cor. on er. Er. bef. *fet. mine* add. by Cor. *fela hy* by Cor. on er. Er. aft. *sprecen.* 18. Er. bef. and aft. *to. to swingellum* part. cov. by d. ink ; *lum* er. betw. *l* and *l. gearo ic eom* by Cor. Er. aft. 7. *min ongean* by Cor. in pl. of er. 19. From *-wisnesse* to *for* by Cor. in pl. of er. The word *cyþe* through some defect in the MS. peeled off but was pasted in again. *sinne* altered (from *synnum* ?) by Cor.

minne   Soþlice mine fiend liebbæþ ł lifiað 7 gestrængode
meo   **20.** *Inimici autem mei   vivent   et confortati*

Sient ofer me 7 gemonigfeældode sindon þæ þe me fiogæþ ł
sunt super me et   multiplicati   sunt   qui   oder-

hatedon on unriht   ðæ þe me edleæniæþ ł agyldon yfelu
unt me   inique   **21.** *Qui   retribuebant michi   mala*

for godon hy tældon me   forðon fylgende rithwisnesse
pro bonis   detrahebant michi quoniam   subsecutus sum

sind ł soðfestnesse   Ne forlet þu me drihten min god
    iustitiam   **22.** *Ne derelinquas me domine deus meus*

ne gewite ðu from me   beheæld on minne fultum
ne discesseris a   me   **23.** *intende in adiutorium meum*

drihten god mine   helo
domine deus salutis meae

38.

    Ic cwæð ic gehælde minne wegæs þet ic ne forlete ł agylte
2. *Dixi   custodiam   vias meas   ut   non delinquam*

on minræ tungæ Ic asette minum muþe geheordunga þonne
in lingua mea Posui   ori meo   custodiam   dum

standað se synfulla ongean me   Ic ǽdumbede 7 geædmed
consistit peccator adversum me   **3.** *Obmutui et humiliatus*

ic eom 7 ic swigeode fram godum 7 min sær geedniwod ys
sum et   silui   a   bonis et dolor meus renovatus est

    hatud   min heortæ on   me 7 on mi[n]re Smeægunge
4. *Concaluit   cor meum intra me et in   meditatione mea*

bierned   fyr   Ic eom sprecende on minre tungon gedo
exardescit ignis   **5.** *Locutus sum   in lingua mea   notum*

me cuþe drihten ende minn 7 getæl ł gerim minræ daga
michi fac domine finem meum et   numerum   dierum meorum

minne added by Cor.   20. *ł lifið* add. by Cor.   *ł hatedon* add. by Cor.
21. *ł agyldon* add. by Cor.   *yfelu, u* by Cor.   *godon* by Cor.   From *hy* to
forðon by Cor. on er.   *rithwisnesse* and the *ł* wh. follows *sind* added by Cor.
22. *gewite ðu* by Cor. on er.   23. *on* by Cor.   38. 2. *Ic cwæð* by
Cor. *ł agylte* add. by Cor. *asette, a-* pref. by Cor. Er. aft. *muþe*. *geheordunga* part. on er.; cov. by d. ink. From *þonne* to *ongean* by Cor. on er.
3. Er. aft. 7. *-med*, fin. *-ed* er. (cf. *-modad* of Vesp. Ps.). *eom 7 ic* by Cor.
on er. *swig-, g* from *c.* *fram godum* by Cor. *geedniwod ys* by Cor. on er.
4. *hatud* by Cor. on er. *mi[n]re*, a let. er. betw. *i* and *r*. Er. bef. *fyr*.
5. From *ende* to *gerim* by Cor. *daga*, orig. = *dægæ*.

hwelc ys þet ic wite hwet wana sie me   On gesihðe
quis est ut sciam quid desit michi   6.   *Ecce*

ealde þu gesettest minne dægæs 7 mine spedæ swæ swæ
veteres posuisti dies meos et substantia mea tanquam

næht beforæn þe is þeah hweþre eæll ydelnessæ eælc
nichil ante te est Veruntamen universa vanitas omnis

man libbende   þeælhþe on godes onlicnesse gænge
homo vivens 7. *quanquam in imagine dei ambulet*

Se mon hweþre on ydel he bioþ gedrefed Geldhordæþ 7 he ne wæt
homo tamen vane conturbabitur Thesaurizat et ignorat

hwam he somnaþ þa   7 nu hwilc is min anbidung
cui congregat ea   8. *et nunc quae est expectatio mea*

hu ne nu drihten 7 sped min swæ swæ næht beforæn
nonne dominus et substantia mea tanquam nichilum ante

þe is   From eællum minum unrihtwisnesse genere me
te est 9. *Ab omnibus iniquitatibus meis eripe me*

hosp 7 unsnytro ł unwisum þu me Seældest   Ic
obprobrium insipienti dedisti me 10. *Ob-*

ædumbude 7 ic ne ontinde minne muð forðæn þu dydest
mutui et non aperui os meum quoniam tu fecisti

astyre fram me witc þine   fram strengo soþlice
11. *amove a me plagas tuas* 12. *a fortitudine enim*

hande þinre ic geteorode on steorum ł onþræwunge For
manus tuae ego defeci in increpationibus Propter

unrihtwisnesse þu nyrwdest mæn 7 aswindan ł weorpian
iniquitatem corripuisti hominem et tabescere

þu didest swæ swæ atterȝoppan sæwle his þah hwæþre all
fecisti sicut aranea animam eius Veruntamen universa

ydelnessæ ælc mon liuiende   gehir god min
vanitas omnis homo vivens 13. *exaudi deus ora-*

hwelc ys by Cor. *þet* orig. = *þette* ? *ic* add. by Cor. *wite hwet* part. cov.
in d. ink by Cor. *wana sie me* by Cor. on er.   6. *On gesihðe ealde* by Cor.
swæ (2nd) by Cor. Er. immed. bef. *næht*. *is* part. cov. by d. ink. *þeah*
hweþre by Cor. on er. *eæll*, fin. let. (e?) er. *eælc* part. on er. *man* cov. by
d. ink. 7. *on* by Cor. on er. *-nesse, -se* add. by Cor.? *gænge*, fin. let. er.
he on er. *bioþ* cov. by d. ink. *-fed*, fin. let. (e?) er. Er. bef. *Gold-*. *hwam*
he somnaþ by Cor.; er. betw. *n* and *a*. *þa* orig. *þæ*; er. aft. it.   8. *an-, a*
from *o* by Cor.; from *-bidung* to *min* by Cor. on er.   9. *-wisnesse* by Cor.
on er. *ł unwisum þu* by Cor. in pl. of er.   10. Er. aft. *þu*. *-st* by Cor. on
er.   11. This v. by Cor. on er.   12. From *fram* to *steorum ł* by Cor. on
er. From *un-* to *nyrwdest* by Cor. on er. Er. bef. *mæn*. From 7 to *-coppan*
by Cor. on er. *þah hwæpre all* by Cor. on er. *-ende*, fin. *e* from some other
let.   13. *gehir*, fin. let. (e?) er. *min*, fin. let. er.

F 2

bed   7   mine bene   mid eærum onfoh   mine
tionem meam et deprecationem meam   auribus   percipe lacrimas
teæræs ne swigæ þu from me forþæn wræcce ic eom mid þe
meas ne   sileas   a   me Quoniam incola ego sum apud te
on eorðæn 7   elþidig   swæ swæ eælle mine fedras   forlet
in terra et peregrinus   sicut   omnes patres mei ·. **14.** *Remitte*
me þet ic bio æcęled er þæm þe ic gange 7   ma   ic ne
michi ut   refrigerer   priusquam   eam   et amplius non
bio
ero

39.

Geanbidigende ic onbad drihtnæs 7 me forlocede ł he beheold
2.   *Expectans   expectavi dominum et   respexit me*
7 gehierde   mine   bene   7 me utgelędde of seæþe
3. *et exaudivit deprecationem meam et   eduxit me   de lacu*
yrmðæ 7 of fenne drosna 7 he gesette   mine fet ofer stæn
miserie et de luto   fecis Et   statuit   supra petram pedes meos
7 gerehte mine stapæs   7 he ondsende on mine muð
*et direxit gressus meos   **4.** et   inmisit   in os meum*
niwne song and ymnæd urum gode Monegæ gesioð 7 ondredæþ
canticum novum   ymnum deo nostro Videbunt multi et timebunt
7 gewenæþ ł gehihtað on drihten   Eædi wer þes ðe
*et   sperabunt   in domino   **5.** Beatus vir cuius*
næma is drihtnes his biht 7 na beseah ł locæde on ydelnesse 7 on
est nomen domini spes eius et non   respexit   in vanitates et in
wedendum leæsingum   Monegæ þu dydest drihten min
*insanias   falsas   **6.** Multa   fecisti tu domine deus*
god þinræ wundræ 7 þinum gepohtum na is hwelc gelic
meus   mirabilia tua   et cogitationibus tuis non est quis similis
þe Ic cyþde 7 ic eom sprecende 7 gemonifældode sien ofer
tibi Adnuntiavi et   locutus sum   et   multiplicati sunt   super

mid add. by Cor. Er. bef. *mine. wræcce ic eom* by Cor. on er.   **14.** *þe
ic gange* by Cor. on er.   *ma* orig. *mæ. bio,* fin. let. er.   **39. 2.** From
Ge- to *ic* by Cor.   *onbad* orig. *onbæd. ł he beheold* by Cor.   **3.** *-rde, d*
from *ð* and fin. *e* by Cor.   *-dde, -de* by Cor. Er. aft. *seæþe.* 7 on er. *fenne
drosna* by Cor. on er. *he* prob. add. by Cor.   *-hte* by Cor. on er. *stapæs, a*
from *e.*   **4.** 7 *he* prob. add. by Cor.   7 cr. bef. *ond-. muð,* accent doubtful.
and, a from *o* by Cor.   *ł gehihtað on* prob. by Cor.   *-ten,* let. cr. betw. *t* and *e.*
5. *ðe* by Cor.   *hiht* in d. ink; *-ht* on er.   *na* in d. ink; let. cr. immed. bef. *n*;
a on er. of another let.   *beseah ł* by Cor. on er.   *-de,* fin. *e* prob. add. by Cor.
on (2nd), fin. let. er.   **6.** *-est, t* prob. add. by Cor.   *na* by Cor. on er.   *hwelc*
by Cor. on er.   *þe* by Cor.   *cyþde, -de* by Cor. prob. in pl. of *e. sien,* fin. let.
(*t* ?) er.

gerym   onsegidnisse 7 tobrengnesse ꞇ ofrunge ðu noldest
numerum   **7.** *sacrificium et   oblationem   noluisti*

soðlice   lichomon   þu   me   fulfremedest   Eæc   swilce
corpus   autem   *perfecisti   michi   Holocausta*

ansægidnisse ꞇ offrunge   fore   scyld ꞇ gylt   na   þu bede
etiam   *pro   delicto   non   postulasti*

þonne ic sægde on gesihðe ic cume On heæfde þere boces
8. *tunc   dixi   ecce   venio   In   capite   libri*

awriten is be me   þet ic dó þinne willæn min god
scriptum est de me   **9.** *ut faciam voluntatem tuam deus meus*

ic wolde 7 þine ǽé ꞇ ewe on midre minre heortæn   Welic
volui et legem tuam in medio cordis mei   **10.** · *Bene*

bodude þine ryhtwisnesse on þere miclæn cierceæn eællæ mine
nuntiavi iustitiam tuam in   ecclesia magna   ecce labia

weleræs ic ne bewerie ꞇ forbeode drihten þu oncnewe   þine
mea   non prohibebo Domine tu cognovisti   **11.** *ius-*

rihtwisnesse na ic gehydde on minre heortæn þine soðfestnesse
titiam tuam non abscondi in   corde meo   veritatem tuam

7 þine helo ic cweð Ic ne behydde þine mildheortnesse 7
et salutare tuum dixi   Non celavi   misericordiam tuam et

þine soþfestnesse from micelræ gemotstowe ꞇ gesomnunga   ðu
veritatem tuam a   synagoga multa   **12.** *Tu*

soðlice drihten ne do þu fior þine mildheortnesse from me
autem domine ne longe facias misericordias tuas a me

þine mildheortnesse 7 þine soðfestnessæ simle hy me onfengon
misericordia tua et veritas tua semper susceperunt me

        Forðæn me ymbseældon yfel þæræ ne is gerim
13. *Quoniam circundederunt me mala quorum non est numerus*

me gegrypon mine unrihtnesse ond na ic ne mihte þet
comprehenderunt me iniquitates meae et non potui ut

ic hie gesæwe hy Gemonifældode sint ofer loccæs mines
viderem   Multiplicati sunt super capillos capitis

---

gerym, let. (g?) er. betw. *e* and *r*.   7. *-idnisse* by Cor. on er. Er. aft. 7.
ꞇ ofrunge add. by Cor. *-est, ꞇ* add. by Cor. (twice). Er. (þone or þane?) bef.
lic-. *ansægidnisse ꞇ* add. by Cor. *scyld ꞇ gylt* by Cor. Er. bef. *na* wh. is
in d. ink.   8. *ic sægde on gesihðe* by Cor. on er. *boces, s* prob. add. by Cor.
9. *wolde* by Cor. on er. *ǽé ꞇ* by Cor. in pl. of er.   10. *ryhtwisnesse* by Cor.
in pl. of er. *ꞇ forbeode* add. by Cor.   11. *rihtwisnesse* by Cor. on er. *na*
by Cor. Er. aft. *ic* (1st). *cweð, e* from *i* by Cor.; orig. = *cwiðe*? *-hydde* by
Cor. on er. *-stowe* by Cor. *ꞇ gesomnunga* by Cor. in pl. of er.   12. *7* er.
bef. *þine* (2nd). *hy* by Cor.   13. *na ic* by Cor. on er. *mihte, e* by Cor. (in
pl. of *on*?).

heæfdes 7 min heorte   me forlet   gelicige   þe
mei   et cor meum dereliquit me   **14.** *Complaceat tibi*

drihten þet þu me generic drihten on mine fultum gelocæ
domine ut   eripias me   domine in auxilium meum respice

Sien gescende 7 gewirfede ł forwandian somod ðæ þe secæþ
15. *Confundantur et   revereantur   simul qui querunt*

mine sæwle ꝥ hi æfyrren hie Sien gecirrede under becling 7
animam meam ut auferant eam   Avertantur   retrorsum et

forscæmien ł ablysien þæ þe me þencæþ yfeles   hy beren
erubescant   qui cogitant michi mala   **16.** *Ferant*

hredlice here gesciendnesse þæ þe me cweðæþ ealæ enlæ
confestim confusionem suam   qui   dicunt michi euge euge

Gehihtæþ 7 blissiæþ þæ þe secæþ þe drihten 7 hie cweðæn
17. *Exultent et letentur qui querunt te domine et   dicant*

simle gemiclæd sie   drihten   ðæ þe lufiæþ þine helo
semper magnificetur dominus   qui diligunt salutare tuum

Ic soðlice wedlæ 7 ðeærfæ eom drihten hævæð hoge ł
18. *Ego vero egenus et pauper sum dominus   curam ha-*

gemenne min gefultum min 7 alysend min þu eart drihten
bet   mei Adiutor meus et liberator meus es tu   domine

ne lætæ þu
ne tardaveris

40.

eadig se þe ongeteþ ofer þone wedlæ 7 þone þeærfæn on dage
2. *Beatus qui intellegit super egenum et   pauperem in die*

yfle drihtæn hi gefriolsæð ł alyseð   drihten geheældeð
malo   liberabit eum dominus   **3.** *Dominus conservet*

hine 7 geliffesteð hinc 7 eædigne gedóþ hine 7 he geclensæð on
eum et vivificet eum et beatum faciat eum et   emundet   in

---

14. *gelicige, ge-* by Cor. on er.; *-ige* by Cor. on er. *on mine* on er. *gelocæ,*
ge- prefixed by Cor.? 15. *gescende, s* wr. over the line prob. by Cor.; *e*
(1st) from *i.* Er. aft. 7. *ł forwandian* add. by Cor. *somod, o* in both cases
from some other let. (e?). *hie* by Cor. *becling* prob. add. by Cor. *furscæmien,*
for- prob. prefixed by Cor.; *n* add. by Cor. *ł ablysien* add. by Cor. 16. *hy*
beren by Cor. in pl. of er. *here,* first *e* from *i.* 17. *-ðæn, n* by Cor. on er.
(of þ?). *-læd, d* add. by Cor. *sie* add. by Cor. 18. *hævæð, v* from something else. *hoge ł* by Cor. *min 7 alysend* by Cor. on er. *þu eart* by Cor. on
er. 40. 2. *eadig* by Cor. *-age* by Cor.; *a* on er. Er. (hiræ?) bef.
yfle; -le in d. ink; fin. let. (s?) er. *ł alyseð* add. by Cor. 3. *- deð, ð* by
Cor. on er. *-teð, ð* add. by Cor. *gedóþ, þ* prob. add. by Cor. *he* prob. add. by
Cor. *sæð, ð* add. by Cor.; er. (hine?) aft. this word.

eordæn his sæwle 7 hine ne seleð on hændæ his fiondæs
terra animam eius et non tradat eum in manus inimici eius

drihten spæde bringeð him ofer bedd sares his
4. *Dominus opem ferat illi super lectum doloris eius*

ælle strele his þu acyrdest on untrumnesse his
universum stratum eius versasti in infirmitate eius

Ic cweð dryhten gemiltsa min hæl sawle mine forðan ic
5. *Ego dixi domine miserere mei sana animam meam quia pec-*

syngode þe   Fynd mine cweðon ł sægdon yfela to me
cavi tibi **6.** *Inimici mei dixerunt mala michi*

hwonne swelteð 7 forwerþeð nama his   7 hy geoden in
quando morietur et periet nomen eius **7.** *Et ingrediebantur*

þ hy gesawan idelu gesprec heorte heora hy gaderedon
ut viderent vana locutum est cor eorum congregaverunt

unryhtwisnesse him 7 hy geodon ut 7 hy sprecon
iniquitatem sibi Et egrediebantur foras et loquebantur

somod on an hy bysmredon ælle fynd mine ongean
8. *simul in unum susurrabant Omnes inimici mei adversum*

me þohton yfelu me   word unrihtwis hy bebudan
me cogitabant mala michi **9.** *verbum iniquum mandaverunt*

ongean me Cwystþu se þe slapð ne geycþ he ł teohað þ
adversum me Nunquid qui dormit non adiciet ut

he arise soðliche mann sybbe minre on ðam ic hyhte
resurgat **10.** *et enim homo pacis mee in quo sperabam*

þæ þe æt minne hlæf he geycte ł monigfeældode ongean me
qui edebat panes meos ampliavit adversum me

underþidnesse ðu soðlice drihten miltsæ me 7
supplantationem **11.** *Tu autem domine miserere mei et*

æwece ł arer me 7 ic agylde hem ł geeædleænie On
resuscita me et retribuam illis **12.** *In*

þam ic oncneow þte þu me woldest forðæn na blissað
hoc cognovi quoniam voluisti me quia non gaudebit

---

seleð, *ð* add. by Cor. -*dæs, s* prob. add. by Cor. 4. MS. *swæde* ; orig. =
swæ? the -*de* add. by Cor. ? From *bringeð* to *on* by Cor. in pl. of er. *his* by
Cor. From begin. of v. 5 to *hyhte* of v. 10 (exactly one page of the MS.) wr.
by one of the Cors. ; *not* on er., shewing that this Cor. was a contemporary of
the scribe who wrote the orig. text. 8. *pohton, h* from something else (o?).
9. *slapð, p* on er. of some other let. 10. *minne,* first *n* dotted. *he* add. by
Cor. -*ycte ł* ins. by Cor. *ongean* on er. 11. *ł crer* add. by Cor. *agylde*
ins. by Cor. *hem ł* by Cor. on er. ; *e* from *i.* 12. *þam, -am* by Cor. on er.
oncneow, e orig. = *æ* ; -*ow* by Cor. on er. ; orig. = *oncnæwe*? *þte* by Cor. on er.
-*est, t* add. by Cor. *na blissað* by Cor. on er.

fiond   min   ofer   me   Fore   minre   unscypenesse
inimicus meus super me   13. Propter innocentiam autem

sodlice þu me onfenge 7 me getrymedest on þinre gesihþe on
meam   suscepisti me et confirmasti me in conspectu tuo in

ecnesse   Gebletsæd drihten god isræhele   æworld 7
aeternum   14. Benedictus dominus deus israel a seculo et

oþþe on worlde si swæ si swæ
usque in seculum   fiat   fiat

41.

        Swæ Se heort wylnæþ to þes weteres willæn swæ wilnæþ
2. *Sicut cervus desiderat ad fontes aquarum   ita   desiderat*

min sæwl to þe drihten   Min sæwle þirsteþ to þæm lifi-
anima mea ad te   deus   3. Sitivit anima mea ad   deum

endæn gode hwænne ic cume 7 etiewe beforæn godes onsiene
    vivum   quando   veniam et apparebo ante   faciem dei

Me weron   mine teæræs hlæfæs on dege 7 on niehte þonne
4. *Fuerunt michi lacrimae meae panes   die ac   nocte dum*

bið cweðend   me elce deg hwer is þin god   þas
dicitur   michi cotidie ubi est deus tuus   5. Haec

ic gemunde 7 ægeæt on me   mine sæwle forðæn ic ingænge
recordatus sum et effudi in me animam meam quoniam ingrediar

on stowe eærdunge ł geteldes wundorlices   oþ   godes hus on
in locum   tabernaculi   admirabilis usque ad domum dei in

stemne blisse ł winsumnesse 7 swegie onddetnesse wistfulgend ł
voce   exultationis   et confessionis sonus   epulan-

simliende   Forhwy sari ł unrot eart þu min Sæwl 7 forwæn
tis   6. Quare   tristis   es   anima mea et quare

gedrefest þu me hyht on god forðæn ic ændette him helo
conturbas me spera in deum quoniam confitebor illi salutare

onsien ł andwlitan mines   7 god min From me silfum
vultus   mei   7. et deus meus A me ipso

Sæwl min gedrefed is   forþan gemindy ic beo þin arihten of
anima mea turbata est propterea memor ero   domine de

---

min by Cor. on er.   13. -est, t prob. add. by Cor.   41. 2. -yln- in
d. ink; y on er.   3. Min, fin. let. prob. er.   4. on prob. ins. by Cor.
(twice). dege, fin. s er. ? niehte, fin. s er. ponne by Cor. on er. me by Cor.
on er. deg, fin. let. (e ?) er.   5. þas by Cor.; orig. word prob. ended in -es.
-unde by Cor. on er.   ł geteldes add. by Cor. blisse ł add. by Cor. wistfulgend ł add. by Cor.   6. -hwy by Cor. on er. eart þu by Cor. hyht by Cor.
on er. ł andwlitan add. by Cor.   7. for-, fin. let. er.; -þan by Cor. part.
on er. ic beo add. by Cor. þin by Cor. drihten by Cor. on er.

eorðan iordænis 7 hermonis from dune unmicelre　　　Dyopnes
terra iordanis et hermonis a monte modico 8. *Abyssus*

diopnesse chieð on stefne geheftræ rihtræ ł wæterædrana
abyssum invocat in voce cataractarum

þinræ eællæ hihþo þine 7 yþa þine ofer me ferdon
tuarum omnia excelsa tua et fluctus tui super me transierunt

　On dege bebeæð dryhten mildheortnesse his 7 on niht
9. *In die mandavit dominus misericordiam suam et nocte*

he gesweotolode Mid me gebed gode lifes mines　　ic cwiþe
declaravit Apud me oratio deo vitae meae 10. *dicam*

gode onfeng min þu ært Forhwi me þu ofergete 7 forhwi me
deo susceptor meus es Quare me oblitus es et quare me

þu utawyltest ł anyldest 7 forhwi unrot ł sári ic gange þonne
reppulisti et quare tristis incedo dum

swencð me fiond　　þonne bioð tobrocene eælle bǽn
affligit me inimicus 11. *Dum confringuntur omnia ossa*

mine me edwitodon þe eærfoþodon ł swencað me midþi
mea exprobraverunt me qui tribulant me um

bið cweþende me þurh Syndrie dægæs hwer is god þin
dicitur michi per singulos dies ubi est deus tuus

　Forhwi unrot is sæul min 7 forwæn þu gedrefest me hyht on
12. *Quare tristis es anima mea et quare conturbas me Spera in*

god forþæn ic ændette him helo ondwlite mines 7 god min
deum quoniam confitebor illi salutare vultus mei et deus meus

42.

dem me god 7 toscead intingæn minne of þiode unhæligre
Iudica me deus et discerne causam meam de gente non sancta

fræm men unrihtwisum 7 facenfullen genere me　　Forðæn
ab homine iniquo et doloso eripe me 2. *Quia*

ðu eært god min 7 strengþo min forwæn me ðu ædrife ł ðu
tu es deus meus et fortitudo mea quare me reppu-

---

unmicelre in d. ink.　8. *Dyopnes diopnesse* by Cor. on er.　About two
lett. er. immed. bef. *chieð. rihtræ ł wæterædrana* by Cor.　9. *on* (2nd)
prob. add. by Cor. *he gesweotolode* by Cor. on er. *lifes mines, -es* in both
cases prob. add. by Cor.　10. *þu ært* by Cor. on er.　From *Forhwi* to *me*
(3rd) by Cor. *fiond* cov. by d. ink.　11. *þonne* by Cor. on er. *ł swencað*
add. by Cor.　12. *-hwi* by Cor. on er. *min*, fin. let. er. *-fest, -st* by Cor.
on er. *hyht* by Cor. in pl. of er. *mines, -es* by Cor.　42. *toscead*, an
er. immed. at end. *unhæligre, un-* by Cor. in pl. of er.; *-igre* by Cor. on er.
-wisum 7 facenfullen by Cor. in pl. of er.　2. *min* (2nd), fin. *e* er. *ł ðu
aryddest* add. by Cor.

aryddest 7 forwæn unrot ic inga þonne swencð me fiond
listi   et   quare tristis incedo dum affligit me inimicus

Asend lioht ðin 7 soðfestnesse þine hy me leddon 7
3. *Emitte lucem tuam et veritatem tuam ipsa me deduxerunt et*

togeleddon on dune hælgæn ðine 7 on eærdunge ðine   Ic
adduxerunt in monte sancto tuo et in tabernaculo tuo   4. In-

ingonge to wifode godes to gode þe geblissiæð giogoðe mine
troibo ad altare dei ad deum qui laetificat iuventutem meam

Ic ændette ðe on heærpæn god god min   forwæn sari
Confitebor tibi in cythara deus deus meus   5. quare tristis

þu ært Sæwl min 7 forwæn gedrefest þu me Gewene ꞇ hyht on
es anima mea et quare   conturbas me   Spera   in

god forðæn ic ændette him helo ondwlitæn min 7 god min
deum quoniam confitebor illi salutare vultus mei et deus meus

43.

god eærum urum we gehierdon faderes ure cyþdon ꞇ
2. *Deus auribus nostris ·audivimus patres nostri annunt-*

bodedon us Weorc ðet þu worhtest on dagum hieræ
iaverunt nobis Opus quod operatus es in diebus eorum

ond on dagum eældum   hand ðin ðiodæ forspilde 7
et in diebus antiquis 3. Manus tua gentes disperdet et

þu plantodest ꞇ wirtwælædæst hie ðu gebigdest ꞇ swenctest
       plantasti   eos   adflixisti

7 þu utædrife hie   Na soðlice on sweorde his
populos et expulisti eos 4. Non enim in gladio suo

hy agon corðæn 7 eærm hioræ ne gehęlð hie Ac
possidebunt terram et brachium eorum non salvabit eos Sed

swiðre ðin 7 eærm þin 7 onliehting andwlitan ꞇ onsien
dextera tua et brachium tuum et inluminatio   vultus

From *ic* to *me* by Cor. in pl. of er.   **3.** *Asend*, fin. let. er.? *-nesse, -se* add. by Cor. *þine, e* add. by Cor. *hy* by Cor. on er. *leddon*, init. *ge-* er.; *-don* by Cor. on er.? *-don* (2nd) in d. ink. *ðine*, let. er. betw. *i* and *n* (twice). **4.** Er. bef. *gio-*. *mine, e* by Cor. in pl. of er. **5.** *sari þu ært* by Cor. in pl. of er. *Sæwl, wl* by Cor. on er. *-est, t* by Cor. on er. *þu* by Cor. *ꞇ hyht* add. by Cor. *-tæn, n* add. by Cor. **43. 2.** *fad-, a* from *e*. *ꞇ bodedon* add. by Cor. *þu worhtest* by Cor. on er. Er. bef. *on* (1st). *dagum*, orig. *dægum* in both cases. Er. bef. *eældum*; *-um* by Cor. on er. **3.** *hand*, orig. *hænd*. *ðin*, fin. let. (e?) er. *7 þu plantodest* add. by Cor. *-lædæst, a*-part of *æ* (1st) from *e*; *ꞇ* add. by Cor. *-dest, t* prob. add. by Cor. *ꞇ swenctest 7 þu ut-* by Cor. in pl. of er. **4.** *Na soðlice* by Cor. in pl. of er. *hy* add. by Cor. *agon* orig. *ægon*. *Ac, c* on er. *andwlitan ꞇ* add. by Cor.

þines forðæn   gelicæde   ðe on him   ðu eært self king min
tui quoniam complacuit tibi in illis   5. *Tu   es   ipse   rex   meus*

7 god min þu ðe behiódest   hęlo   isrhel ł iæcobe   On
et deus meus   qui   mandas salutem   iacob   6. *In*

þe fiond   ure   we windwioð 7 on nomæn þin we forhogyen
te inimicos nostros ventilabimus et in nomine tuo   spernemus

onærisonde on us   Ne soðlice on bogan minum ic gewene
insurgentes in nos   7. *Non enim in arcu   meo   sperabo*

7 sweord min   ne geheleð me   ðu gefriolsedes soðlice us
et gladius meus non salvabit me   8. *Liberasti   enim   nos*

of ðæm swencendum us 7 þa þe us fiodon ðu gescyndest
ex   affligentibus   nos et eos qui nos oderunt   confudisti

On gode we beoþ herede alne deg 7 on namæn þinum we
9. *In deo   laudabimur   tota die et in nomine tuo   con-*

ændetteþ on worolde   Nu soðlice ðu aneddest 7 ðu
fitebimur in secula   10. *Nunc autem   reppulisti et*

gescindest ł drefdest us 7 ne utgængest god on megnum
confudisti   nos et non egredieris deus in virtutibus

urum   ðu acyrdest us on beclinc fore fiondum urum 7
nostris   11. *Avertisti nos retrorsum prae inimicis nostris et*

þa þæ fiodon ł hatedon us hyo reafodon him   þu geseældest
eos qui   oderunt   nos diripiebant sibi   12. *Dedisti*

us swæ swæ Sceæp mettæ 7 on ðiodum ðu us tostenctest
nos tanquam oves escarum et in gentibus   dispersisti nos

ðu sældest ł cyptest   folc   þin buton wiorðe 7 ne wes
13. *Vendidisti   populum tuum sine   precio et non fuit*

menigo on stirengum ł behwearfum hioræ   ðu gesettest
multitudo in   commutationibus   eorum   14. *Posuisti*

us on   edwite   neæhgeburum urum of leahtrum 7 hyrwnesse
nos in opprobrium   vicinis   nostris   derisum et   con-

þines, -es by Cor.   -æde, d from ð and e add. by Cor.   5. self prob. add.
by Cor.; fin. let. er.? þu ðe by Cor.; er. betw. these words. -est, t add. by
Cor.   israhel ł add. by Cor.   6. we add. by Cor.   Word of about two lett.
er. betw. wind- and -wioð. -nde by Cor. in pl. of er.   7. Er. aft. Ne. From
on to ic add. by Cor.   8. -est, t add. by Cor.? 9. we beoþ herede by Cor. on
er.   deg, fin. let. er.   nam- orig. næm-.   Er. immed. bef. ænd-.   10. aneddest by Cor. on er.   ł drefdest add. by Cor.   -gest, st by Cor.   11. acyr-
by Cor. in pl. of er.   ł hatedon add. by Cor.   hyo reafodon prob. by
Cor. on er.   13. sældest on er.   ł cyptest add. by Cor.   ł behwearfum add.
by Cor.   14. -est, t add. by Cor.? neæhgeburum, -hgeburum prob. add.
by Cor.; the orig. word was prps. neæn, h being from the last n.   of by Cor.
on er.

ł hogunge ðam ðæ on ymbegænge ure sindon ðu gesettest
temptum his qui in circuitu nostro sunt 15. *Posuisti*

us on gelicnesse ðiodum æwendnesse ł styringe heæfdes on
nos in similitudinem gentibus commotationem capitis in

ðiodum ł folcum Alne dei scamu min ongean me is 7
plebibus 16. *Tota die verecundia mea contra me est et*

gescindnes onsien ł andwlitan mines oferwreah me Fram
confusio vultus mei operuit me 17. *A*

stemne hyspendes 7 ongeansprecendes from onsine fiondæs 7
voce exprobrantis et obloquentis a facie inimici et

from ehtendes ðæs eællæ comon ofer us 7
persequentis 18. *Haec omnia venerunt super nos et*

ofergitende we ne sindon ðe 7 unrihtlice we ne deden on
obliti non sumus te et iniquae non egimus in

cyþnesse ðine 7 ne gewat on bec heorte ure
testamento tuo 19. *et non recessit retro cor nostrum*

7 ðu aheldest stigæ ł siþfatu uræ from ðinum wege
Et declinasti semitas nostras a via tua

forðæn ðu geeæðmeddest us on stowe geswencednesse 7
20. *quoniam humiliasti nos in loco afflictionis et*

oferwreah us scadu deæþes Gif we sien ofergitende
operuit nos umbra mortis 21. *Si obliti sumus*

nomon godes ures 7 gif we âþeniæð hænde ure to gode
nomen dei nostri et si expandimus manus nostras ad deum

fremdum hwu ne god secæþ ðæs he eællengæ cnaweð
alienum 22. *Nonne deus requiret ista ipse enim novit*

diglæ heortæn Forðæn fore ðe deæde we bioþ gewordene
occulta cordis Quoniam propte[r] te morte afficimur

elce deg we bioþ gewenende swæ scep acweællednesse
tota die estimati sumus ut oves occisionis

ł hogunge prps. add. by Cor. *ðam, -am* by Cor. on er. 15. *-est, ł* add.
by Cor. *ł styringe* add. by Cor. *ł folcum* add. by Cor. 16. *ongean* by
Cor. on er. *ł andwlitan* add. by Cor. *mines, -es* add. by Cor. *oferwreah* by
Cor. on er. 17. *Fram* by Cor. on er. *hyspendes* by Cor. on er. *ongeansprecendes* by Cor on er. *-dæs, s* prob. add. by Cor. *-des, s* by Cor. in pl. of
er. 18. *we* add. by Cor. *ðe, ð* from some other let. Er. bef. *unrihtlice,
-tlice* by Cor. on er. *deden, e* (1st) on er.; second *d* from *ð.* 19. *gewat*
orig. *gewæt. aheldest* by Cor. on er. *ł siþfatu* add. by Cor. 20. *geswenced-,
-ed-* wr. over the line by Cor. *oferwreah* by Cor. on er. *-cadu* by Cor. on er.
21. *âþeniæð, â* prob. orig. *æ; -þ-* by Cor. Er. bef. *fremdum.* 22. *hwu ne*
on er. *cnaweð* by Cor. *diglæ,* about two lett. immed. bef. and one let.
immed. aft. this word er. *deæde,* second *d* from *ð.* *we* by Cor. *deg,* fin. *e*
er. Er. aft. *swæ. -lednesse* by Cor. on er.

Aris   forwæn   slepest   þu   drihten   æris   ne   anyd   þu   †
23. *Exsurge   quare   obdormis   domine   exurge   et   ne   repell-*

7   ne   ædrif   þu   us   oððe   ón   ende   Forwæn   onsîéne   þine
as   nos   usque   in   finem   **24.**   *Quare   faciem   tuam*

æhwirfst   þu   ofergitest   unspede   †   wedlæn   ure   7   eærfoðnesse   †
avertis   oblivisceris   inopiam   nostram   et   tribula-

swinc   ure   Forðæn   geeæðmæd   is   on   duste
tionem   nostram   **25.**   *Quoniam   humiliata   est   in   pulvere*

sæule   ure   etfylhð   †   clyuode   on   eorðæn   wamb   †   innoð   ure
anima   nostra   adhesit   in   terra   venter   noster

Æris   drihten   gefultumæ   us   7   alys   †   friolsæ   us   fore
26. *Exsurge   domine   adiuva   nos   et   libera   nos   propter*

nomæn   ðinum
nomen   tuum

44.

belcette   heorte   min   word   god   cwiðe   ic   wiorc   mine
2. *Eructavit   cor   meum   verbum   bonum   dico   ego   opera   mea*

kininge   Tunge   min   writingfeþere   gewriteres   hredlice   writendes
regi   Lingua   mea   calamus   scribe   velociter   scribentis

Wlitig   heow   fore   beærnum   mænnæ   ægoten   is   gifu
3. *Speciosus   forma   pre   filiis   hominum   diffusa   est   gratia*

on   welrum   þinum   Forðæn   gebletsode   þe   god   on   ecnesse
in   labiis   tuis   Propterea   benedixit   te   deus   in   aeternum

to   begirdænne   sweorde   ðinum   ymb   þæ   lendeno   mihtigliche   †
4.   *accingere   gladio   tuo   circa   femur   poten-*

þeoh   riclicost   Wlite   ðinne   7   fegernesse   diue   beheæld
tissime   **5.** *Specie   tua   et   pulchritudine   tua   intende*

gesundfullice   forðgæwit   7   rixæ   Fore   Soðfestnesse   7
prospere   procede   et   regna   Propter   veritatem   et

geþwernesse   7   rihtwisnesse   7   geledeþ   þe   wundorliche   swiðre
mansuetudinem et   iustitiam   et   deducet   te   mirabiliter   dextera

23. *Aris* = orig. *Æris.* -est þu add. by Cor.   þu us add. by Cor.   24.
onsîéne, fin. e prob. add. by Cor.   þine add. by Cor.   Er. bef. æhwirfst;
† add. by Cor.   þu add. by Cor.   -est, -st by Cor. on er.   unspede † add. by
Cor.; † on er.   -nesse, se add. by Cor.   25. † clyuode add. by Cor.   wamb †
add. by Cor.   26. alys † add. by Cor.   44. 2. belcette by Cor.
heorte, fin. e prob. add. by Cor.   writingfeþere, by Cor. on er.   -eres add. by
Cor.   3. -ig in pl. of er. by Cor.†   -ow by Cor. on er.   -ode by Cor.   þe
by Cor.   4. Er. bef. mihtigliche; -igliche by Cor. on er.   5. gesundfullice by Cor. on er.   -wit on er.   rixæ, æ from e.   rihtwis- by Cor. on er.
Er. aft. 7.   þe add. by Cor.   -liche add. by Cor.

ðin   strelæ ł flane ðine sceærpe ðes mihtigestæn folc
tua   **6.**   *Sagittae   tuae   acute   potentissime   populi*

under ðe gefealleþ on heortæn   find   þes kinges   Setle
sub   te   cadent   in   cordae inimicorum   regis   **7.** *Sedes*

þin god on woroldæ world gierd riht   is   gird rices   þines
tua deus   in   seculum   seculi virga   recta   est   virga regni   tui

ðu lufodest rihtwisnesse 7 þu fiodest ł hatudest unrihtwisnesse
8.   *Dilexisti   iustitiam   et   odisti   iniquitatem*

foreðæn smirede ðe god god ðin of ele blisse   fore   efnlinge
propterea   unxit   te   deus deus tuus   oleo laeticiae   pre   consortibus

þine   Murræ 7 swete dropen 7 swete wirt from   girelæn
*tuis   **9.**   Mirra et   gutta   et   cassia   a   vestimentis*

ðinum of   stapum   ælpenbanenum of ðam   gelustfulladon
tuis   a   gradibus   eburneis   ex quibus te   delectaverunt

dohtre ciningæ on arwur[ð]nisse ðiure Etstod Sio cwen
10.   *filiae   regum   in   honore   tuo Adstitit   regina*

ðeræ swiðræn þines on girelæn   of golde   ymbgyrd   mislicnisse
a   dextris   tuis in vestitu   deaurato circumamicta varietate

Gehier dohtor 7   gesioh 7 onhild   eære   þin 7   ofergit
11.   *Audi   filia   et   vide   et inclina aurem tuam et obliviscere*

folc   ðin   7   hus   federes   þines   Forðæn
*populum   tuum   et   domum   patris   tui   **12.** Quoniam*

gewilnæde   kining   wlite ł hiw   ðinne   forðæn   he is   drihten
concupivit   rex   speciem   tuam   quia   ipse est   dominus

god ðin 7   hine gebiddæþ   dohtore tire on   læcum
*deus tuus et   adorabunt eum   **13.** filiae   tyri   in muneribus*

Onsin ł   andwliton ðin   bioð   biddende   eællæ   welige folces
Vultum   tuum   deprecabuntur   omnes   divites   plebis

eæl   wuldor his dohtora ciningæ from on innen On fnedum
14. *omnis gloria eius   filiae   regum   ab   intus   In fimbriis*

---

6. *ł flane* add. by Cor.   *under* by Cor. on er.   MS. has *heortæn on*, but marked for transposition.   7. *Setle*, fin. e prob. add. by Cor.   8. *lufodest*, *ł* prob. add. by Cor.   *rihtwis-* by Cor. on er.   *fiodest, ł* add. by Cor.   *ł hatudest* add. by Cor.   *-wisnesse* add. by Cor.   *of* add. by Cor.   *blisse fore* add. by Cor.   *efnlinge* by Cor. on er.   9. *swete dropen 7 swete wirt* by Cor. on er.   *of stapum* by Cor. on er.   From *æl-* to *ðam* by Cor. in pl. of er.   *-don* by Cor.   10. *dohtre* by Cor.; er. aft. it.   *on arwurnisse* by Cor. on er.   *-od* by Cor. on er.   *-gyrd* by Cor. on er.   *-nisse* by Cor. on er.   11. *Gehier*, fin. let. er.   *dohtor* by Cor. on er.   Er. immed. aft. *-git.*   7 by Cor. on er.   *federes, -es* add. by Cor.   12. *-de* by Cor. on er.   *ł hiw* add. by Cor.   13. *dohtore* by Cor. on er.   *ł andwliton* add. by Cor.   14. *eæl*, fin. *-le* er.?   *dohtora* by Cor. on er.   *on* by Cor. on er.   *-nen* by Cor. on er.   *fnedum* by Cor. on er.

gyldenum   ymbgyrd ꝉ cæfed   missenlihnesse To bioð
aureis   **15.**   *circumamicta*   *varietate*   *Addu-*

geledde kininge femnæn ꝉ medenan efter ðon nixtum his
centur   *regi*   *virgines*   *post* *eam* *proxime* *eius*

to bioð borene ðe   on blissæ ⁊ on hyhte ꝉ gefægnunge
adferentur tibi   **16.** *in laetitia et*   *exultatione*

hy bioð geledde on temple kininges   Fore federum ðinum
adducentur *in templum regis*   **17.** *Pro patribus tuis*

cynnede sint ðe beærn þu gesetest hie eældormen ofer eælle
nati   *sunt tibi filii*   *constitues* *eos* *principes super omnem*

eorðæn   Gemindyge bioð næmon þin drihten on eællum
terram   **18.** *Memores erunt nominis tui domine in   omni*

cneorisse ⁊ cynne   Foreðæn   folc   ondettæþ   ðe on
generatione et progenie Propterea   populi confitebuntur tibi in

ecnesse ⁊ on worold aworlde
aeternum et in seculum seculi

45.

God ure gescildent ꝉ frofr ⁊ megen fultumend on swincum
2. *Deus noster   refugium   et virtus   adiutor in   tribu-*

ꝉ eærfoþnessum þæ gemetton us sw ðe   Forðæn
lationibus   quae invenerunt nos nimis   **3.** *Propterea*

we ne ondredæð þonne beoð gedrefed eorðe ⁊ bioð ofer-
non timebimus   dum   conturbabitur terra et trans-

farende ꝉ borene dunæ on heortæn sæs   Swegdon ⁊
ferentur   montes in   cor   maris   **4.** *Sonaverunt et*

gedrefede Sint wetere his gedrefede sint dunæ on Strangnysse
turbate   sunt aquae eius conturbati sunt montes in   fortitudine

his   Streæmæs ꝉ flodes onres geblissæþ ceæstre godes
eius **5.** *Fluminis   impetus laetificat civitatem dei*

he gehælgæde geteld ꝉ eærdungstowe his þu hihsta   god
sanctificavit   tabernaculum   suum altissimus   **6.** *deus*

15. -gyrd ꝉ cæfed by Cor. oñ er. -senlihnesse by Cor. prob. in pl. of er.
ꝉ medenan add. by Cor.   16. ꝉ gefægnunge hy add. by Cor.   17. -st add. by
Cor.   18. -dyge, -ge prob. add. by Cor. cneorisse add. by Cor. cynne by Cor.
on er.   45. 2. -ent ꝉ frofr add. by Cor. to er. immed. bef. ful-. swincum ꝉ
add. by Cor. Er. (on?) immed. bef. gemetton.   3 Forðæn, let. (e?) er. aft. r.
þonne beoð by Cor. in pl. of er. -fed, fin. e er.   ꝉ borene add. by Cor. sæs,
second s from some other let.; orig. = sæwe?   4. wetere, fin. e prob. add.
by Cor.   5. ꝉ flodes onres by Cor. in pl. of er. geteld ꝉ prob. add by Cor.

on midle hise ne bi∂ onwenden ꞇ astired gefultumat hie god
in medio eius   *non commovebitur*   *Adiuvabit cam deus*

andwlitan ꞇ onsine his   gedrefede sint ∂iodæ 7 onhilde
    vultu   *suo*   **7.** *conturbatae sunt gentes et inclinata*

sint rice Selde stefne his se hihsta 7 astyred is eorþe
sunt regna dedit vocem suam altissimus et mota est terra

    drihten megene mid us onfeng ure god iacobes
8. *Dominus virtutum nobiscum susceptor noster deus iacob*

    Cumæþ 7 gesio∂ wiorc drihtnes þa he gesette foretacne
9. *Venite et videte opera domini quae posuit prodigia*

ofer eor∂an   Afyrrende gefioht o∂∂et to endes eor∂an
super terram   **10.** *Auferens bella usque ad fines terrae*

bogæ he forbryte∂ 7 gebric∂ wepnæ 7 scylde he forbernþ
arcum conteret et confringet arma et scuta comburet

on fyre   geemtiæþ 7 gesio∂ for∂æn þ ic eom god ic bio
igni   **11.** *Vacate et videte quoniam ego sum deus exal-*

uphæfen on ∂iodum 7 bi∂ uphæfen on eor∂æn   drihten
tabor in gentibus et exaltabor in terra   **12.** *Dominus*

megen mid us onfeng ure god iacobes
virtutum nobiscum susceptor noster deus iacob

46.

ælle ∂io∂æ heofæ∂ ꞇ blissiad hændum winsumiæþ gode on
2. *Omnes gentes plaudite manibus iubilate deo in*

stefne hihte ꞇ blisse   For∂æn god heah egeslic 7
voce exultationis   **3.** *Quoniam deus summus terribilis et*

cing micel ofer eulle godas   he Underþeod folc
rex magnus super omnes deos   **4.** *Subiecit populos*

us 7 ∂iodæ under fet urc   he Gecæs us on
nobis et gentes sub pedibus nostris   **5.** *Elegit nos in*

yrfeweærdnesse him hiw iacobes ∂one he lufode   Æstigæþ
haereditatem sibi speciem iacob quem dilexit   **6.** *Ascendit*

---

6. *ꞇ astired* add. by Cor. *hie, e* from some other let.? *andwlitan ꞇ* add. by Cor.   7. *Selde, -de* by Cor. on er. *se,* fin. let. er. *astyred* by Cor. on er. 9. *þa he* by Cor. in pl. of er. *-tacne* by Cor.   10. *endes, s* prob. add. by Cor. *he forbryte∂* by Cor. on er. *gebric∂, ∂* by Cor. in pl. of er. *wepnæ, æ* prob. add. by Cor. *on fyre, on* and *-e* add. by Cor.   11. *þ* add. by Cor. *ic* (2nd) by Cor. on er. *bio, o* from *d* or *∂*.   46. 2. *alle* by Cor. *ꞇ blissiad* add. by Cor. *ꞇ blisse* add. by Cor.   3. *heah* by Cor. on er. *godas, s* prob. add. by Cor.   4. *he* pref. by Cor. *-þeod* on er.   5. *he* pref. by Cor. (twice). *Gecæs,* let. (s?) er. betw. *e* and *c*.

god on winsumnesse ł dræme 7 drihten on stefne bimæn
deus in   iubilatione   et dominus in   voce   tube .

Singæð gode ure singæþ singæþ kininge urum singæþ
7. *Psallite deo nostro psallite psallite regi nostro psallite*

Forðæu kining ælre eorðæn god is singæþ snytro ł
8. *Quoniam rex omnis terrae deus psallite sapi-*

wislicbe   Rixæþ drihtæn on ofer eælle þiodæ god
enter   **9.** *Regnabit dominus   super omnes gentes deus*

sitt ofer setle hæligam his   Eældormen folces tosomne
sedet super sedem sanctam suam **10.** *Principes populi con-*

becomen mid gode abræhæmes forðæn godas strænge on eorþen
venerunt cum deo abraham quoniam dii fortes   terrae

swiþe upæhæfen sindon
nimium elevati sunt

47.

Michel drihten 7 hergendlic swiðe on ceæstre godes
2. *Magnus dominus et laudabilis nimis in civitate dei*

ure on dunæ hælie his   gebredende hyhtes   eælle
nostri in monte sancto eius **3.** *Dilatans exultationes universae*

eorðe munt ł dune sion siden norðdeles ceæster kininges miceles
terrae mons syon latera aquilonis civitas regis magni

god on stepum his bioð gitende ł cnawen þonne he onfoð
4. *Deus in gradibus eius dinoscitur dum suscipiet*

hie   Forðæn eællengæ kininges eorðe gesomnede beoð
eam **5.** *Quoniam ecce reges terrae congregati*

ł sint 7 togedere comen on ænum   hy gesiende þa
sunt et convenerunt in unum **6.** *Ipsi videntes tunc*

wundriende sint gedrefede sint 7 onfarede ł astyrede sint
admirati sunt conturbati sunt et commoti   sunt

firhto ł bifung gegripþ hie ðer Sar swa swæ
7. *tremor apprehendit eos Ibi dolores sicut*

6. ł *dræme* add. by Cor.   8. *ælre* by Cor. on er. *is* add. by Cor. ł *wis-*
liche add. by Cor.   9. *on*, aft. this word is an er. wh. glosses *in æternum* (wh.
has a red line drawn through it for er.); prob. *on* should have been er. too.
10. Er. bef. *folces*. *tosomne becomen* by Cor. on er. *on* add. by Cor. *eorþen*,
n add. by Cor.   47. 2. *Michel* by Cor.   3. -*ende*, fin. *e* add. by Cor.
hyhtes by Cor. on er. *munt* ł add. by Cor. *siden norðdeles* by Cor. in pl. of
er.   4. *bioð* from something else. ł *cnawen* add. by Cor. *þonne he* by Cor.
prob. in pl. of er.   5. *beoð* ł add. by Cor. *togedere comen* by Cor. on er.
6. *hy*, *y* from *i* by Cor. *þa* orig. prob. = *þæ*. ł *astyrede* add. by Cor.   7.
ł *bifung* add. by Cor.; fin. let. er. *Sar* orig. = *Sær* (accent doubtful). *swa*
add. by Cor.

G

æcniendes   on gastæ swiþe brecende scypa tharsis
parturientis   **8.** *in spiritu vehementi conterens naves tharsis*

   swæ we gehirdon swæ 7 we gesæwon on ceæstre drihten
9. *Sicut audivimus ita et vidimus in civitate domini*

megene on ceæstre godes ure god gestæðolode hy on
virtutum in civitate dei nostri deus fundavit eam in

ecnesse   We onfengon god mildheortnesse þine on
aeternum **10.** *Suscepimus deus misericordiam tuam in*

middæn temple þin   Efter nomæn ðinum god swæ
medio templi tui **11.** *Secundum nomen tuum deus ita*

7 lof þin on ende eorðæn rihtwisnesse full is swiðræ ðin
et laus tua in fines terrae iustitia plena est dextera tua

blissiæþ munt Ɨ dún syon 7 hihtæþ Ɨ fæogen dohtre iudæn
12. *Laetetur mons syon et exultent filiae iudae*

for dome þinc drihten   Ymbsellæð sion 7 bewindæþ
propter iudicia tua domine **13.** *Circundate syon et complec-*
Ɨ ymbclyppað hy secgæþ Ɨ cyþað on stepelum his   settæþ
timini eam narrate in turribus eius **14.** *ponite*

heortæn eowræ on megen his 7 todelcð stepæs his ðette
corda vestra in virtute eius et distribuite gradus eius ut

gesegæn Ɨ cyþen on cneowrisc Ɨ cynrede oðrum   Forðan
enarretis in progeniae altera **15.** *Quoniam*

þes is god ure on ecnesse 7 on worold aworolde 7 he
hic est deus noster in aeternum et in saeculum saeculi et ipse

gerecet us on worolde
reget nos in secula

48.

gehyrað ðæs eælle ðiodæ mid eærum onfoð þæ ðe eærdiæþ
2. *Audite haec omnes gentes auribus percipite qui habitatis*

on ymbwirft   7 gefylce eorðware Ɨ eordcende 7 bcærn
orbem **3.** *Quique terrigene et filii*

æcniendes add. by Cor. on er.   8. *scypa* by Cor.; er. bef. it.   9. *we*
(2nd) by Cor. wr. over the line. *megene,* fin. *e* add. by Cor. *-lode* by Cor. on
er. *hy, y* from *i* by Cor.; er. immed. aft. it.   11. *rihtwisnesse* by Cor. on
er.   12. *dohtre* by Cor. on er. *for,* fin. let. (e?) er. Er. bef. *dome, þine,*
e prob. add. by Cor.   13. Ɨ *ymbclyppað* add. by Cor. *hy, y* from *i* by Cor.
Ɨ *cypað* add. by Cor. *on stepelum* by Cor. on er.   14. *todeleð* by Cor. on er.
Ɨ *cyþen* add. by Cor. *-e* Ɨ *cynrede oðrum* add. by Cor.   48. 2. *gehyrað*
by Cor. *mid* add. by Cor. *ðe* add. by Cor. *on* by Cor.   3. From 7 (1st)
to *-cende* by Cor. on er. (MS. = *gefylce.*)

mænnæ semed on æn welig 7 þeærfæ   Muð min
hominum simul in unum dives et pauper   **4.** *Os meum*

sprecð snytro ł wisdom 7 smeæung ł gemynd heorte minre
loquetur sapientiam et meditatio cordis mei

gleawnisse ł wisdom   Ic Onhilde to gelicnesse eære
prudentiam   **5.** *Inclinabo ad similitudinem aurem*

min ic ontine on spaltere foregesetenesse minre   To
meam aperiam in psalterio propositionem meam   **6.** *Ut*

hwon ic ondrede on dege yfelæn unrihtwisnesse spuran mine
quid timebo in die mala iniquitas calcanei mei

ymbseælde me   ðæ þe getriwæð on megene heora
circumdedit me   **7.** *Qui confidunt in virtute sua*

witoþlice on genihtsummunga ł fulsumnesse welenæ hiræ
quique in abundantia diviciarum suarum

bioð wuldriende   broðor ne ælisede ælisede mon ne
gloriabuntur   **8.** *Frater non redemit redemit homo non*

seleð gode gecwemnesse ł licungæ his   ne wiorþ
dabit deo placationem suam   **9.** *nec precium*

alisnesse saul his 7 sceal swinccan on ecnesse
redemptionis anime suae et laborabit in aeternum

7 lifæþ on ende   Forðæn ne gesihþ forwird
10. *et vivet in finem*   **11.** *Quoniam non videbit interitum*

þonne he gesihþ wise ł snitro sweltende somed unwis ł snitro
cum viderit sapientes morientes simul insipiens

7 disig forwiorðæþ 7 hi forletæþ fremdæn welæn heræ
et stultus peribunt Et relinquent alienis divitias suas

7 birigene heræ hus heræ on ecnesse Eærdungæ ł
12. *et sepulchra eorum domus eorum in aeternum Taberna-*

geteld hioræ on cneowrisse ł on cynrene 7 forecneowrisse
cula eorum in generatione et progeniae

gecigæþ nomæn hiræ on eorðum hiræ   7 mon
invocabunt nomina eorum in terris ipsorum   **13.** *Et homo*

---

4. *sprecð, ð* by Cor. on er.   *ł wisdom* add. by Cor.   *ł gemynd* add. by Cor.
gleawnisse ł add. by Cor.   5. *Ic* pref. by Cor.   6. *hwon* on er.   *-wisnesse*
by Cor. on er. Er. bef. *mine.*   7. *þe* add. by Cor.   *heora* prob. by Cor. in
pl. of er.   *-unga ł fulsumnesse* by Cor. part. on er.   8. *ælisede* (twice), *d*
from ð?, fin. *e* add. by Cor.?   About two lett. (*se*?) er. immed. bef. *mon.*
gecwemnesse ł add. by Cor.   9. *7 sceal swinccan* by Cor. on er.   11. *þonne*
he by Cor. in pl. of er.   *wise ł* add. by Cor.   *-wis ł* add. by Cor.   *disig,* fin. let.
(*e*?) er.   *fremdæn,* let. er. aft. *e.*   *heræ, e* from *i* by Cor.   12. *-gene,* fin. *e*
add. by Cor.   *heræ, e* from *i* by Cor. (twice).   *ł geteld* add. by Cor.   *ł on*
cynrene by Cor. part. on er.   *eorðum* by Cor. on er.

mid wiorðmynde wes ne ongiet efenameten ł wiðmeten is
cum in honore esset non intellexit comparatus est

nietenum unwisum ł unsnytrum 7 gelic geworden is him
iumentis insipientibus et similis factus est illis

ðes weg hioræ æswic ł wroht him 7 efter þæm on muðe
14. *Haec via eorum scandalum ipsis et postea in ore*

hiræ bletsiæþ   swæ swæ scep on helle gesette sindon
suo benedicent **15.** *Sicut oves in inferno positi sunt*

7 deæþ misfedeþ ł fritt hii 7 begitæþ hii soðfeste ðe on
et mors depascet eos Et obtinebunt eos iusti in

uhttide ł in morgentid 7 fultum hiræ eœldæþ on helle
matutino et auxilium eorum veterascet in inferno

7 fram wuldor hiræ onweg adrifene sint   þeah hweþre
et a gloria sua expulsi sunt **16.** *Verumtamen*

god gefriolsæþ sawle mine of hænde helle midþi
deus liberabit animam meam de manu inferi dum

he onfehð me   Ne ondred þu þe þonne welyg geworden
acceperit me **17.** *Ne timueris cum dives factus*

bieð mon 7 þonne gemonifalded bið wuldor hus his
fuerit homo et cum multiplicata fuerit gloria domus eius

Forðæn na þonne he swylteð onfehþ ðæs eallæ
18. *Quoniam non cum morietur accipiet haec omnia*

ne semed astæh adúne mid him wuldor hus his
neque simul descendit cum eo gloria domus eius

Forðan sæwl his on life his bið gebletsad 7 bið
19. *Quoniam anima eius in vita ipsius benedicetur et con-*

geandette þonne ðu weldest him   7 ingeð oðþe
fitebitur tibi dum benefeceris ei **20.** *Et introibit usque*

on forekinred fedræ hioræ 7 oððet on eccnesse ne gesioþ
in progeniem patrum suorum et usque in aeternum non videbit

lioht   7 man þa he on weorðscipe ł are wes ne
lumen **21.** *Et homo cum   in honore esset   non*

---

13. -*mynde, y* from *i* by Cor. *efenameten* by Cor. on er. *ł wiðmeten* add. by Cor. -*enum, um* prob. add. by Cor. *unwisum ł* add. by Cor. 14. *weg* from *wei?* *æswic* by Cor. on er. *ł wroht* add. by Cor. 15. *swœ* (2nd) add. by Cor. *mis-* pref. by Cor. *ł fritt* add. by Cor. -*tide ł in morgentid* by Cor. *on helle* add. by Cor. *onweg adrifene* by Cor. on er. 16. *helle* by Cor. *he* add. by Cor. 17. *þonne* by Cor. on er. (twice). -*falded, ed* add. by Cor. 18. From *na* to -*teð* by Cor. in pl. of er. *astæh,* accent doubtful. *adúne* add. by Cor.; accent doubtful. *mid, d* from *ð.* 19. *gean-,* er. betw. *e* and *a.* 20. *oðþe,* fin. let. er. 21. *man, a* from *o.* From *þa* to *wes* on er.

ongiet he   gemetfest ꞇ efenmeten   is nietenum   unsnytrum ꞇ
intellexit   comparatus   est iumentis   insipi-
unwise 7 gelic geworden is his
entibus et similis   factus   est illis

49.

God   goda   drihten   sprecende is 7 chigð ꞇ cleopede eorðæn
Deus deorum dominus   locutus   est et   vocavit   terram
From sunnæn upgange oððe   setlgange   of sione hyow
A   solis   ortu usque ad occasum   2. ex syon species
his wlites   god openliche cimeþ god ure 7 ne
decoris eius   3. Deus manifeste veniet deus noster et non
swigoð   Fyr on gesihþe his   birnþ 7 ymbegænge his
silebit Ignis in conspectu eius ardebit et in circuitu eius
storm st[r]ang   to he gechigde hefon   up 7 eorðæn
tempestas valida   4. Advocavit caelum sursum et terram
ðet he sceæwie   folc his   gesomniæð hredlice hælige
discerneret populum suum   5. Congregate illic sanctos
his ðæ geendebyrdan cyþnesse his ofer offrungæ ꞇ æsegdnessæ
eius qui ordinaverunt testamentum eius super   sacrificia
7 Cypað hefonæs rihtwisnes his forðæn god demæ is
6. Et adnuntiabunt caeli   iustitiam eius quoniam deus iudex est
Geher folc min 7 sprece to israehele 7 ic cyðe ðe
7. Audi populus meus et loquar israel   et testificabor tibi
ðætt god god þin ic eom   Na ofer æsegðnessæ
quoniam deus deus tuus ego sum   8. Non super sacrificia
þin ic þræwie þe ofrungæ ꞇ onsegdnisse eællængæ ðine on gesiehðe
tua arguam te   holocausta   autem tua in conspectu
minre sint simle   Ic ne onfó of huse þinum ceælfru
meo sunt semper 9. Non accipiam de domo tua vitulos
ne of ewedum ðinum buccæn   Forðæn mine sint
neque de gregibus tuis hyrcos 10. Quoniam meae sunt

. **49.** *God goda* by Cor. ꞇ *cleopede* add. by Cor. *setlgange* prob. by Cor.
on er.   **2.** *wlites, s* prps. add. by Cor.   **3.** *openliche* by Cor. on er.
swigoð, fin. let. er.; *ð* prob. from *d* by Cor. *storm st[r]ang* by Cor. in pl. of
er.   **5.** *-endebyrdan* by Cor. *offrungæ ꞇ* add. by Cor.   **6.** *-það* by Cor.
on er. *rihtwisnes* by Cor. on er.   **7.** *-her, e* from *i* by Cor.; fin. let. prps.
er.   *ðætt* by Cor. on er.   **8.** *Na, a* by Cor.? ꞇ *onsegdnisse* add. by Cor.
ðine, e add. by Cor.   **9.** *Ic ne onfó* by Cor. in pl. of er.   *-ru* add. by Cor.
-cæn, n add. by Cor.

eælle   wildedeor   on   wudæ   nietenæ   on   dunum   7   oxæn
omnes   *fere*   *silvarum*   *iumenta*   *in*   *montibus*   *et*   *boves*

   Ic oncneow   cælle   ða   flegende   ł fugulæs   hefonæs   7   hiw
11.   *Cognovi*   *omnia*   *volatilia*   *caeli*   *et*   *species*

landes mid me is   gif ic hingrie ic ne segge þe min
agri   *mecum est*   **12.** *Si*   *esuriero*   *non dicam tibi meus*

is soðliche ymbhwirft eorðæn 7   filnes   his   Is ðes wén ðet
est enim   *orbis*   *terrae et plenitudo eius*   **13.**   *Nunquid*

ic ete   flesc   feærræ   oþþe   blod   buccænæ ic drince
manducabo carnes taurorum aut sanguinem hyrcorum   potabo

   offra   gode onsegdnesse   lofes   7   ic gild   ðæm hihstæn
14. *Immola*   *deo*   *sacrificium*   *laudis et*   *redde*   *altissimo*

gehat þin·   Gechige me on dci geswinkes ł eærfoðnesse
vota tua   **15.** *Invoca*   *me in die*   *tribulationis*

þin þet ic generie ðe 7 ðu gemiclæst me   To þam senfullæn
tuae ut eripiam te et magnificabis me   **16.**   *Peccatori*

soðlice cweð god forwæn þu segst rihtwisnesse mine 7 genimest
autem dixit deus quare tu enarras iustitias meas et adsumis

cyðnesse   min ðurh muð ðinne   ðu soðlice fiodes
testamentum meum per os tuum   **17.** *Tu*   *vero*   *odisti*

þiodscipe ł lare 7 þu awirpe spræce ł word mine efter ðe   Gif
disciplinam et proiecisti sermones meos post te   **18.** *Si*

ðu gesage ðiof   samed   þu urne mid him 7 mid unrihtemeðe
videbas furem simul currebas cum eo et cum adulteris

   dæl   þine þu setest   Muð ðin genihtsumæde of hete ł niþæ
portionem tuam ponebas **19.** *Os tuum*   *abundavit*   *nequitia*

7 tunge þin sang ł leoðrade facen ł sær   Sittende   wiþ
et lingua tua concinnavit dolum   **20.** *Sedens adversus*

broðor þine þu tildest 7   wið   sunu modor þinre þu settest
fratrem tuum detrahebas et adversus filium matris tuae ponebas

geswic ł flit   þæs ðu didest 7 ic swigude þu gewendes
scandalum   **21.** *Haec*   *fecisti et*   *tacui*   *existimasti*

---

10. *wildedeor on* by Cor. in pl. of er.   11. *ða flegende ł* add. by Cor.
landes, a from *o* by Cor.   12. *segge* by Cor. on er.   *soðliche* by Cor. on er.
14. *offra* by Cor. on er.   *gild*, fin. let. er.   *gehat*, orig. = *gehæt* ł   15.
Gechige, Ge- by Cor. on er.; second *g* from some other let. by orig. scribe.
geswinkes ł by Cor. in pl. of er.   16. *To þam sen-* by Cor. on er.   *rihtwis-*
by Cor. on er.   *genimest* by Cor. on er.   17. *ł lare* add. by Cor.   *spræce ł*
word by Cor. in pl. of er.   *ðe* by Cor. on er.   18. *-sage* by Cor. in pl. of er.
samed, a from *o*. Er. bef. *dæl*. *-st* add. by Cor.   19. *-æde, d* prob. on er. of
another let. *of* add. by Cor.   *ł niþæ*, the *ł* and *-æ* add. by Cor.   *sang ł leoðrade*
by Cor. in pl. of er.   *facen ł* add. by Cor.   20. Er. aft. *þu*.   *-ldest* by Cor.
on er.   *þu settest* by Cor. on er.   *ł flit* add. by Cor.   21. *didest, t* add. by Cor.

unrihtnessæ þet ic bio ðe   gelic   Ic þræge þe 7 ic gesette þa
iniquitatem quod ero tibi similis Argucm te et statuam illa

ongen onsiene þin   ongitæð ðæs eælle þa ofergitelieð
contra faciem tuam **22.** *intelligite haec emnes qui obliviscimini*

drihten ne hwonne gereafie 7 ne siə se alise ł anerige
dominum ne quando rapiat et non sɪt qui eripiat

Æsegdnessæ lofes wiorðæð ł úreð me onɪ þer siðfet is on ðæm
23. *Sacrificium laudis honorificabit me et illic iter est in quo*

ic ettiewe him helo godes
ostendam illi salutare dei

50.

gemiltsa me god   efter   þere micelrə mildheortnesse ðinre
3. *Miserere mei deus secundum magnam misericordiam tuam*

Ond efter micelnesse ł manege mildɛunga þinræ adilgæ
Et secundum   multitudinem   miserationum tuarum dele

unrihtwisnesse minre   Ma þweach me from unrihtwisnesse
iniquitatem meam **4.** *Amplius lava me ab iniustitia*

minre 7 from egyltum ł scylde minre clensæ me   Forðæn
mea et a   delicto   meo mundɑ me   **5.** *Quoniam*

unrihtwisnesse minre ic ongite ł ancnáwa 7 egylt ł scyld min
iniquitatem meam ego agnosco et delictum meum

beforæn me is simle   ðe anum ic sinəgode 7 yfel beforæn
coram me est semper **6.** *Tibi soli peccavi et malum coram*

þe ic dyde þet þu beo gerihtwisad ou wordum þinum 7
te feci ut iustificeris in sermonibus tuis et

oferswiðe ðu midþi ðu demed eart   Eællengæ witoðlice on
vincas dum iudicaris **7.** *Ecce enim in*

unrihtwisnesse geeæcnod ic eom 7 on egyʟtum cende me moder
iniquitatibus` conceptus sum et in delictis peperit me mater

---

prœge, -ge by Cor. on er.ł *þa ongen* by Cor. on er. *onsiene,* fin. *e* prob.
add. by Cor. **22.** *þa* by Cor. on er. *-lieð* by Cor. in pl. of er. *ne hwonne*
by Cor. on er. *-eafie* by Cor. on er Er. immed. aft. *se.* ł *anerige* add. by
Cor. in pl. of er. **23.** *lofes, es* add. by Cor.ł ł *áreð* add. by Cor.
50. 3. *gemiltsa me god* by Cor. *micelre, re* add. by Cor.ł *ðinre* by Cor.ł
ł *manege* add. by Cor. *-sunga* on er. by Cor.ł *-wisnesse* by Cor. on er.
minre, re prob. add. by Cor. **4.** Er. aft. *Ma. þweach* by Cor. *unrihtwis-*
nesse by Cor. on er. ł *scylde* add. by Cor. **5.** *-wisnesse* add. by Cor. ł *an-*
cnáwa add. by Cor. Er. aft. **7.** ł *scyld* prob. add. by Cor. **6.** *ic* add. by
Cor. *sine-,* init. *ge* er. *ic* (2nd) add. by Cor. *bee gerihtwisad* by Cor. in pl.
of er. *ðu* add. by Cor. *-ed, d* by Cor. on er. of another let. *eart* add. by
Cor. **7.** Er. aft. *-nesse. ic eom* by Cor. *cende, ce* prob. by Cor. on er.

min   Eællenga witoþlice soðfestnesse ðu lufodes ungewissa 7
mea   8. *Ecce   enim   veritatem   dilexisti   incerta   et*

ðæ   dihlu wisdomes ł snitro þines   þu gecyþdes   me
occulta   sapientiae   tuae   manifestasti michi

ðu astregdest me myd ysopo 7 ic beo geclensod þu þweæhst me 7
9. *Asperges   me   ysopo   et   mundabor   lavabis   me et*

ofer snæw ic bio gehwitad   gebiernesse min þu selest gefeæn
super nivem   dealbabor   10. *Auditui   meo   dabis gaudium*

ond blisse   7 hihtæþ ł gefeogað bæn eædmodæn   Ahwirf ł acer
et laetitiam et   exultabunt ossa humiliata 11. *Averte*

onsiene ðine from synnum mine 7 eælle unrihtwisnessæ mine
faciem tuam a   peccatis meis et omnes   iniquitates   meas

adilgæ   heorte clene scype on me god 7   gæst rihtne
dele   12. *Cor mundum crea in me deus et spiritum rectum*

geniwæ on innoðe minum   Ne æwiorp ðu me from onsine
innova in visceribus meis 13. *Ne   proicias me   a   facie*

ðinre 7 gæst hæligne þinne ne æfyrre þu from me   Agild
tua et spiritum sanctum tuum ne auferas a   me 14. *Redde*

me   blisse   helo ðine 7 of gæste eældordomlican getrime
michi laetitiam salutaris tui et spiritu   principali   confirma

me   Ic lere ðæ unrihtwisan wegæs þine 7 þa arleæsæ to þe
me 15. *Docebo   iniquos   vias tuas et   impii   ad te*

beoð gecirrede   Gefriolsæ me of   blodum   god god
convertentur   16. *Libera   me de sanguinibus deus deus*

helo mine 7 winsumæð tungæ min rihtwisnesse ðine
salutis meae et exaltabit lingua mea   iustitiam   tuam

drihtæn weleræs mine ðu untyn 7 muð min   segeð ł
17. *Domine labia mea aperies et os meum   ad-*

bodaþ ł cyþeð lof þin   Forðæn gif ðu woldest
nuntiabit laudem tuam   18. *Quoniam si   voluisses*

onsegdnesse ic seælde witodlice offrengæ soðlice   ne
sacrificium dedissem utiquae holocaustis autem   non

gelustfullæst þu   Onsegdnesse gode   gæst   geswenced ł
  delectaberis   **19.** *Sacrificium   deo spiritus   contribu-*

geunrotsod heorte forgnidene 7 ðæ eæðmodæ god ne forhogad
  latus   cor   contritum et   humiliatum deus   spernit

    Estelice do drihten on góde willæn þines sion þett sien ge-
20. *Benigne fac domine in bona voluntate tua syon ut   aedifi-*

tymbrede   weællæs   hierusælem   ðonne   þu onfehst
  centur   muri   hierusalem   **21.** *Tunc   acceptabis*

offrunge ł onsegdnesse of rihtwisnesse bringas ł oflaten ond
  sacrificium   iustitiae   oblationes   et

offrunge ðonne onsetteð ofer wifod ðin ceælfre
holocausta tunc inponent super altare tuum vitulos

51.

    hwet wuldræst ðu on níþe ł on yfelnisse þu ðe mihtig ært on
3. *Quid   gloriaris   in   malitia   qui potens es in*

unrihtwisnesse   Ealchæ dege on   unrihtwisnesse   ðohte
  iniquitate   **4.** *Tota   die   iniustitiam   cogitavit*

tungæ þin swa swæ scersæx scearpe þu dydest faken
lingua tua   sicut novacula acuta fecisti dolum

    ðu lufedest heteni∂ ł yfelnysse ofer   godnesse unrihtwisnesse
5. *Dilexisti   malitiam   super benignitatem iniquitatem*

mæ ðone gesprecæn rihcwisnesse   ðu lufedest ealle word
magis quam   loqui   aequitatem   **6.** *Dilexisti omnia verba*

fortrugadnysse ł hryres on tungan facenfulre   Foreðæn
  precipitationis   in   lingua   dolosa   **7.** *Propterea*

tobreche ł toweorpð þe god on ende útaluceð þe 7 útadrifeð þe
  destruet   te deus in finem evellet   te et emigrabit te

of ðinre Eardunge ł tilde 7 wyrtwelæ ðin of eordæn lifigendra
  de   tabernaculo tuo   et radicem tuam de terra viventium

---

19. *On-* by Cor. ? From *geswenced* to *-dene* by Cor. in pl. of er.   *eæðmodæ*,
fin. let. er.   *forhogad* by Cor. on er.   20. *þett, t* (2nd) from some other let.
by Cor.   *sien, en* by Cor.   21. *offrunge ł* add. by Cor.   From *of* to *oflaten*
by Cor. in pl. of er.   *-re* add. by Cor.   51. 3. *hwet* by Cor.   *ðu* by Cor.
Er. aft. *on* (1st).   *yfelnisse* by Cor. on er.   *þu* by Cor.   *ðe, ð* by Cor. on er.
ært on add. by Cor.   *-wisnesse* by Cor.   4. *unrihtwisnesse ðohte* by Cor. on
er.   *swa* by Cor.   *scersæx* by Cor. on er.   *þu* add. by Cor.   *faken* by Cor. aft.
er.   5. *ł yfelnysse* add. by Cor.   *god-* on er.   *-cæn, n* prob. add. by Cor.
rihcwisnesse by Cor. on er.   6. *-est, t* add. by Cor.   *fortrugadnysse ł* by
Cor. on er.   *facenfulre* by Cor. part. on er. ?   7. *ł toweorpð* add. by Cor. ?
Er. bef. and aft. *út-* (1st).   *ł tilde* add. by Cor.   *ef, f* in d. ink on er. of
another let.

gesioð ðæ soðfestæn 7 ondreðæð 7 ofer hine hlethað 7
8. *Videbunt iusti et timebunt et super eum ridebunt et*

cweðæð Eællengæ man se ne gesette god to fultome him
dicent **9.** *Ecce homo qui non posuit deum adiutorem sibi*

æh gewenæde ł hyhte on manifeldnesse welena here 7
sed speravit in multitudine divitiarum suarum et

strongað on idelnesse his Ic eallengæ swæ swæ eletreow
prevaluit in vanitate sua **10.** *Ego autem sicut oliva*

westmberende on huse drihtnes ic gehihte on mildheortnesse godes
fructifera in domo domini speravi in misericordia dèi

mines on ecnesse 7 on world aworlde Ic ondette þe
mei in aeternum et in seculum seculi **11.** *Confitebor tibi*

drihten on world forþon ðu geworhtes 7 ic onbide naman ðinne
domine in seculum quia fecisti et expectabo nomen tuum

forðan gód is beforan gesihðæ haligra ðinra
quoniam bonum est ante conspectum sanctorum tuorum

52.

cwæþ se vnsnoter ł se unwise on heortan his ne is god
Dixit insipiens in corde suo non est deus

gewemde sindon 7 onscunienliche gewordene sindon on
2. *corrupti sunt et abominabiles facti sunt in*

hiora willum Ne his se þe do god ne is oþðæ on
voluntatibus suis Non est qui faciat bonum non est usque ad

anne drihten of hefeon foreseah ofer bearn monna
unum **3.** *Dominus de caelo prospexit super filios hominum*

þ he gesio gif is ongetende oþþe secende god Ealla
ut videat si est intelligens aut requirens deum **4.** *Omnes*

onhyldon somed unnytte gewordene syndon ne his se þe
declinaverunt simul inutiles facti sunt non est qui

deþ god ne his oðþe on ænne hwu ne oncnewæþ
faciat bonum non est usque ad unum **5.** *Nonne cognoscent*

---

8. *hlethað* add. by Cor.; er. aft. it. 9. *man*, about two fin. lett. er.
ł *hyhte* add. by Cor. *manifeld-* pref. by Cor.; er. immed. bef. -*nesse.*
strongað by Cor.; er. aft. it. 10. *swæ* (2nd) add. by Cor. -*treow* prob. on
er. -*hihte* by Cor. on er. 11. *forþon, for-* pref. by Cor.; -*þon,* one (or
two?) fin. lett. er. *onbide, d* from ð. 52. ł *se unwise* prps. add. by Cor.
2. *gewemde* by Cor. on er. *onscunienliche* by Cor. in pl. of er. 3. *þ* by Cor.
on er. *he* by Cor. on er. *gesio,* fin. let. er. *is* in pl. of er. *oþþe,* fin. let. er.
4. Er. immed. bef. *unnytte;* -*te* prob. by Cor. on er. Er. bef. *deþ. on ænne*
add. by Cor.? 5. *hwu ne* by Cor. in pl. of er.

ealle þa ðe wirced unrihtwisnesse þa ðe forswelgað folc
omnes qui operantur iniquitatem qui devorant plebem

min swæ swæ mete hlæfes god ne gechigdon ðer
meam sicut escam panis 6. *deum non invocaverunt illic*

hy forhtodan ꝺ cwacedan of ege þer ne wæs nan ege Forðan
trepidaverunt timore ubi non erat timor Quoniam

god tostencæþ bæn manna him liciendræ ꝺ cwemendra gescinde
deus dissipat ossa hominum sibi placentium confusi

syndon forðon god forhogode hie hwylc seleð of Sion
sunt quia deus sprevit eos 7. *Quis dabit ex syon*

hęlo israhele þanne acerreð drihten heftnied folces his
salutare israel dum avertit dominus captivitatem plebis suae

hyhteð iacob 7 blissæð israhel
Exultabit iacob et laetabitur israel

53.

God on næmæn þinum hælne me gædó 7 on mægne þine
3. *Deus in nomine tuo salvum me fac et in virtute tua*

gefriolse me god gehir gebed minæ mid eærum
libera me 4. *Deus exaudi orationem meam auribus*

onfoh word muðes mines Forþan fremde onærison
percipe verba oris mei 5. *Quoniam alieni insurrexerunt*

on me 7 strange sohten sawle mine 7 næ foregesetton
in me et fortes quesierunt animam meam et non proposuerunt

god beforæn onsine ꝺ sihðe his Eællcngæ soðlice god
deum. ante conspectum suum 6. *Ecce enim deus*

gefultumæð me 7 dryhten onfeng is sæwle minre
adiuvat me et dominus susceptor est animae meae

æhwyrf yfele of findum minum 7 on soþfestnesse ðinre
7. *Averte mala inimicis meis et in veritate tua*

forspil hie wilsumlice ic offrie ðæ 7 ic ondette
disperde illos 8. *Voluntariae sacrificabo tibi et confitebor*

-*wisnesse* by Cor. in pl. of er. *ðe* add. by Cor. *swæ* (2nd) add. by Cor.
-*es* add. by Cor. 6. -*don* (1st) by Cor. on er. *hy* add. by Cor. -*todon* by
Cor. on er. *ꝺ cwacedan of* add. by Cor. *nan* add. by Cor. *manna* orig. =
mannæ. ꝺ cwemendra add. by Cor. *forhogode* prps. by Cor. in pl. of er.
7. *hwylc* by Cor. on er. *þanne acerreð* by Cor. on er. *israhel, l* by Cor. in pl.
of er. 53. 4. *gehir,* fin *e* er. 5. *ꝺ sihðe* add. by Cor.? 7. *æhwyrf,*
fin. *e* er. -*spil* by Cor. in pl. of er. 8. *wilsumlice, s* from *l* (by Cor.?);
-*lice* add. by Cor.? Er. aft. *ic* (1st). *offrie* by Cor.?

nomæn ðinnum drigten forðæn god he is   Forðæn
nomini   tuo . domine quoniam bonum est   9. Quoniam
of ællum eærfoþnesse ł geswince ðu gencredest me 7 ofer
ex omni   tribulatione   eripuisti   me et super
fiend mine foreseah eagæ ðin
inimicos meos respexit oculus tuus

54.

    gehyr god gebed   min 7 ne forsioh   bene
2. *Exaudi deus orationem meam et ne despexeris deprecationem*
mine   beheæld on me 7 gehir me geunrotsod ic eom on
meam   3. intende in me et exaudi me Contristatus sum in
ymbhwyrfte ł geswynce minum 7 gedrefed ic eom   fram
exercitatione   mea et conturbatus sum   4. a
stemne fendes 7 from earfoðnesse ðes synfulles Forðan
voce inimici et a tribulatione peccatoris. Quoniam
hy onhyldon on me unrihtwisnesse 7 on erra hefigmode hy wæron
declinaverunt in me iniquitates et in ira molesti erant
me   min heorte gedrefed is on me 7 fyrhto deæþes
michi 5. Cor meum conturbatum est in me et formido mortis
gefyl ofer me   ege 7 fyrhto comon ofer me 7
cecidit super me   6. Timor et tremor venerunt super me et
bewrigon me ðistro   7 ic cweð hwilc seleð me
contexerunt me tenebrae   7. Et dixi quis dabit michi
fyþræ swæ culfre 7 ic flio 7 reste   eællenge
pennas sicut columbe et volabo et requiescam 8. Ecce
ic aferrode flionde 7 ic wunode on westene   ic onbidede
elongavi fugiens et mansi in solitudine 9. expectabam
him ðe me heælne dyde from medmiclum mode 7 hreohnesse
eum qui me salvum faceret a pusillo animo et tempestate
    Afyl drihten 7 todel tungæn hioræ forðæn ic geseac
10. *Precipita domine et divide linguas eorum quoniam vidi*
unrihtwisnesse 7 wiþorcwidolnesse on ceæstre   deges 7
iniquitatem et contradictionem in civitate 11. die ac

Er. bef. *god.* 9. ł *geswince* add. by Cor. ? -*dest* add. by Cor. ? *eagæ*, fin.
let. er.   54. 2. Er. bef. *bene.* 3. *gehir*, fin. e er. -*hwyrfte*, er. betw.
f and *t.* 4. *fend-*, e from *i.* Er. aft. *ðes.* Er. aft. *hy.* erra, e from *i.*
From *hefig-* to *me* prob. on er. 5. *gefyl*, fin. let. er. 7. *cweð*, e from *i.*
flio, er. at end. Er. bef. *reste.* 8. *ic aferrode* by Cor. on er. 9. *heælne*,
er. betw. *n* and *e.* 10. *todel*, fin. æ er. *geseac*, e from *i* by Cor.; -*ac* by
Cor. ? -*wisnesse* on er.

nichtes Ymbseleð hie ofer weælles his unrihtwisnes 7 swinc
nocte Circundabit eam super muros eius iniquitas et labor

on midle his 7 unrihtwisnesse 7 ne geteorade of
in medio eius **12.** *et iniustitia Et non defecit de*

stretum his gestreone ł gauel 7 facne forðan gif
plateis eius usura et dolus **13.** *quoniam si*

fiond min wyrgde me ic hit forbære witoðlice 7
inimicus meus maledixisset michi subportassem utique Et

gif ðes þe hatude me ofer me ma miclæn sprece
si is qui oderat me super me magna locutus fuisset

ic hyddo me witodlice fram him þu soðlice mon
absconderem me utique ab eo **14.** *Tu vero homo*

anes modes heretogæ mín 7 cuðæ min ðu þe semæð
unanimis dux meus et notus meus **15.** *qui simul*

mid me swete gripe mettæs on huse drihtnes we geodon
mecum dulces capiebas cybos in domo domini ambulavimus

mid sibbe Cumæð deæð ofer hie 7 adune æstygæð
cum consensu **16.** *Veniat mors super illos et descendant*

on helle liuiænde Forðan hete ł nið on gisthusum hiora
in infernum viventes Quoniam nequitia in hospitiis eorum

on midle hiora Ic soðlice to drihtne clypede 7
in medio ipsorum **17.** *Ego autem ad dominum clamavi et*

dricten geherde me On efen 7 on morgæn 7
dominus exaudivit me **18.** *Vespere mane et*

on midne dei ic cyþe 7 bodige 7 he gehereð stemnæ
meridie narrabo et adnuntiabo et exaudiet vocem

míne gefriolsæþ on sybbe sawule mine from þisum ðæ
meam **19.** *Liberabit in pace animam meam ab his qui*

nealecæð me forðam betweox monegæ wes mid me
adpropiant michi quoniam inter multos erat mecum

gehire god 7 geeæðmetdeþ hy þe is beforan woruld 7
20. *Exaudiet deus et humiliabit eos qui est ante secula et*

---

11. *-wisnes* by Cor.? 12. *unrihtwisnesse, -riht-* by Cor.; *-wis-* in pl. of
er. *geteorade* on er. by Cor.? *facne, e* prob. add. by Cor. 13. Er. bef.
me. Er. aft. *ðes. þe hatude* in pl. of er. by Cor.? *ma* in d. ink on er.
sprece, er. at end. *hyddo,* init. *ge-* er.; fin. *n* er. Er. aft. *-lice.* 14.
anes modes orig. = *œnes moðes.* 15. *þe* add. by Cor. *-eodon* by Cor. on er.
Er. aft. *sibbe.* 16. *ł nið* add. by Cor. 17. *geherde, e* (2nd) from *i.*
18. *bodige 7 he gehereð* by Cor. on er. 19. *-sæþ, þ* prob. add. by Cor. Er.
(*þe?*) bef. *ðæ. betweox, e* (2nd) from *i*; *-ox* by Cor. on er. *wes* by Cor. in pl.
of er. 20. From *-deþ* to *ecnesse* by Cor. in pl. of er.

wunaþ on ęcnesse Ne is sodlice him styrung ł awendednis
manet in aeternum Non est enim illis   commutatio

7 ne hi ondredon god   he æðeneð hand his on
et non timuerunt deum 21. extendit manum suam in

ędleænunga him hy besmiton weron cyðnesse his   hy
retribuendo illis contaminaverunt testamentum eius 22. di-

todelede sindon from irra andwlitæ his 7 togenealæhð heorte his
     visi sunt ab ira vultus eius et adpropiabit cor eius

hy hnescodon spręca here ofer ele 7 hi sindon flana
  Mollierunt sermones suos super oleum et ipsi sunt iacula

     aweorp on gode geðoht þinne 7 he þæ fedæt na
23. *Iacta in deum cogitatum tuum et ipse te enutriet Non*

he seleð on ęcnesse ł effre yðgunga rihtwisum   ðu
   dabit in   aeternum   fluctuationem iusto 24. tu

soðlice god geledest hie on ðone seæð ł on pyt forwirðe weræs
   vero deus deduces eos in   puteum   interitus Viri

bloda 7 facenfulle na healfe getillað ł gemidliat dagæs hira
sanguinum et dolosi non   dimidiabunt   dies suos

ic soðlice on ðæ gewene drihten
ego vero in te sperabo domine

55.

gemildsa me driyhten forðæn   træd me mæn ealnæ
2. *Miserere michi domine quoniam conculcavit me homo tota*

dęi fiohtende swencte ł earfoðaþ me   Tredon mè
die bellans   tribulavit me 3. Conculcaverunt me

fiend mine ealnæ dęi   from hyhðo ðes deges Forðan
inimici mei tota die 4. ab altitudine diei Quoniam

monige þe fiohteð wið me ondredeð ic soðlice on ðæ gewene
multi qui debellant me timebunt ego vero in te sperabo

drihten   on gode ic herie word mine elce dege on
domine 5. In deo laudabo sermones meos tota die in

<hr />

soðlice, d from ð ? ł awendednis add. by Cor. 21. he add. by Cor. -neð
from -nede by Cor. -unga by Cor. on er. besmiton on er. 22. sindon, d
from ð. togenealæhð on er. From hy (2nd) to here by Cor. on er. flana on
er. 23. aweorp, a prob. pref. by Cor.; a fin. let. er. From na to effre by
Cor. on er. rihtwisum on er.; ł wr. over the line. 24. -est add. by Cor.
na healfe getillað on er.   55. 2. gemildsa by Cor. me, er. immed. at
end. træd by Cor. on er. mæn, let. er. immed. bef. this word. Er. bef. fioh-;
init. ge- er.?; er. of about one let. betw. i and o; -ende prob. add. by Cor.
swencte ł add. by Cor. -foðaþ, let. er. betw. o and ð. 4. Two lett. er. bef.
þe. 7 er. bef. fiohteð; ð by Cor. wið add. by Cor.

gode ic wene ic ne ondręde hwet do   ꝥe mon   Ęlche
deo sperabo non timebo quid faciat michi homo 6. *Tota*

dęge word mine onscunedon ongean me ealla gerun ꞇ geþeæht
die verba mea execrabantur adversum me omnia   consilia

hiræ on yfel   Oneardigaꝺ 7 gehydæꝺ hie
eorum in malum 7. *Inhabitabunt et abscondent ipsi*

sporetengæ ꞇ hælspuran mine gehealdæꝺ swa swa onbidode
calcaneum   meum observabunt sicut expectavit

sawle min   fore næwihta hale þu dest hie on yrra
anima mea 8. *pro nichilo salvos facies eos in ira*

folc þu gebricest god   lif min ic segede ꝺæ
populos confringes Deus 9. *vitam meam nuntiavi tibi*

ic gesette teæras mine on ꝺinre gesihꝺe swa swa on behate
posui lacrimas meas in conspectu tuo sicut in promissione

ꝺinre   syen gecirrede mine fiend on becling on swa
tua 10. *Convertantur inimici mei retrorsum in qua-*

hwilcum dege ic þe gecige eallenge ic ancnewa forꝺan god
cumque die invocavero te ecce agnovi quoniam deus

min ꝺu eart   On gode ic heriga word 7 on drihtne
meus es tu 11. *In deo laudabo verbum et in domino*

ic heriga word on god ic gewene ic ne ondredæ hwet
laudabo sermonem in deo sperabo non timebo quid

dô me mæn   On me syndon god gehat þa
faciat michi homo 12. *In me sunt deus vota quae*

ic agildæ herenesse ꝺæ   Forꝺæn ꝺu generedest sawl
reddam laudationes tibi 13. *quoniam eripuisti animam*

min of deaþe egan mine fram tearum fet mine fram
meam de morte oculos meos a lacrimis pedes meos a

slide þeꝺ ic licige beforan drihten on liohte lifigendra
lapsu ut placeam coram domino in lumine viventium

56.

Gemildsa me god mildsa me forꝺan on ꝺe getriwæꝺ
2. *Miserere mei deus miserere mei quoniam in te confidit*

5. *do* on er.   6. *onscunedon ongean* by Cor. in pl. of er.   *gerun* ꞇ add. by
Cor.   7. ꞇ *hælspuran* add. by Cor.   *onbidode* by Cor. from *onbit*! *min*, fin.
e er.   8. *dest*, init. *ge-* er.ꝺ; ꞇ add. by Cor.ꝺ *hie* add. by Cor.   9. *ic*
pref. by Cor. (twice). *-de, d* from ꝺ; *e* add. by Cor.   *on behate* by Cor. on er.
10. *sy-* on er. *-ecir-* on er.   *mine, -ne* on er.   11. *heriga* (twice) fin. lett.
(ꝺꝺ) er.   12. *þa* by Cor. *-nesse*, fin. *e* by Cor.   13. *-est*, ꞇ add. by Cor.
mine (2nd) by Cor.   *þeꝺ ic* by Cor.   56. 2. *Gemildsa* by Cor.

saul min 7 on scuadwe fiðra ðinre ic wene oððet forð-
anima mea et in umbra alarum tuarum spero donec trans-
gewite unrihtwisnesse   ic scel clypien to godæ ðam
eat   iniquitas   3.   Clamabo   ad deum al-
hyhstum 7 to drihten se ðæ god dæde me   he Sende
tissimum et ad dominum qui benefecit michi 4. Misit
of heofonum 7 gefriolsede ł lisde me he sealde on   edwite
de caelo et liberavit me dedit in obprobrium
þa fortredende me Sende god mildheortnesse his 7 soðfest-
conculcantes me Misit deus misericordiam suam et veri-
nesse his   saule mine he generede of middele
tatem suam 5. animam meam eripuit de medio
hwælpæ leonæ ic slæp gedrefed bearn mannæ teð
catulorum leonum dormivi conturbatus Filii hominum dentes
hiræ wæpn 7 strelæ ł arwen 7 tunga hira sweord scearpe
eorum arma et sagittae et lingua eorum machera acuta
     Upahefe ofer hefonæs god 7 ofer ealle eorðan wuldor
6. *Exaltare super caelos deus et super omnem terram gloria*
ðin   grino hi gearwodon fotum mine 7 hy gebygdon
tua   7. Laqueos paraverunt pedibus meis et incurvaverunt
saulæ minæ hy dulfon beforan ænsinæ minre pit ł seæð
animam meam Foderunt ante faciem meam foveam
7 hie fiollon on hine   gearwæ heortæ min god
et ipsi inciderunt in eam 8. Paratum cor meum deus
geærwæ hertæ min ic singæ 7 seælm ic cwiðæ drihtne
paratum cor meum cantabo et psalmum dicam domino
     aris wuldor min aris Saltere 7 hearperas ic arise
9. *Exurge gloria mea exurge psalterium et cythara exurgam*
on morgen   ic ondette ðæ on folc drihten sealm
diluculo   10.   Confitebor tibi in populis domine psalmum
ic cwiðæ ðe betwioh ðiodum   Forðan gemiclod is
dicam tibi inter gentes 11. Quoniam magnificata est

-dwe add. by Cor.? *-wisnesse* prob. add. by Cor.   3. *ic scel clypien* by
Cor. on er.; *l* (2nd) wr. over the line. *dæde* (or *dæðe*?), fin. *e* add. by Cor.
4. *-friolsede*, *de* by Cor. on er. *ł lisde* add. by Cor. *þa for-* add. by Cor.
-heortnesse, *e* er. betw. *t* and *n*. *-nesse* (2nd), *se* add. by Cor.   5. *-de*, *d*
from *ð* and *e* add. by Cor.? Er. bef. *gedrefed*; fin. *d* from *ð*? *ł arwen* add.
by Cor. *sweord* prob. by Cor. in pl. of er.   6. *-ahefe* by Cor. in pl. of er.
7. *grino*, init. er. of about two lett. made. *hi* in d. ink prob. add. later. *hy
gebygdon* by Cor. in pl. of er. *hy* (2nd) by Cor. Er. immed. bef. *fiollon*.

oððæ to hiofenum mildheortnes ðin 7 oððæ to wolcnæ soðfestnes
usque ad caelos misericordia tua et usque ad nubes veritas

ðin   Upæhefe ofer hefonæs god 7 ofer eællæ eorðæ
tua   **12.** *Exaltare super caelos deus et super omnem terram*

wuldor ðin
gloria tua

57.

Gyf soðlice gewitodlice rihtwisnessæ gesprecæð rihte demæð
2. *Si vere utique iustitiam loquimini iuste iudicate*

bearn manne   7 soðlice on heortæn unrichtwisnesse
filii hominum **3.** *Et enim in corde iniquitates*

ge bioð wyrchende on eorðan unrihtwisnesse handæn eowre
operamini in terra iniquitatem manus vestrae

midswegæ ł syrwað   Afremdodæ sinðon ðæ senfullen
concinnant **4.** *Alienati sunt peccatores*

of innoðæ hy gedwolodon of innoðe ł wombe sprecendæ synðon
ab utero erraverunt a ventre locuti sunt

leæsingæ   yrre him efter gelicnesse nedræn swæ
falsa **5.** *Ira illis secundum similitudinem serpentis sicut*

nedræn deafe 7 fordemmende eæran hira   ðæ ne
aspidis surdae et obturantis aures suas **6.** *quae non*

gehiræð stemne wigeleren ł galendra 7 ætrene ðæ þe beoð
exaudiet vocem incantantium et venefici quae

gewigelode ł begalene fram wisvm ł snytro   god tobriceð
incantantur a sapiente **7.** *Deus conteret*

teð hiræ on muðæ hiræ wongtæð ł weohlan leonæ gebriceð
dentes eorum in ore ipsorum molas leonum confringet

drichten   to næwihte hy becymeð swa swa weter
dominus **8.** *Ad nichilum devenient velut aqua*

irnende aþeneð bogæn his oððe hit bið geuntrumod
decurrens intendit arcum suum donec infirmetur

H

swæ swæ weax meltende bioð æfirredæ ofer hie gefil fyr
9. *Sicut cera liquefacta auferentur super eos cecidit ignis*

7 ne gesioð sunnæ Ærðæn þe forðleden ðornes
et non viderunt solem 10. *Priusquam producant spinae*

eowre telgan ł wefeðorn swæ swæ ða lifiendæ swæ on irra
vestrae ramnos sicut viventes sic in ira

geforswilgeð hie blissæð soðfeste þonne he gesiehð
obsorbet eos 11. *Laetabitur iustus cum viderit*

, wrece arleæsra hændæ his he ðwihð on blode
vindictam impiorum manus suas lavabit in sanguine

senfulra ł firenfulræ 7 cwið mon gif witoðlice is
peccatorum 12. *Et dicet homo si utique est*

westm rihtwisum witoðlice is god demende hie on eorðæn
fructus iusto utique est deus iudicans eos in terra

58.

Nere me of minum fiondum god min 7 from ðæm arisendum
2. *Eripe me de inimicis meis deus meus et ab insurgentibus*

on me ålys me Genere me fram wyrcendum unriht-
in me libera me 3. *Eripe me de operantibus iniqui-*

wisnesse 7 fram werum blodæ hel me Forðæn
tatem et de viris sanguinum salva me 4. *Quia*

eallengæ hy ofþrycton saul min onhruron on me strange
ecce occupaverunt animam meam irruerunt in me fortes

7 na unrihtwisnesse min ne synnæ min drihten
5. *neque iniquitas mea neque peccatum meum domine*

butan unrihtwisnesse ic ern 7 ic gereht wæs Aris on
Sine iniquitate cucurri et dirigebar 6. *exurge in*

minum geænrynum 7 gesyoh 7 ðu drihten god megena
occursum michi et vide et tu domine deus virtutum

---

9. Er. bef. *bioð. gefil,* a fin. er. made. Er. bef. *ne.* 10. *forðleden, ge*
er. betw. *ð* and *l.* *ł wefeðorn* add. by Cor.; *e* (1st) from *æ.* *swæ* (2nd) add.
by Cor. *-dæ,* fin. let. er. *geforswilgeð* by Cor. on er. 11. *þonne he* by
Cor. on er. *he* (2nd) add. by Cor. *ðwihð* by Cor. on er. *senfulra ł* add. by
Cor. 12. *cwið,* fin. *e* er. *riht-* by Cor. on er. 58. 2. *Nere* by Cor. *of,*
f by Cor. on er.ł *ålys* by Cor. on er. 3. *fram* by Cor. in pl. of er. *-wis-*
nesse by Cor. on er. *fram werum* by Cor. on er. *hel* orig.= *gehęle.* 4. *hy*
ofþrycton by Cor. on er. 5. 7 *na* by Cor. on er. *-wisnesse* by Cor. on er.
ne by Cor. on er. *min,* fin. let. er. *-wisnesse ic ern* by Cor. in pl. of er.
gereht, ht by Cor on er. 6. *rynum, r* from *w. gesyoh, h* by Cor. on er.
mẹgena, a add. by Cor.

god isræl beheald to geneosienne ealla ðiodæ na þu mildsast
deus isræl Intende ad visitandas omnes gentes non miserearis

eallum ðæ ðe wirceð unrihtwisnesse   Sin gecirrede
omnibus qui operantur iniquitatem   7. Convertentur

to efenne 7 hunger þrowigen swæ hundes 7 ymbyrnað
ad vesperum et famem pacientur ut canes et circuibunt

ceæstre   Eallenga hie spreceð on muðe heore 7
civitatem   8. Ecce ipsi loquentur in ore suo et

sweord is on welerum hiræ Forðæn hwylc gehyrde   7
gladius est in labiis eorum Quoniam quis audivit   9. et

þu dryhten bismrast ł spest hie for naht þu heafst eallæ
tu domine deridebis eos pro nichilo habebis omnes

ðiodæ   Strengðo mine to ðæ ic gehalde forðan
gentes   10. Fortitudinem meam ad te custodiam quia

ðu god onfeng min ært   god min mildheortnes
tu deus susceptor meus es   11. deus meus misericordia

his forecumeð me   god min opiwe me gód
eius preveniet me   12. Deus meus ostende michi bona

betweox fiend mine ne cwealle ðu hie ðylęs hyo ofergeten
inter inimicos meos ne occideris eos ne quando obliviscantur

æs ł ewę þine Tostenc hie on megene þinum 7 tobręc hie
legis tuae Disperge illos in virtute tua et destrue eos

scilden min drihten   Scyldes ł Agyltas muðes hira
protector meus domine   13.   Delicta oris eorum

word ł spræce welera hira 7 hy bioð gegrypene on
sermo labiorum ipsorum et conprehendantur in

oferhyda hera 7 of scununga 7 leasungæ hy bioð adrifene ł anedde
superbia sua et de execratione et mendatio conpellantur

on irræ geEndunge 7 hy ne bioð 7 hy witen þet god
14. in ira consummationis et non erunt Et scient quia deus

---

7 er bef. *beheald*; *d* from ð. *geneosienne, ge-* by Cor. in pl. of er.; *g* from some other let.; *e* (2nd) by Cor. from *i*; *-ne* by Cor. on er. *ðiodæ, d* from ð. *na þu mildsast* by Cor. on er. *-wisnesse* by Cor. on er. 7. *-gen*, about two fin. lett. er. *-yrnað* by Cor. on er. 8. *spreceð, ð* by Cor. on er. *heore* by Cor. on er. 9. *bismrast*, about two init. lett. er. *ł spest* add. by Cor. 7 er. bef. *for*; fin. let. (e ?) er. *naht*, fin. let. er ? *þu* add. by Cor. 10. *ært* by Cor. on er. 11. *-ð me* add. by Cor. 12. *betweox* by Cor. *hyo* add. by Cor. *æs ł* add. by Cor. *Tostenc*, fin. *e* er ? *megene*, fin. *e* by Cor. on er. 13. *Scyldes ł* add. by Cor. *Ag-* orig.= *Æg-*. *ł spræce* add. by Cor. *hy* add. by Cor. (twice). *hera* by Cor. on er. *of scununga* by Cor. on er. *ł anedde* add. by Cor. 14. *hy* (2nd) add. by Cor. *-en* by Cor. on er. *þet* by Cor. on er.

wealdeþ ˙ iacobes 7 enda eorðan   Sien gecirrede to
dominabitur iacob et finium terrae   **15.** *Convertentur ad*

efenne   7   hunger biða þrowigende swa hundæs 7 ymbgangæð
vesperam et famem   pacientur   ut   canes et circuibunt

ceastre   Eallengæ hie bioð tostencede ł tofarene to
civitatem   **16.** *Ecce ipsi   dispergentur   ad*

etanna   gif soðlice hy ne bioð gefillede 7 gnorniæð
manducandum   si   vero   non fuerint   saturati et   murmu-

ł murcniað   Ic Soðlice singe megen   ðinum 7
rabunt   **17.** *Ego autem cantabo virtutem   tuam   et*

ic upæhebbe on mergen mildheortnesse þine Forðæn geworden
exaltabo   mane   misericordiam tuam   Quia   factus

þu eart onfeng min 7 gescild min on dege earfoþnessæ
es   susceptor meus et refugium meum in   die   tribulationis

mine   fultumend min þe ic singe Forðæn þu god
meae   **18.** *adiutor meus tibi psallam   Quia   tu deus*

onfeng min ært god min mildheortnes min
susceptor meus es deus meus misericordia mea

59.

god ðu adrife us 7 tobrece us irre ðu ært 7 mildsod
3. *Deus reppulisti nos et destruxisti nos iratus es   et misertus*

ært us   ðu astiredest eorðæn 7 ðu gedrefdest hie hæl
es nobis   **4.** *Commovisti terram et   conturbasti eam sana*

unrotnesse hire forðan æstyræð hýo is   ðu oðiewdes folce
contritiones eius quia   mota est   **5.** *Ostendisti populo*

ðinum herdnes þu drænctest us of wine onbryrdeduesse
tuo   dura   potasti   nos   vino   compunctionis

ðu sealdes ondredendum þe getæcnunge þet hie flion from
6. *Dedisti   metuentibus   te significationem ut   fugiant   a*

onsine bogan þet syn friolsede ł alysed gecorene ðine   hælnæ
facie arcus ut   liberentur   electi   tui   **7.** *Salvum*

-*deþ, þ* by Cor. on er.   *enda,* init. *ge-* er. ; *a* from some other let. (u ł) ; fin.
let. er.   **15.** *Sien* or *Sen* ? Er. aft. *swa.*   **16.** *ł tofarene* add. by Cor.
7 er. bef. *to.*   *ł murcniað* add. by Cor.   **17.** *megen,* fin. *e* er.   *þu eart* by
Cor. in pl. of er.   *dege,* altered by Cor. from *dęi* ?   **18.** *ic* add. by Cor.   Er.
bef. *singe. ært* by Cor. on er.   **59. 3.** *god* by Cor.?   *ðu ært* by Cor.
-*sod ært* by Cor. on er.   **4.** *astiredest* by Cor. on er.   *eorðæn, n* add. by
Cor.?   *est* (2nd), *t* add. by Cor.   *hire* by Cor. on er.   *hýo is* by Cor. in pl. of
er.   **5.** *-ænctest* by Cor. on er.   *-yrdednesse* by Cor. on er.   **6.** *bogan, n*
prob. add. by Cor.   *þet,* fin. *te* er.?   *syn,* about two fin. lett. er.   *ł alysed*
add. by Cor.   *ðine, e* add. by Cor.

me do of swiðren þinre 7 gehir me　　　　　god　　sprec　on.
me fac　dextera　tua　et exaudi me　　8. *deus locutus est in*

halgum　his　blissige　7　ic　todele　swæ lyllæ　7　holedene
sancto　suo　laetabor　et　dividam　sicimam　et convallem

eærdungæ ł teldum　　　　　Min　is　helm　7　min　is to
tabernaculorum　metibor　9. *Meus　est galaad et meus est*

wunienne 7 to onfonne strengðo heæfedes mines Iudæ kynig min
manasses et　effrem　fortitudo capitis　mei　Iuda rex　meus

næmæ　　hyhte min on fnestum him ic aðenie scoe ł scyeuange
10. *moab olla spei meae in　idumea　extendam　calciamentum*

mine　me　næmæ underðiedde sinðon　　h[w]ylc geleded me
meum michi allophili　subditi　sunt　11. *Quis　deducet me*

on　ceæstre gestrangode　oððe　wilc　geleded　me　oððe　on
in　civitatem　munitam　aut　quis　deducet　me　usque in

ða eorðlican þing　　Nealles þu god þe aneddest us 7　na
idumeam　12. *Nonne　tu deus qui reppulisti nos et non*

þu utgæst god on megenum urum　　Sele us　　fultum
egredieris deus in virtutibus nostris　13. *Da nobis auxilium*

of eærfoðnessum 7 idel helo mannæ　　On gode we doð
de　tribulatione et vana salus hominis　14. *In　deo　faciemus*

megen 7 he to nawiht geledcþ þa swenzende ł dreccende us
virtutem et ipse ad nichilum deducet　tribulantes　nos

60.

gehyr　god　　bene　　mine beheæld gebeda　min
2. *Exaudi deus deprecationem meam intende orationi meae*

from enðe eorðæn to ðæ ic clipode midðy bið genirwed hiorte
3. *a finibus terrae ad te clamavi dum　anxiaretur　cor*

min on stanæ þu upæhofe me　　ðu geleddest me forðæn
meum in petra exaltasti　me　4. *Deduxisti　me　quia*

<hr>

7. of add. by Cor.　-n þinre add. by Cor.　gehir. fin. e er.　8. Er. aft.
sprec. -ige 7 ic by Cor. in pl. of er.　holedene add. by Cor.　t teldum add. by
Cor.　9. kynig, about two fin. lett. er.　10. ic add. by Cor.　-ie by Cor. on
er. scoe ł scyeuange add. by Cor.　11. gestrangode add. by Cor.　From on
(2nd) to þing add. by Cor.　12. þe aneddest add. by Cor.　na þu utgæst
prob. add. by Cor.　meyenum by Cor. part. on er. ?　13. 7 idel add. by
Cor.　14. gode, fin. s er.　megen by Cor. part. on er.　-þ add. by Cor.
Rest of verse by Cor. prob. in pl. of er.　60. 2. gehyr by Cor.　-da by
Cor. in pl. of er.　3. ende or enðe ? -ode by Cor. on er.　Er. bef. hiorte. on
by Cor. on er.　4. -est, t add. by Cor.

geworden ært hyht min torr ł stepel strengnesse of ansene fiondæs
factus   es   spes mea   turris   fortitudinis   a   facie inimici
   Ic oneærdie on   eærdunge ðine on woroldæ ic beo scilded on
5. *Inhabitabo   in   tabernaculo tuo   in   secula   protegar   in*
wrignesse fyðræ þynræ   Forðæn ðu god ðu gehyrdest
velamento alarum tuarum   **6.** *Quoniam tu deus   exaudisti*
   gebed   mine ðu sealdest yrfewirðnese ondredendum næmæn
orationem meam   dedisti   haereditatem   timentibus   nomen
ðinne   dagæs ofer dagæs kyninges þu geæcest ger his oððet
tuum   **7.** *Dies super dies   regis   adicies annos eius usque*
on dege woroldæ 7 worolde   þurhwuniæð on ecnesse on
in diem saeculi et saecula   **8.** *permanebit in aeternum in*
gesihðæ godes Mildheortnesse 7 soþfestnesse wylc seceð hyræ
conspectu dei Misericordiam et veritatem   quis requiret eorum
   swæ ic singe namæn ðine god on worolde woruld ðæt ic gieldæ
9. *sic psallam nomini tuo deus in seculum seculi ut reddam*
gehæt min of dege on dege
   vota mea de die in diem

61.

hu ne nu godæ underþeod beoð sawl min fram him soðliche
2. *Nonne   deo   subdita   erit anima mea ab ipso   enim*
hele min   he is god min 7   helo   min
salutare meum   **3.** *Et enim ipse est deus meus et salutaris meus*
fultumend min   ne   beo ic ma gestired   hwu lange
adiutor meus non   movebor amplius   **4.** *Quo usque*
onhreosæ ge on man   ge oncweælðeð eælle swæ swæ wagum
irruitis in homines   interficis universos tanquam parieti
onhyldon 7 stangaderunge onheldum   þah hwæþre
inclinato et   maceriae   inpulsae   **5.** *Verumtamen*

ært add. by Cor.   *ł stepel* add. by Cor.   *-nesse* by Cor.; *-ne-* on er.   *of*
add. by Cor.   *an-, a* from *o* by Cor.   *-dæs, s* add. by Cor.   **5.** *ic beo* by
Cor. in pl. of er.   *scilded,* init. *ge-* er.; fin. *d* add. by Cor.   **6.** *-est, t* add.
by Cor. (twice).   *-nese,* fin. *e* add. by Cor.ł *-endum* by Cor.   **7.** *dagæs*
orig. = *dægæs* (twice).   *þu geæcest ger* add. by Cor.   *-olde, e* add. by Cor.ł
8. MS. = soþwestnesse.   **9.** *ic* prob. add. by Cor.   Er. bef. *namæn;* fin. *n*
add. by Cor.   *-olde, d* from *ð.   woruld* add. by Cor.   *of, f* by Cor. prps. from
b.   dege, ge prob. by Cor. in pl. of er. of one let.   **61. 2.** *hu ne nu* by
Cor.   From *un-* to *sawl* by Cor.   From *fram* to *min* by Cor.   **3.** *he is god*
by Cor.ł   *min* (1st) by Cor. on er.   *min* (2nd) fin. let. er.   *ful-,* init. lett. er.
From *min* (3rd) to end of verse by Cor. in pl. of er.   **4.** *hwu lange* by Cor.
in pl. of er.   *ge* by Cor.   *man,* two (or three) fin. lett. er.   *ge oncweælðeð, ge-*
pref. by Cor.; fin. *ð* add. by Cor.   *wagum* add. by Cor.   From *stan-* to end of
verse by Cor. part. on er.   **5.** *þah hwæpre* by Cor. in pl. of er.

weorþunge min hy þohton anydan ꝉ udrifon ic arn   on þurst
honorem meum cogitaverunt   repellere   cucurri   in sitim

of muðe 7 he sie hy blctsodon 7   hyræ heorten hy yfel-
ore   suo   benedicebant et corde   suo   male-

cweðon ꝉ wyrgden   Soðlice hweðre goðe underðid bið sawul
dicebant   **6.** *Veruntamen deo subdita erit anima*

mine forðæn from him is geðylð min   7 soðlice he is
mea quoniam ab ipso est pacientia mea   **7.** *Et enim ipse est*

god min 7   helo   min fultumend min ic ne afeorrie
deus meus et salutaris meus   adiutor   meus non emigrabo

On godæ helo   min 7 wuldor min god fultumes mines 7
8. *In deo salutare meum et gloria mea deus auxilii mei et*

hyht min on gode is   hyhtað on hine ealc gemeting ꝉ
spes mea in deo est   **9.** *Sperate in eum omnis   con-*

efenmeteð folces ageotað beforæn him heortæ eowra forðan god
ventus plebis effundite coram illo corda vestra quia deus

fultum ure is   Soðlice idle suna ꝉ bearn mænnæ
adiutor noster est **10.** *Verumtamen vani   filii   hominum*

lease bearn mannæ on wegum ðet hy beswicen hye of
mendaces filii hominum in stateris ut   decipiant ipsi de

idelnesse on þ selfe   Nellen ge wenæn ꝉ hyhten on
vanitate in id ipsum **11.** *Nolite   sperare   in*

unrihtwisnessum 7 on gereaflacum nellen ge gytsian welæn
iniquitate et in rapinis   nolite concupiscere Diviciae

gif hio flowen nellen ge heortan tosetten   ane siðe sprec
si affluant nolite   cor apponere   **12.** *semel locutus est*

god twa þas ic gehyrde Forðæn mihte ꝉ anweald godes is
deus duo haec audivi Quia   potestas   dei est

From *weorþ*- to -*dan* ꝉ (except *min*) by Cor. *ic* by Cor. on er. *arn on*
þurst of add. by Cor.? *muðe, e* add. by Cor.? *he, e* from *i.* *sie hy* crowded
in by Cor.? -*en hy* add. by Cor.? ꝉ *wyrgden* add. by Cor.   7. *soðlice he*
add. by Cor. Er. bef. *ful*-. *min ic* by Cor. *afeorrie* by Cor. in pl. of er.
8. *min* (1st) fin. *e* er.   9. *hyhtað on hine* by Cor. *gemeting* ꝉ add. by Cor.
ageotað add. by Cor.   10. *suna* ꝉ add. by Cor. *lease, se* by Cor. in pl. of er.
wegum by Cor. on er. *ðet,* two fin. lett. er.? *hy* add. by Cor. -*swicen* by
Cor. on er. *of* by Cor. on er. on *þ selfe* add. by Cor.   11. *Nellen* by Cor.
part. on er. *wenæn,* init. *ge* er.; fin. *n* by Cor. on er. of ð? ꝉ *hyhten on* add.
by Cor. -*wis*- wr. over the line by Cor. From -*reaf*- to *gytsian* by Cor. in
pl. of er. From (3rd) *nellen* to -*setten* by Cor. part. in pl. of er.   12. *ane siðe*
by Cor. *sprec,* several fin. lett. er. Er. bef. *god.* *twa þas ic gehyrde* add.
by Cor. -*e* ꝉ *anweald* add. by Cor.

7 ðæ dryhten mildheortnesse forðæn ðu geldest sendrigum
13. *et tibi domine   misericordia   quia   tu   reddes   singulis*
efter   weorc hioræ
secundum opera eorum

62.

god god min to þe of liohte ic wecie ðyrste on ðæ sæul
2. *Deus deus meus ad te de luce   vigilo Sitivit in te anima*
min hu monifealdlice 7 flǽsc min   on westene 7 on wege
mea quam multipliciter et caro mea   3. In deserto et in invio
7 on weterige swæ on haligum ic atawede þe dæt ic gesage
et in aquoso sic in sancto   apparui tibi ut   viderem
megne ðin 7 wuldor þin   Forðæn selre is milðheortnes
virtutem tuam et gloriam tuam   4. Quia melior est misericordia
ðin ofer lyf weleres mine herigæð ðæ   Swæ ic bletsye ðe
tua super vitam labia   mea laudabunt te   5. Sic benedicam te
on lyfe mine 7 on namæn ðinum ic upæhebbæ hænd mine
in vita mea et in nomine tuo   levabo   manus meas
Swæ swa mid seime 7 mid fetnesse gefelled beoð sawul min 7
6. *Sicut   adipe   et pinguedine   repleatur   anima mea et*
weleres upahefednysse herigað næman þinne   Swæ gemindig
labia   exultationis laudabunt nomen tuum   7. Sic   memor
ic wæs ðines ofer bedd   min on uhtlicum ł degrede ic smeæ-
fui   tui super stratum meum in   matutinis   medi-
gede on þe   forðæn þu gewurðen ært felstend min 7 on
tabor in te   8. quia   factus es   adiutor meus Et in
oferbrædelse fiðræ ðinræ ic blissige   togeþeodde saul
velamento alarum tuarum exultabo   9. adhesit   anima
min efter þe me onfeng swiðra þin   hyo soðlice on
mea post te me suscepit dextera tua   10. Ipsi vero   in

---

13. *sendrigum efter* add. by Cor.   62. 2. *god* (1st) by Cor. *of*, *f* by
Cor. prob. from some other er. let. *ic* add. by Cor. *-ie* by Cor. on er. *-lice*
by Cor. in pl. of one er. let.   3. *on westene* by Cor. on er. *-ige* by Cor. From
on to *þe* by Cor. in pl. of er. *-age* by Cor. on er.   5. *ic* add. by Cor. *ðe*
orig. = *ðæ*. *mine*, *e* add. by Cor. (twice).   6. *swa* add. by Cor. *mid seime*
by Cor. on er. *mid* (2nd) by Cor. on er. *gefelled beoð* add. by Cor. *upahe-*
fednysse by Cor. in pl. of er. *herigað*, er. immed. bef. *h* ; *-igað* by Cor. on er.
7. *-dig* by Cor on er. *wæs* by Cor. on cr. *bedd* add. by Cor. *min*, fin. let.
er. *ł degrede* add. by Cor. *-gede*, *de* add. by Cor.   8. From *þu* to *min*
by Cor. in pl. of er. 7 *on oferbrædelse* add. by Cor. *ic blissige* add. by Cor.
9. *togeþeodde* add. by Cor. *þe* add. by Cor. *onfeng* add. by Cor.   10.
From *hyo* to *sohtan* add. by Cor.

idel sohtan   saul   min hy ingað on þa neoþeran eorðæn
vano quesierunt animam meam introibunt in inferiora terrae

     hyo beoð sæld on hand sweordes 7 dæles foxa hy beoð
11.   *tradentur   in manus   gladii   et partes vulpium erunt*

     kining soþlice blissað on drihtne herigað eælle ðæ þe
12.   *Rex   vero   laetabitur in domino laudabuntur omnes qui*

sweriæð on hine fordæn   fordett is muð sprecendræ unriht
iurant in eo   quia obstructum est os loquentium iniqua

63.

     Gehyr god   gebed   min þanne ic bio geeærfoðod í swenced
2. *Exaudi deus orationem meam cum   tribulor*

from ege fyondæs genere saul   min   ðu bewruge me
a timore inimici eripe animam meam.   3. *Protexisti me*

from gencyme í metinge warigendra from menigo wyrcendra
a   conventu   malignantium a multitudine operantium

unrihtwisnesse   Forðæn hy hwetten swæ sweord tungen
iniquitatem 4. *Quia   exacuerunt   ut gladium linguas*

heora hy onðenedon í beheoldon bogæn ðing biter   þet
suas   intenderunt   arcum rem amaram 5. *ut*

hy scotigen í strelien on dygelnesse þa unwemme   Ferlice
sagittent   in occultis inmaculatum 6. *Subito*

scotigen hine 7 ne ondredon hy trymedon him word   yfel
sagittabunt eum et non timebunt firmaverunt sibi verbum malum

hy geteældon í fliton þ hy hydden grino hy cweðon hwylc
disputaverunt   ut absconderent laqueos dixerunt quis

gesihð hie   hy Smeageden unrihtwisnesse hy geteorodon
videbit eos 7. *Scrutati sunt   iniquitatem   defecerunt*

From *hy* to *neoþeran* add. by Cor.   *eorðæn, n* add. by Cor.   11. This
v. add. by Cor.   12. From *kining* to *herigað* add. by Cor.   *þe* prob. add.
by Cor.   *fordett* add. by Cor.   Word of about two lett. er. bef. *unriht*.
63. 2. *Gehyr* prob. by Cor.   *þanne* by Cor. in pl. of er.   *í swenced* add. by
Cor.   *fyondæs, o* from some other let.; *s* add. by Cor.   3. *bewruge me* by
Cor. in pl. of er.   *í metinge warigendra* by Cor. on er.   *-wisnesse* by Cor. on
er.   4. *hy hwetten* by Cor. on er.   *heora hy on-* by Cor. in pl. of er.   *í beheoldon* add. by Cor.   *ðing biter* by Cor. on er.   5. *-tigen* by Cor. on er.
í strelien add. by Cor.   *-se* by Cor. (orig. = -sum ?).   *-me* by Cor. on er.   6.
Ferlice by Cor. on er.   *-tigen* by Cor. on er.   *hy* (1st and 2nd) pref. by Cor.
í fliton þ add. by Cor.   *hy* (3rd) by Cor. on er.   *hydden*, two lett. er. immed.
bef. it; *n* add. by Cor.   *grino*, init. ge- er. ? *hy* (4th) add. by Cor.   7. *hy*
add. by Cor.   *-den* by Cor. on er.   *-wis-* add. over the line by Cor.   *hy*
geteorodon by Cor. in pl. of er.

smeagenðe ł scrudniende smeægunge   Togenealehte   mæn   to
   scrutantes   *scrutinium*   *Accedet*   *homo ad*

heorton heagre   7 bioð upahafen god   Strelæ   cilde
   cor   altum   8. *et exaltabitur deus Sagittae parvulorum*

gewordene sinðon wunden ł witu heræ   7 fore   naht
   factae   sunt   plage   eorum   9. *et pro nichilo*

hefðo weron ongean hie tungan   hera   gedrefede sint
habitae sunt   contra   eos   linguae ipsorum Conturbati sunt

ealle ðæ þe gesegen hie   7 ondrędde ælc   man 7
omnes qui videbant eos 10. *et   timuit   omnis homo et*

hy bebodedan   weorc   godes 7 deda   his   hy ongietæn
adnuntiaverunt   opera   dei   et facta   eius   intellexerunt

   blissiæþ rihtwis   on   drihten 7 gehihteð on hine 7
11. *Letabitur iustus   in   domino et sperabit   in   eo   et*

beoð geherede eallæ rihtwise heorte
laudabuntur omnes   recti   corde

64.

þe geriseð ymen ł lofsang god on sion 7 ðæ bið agolden
2. *Te   decet   hymnus   deus in syon et tibi   reddetur*

gehæt ł lest on hierusalem   gehier . gebed   min   to ðæ
votum   in ierusalem   3. *Exaudi orationem meam ad te*

ealc flesc cymeð   word unrihtwisra strangoden ł rihsodon
omnis caro veniet   4. *Verba iniquorum   prevaluerunt*

ofer   us 7 arleasnæsse urum ðu gemiltsast   eadig
super nos et impietatibus nostris tu propitiaberis   5. *Beatus*

ðane ðu gecure 7 name ł afenge oneardæþ on geteldungum
quem   elegisti   et   adsumpsisti inhabitabit in   tabernaculis

---

ł *scrudniende* add. by Cor.   Aft. -*gunge*, ' ł something' no longer legible—
prob. for the Latin. *Togenealehte* by Cor. on er. *heagre* by Cor.   8.
-*ahafen* orig. = *ahæfen* ł *wunden* ł add. by Cor. *heræ, e* from *i*.   9. -*naht*,
fin. *e* er. *ongean* by Cor. in pl. of er. *hera, e* from *i*. *gesegen, -sege-* altered
by Cor. from something else ; *n* add. by Cor.   10. -*e ælc* by Cor. on
er. *bebodedan* by Cor. on er. *weorc, e* from *i* (by Cor. ?). *deda* by Cor. on
er.   11. -*siæþ, þ* add. by Cor.? *rihtwis* by Cor. on er. From *gehihteð* to
beoð by Cor. ; *gehihteð* on er. -*ede*, first *e* from *i* ; *de* by Cor. on er. -*wise* by
Cor. on er.   64. 2. *þe geriseð* by Cor. ł *lofsang* add. by Cor. *agolden*,
init. *a* and fin. -*en* on er. ł *lest* add. by Cor.   3. *gehier, i* dotted ; fin.
let. (*e* ?) er. *flesc*, let. er. betw. *l* and *e*.   4. -*wisra* by Cor. on er. *strangoden* ł *rihsodon* by Cor. in pl. of er. Er. bef. *ar-*. *gemiltsast* by Cor. on er.
5. ł *afenge* add. by Cor..

ðinum   We beoð gefelled   on   godum   huses   þines   hælig   is
tuis   Replebimur   in   bonis   domus   tuae   sanctum est

te[m]pel   ðin   wundorlic   on efennesse   gehir   us   god
templum   tuum   6. mirabile   in equitate   Exaudi   nos   deus

helo   ure   hyht   ealræ   ende eorðæn 7 on sęwe ꝼ sæ   feor
salutaris noster spes omnium finium terrae et in   mari   longe

gearwienda dunæ on megene ðinum begierd of anwalde ꝼ mihte
7. *Preparans montes in virtute   tua   accinctus   potentia*

þu   drefest   grund ꝼ diop   sæs   sweig   yða   hire hwa
8. *qui conturbas   fundum   maris   sonum   fluctuum   eius quis*

arefneð bioð gedrefede ðioda   7 ondrędað ealle ða þe
sustinebit Turbabuntur gentes   9. et timebunt omnes   qui

eardiæð   on   endes   eorðæn   fram   tæcnum   ðinum   Utgæng
habitant   fines   terrae   a   signis   tuis   Exitus

uhtlecæn ꝼ degredes   on   efene   ðu gelustfullæst ꝼ blissað
matutini   et   vespere   delectaberis

ðu niosodest eorðæn 7 ondrenctest hie ðu monigfældodest
10. *visitasti   terram et   inebriasti eam   multiplicasti*

to geweligan hie Stræm ꝼ flod godes gefylled is of wętere
locupletare   eam   Flumen   dei   repletum est   aqua

þu gearwodest mete hiræ forðæn swæ is geærwung ðin
parasti   cibum illorum quia   ita est   preparatio tua

his reneles drencende gemonigfæld cneowrissa his on
11. *Rivos eius   inebrians   multiplica generationes eius   in*

dropungan his he blissæð ðanne he bið upcumen   ðu blet-
stillicidiis suis laetabitur dum   exorietur   12. Bene-

sest trendel geræs estinesse ꝼ medemnesse ðinre 7 feldes ðine
dicens coronam anni   benignitatis   tuae et campi tui

---

beoð by Cor. on er. -*es þines* add. by Cor.   6. -*lic*, fin. let. er. *on
efennesse* by Cor. on er. *gehir*, fin. let. (e ?) er. ꝼ *sæ* add. by Cor. *feor* by
Cor. on er.   7. *gearwienda* by Cor. on er. *begierd, i* dotted. *of* by Cor.
on er. *anwalde* ꝼ add. by Cor.   8. *grund* ꝼ *diop sæs* by Cor. in pl. of er.
sweig, g add. by Cor. -*a hire hwa* prob. by Cor.   9. -*diæð* or -*diað? on*
prob. add. by Cor. *endes, s* add. by Cor. ? ꝼ *degredes* add. by Cor. over the
line. ꝼ *blissað* add. by Cor.   10. -*est* (1st), ꝼ add. by Cor. ? *ondrenctest*,
first *e* on er.; -*test* on er. by Cor. ? -*fældodest, ge* er. bef. *f* ?; ꝼ prob. add. by
Cor. *to geweligan* by Cor. in pl. of er. ꝼ *flod* add. by Cor. *of* add. by Cor.
-*e þu* add. by Cor. -*est* (4th) ꝼ add. by Cor. Er. bef. *swæ*.   11. *his* by Cor.
in pl. of er. *reneles drencende* by Cor. in pl. of er. *gemonigfæld, ge* prob.
pref. by Cor.; let. (e ?) er. betw. *g* and *f*; fin. let. er. -*rissa, a* add. by
Cor. ? *his, s* by Cor. in pl. of er. *on dropungan* by Cor. in pl. of er. *he* add.
by Cor. ? *ðanne he* add. by Cor.; these two words misplaced but marked for
transposition.   12. *trendel* by Cor. on er. ꝼ *medemnesse* add. by Cor. *feldes,
es* prob. add. by Cor. *ðine, e* prob. add. by Cor.

bioð gefylled of genihtsumnesse   Fettigað endes on westene
replebuntur   ubertate   13. *Pinguescent fines   deserti*

7 of blissunga beorges beoð ymbgert   Gescrydde sinðon
et exultatione   colles   accingentur   14. *Induti   sunt*

rammas sceæpæ 7 denæ genihtsumiað of hwetes 7 soðlice
arietes   ovium et convalles habundabunt   frumento   etenim

hy clypiað 7 imen ł lofsang cweðæð
clamabunt et   hymnum   dicent

65.

Herigað gode eal eorða   seælm cweðað naman his
Iubilate deo omnis terra   2. *psalmum dicite nomini eius*

sellað wuldor lofe his   cweðæð ł secgað gode hu
date gloriam laudi eius   3.   *Dicite   deo quam*

egeslecu sinðon wiorc ðin on manigfealnesse mægenes ðines
terribilia   sunt opera tua in · multitudine   virtutis tuae

liogenð ðe fiend ðine   Eal eorða gebide ðe 7
mentientur tibi inimici tui   4. *Omnis terra adoret te et*

ic singe ðe psalmsang . he secge næmon ðinne þu hyhsta
psallat tibi psalmum   dicat   nomini tuo   altissime

Cumæð 7 gesioð wiorc drihtnes hu   egeslic is on geðcahte
5. *Venite et videte opera domini quam terribilis in consiliis*

ofer bearn mænnæ   Se gehwyrfð ł cyrde sewe ł sæ
super filios hominum   6. *Qui   convertit   mare*

on drege land 7 stræam ł flodas he oferfor mid fotum ðer
in aridam et   flumina   pertransibit   pede   ibi

we blissiæð on ðet selfe   Se weældeð on megne his
laetabimur in id ipsum   7. *Qui dominatur in virtute sua*

-*led*, fin. lèt. (e?) er.   *of genihtsumnesse* by Cor. on er.   13. *Fettigað* by
Cor.   *endes, s* prob. add. by Cor.   *of blissunga beorges* add. by Cor.   *beoð*
ymbgert by Cor. on er.   14. *Gescrydde* prob. by Cor.   *rammas* by Cor. on
er.   *-að* (1st) prob. by Cor. on er.   *of* prob. add. by Cor.   *hwetes*, two init.
lett. er.?   *hy* add. by Cor.   *ł lofsang* add. by Cor.   65. *Herigað* by
Cor.   *eal*, fin. let. er.   *eorða*, fin. let. er.   2. *lofe* by Cor.   3. *ł secgað*
add. by Cor.   From *on* to *mægenes* by Cor. in pl. of er.   *ðines, s* add. by Cor.?
liogenð, *n* dotted ; *ð* from *d* by Cor. ; fin. let. (e?) er.   4. *Eal*, two fin. lett.
er.   *eorða*, fin. let. er.   *psalmsang he secge* by Cor. in pl. of er.   *þu* add. by
Cor.   *hyhsta*, fin. let. (n?) er.   6. Er. bef. *ge-*.   *ł cyrde* add. by Cor.   *ł sæ*
add. by Cor.   *on drege land* by Cor. in pl. of er.   *ł flodas* add. by Cor.   *he*
oferfor mid by Cor. in pl. of er.   *we* add. by Cor.   -*siæð*, *ð* from *d* by Cor.
7. -*deð*, *ð* by Cor. on er.

on   ecnesse   eægæn   his   ofer   ðiodæ   gelociað   þa   on   erra
in   aeternum   oculi   eius   super   gentes   respiciunt   qui   in   ira

forðgeclypiað   na   hi   beoð   upahafen   on   him   selfum   blet-
provocant   non   exaltentur   in   semetipsis   8. *Bene-*

siað   dioðæ   god   urne   7   gehlystað   stefne   lofes   his
dicite   gentes   deum   nostrum   et   obaudite   vocem   laudis   eius

   Se   þe   gesette   saul   mine   to   lyfe   7   ne   seælde
9. *Qui   posuit   animam   meam   ad   vitam   et   non   dedit*

to astyrigenne   fet   mine   Forðan   ðu   fandedest   us
   commoveri   pedes   meos   10. *Quoniam   probasti   nos*

god   of   fyre   us   ðu   amerodest   swa   swæ   mid   fyre   bið   amerod
deus   igne   nos   examinasti   sicut   igne   examinatur

seolfor   þu   geleddest   us   on   gegrino   ðu   gesettest
argentum   11. *Induxisti   nos   in   laqueum   posuisti*

eærfoðnessæ   ł   swinc   on   rycge   ure   þu   ongesettest
   tribulationes   in   dorso   nostro   12. *inposuisti*

men   ofer   hcæfod   urræ   We   ferðon   þurg   fyr   7
homines   super   capita   nostra   Transivimus   per   ignem   et   aquam   et

þu   led   us   on   celnessum   ł   frofr   Ic   ingænge   on
induxisti   nos   in   refrigerium   13. *Introibo   in*

hus   ðin   on   offrunge   ł   asægdnissum   ic   gielde   ðe   gehæt   ł   lest
domum   tuam   in   holocaustis   reddam   tibi   vota

mine   ðæ   gestihtedon   ł   deldon   lippan   ł   weleræs   mine
mea   14. *quae   distinxerunt   labia   mea*

þæs   sprec   muð   min   on   earfoðnesse   ł   on   geswince   min
Haec locutum est   os   meum   in   tribulatione   mea

   offrungæ   ł   onsegdnesse   ic   bringe   ðe
15.   *holocausta   medullata   offeram   tibi   cum   incensu*

7   rammum   ic   bringe   ðe   oxæn   mid   buccum   Cumæð
et   arietibus   offeram   tibi   boves   cum   hyrcis   16. *Venite*

---

gelociað þa by Cor.   *erra, e* from *i*.   From *forð-* to *upahafen* by Cor. in pl.
of er.   8. *gehlystað* by Cor. on er.   9. *astyrigenne* by Cor. on er.   10.
fandedest by Cor. on er.   *of* add. by Cor.   *amerodest* by Cor. in pl. of er.
swa add. by Cor.   *mid* add. by Cor.   *amerod* prob. by Cor. on er.   *-or* by
Cor. on er.   11. *þu* by Cor.?   *-dest* by Cor. in pl. of *e* ?   *-est* (2nd), *t* add.
by Cor.   *ł swinc* add. by Cor.   *rycge*, init. *h* er.   *ure* by Cor. (from *urre* ?).
12. *þu* by Cor.?   *-est, st* add. by Cor.   Gloss to *et aquam* er.   MS. = *þu 7, þu*
being add. by Cor. in wrong pl.   *led*, init. and fin. er. made.   *ł frofr* add. by
Cor.   13. *ł asægdnissum* add. by Cor.   *ł lest* add. by Cor.   *mine, e* add. by
Cor.   14. *ł deldon lippan ł* add. by Cor.   Er. aft. *sprec*.   *ł on geswince* add.
by Cor.   15. *ł onsegdnesse* add. by Cor.   Gloss to *medullata* er.   Gloss to
cum incensu er.   *rammum* by Cor. on er.   About two lett. er. bef.
bringe.

7 gehiræð me 7 ic segge ł cyþe iow eælle þæ ondredæð
et audite me et narrabo vobis omnes qui timetis

drihten hu monegæ he dyde saul mine to him
dominum quanta fecit anime meae 17. *Ab ipso*

mid muðæ minum ic clepode 7 ic upæhebbe under tungæn minre
ore meo clamavi et exaltavi sub lingua mea

Unrihtwisnesse gyf ic geseah on heortan mine ne gehireð
18. *Iniquitatem si conspexi in corde meo non exaudiet*

drihten Forðæn geherde me god 7 he behyold stefne
deus 19. *Propterea exaudivit me deus et intendit voci*

of bene mine Gebletsæd beo drihten se ðe ne
deprecationis meae 20. *Benedictus dominus qui non*

asterede bene mine 7 mildheortnesse his fram me
amovit deprecationem meam et misericordiam suam a me

66.

God gemiltsie us 7 gebletsie us onliohte he *andwlitæn*
2. *Deus misereatur nobis et benedicat nos illuminet vultum*

his ofer us 7 mildsa us ðet we oncnæwen· on
suum super nos et misereatur nobis 3. *Ut cognoscamus in*

eorðæn weg þinne on eallum ðiodum helo ðine
terra viam tuam in omnibus gentibus salutare tuum

Ændetten ðe folc god ondettæn ðe folc ealle
4. *Confiteantur tibi populi deus confiteantur tibi populi omnes*

blissian 7 fægnien ł hyhtæn ðiodæ forðan ðu demest
5. *Laetentur et exultent gentes quoniam iudicas*

folc on emlicnesse ł efnesse 7 ðiodæ on corðæn gerecest
populos in aequitate et gentes in terra dirigis

Ændettæn ðe folc god andettæn ðe folc ealle
6. *Confiteantur tibi populi deus confiteantur tibi populi omnes*

---

16. *ł cyþe* add. by Cor. *he* wr. over the line. *dyde,* second *d* from ð. 17. *to him mid* by Cor. in pl. of er. *clepode, e* from *i*; *-ode* prob. by Cor. in pl. of er. 18. *-wis-* wr. over the line by Cor.? *ic geseah* by Cor. on er. Er. bef. *gehireð*; ð add. by Cor. 19. *geherde* altered by Cor. from *gehire*. *7 he behyold* by Cor. on er. *of* add. by Cor. 20. *-sæd, d* from ð. *beo* add. by Cor. *ðe ne asterede* by Cor. in pl. of er. 66. 2. *God* by Cor. *he* add. by Cor. *-æn, n* add. by Cor. *ofer, o* on er. 3. *7* er. bef. *ðet. we* by Cor. on er. *-wen, n* add. by Cor. 4. *-ten, n* add. by Cor. *-tæn, n* by Cor. on er. 5. *-ian, n* by Cor. on er. *7 fægnien ł* by Cor. part. on er. *-tæn, n* by Cor. prob. on er. *-est* (1st) by Cor. on er. *ł efnesse* add. by Cor. *-est* (2nd), *et* by Cor.? 6. *-tæn, n* by Cor. on er. (twice).

eorðæ gef ł sealde westm hira bletsige us god god ure
7. *terra*   *dedit*   *fructum suum Benedicat nos deus deus noster*

bletsige us god 7 ondredon hine eælle endes eorðæn
8. *et benedicat nos deus et metuant eum omnes fines terrae*

67.

Arise god 7 beon todrefed fiend his 7 flion from
2. *Exurgat deus et dissipentur inimici eius et fugiant a*

ænsine his ðæ ðe hatodon hine   Swæ swa teorode smic
facie eius qui oderunt eum   3. *Sicut defecit fumus*

hy geteorien swæ swa floweð weæx frcm ænsine fyres swæ
deficiant sicut fluit cera a facie ignis sic

forweorðen synfullæn from ænsine godes   7 soðfeste
pereant peccatores a facie dei   4. *et iusti*

bioð simlende Gehihtað on gesihðæ godes 7 bioð gelustfullod
epulentur Exultent in conspectu dei et delectentur

on blissæ   Singe god seælm cweðæð næman his
in laetitia   5. *Cantate deo psalmum dicite nomini eius*

wæg ł siþfet doð him ðe astæg ofer westdæl drihten
iter facite ei qui ascendit super occasum dominus

næma is him Gefahnieð on gesihðe his bioð gedrefede from
nomen est ei Gaudete in conspectu eius turbabuntur a

ænsine his   federes Stiopcildæ 7 demen widewenæ
facie eius   6. *patres orphanorum et iudices viduarum*

God on stowe hælig his   god ðe eærdien deð
Deus in loco sancto suo   7. *deus qui inhabitare facit*

anmode on huse Se geledeð gebundene on strangnesse
unanimes in domo Qui educit vinctos in fortitudine

gelice 7 þa þe on irræ forðgecigæð þa eardæð on byrgenne
similiter et eos qui in ira provocant qui habitant in sepulchris

---

7. eorðæ, fin. let. er. *gef* ł prob. add. by Cor. *hira, ra* by Cor. in pl. of an
er. let. Er. aft. *ure*.   8. *endes, s* prob. add. by Cor.   67. 2. *Arise*
by Cor. *beon todrefed* by Cor. on er.   Er. bef. *flion. ðe hatodon* by Cor. in
pl. of er.   3. *swa* add. by Cor. *teorode* prps. by Cor.   *hy geteorien* by Cor.
in pl. of er. -*eð* by Cor. prob. on er.   *fyres, es* add. by Cor.   *syn-* by Cor. in
pl. of er.   *godes, s* prob. add. by Cor.   4. -*lod, d* from ð.   5. *wæg* ł *sipfet*
by Cor. *ðe, e* from *o. astæg, a* from *œ* ?   *westdæl* add. by Cor.   *Gefahnieð*
add. by Cor.   6. *federes, es* prob. add. by Cor.   *widewenæ*, first *e* prob. add.
by Cor.   7. -*ien* by Cor. on er.   *anmode* orig. = *anes modes?*   *geledeð*
altered by Cor. from *gelet?* *gebundene* add. by Cor.   From *on* to *þe* by Cor.
in pl. of er.   *forðgecigæð*, first ð from *e* by Cor. ; second *g* altered to ð by Cor.,
but ð er. again.   *þa* by Cor. on er.

god þanne þu utgest beforan folce ðine þonne þu færst
8. *Deus dum egredieris coram populo tuo dum transgredieris*

þurh westen eorðe astyred is 7 soðlice hefonæs
per desertum **9.** *terra mota est Etenim caeli*

drupon from ansiene godes dune from ansine godes
distillaverunt a facie dei mons syna a facie dei

israela Ren wilsumne asyndriende god yrfeweærd-
israel **10.** *Pluviam voluntariam segregans deus haeredi-*

nesse ðinre 7 soðlice geuntrymed is ðu soðlice fulfremedu ða
tati tuae et enim infirmata est tu vero perfecisti eam

Nietenæ ðine oneardiað on ðam du gearwodest on
11. *Animalia tua inhabitabunt in ea parasti in*

swetnesse ðine ðeærfæ god drihten seleð word
dulcedine tua pauperes deus **12.** *Dominus dabit verbum*

þam godspellendum megene monige kining megnæ
evangelizantibus virtute multa **13.** *rex virtutum*

þas gecorenen 7 hiow huses todelen reaflac gif ge
dilecti et species domus dividere spolia **14.** *Si dor-*

slapæð betweoxon midde winde fiðrum culfran ouerselfrede
miatis inter medios cleros pennae columbae deargentate

7 ða eftran hriccg his on hiwe goldes Midðy ðe
et posteriora dorsi eius in specie auri **15.** *Dum*

sceæwæð ðes hefenlecæn kiniges ofer hine snaw bioð gehwittod
discernit caelestis reges super eam nive dealbabuntur

on selmon ðun godes ðun berende ł nihtsum
in selmon **16.** *Montem dei montem uberem*

dun gerenned ł runnen dun fétt Towon
mons coagulatus mons pinguis **17.** *Ut quid*

onfengon ge dunæ ł munt berende ł genihtsume dun
suscepistis montes uberes mons

---

8. *þanne þu utgest* by Cor. on er. *þonne þu færst þurh* by Cor. in pl. of er.
9. *drupon* by Cor. on er. *ansiene*, first *e* wr. over the line prob. by Cor. (or is
it *ansene* with first *e* from *i* by Cor.?). *dune, e* add. by Cor. 10. *-mne* by
Cor. in pl. of er. *asyndriende* by Cor. in pl. of er. *ða* orig. = *ðæ*? 11.
From *on-* to *ðam* by Cor. in pl. of er. *gearwodest*, first *e* dotted by Cor.; *t*
add. by Cor. 12. *þam* add. by Cor. *megene*, fin. *e* add. by Ccr. 13. *þas
gecorenen* 7 by Cor. in pl. of er. *hiow, o* from *e* ł *huses, es* add. by Cor.
14. *betweoxon midde* by Cor. on er. *culfran ouer selfrede* by Cor. in pl. of er.
-a eftran by Cor. on er. 15. MS. = *sceæpæð*. *-tlod* in d. ink; *o* on er.?
16. *ł nihtsum* add. by Cor. *ł runnen* add. by Cor. 17. *To-*, let. (h?) er.
immed. aft o. *ge* er. immed. bef. *on-* ł *ge* prob. add. by Cor. *dunæ, d* from *ð*.
ł munt add. by Cor. *ł genihtsume* add. by Cor.

on ꝧæm wel gelicode gode to eærdiæn on him 7
in quo bene placitum est deo habitare in eo et

soꝧlice drihten eærdaꝧ oꝧ on endæ   Ryne godes
enim dominus habitabit usque in finem   **18.** *Currus dei*

tien ꝧusendæ monigfæld þusendæ blissiendra drihten on hī
decem milium multiplex milia laetantium Dominus in illis

on sinæi on ꝧere halgon   astigende on heahnesse
in syna in sancto   **19.** *ascendens in altum*

gehæftne he ledde hæftned he gæf gife monnum 7 soꝧlice
captivam duxit captivitatem dedit dona hominibus Et enim

ꝧæ ne geliefæþ oneardian on him drihten god   ge-
qui non credunt inhabitare in eo dominus deus   **20.** *bene-*

bletsod gebletsod drihten of dege on deg gesund weg ꝉ siþfet
dictus benedictus dominus de die in diem Prosperum iter

dæþ us god helo ure   god ure god hæle
faciat nobis deus salutaris noster   **21.** *deus noster deus salvos*

to donne 7 dryhtnes utgong deæþes   Soꝧlice
faciendi et domini exitus mortis   **22.** *Verumtamen*

god scel tobrecen hefodo fiondæ his hnoll loccæs
deus conquassavit capita inimicorum suorum verticem capilli

þurhgængende on scyldum ꝉ on gyltum his   Cweþ
perambulantium in delictis suis   **23.** *Dixit*

drihten of bassæn ic gecirræ ic cirre on diæpan ꝉ on grunde
dominus ex basan convertam convertam in profundum

sæs   oꝧꝧet biꝧ awescen ꝉ dyped fot ꝧin on blode
maris   **24.** *donec intinguatur pes tuus in sanguine*

Tunga hundæ þinra of fiendum from him   gesewene
Lingua canum tuorum ex inimicis ab ipso   **25.** *visi*

sindon stepes ꝧine god on stepum godes mines kininges ꝧe
-sunt ingressus tui deus ingressus dei mei regis qui

is on hælgon his   Forecomon æældermæn togeþiedde
est in sancto ipsius   **26.** *Prevenerunt principes coniuncti*

---

gelicode by Cor. on er. to- add. by Cor. oꝧ on by Cor. in pl. of er.
18. -fæld, fin. let. (e?) er.   19. From on (1st) to gæf by Cor. in pl. of er.
20. gesund weg ꝉ add. by Cor.   21. hæle, e prob. add. by Cor. dryhtnes, es
add. by Cor.; let. er. betw. t and n.   22. scel to- add. by Cor.; -brec-, init.
ge er.?; en add. by Cor.?   fiondæ, o from d by orig. scribe. on scyldum ꝉ
add. by Cor. Er. after on (2nd).   23. gecirræ, a fin. let. er.? ic (2nd)
add. by Cor. cirre, a fin. let. er.? ꝉ on grunde sæs by Cor. in pl. of er.
24. awescen, a orig.= æ; let. er. betw. a and w; ꝉ by Cor. on er. ꝉ dyped
add. by Cor. fiendum, e by Cor. on er.   25. ꝧe by Cor. in pl. of er. Er.
aft. on (last).

I

singendum on midle gingra gliewmedene ł plegiendra mid
psallentibus in medio iuvenum   timpanistriarum

timpanan   on circum bletsioþ drihten god of
27. *in aecclesiis benedicite dominum deum de*

willum israhele   dær wuneð beniamin se gungesta on
fontibus israel   **28.** *Ibi   beniamin adolescentior in*

firhto eældermæn iuda herctogæ ł latþeowes hiræ eældras
pavore principes iuda   duces   eorum principes

of zabulon 7 eældermen neptalim   bebioð god megne
zabulon et principes neptalim   **29.** *Manda deus virtuti*

þine getremæ ðis god þet þu ƿrohtest on us   from
tuae confirma hoc deus quod operatus es in nobis   **30.** *a*

templum hælgen þine þet is on ierusalem ðe brengæn
templo sancto tuo quod est in ierusalem tibi offerent

kininges læc   þu oferþrawæst wildeor wude
reges munera   **31.** *Increpa   feras   silvarum*

gemot fearra betweoxon chun þes folches ꝥ na beon
concilium taurorum inter vaccas populorum ut non exclu-

utalocen ða þæ acunnode sindon of seolfre Tostenc ðioda
dantur hi qui probati sunt argento Dissipa gentes

þæ gefioht willæþ   cumæð erendracen of egiptum
quae bella volunt   **32.** *venient legati ex egypto*

7 redlingum forecymð hand his gode   Rice eorðen
ethyopia preveniet manus eius deo   **33.** *Regna terrae*

singað gode singad drihtne singað gode   ðe æstæg
cantate deo psallite domino psallite deo   **34.** *qui ascendit*

ofer heofænas hæofæna on æstdele Æallægga he seleð stefne
super caelos caelorum ab oriente Ecce dabit vocem

his stefne megnes his   sellæð wiorþunge gode Ofer
suam vocem virtutis suae   **35.** *date honorem deo Super*

israhelæ michelnesse his 7 megen his on wolcnum
israel magnificentia eius et virtus eius in nubibus

---

26. From *gliew-* to *timpanan* by Cor. in pl. of er.   28. *ƿuneð beniamin
se gungesta* by Cor. in pl. of er.   *ł latþeowes* add. by Cor.   *-dras of zabulon*
by Cor. in pl. of er.   29. *getremæ*, second *e* by Cor. in pl. of two er. lett.   *þu
ƿrohtest* by Cor. in pl. of er.   30. Er. aft. *from.   kininges, s* add. by Cor. ł
31. *fearra betweoxon* by Cor. in pl. of er.   From *þ* to *-ode* by Cor. in pl. of er.
of add. by Cor.   Three (or four) lett. er. immed. aft. *Tostenc.*   32. *erendracen of* by Cor. in pl. of er.   33. *singað* or *singæð* ł (3rd).   34. *ðe* orig. =
ðæ. hæofæna, fin. let. er.; two lett. (on ł) er. bef. this word.   35. *michelnesse* by Cor. in pl. of er.   *megen, en* by Cor. on er.

Wundorlic god on hælgum his   god isræhelæ he seleð
36. *Mirabilis deus in sanctis suis deus   israel ipse dabit*
megen 7 strangnesse folces his gebletsad beo god
virtutem et fortitudinem plebis suae   benedictus deus

68.

halne me do god forðan   ingeodon wæteres oððe to
2. *Salvum me fac deus quoniam introierunt aquae   usque ad*
saule minre   afestnod ic æm on lame ł slim dipæ 7 ne
animam meam **3.** *infixus sum in   limo   profundi et non*
is sped   ic cam on deopnesse sæs ł sewe 7 hriohnes besencte
est substantia Veni in altitudinem   maris   et tempestas demersit
me   Ic swanc chigende hase beoð geworðen Goman mine
me **4.** *Laboravi clamans rauce   factae sunt   fauces meae*
geteoroden egan mine mydþi ic wene on god min   Gemonig-
defecerunt oculi mei   dum   spero in deum meum **5.** *Multipli-*
fælldæ synðon ofer loccæs heafdes mines þæ ðe fiogædon ł hatedon
cati sunt super capillos capitis mei   qui   oderunt
me buton gewryhtum Gestrængode sincon ofer me þa ðe
me   gratis   Confortati sunt super me qui
ehttæð me   fiend mine unrihtlice þa ic ne reafode þa
me persequuntur inimici mei   iniuste quae non rapui tunc
ic ageald ł tolesde   god þu wast unwisdom minne 7
exsolvebam **6.** *Deus tu scis insipientiam meam et*
gyltas ł scyldes mine from þe ne sinðon behidde   Ne
delicta   mea a te non sunt abscondita **7.** *Non*
scamigen on me þa þe onbiduþ drihten god megena ne
erubescant in me qui te expectant domine deus virtutum non
forwandien ł scunien ofer me ða þe secæþ þe god isræhelæ
revereantur super me qui requirunt te deus israel

---

36. -*lic* add. by Cor.   *strangnesse*, *a* from *e* by Cor.; -*nesse* by Cor. on er.
-*d beo* add. by Cor.   **68.** 2. From *halne* to *forðan* by Cor.?   *ingeodon*
wæteres by Cor. in pl. of er.   3. From *afestnod* to *slim* prps. by Cor.   From
ic (2nd) to *ł* by Cor.   *hriohnes*, *h* (2nd) wr. over the line.   4. *swanc* by Cor.
on er.   From *hase* to *-oden* by Cor. in pl. of er.   -*þi*, *a* fin. let. (e?) er.   5. *ðe*
add. by Cor. (twice).   *fiogædon*, *d* from *ð*; -*on* prob. add. by Cor.   *ł hatedon*
add. by Cor.   *buton gewryhtum* by Cor. on er.   *ehttæð*, first *t* dotted by Cor.;
ð from *t* by Cor.   *unrihtlice* by Cor. on er.   *þa* orig. *þæ*. From *ic* (1st) to
tolesde by Cor. in pl. of er.   6. *gyltas*, init. *æ* er.?   *ł scyldes* add. by Cor.
7. -*igen*, *g* from *e*; *n* add. by Cor.   *megena*, *a* add. by Cor.   *forwandien ł*
scunien by Cor.   *ða*, *a* prob. by Cor. on er.

Forðæn   fore   ðe   ic forbær   hosp ł edwite   oferwreah
8. *Quoniam   propter   te   subportavi   improperium   operuit*

mid scæme   ansiene   mine   fremde   geworden   ic eom
*reverentia   faciem   meam   **9.** exter   factus   sum*

broþrum   minum   7   gyst ł cume   beærne   moder   minre
fratribus   meis   et   hospes   filiis   matris   meae

Forðæn   hatheortnesse ł wodnesse   huses ðines eteð   me 7
10. *Quoniam   zelus   domus tuae comedit me et*

edwit ł hosp   edwittendræ   ðe   gefiollon   ofer   me   7
*obprobria   exprobrantium tibi   ceciderunt   super   me   **11.** Et*

ic oferwreah on festone   sæule   minre 7   geworden is   me   on
operui   in ieiunio animam   meam et   factum   est michi   in

edwit   7   ic sette   hregl   min   heren   7
*obprobrium   **12.** Et   posui   vestimentum   meum   cilicium   et*

geworden ic eom   him   on   bispel   ongean   me
*factus   sum   illis   in   parabolam   **13.** Adversum me*

fliton   þa þe   seton   on gatum 7   on me   sungon   þæ þe
exercebantur   qui sedebant in   porta   et   in me psallebant   qui

druncon   win   Ic soðlice   gebed   min   to þe
*bibebant   vinum   **14.** Ego vero   orationem   meam   ad te*

drihten   tid   wellicungæ god on   monige   mildheortnesse ðinre
domine   tempus beneplaciti deus in   multitudine misericordiae   tuae

gehier me on soðfestnessé   helo ðine   Genere me of fenne
*exaudi me in   veritate   salutis tuae   **15.** Eripe me de luto*

ðet na ic onclyuie gefriolsa me   of ðam   hatigende me 7 of
ut non inheream libera me ex   odientibus   me et de

diopæ ł grunde   wetræ   ne me besenca hreohnæssa
*profundo   aquarum   **16.** non me demergat   tem-*

---

8. *forbær hosp ł* by Cor. in pl. of er.   From *ofer-* to *ansiene* by Cor. in pl. of er.   *mine, e* add. by Cor.   9. *fremde* by Cor. on er.   *gyst* by Cor. on er. *ł cume* add. by Cor.   *beærne*, fin. *e* prob. add. by Cor.   10. *-eortnesse ł* by Cor. on er.   *wodnesse, se* add. by Cor.   *huses ðines, -es* add. by Cor. in both cases; first *e* from a false let.   *ł hosp* add. by Cor.   *edwitt-*, let. er. betw. *ł* and *ł*.   11. *7 ic oferwreah on* by Cor. in pl. of er. *-one, e* add. by Cor.   on (2nd), *n* from some other let. by orig. scribe.   12. *heren, n* prob. add. by Cor.   *bispel* by Cor. in pl. of er.; *s* er. bef. the *s*.   13. *ongean* by Cor. in pl. of er.   *fliton* by Cor. in pl. of er.   *þa, a* by Cor. on er.   14. *to þe drihten* by Cor. in pl. of er.   *ðinre, re* add. by Cor.ł   *gehier*, fin. let. er.   15. *fenne* by Cor. on er.   *na ic onclyuie* by Cor. in pl. of er.   *of ðam hatigende* by Cor. in pl. of er.   *diopæ, o* in darker ink.   *grunde*, fin. *e* repeated, but one er.   16. *ne* by Cor. in pl. of er.   *besenca*, fin. let. er. ł   *hreoh-, h* (2nd) by Cor. wr. over the line.

ł storm wetræs 7 na forswelge me dypan ł grund nene
pestas aquae Neque obsorbeat me profundum neque

genyrwe ofer me pit ł seæð muð hira gehier me
urgeat super me puteus os suum 17. *Exaudi me*

drihten forðan medema ł estelic is mildheortnes ðin efter
domine quoniam benigna est misericordia tua secundum

manege mildsunge þinra locæ on me Ne
multitudinem miserationum tuarum respice in me 18. *Ne*

æhwyrfæ þu ænsiene ðine from cnihte þinum forðæn
avertas faciem tuam a puero tuo quoniam

ic eom geeærfoðod hredlice gehier me beheæld Sawle
tribulor velociter exaudi me 19. *Intende anime*

mine 7 gefriolsæ hie fore fiondum minum genere me
meae et libera eam propter inimicos meos eripe me

ðu soðlice wæst edwit min gescindnesse 7
20. *Tu enim scis inproperium meum confusionem et*

scæmæ mine on gesigðe þinræ sindon eællæ
verecundiam meam 21. *in conspectu tuo sunt omnes*

swencende me edwit ł hosp onbad heorte min 7 yrmðe
tribulantes me Inproperium expectavit cor meum et miseriam

7 ic þolode se þæ somed mid me weron geunrotsod 7 ne wes
et sustinui qui simul mecum contristaretur et non fuit

frefrende me þone ic sohte 7 ne gemette 7
et consolantem me quesivi et non inveni 22. *Et*

hy seælden on mete minum geæłłæn 7 on ðurste mine drincten
dederunt in escam meam fel et in siti mea potaverunt

me mid ecede beo bord ł mese hieræ beforan him on
me aceto 23. *Fiat mensa eorum coram ipsis in*

grine 7 on eadleæningæ 7 on beswice Æðystrode sien
laqueum et in retributionem et in scandalum 24. *Obscurentur*

ł storm add. by Cor. *wetræs, s* add. by Cor. *7 na forswelge* by Cor. in pl.
of er. About two lett. (gloss to *pro-*?) er. bef. *dypan*. *ł grund* add. by Cor.
genyrwe by Cor. on er. *pit ł* add. by Cor. 17. *gehier, i* dotted; fin. let.
er. *medema ł* add. by Cor. *ðin,* fin. -*re* er. ? *manege* by Cor. in pl. of er.
-*deunge* by Cor. prps. on er. 18. *þu* add. by Cor. -*ene,* fin. *e* add. by Cor.
gehier, fin. let. (*e?*) er. 20. *edwit,* fin. let. (*e?*) er.; er. (on?) bef. this
word. *min,* fin. let. er. 21. *swencende* by Cor. on er. *edwit,* fin. *e* er.;
er. (on?) bef. this word. *ł hosp* add. by Cor. *onbad* prob. orig. = *onbæd.*
yrmðe, ðe add. by Cor.; er. aft. this word. *ic þolode* by Cor. on er. *se* add.
by Cor. *somed, o* by Cor. from *e?*; *d* from ð. *mid, d* from ð. -*otsod* by Cor.
on er. 22. *hy seælden, hy* and fin. *n* add. by Cor. ? *on ðurste* by Cor. in pl.
of er. -*ten* add. by Cor. *mid* by Cor. wr. over the line. 23. *beo bord ł*
mese by Cor. in pl. of er. *grine,* two init. lett. er. ? *be-, e* from *i* by Cor. ?
24. -*rode, d* from ð.

eægæn hioræ ꝥ hi ne gesion 7 hricg hira simle gebyged
oculi eorum ne videant et dorsum illorum semper incurva

Ægiot ofer hi yrræ ðin 7 abylgnes yrres ðines
25. *Effunde super eos iram tuam et indignatio irae tuae*

gegripe hie Sy eærdung hiræ awest 7 on eardung-
apprehendat eos **26.** *Fiat habitatio eorum deserta et in taberna-*

stowum hira ne sie ðe oneardige Forðæn ðone ðu
culis eorum non sit qui inhabitet **27.** *Quoniam quem tu*

sloge hie hehtende sinðon me 7 ofer sær wundæ
percussisti ipsi persecuti sunt et super dolorem vulnerum

minræ hy geyhton Tosete unrihtwisnesse ofer unriht-
eorum addiderunt **28.** *Appone iniquitatem super iniqui-*

wisnesse hiræ ꝥ hy na ingan on þine rihtwisnesse
tatem ipsorum et non intrent in tuam iustitiam

Sien hy adilgode of bocum lifiendræ 7 mid rihtwisum ne
29. *Deleantur de libro viventium et cum iustis non*

bíon hy awriten þeærfæ 7 særi ic eom 7 helo ænsiene
scribantur **30.** *Pauper et dolens ego sum et salus vultus*

ðine god onfeng me Ic herie næmæn godes mines mid
tui deus suscepit me **31.** *Laudabo nomen dei mei cum*

sange 7 ic miclige hine on lófe 7 licæð gode ofer
cantico et magnificabo eum in laude **32.** *Et placebit deo super*

ceælf geong ł niwe hornæs forðledende 7 neglæs ł clawa
vitulum novellum cornua producentem et ungulas

Gesion ðeærfen 7 blissigen secæþ drihten 7 lifað saule
33. *Videant pauperes et laetentur querite dominum et vivet anima*

eowra Forðæn gehirde ðeærſæn drihten 7 gebundene
vestra **34.** *Quoniam exaudivit pauperes dominus et vinctos*

his he ne forhygoda herigen hienc hefonæs 7 eorðe sê
suos non sprevit **35.** *Laudent eum caeli et terra mare*

ꝥ *hi ne gesion* by Cor. on er.   25. *abylgnes, a* orig. *æ*; *-ylgnes* by Cor.
yrres, s add. by Cor. *gegripe,* fin. let. er.; 7 er. bef. this word.   26. *sy* by
Cor. on er. *awest* by Cor. in pl. of er.? *-ung-,* fin. *e* er.?; *-stowum* prob. add.
by Cor. *ðe* add. by Cor. *-ige* by Cor. on er.   27. Er. (gloss to *per-*?) bef.
sloge. me, the Latin to this is er. *hy geyhton* by Cor. on er.   28. *unriht-*
wisnesse by Cor. on er. (twice). ꝥ *hy na ingan* by Cor. in pl. of er. *rihtwis-*
nesse by Cor. on er.   29. *hy adilgode* by Cor. in pl. of er. *of, f* by Cor.
(altered from *b*?). *rihtwisum* by Cor. on er. *hy awriten* by Cor. on er.
30. *særi, i* prps. add. by Cor. *-ene,* fin. *e* add. by Cor. *ðine, e* add. by Cor.
31. *-es* add. by Cor. (twice). *-lige, g* from *e* by orig. scribe.   32. *gode, e*
add. by Cor. *geong ł* add. by Cor. *-ledende* by Cor. on er. *ł clawa* add. by
Cor. 33. *-gen* by Cor. on er. *-að* by Cor. on er. *eowra* orig. = *eowræ.*
34. *-de* by Cor. on er. *forhygoda* by Cor. in pl. of er.   35. *-en* by Cor. on er

7 eallæ ða on him sindon   Forðon god hale gedeþ
et omnia quae in eis sunt   **36.** *Quoniam deus salvam faciet*

Sion 7 bioð getimbreðe ceæster iudeæ 7 oneærdiæþ ðer 7
syon et aedificabuntur civitates iudae et inhabitabunt ibi Et

yrfweærðnæssæ hy secæð hy   7 sæd þeowæ his
haereditate adquirunt eam   **37.** *et semen servorum eius*

agun ł besittað hy 7 ðæ ðæ lufieð næmæ his oneærdiæð
possidebunt eam et qui diligunt nomen eius inhabitabunt

on hire
in ea

69.

god on fultum   mine beheæld drihten 7 to gefultomiende
2. *Deus in adiutorium meum intende domine   ad adiuvandum*

me efste   Sien gesciende 7 forwandian ł scunian
me festina   **3.** *Confundantur et   revereantur*

fiend mine þa ðæ secæð sæule mine   Sien gecirde
inimici mei qui querunt animam meam   **4.** *Avertantur*

on bæcling 7 scæmiæn ðæ þe þencæd me yfel Sien gecirrede
retrorsum et erubescant qui cogitant michi mala Avertantur

hræþe 7 scæmiende þa ðe cweðæþ me eowlæ eowlæ
statim et erubescentes qui dicunt michi euge euge

biehtæð 7 blissiæd þa þe secæþ ðe dryhten 7 cweðæð
5. *Exultent et laetentur qui querunt te domine et dicant*

simle si gemiclod drihten þæ þe luħgað helo þine
semper magnificetur dominus qui diligunt salutare tuum

Ic soðlice wędlæ 7 þearfa eom god fylste me Fultomond
6. *Ego vero egenus et pauper sum deus adiuva me Adiutor*

min 7 friolsiend ł alysend min ært ðu drihten ne letæ þu
meus et liberator meus es tu domine ne tardaveris

70.

God on þe ic gewene drihten ne bio ic scended on eacnes
Deus in te speravi domine ne confundar in aeternum

36. *hale*, a orig. = æ; fin. *e* by Cor. *hy* by Cor. on er. (twice). 37. *sæd*
by Cor. on er. *agun* ł add. by Cor. *hy* by Cor. on er. *lufieð*, orig. = *lufiæð*.
hire, *e* by Cor. in pl. of er.   69. 3. *forwandian* ł *scunian* by Cor. 4.
þe add. by Cor. *þa* orig. = *þæ*. *ðe* add. by Cor. 5. *þa* orig. = *þæ*. *þine* by
Cor. on er. 6. *fylste me* by Cor. in pl. of er. ł *alysend* add. by Cor. *ært*
by Cor. on er. *letæ* orig. = *lætæ*.   70. *ne bio ic scended* by Cor. on er.

on þinre rihtwisnesse gefriolse me 7 genere me Onhyld to
2. *in   tua   iustitia   libera   me et eripe me Inclina ad*

me eæræ þin 7 gefrilsæ ł alys me   beo ðu me on
me aurem tuam et   libera   me   3. esto michi in

god   scildend 7 on stowe getrymede þet þu halne me   do
deum protectorem et in locum munitum ut   salvum me facias

Forðæn   trymnes   min 7 gescild ł gener min ært þu
Quoniam firmamentum meum et   refugium   meum es   tu

god min genere me of hande firænfulra synfulles 7 of hænde
4. *deus meus eripe me de manu   peccatoris   et de manu*

ongean æwe ł æ dondes 7 unrihtwises   Forðæn þu eært
contra   legem   agentis et   iniqui   5. Quoniam tu es

geðyld   min drihten hyht min fram giogædhæde minum
patientia mea domine spes mea   a   iuventute   mea

On þe ic eom getriemed of innoþe of wambe l innoðe
6. *In te confirmatus sum   ex   utero de   ventre*

modor minre þu eart min scildend on þe sang min
matris meae tu es   meus protector in te decantatio mea

simle   Swa swa foretacen ic eom geworðen monegum 7
semper   7. Tanquam prodigium   factus sum ·   multis et

þu fultumend strang   Sie gefillæd muð min of lofe þin þet
tu adiutor fortis   8. Repleatur os meum laude tua ut

ic mege singæn wuldor þin æle deg   micelnes ðin
possim cantare gloriam tuam tota die magnificentiam tuam

Ne awiorp þu me on tyde   yldo   midþi ðe ateorað
9. *Ne proicias me in tempore senectutis   dum   defecerit*

megen min ne forlet ðu me   Forðæn cweðon fiend
virtus mea ne derelinquas me   10. Quia dixerunt inimici

mine yfel me 7 þa ðe gehioldon sæwle mine geðeæhtunge
mei mala michi et qui custodiebant animam meam   consilium

---

2. *rihtwisnesse* by Cor. on er.   ł *alys* add. by Cor.   3. *beo* by Cor. on er.
getrymede prob. by Cor. on er.   þu add. by Cor.   *halne* orig. = *hælne*. About
two lett. er. immed. bef. *do.*   *min* (1st), fin. let. er.   ł *gener* added by Cor.
ært þu by Cor. in pl. of er.   4. *of, f* by Cor. from some other let. (twice).
synfulles add. by Cor.   *hænde*, fin. *e* add. by Cor. ł   *ongean* by Cor. on er.
ł *æ* add. by Cor.   *dondes* by Cor. on er.   Er. after 7.   *-wises* by Cor. on er.
6. *of* (1st), *f* by Cor. from some other let.   *of* (2nd) by Cor. on er.   ł *innoðe*
add. by Cor.   MS. = *scildend min*, but marked for transpos.; MS. = *protector
meus* also marked for transpos.   *sang*, about two init. lett. er.; *a* orig. = *æ*;
fin. let. er.   *min*, a fin. er. made.   7. *Swa* (1st) orig. = *swæ.*   *swa* (2nd) add.
by Cor.   *-cen* prob. by Cor. on er.   8. *æle* by Cor. on er.   *deg, g* from ł prob.
by Cor.   9. *awiorp* orig. = *æwiorp.*   *ateorað* by Cor. on er.   10. *cweðon,*
ℕ by Cor. on er. of another let.   *þa ðe* by Cor. in pl. of er.

hy didon on   æn   Cwæðonde god   forlet   hine
fecerunt in unum   **11.** *Dicentes deus dereliquit eum*

fylgæð ł ehtað 7   gegripæþ   hine forþan ne   is   se genere
persequimini et comprehendite eum quia non est qui eripiat

hine   god ne afiorre þu fram me   god min on
eum   **12.** *Deus ne elonges a me deus meus in*

fultome minne locæ   Sien gescinde 7   geteregien
auxilium meum respice   **13.** *Confundantur et deficiant*

telende   saule mine syn oferwrigene gescindnesse 7 scæme
detrahentes animae meae operiantur confusione et pudore

þæ þe secæð yfele me   Ic eallengæ simle on ðe
qui querunt mala michi   **14.** *Ego autem semper in te*

ic gewene drihten 7   ic yce ofer eællæ   lóf   þin
sperabo domine et adiciam super omnem laudem tuam

Muð min forecyðen scal rihtwisnesse þine æle deg   helo
15. *Os meum pronuntiabit iustitiam tuam tota die salutare*

ðine Forðæn ic ne oncnew ceæpunga   ic ingange
tuum Quia non cognovi negotiationes   **16.** *introibo*

on mihte drihten dryhten ic gemindig beo rihtwisnesse þine
in potentias domini Domine memorabor iustitiae tuae

ænre   god þu lerdest me from giogæðhædæ minum
solius   **17.** *deus docuisti me a iuventute mea*

7 oððe nu ic cyðe wundru ðine   7 oððe on
et usque nunc pronuntiabo mirabilia tua   **18.** *et usque in*

yldo 7 yldrene god ne forlet þu . me Oððet ic cyðæ ł bodige
senectam et senium deus ne derelinquas me Donec annuntiem

eærm ðinne cneowrisse ælcre þe toweærd is Mihte
brachium tuum genera[ti]oni omni quae ventura est Potentiam

ðin   7 rihtwisnesse þin god oððet on þa hyhstan
tuam   **19.** *et iustitiam tuam deus usque in altissima*

---

11. *god,* fin. let. er.   *forlet,* about two fin. lett. er. ?   *ł ehtað* add. by Cor.
forþan on er. by Cor. ?   *genere,* fin. *e* add. by Cor. ?   12. *ne* on er. by Cor. ?
-re þu add. by Cor.   13. *ges-, s* add. by Cor. over the line.   *geteregien
telende* by Cor. in pl. of er.   *saule, e* add. by Cor.   *syn oferwrigene* by Cor. on
er.   14. *ic yce* by Cor. on er.   15. *-en* by Cor. in pl. of er.   *scal* by Cor.
rihtwisnesse þine æle by Cor. on er.   *deg,* fin. let. er.   *ic* prob. add. by Cor.
16. *ic* (2nd) by Cor. on er.   *beo* prob. by Cor.   *rihtwisnesse* by Cor. on er.
ænre, re add. by Cor. ?   17. *oððe, a* fin. let. (t ?) er.   *ic* by Cor. on er.   *-ru*
by Cor. on er.   *ðine, e* add. by Cor.   18. *oððe,* fin. let. (t ?) er.   7 er. bef.
cyðæ. ł bodige add. by Cor.   *-risse, e* add. by Cor.   *ælcre þe* by Cor. on er.
ðin, a fin. let. er.   19. *rihtwisnesse* by Cor. on er.   *þin,* fin. let. (e ?) er.   *þa*
(1st), fin. let. (m ?) er.

þa þu worhtes miclan   god hwilc gelic þe   hu
quae   fecisti   magnalia deus quis similis tibi   **20.**

monige þu iewdest me   eærfoþnesse ł geswin[c] monige 7
Quantas   ostendisti michi   tribulationes   multas et

yfela 7 gehwyrfed þu geliffestedest me 7 of niowolnesse ł grunde
malas et conversus   vivificasti   me et de   abyssis

eorðæn eft þu geleddest me   ðu gemonigfaldodest
*terrae iterum   reduxisti   me   **21.** Multiplicasti*

rihtwisnesse ðine 7 gehwierfed þu lærdest me   7 ic
*iustitiam   tuam et conversus   exortatus es me   **22.** et ego*

ændette þe on fatum salmesængæ soðfestnesse þine ic singe
confitebor tibi in vasis   psalmorum   veritatem   tuam psallam

þe on heærpæn god hælig isræhele   Gefioþ
*tibi in cythara deus sanctus   israel   **23.** Gaudebunt*

weleræs mine midþi ic singe ðæ 7 sæul mine ðæ þu
labia mea dum cantavero tibi et anima mea quam re-

alisdest   ac 7 tunga min sceal smeagen rihtwisnesse
*demisti   **24.** Sed et lingua mea meditabitur   iustitiam*

ðine þanne gescinde 7 ofscamede bioð ða ðe secæþ yfelu
tuam dum confusi et reveriti fuerint qui querunt mala

me
michi

71.

god   dom   þiune kinege geof 7 rihtwisnesse ðine suna
2. *Deus iudicium tuum   regi   da et iustitiam   tuam fil-*

ł beærn kininges To demænne folc   þin on ðine rihtwisnesse
-io   regis   Iudicare   poþulum tuum in tua   iustitia

7 ðeærfæn ðine on domo   Onfon   muntes ł dunæ
*et pauperes tuos in iudicio   **3.** Suscipiant   montes*

sibbe folces þines 7 hyllæ ł beorgas rihtwisnesse   On
*pacem populo tuo et   colles   iustitiam   **4.** In*

þa (2nd)=orig. þœ. Er. bef. *miclan.*   20. *iewdest,* about two init. lett.
er. ł *geswin* add. by Cor. *yfela, a* add. by Cor. *-dest* (2nd) by Cor. in pl.
of er. ł *grunde* add. by Cor. *-dest* (3rd), *ł* add. by Cor.   21. *rihtwisnesse*
by Cor. on er. *þu lærdest* by Cor. in pl. of er.   22. *fatum salme* by Cor. in pl.
of er.   24. *ac* by Cor. on er. ; Cor. first wrote *œc.* From *sceal* to *-nesse* by Cor.
in pl. of er. *þanne* by Cor. on er. *ofscamede* by Cor. on er. ðe orig. = ðœ.
71. 2. From *kinege* to *-nesse* by Cor. in pl. of er. *suna ł* add. by Cor. *rihtwisnesse* by Cor. on er.   3. *Onfon,* fin. *n* by Cor. on er. let. *muntes ł* add.
by Cor. ł *beorgas* add. by Cor. *rihtwis-* by Cor. on er.

his rihtwisnesse he demð þearfan þyses folces 7 hale he deþ
sua   iustitia   iudicabit   pauperes huius poṗuli et salvos faciet

beærn þeærfænæ 7 geeædmedeþ hearmcweðendre   7
filios   pauperum Et humiliabit   calumṗniatorem   5. et

þurhwuniæþ ṃid sunnan 7 beforæn monam on   world   worulde
permanebit cum   sole et ante   lunam in saeculum saeculi

    7 he adune stah swæ   ren   on ueht Í flys 7 swæ dropunga
6. *Et   descendit   sicut pluvia in   vellus   et sicut stillicidia*

dreopenda ofer eorðæn   asprigð on dagæs his riht-
stillantia super terram   **7.** *Orietur in diebus eius ius-*

wisnesse 7 genihtsumnes sibbe oððet biþ upahauen munæ
titia   et   abundantia   pacis donec   extollatur   luna

    7 he walt from sæ oððet sæ 7 from flode
8. *Et dominabitur a   mari usque ad mare et   a   flumine*

oððet ða uteræn Í gemere ymbhwyrftes eorðe   beforæn
*usque ad   terminos   orbis terrae   **9.** Coram*

him feallað sielhearwæn 7 fiend his eorðen licciæð
illo procident ethyopes et inimici eius terram lingent

    kininges of tarsis 7 iglonde læc brohton kininges
10. *Reges   tharsis et insulae munẹra offerent reges*

of arabe 7 feredæ giefæ togeledæþ   7 gebiddaþ hine
arabum et saba dona adducent   **11.** *Et adorabunt eum*

eællæ kininges of eorðæn eællæ ðῑodæ þeowigæþ him
omnes reges terrae omnes gentes servient ei

    Forðæn he friolsede þeærfæn from mihtige Í ricum 7 wedlen
12. *Quia   liberabit   pauperem a   potente   et inopem*

þæm ne wes fultumend   he aræþ ðeærfan 7 wẹdlen
cui non erat adiutor   **13.** *Parcet pauperi et inopi*

    7 saulæ ðearfanæ hale gedeð   Of   7
et animas pauperum salvas faciet   **14.** *Ex usuris et*

---

4. *rihtwisnesse he demð* by Cor. in pl. of er. *hale*, orig.= *hæle* ; er. bef.
this word. *he* add. by Cor. *-eæd-*, *d* by Cor. on er. let. (þ ?). *-cweðendre* by
Cor. in pl. of er. 5. *worulde* by Cor. 6. *he ɪdune stah* by Cor. in pl. of
er. *ueht Í flys* by Cor. in pl. of er. *dropunga dreopenda* by Cor. in pl. of er.
7. *asprigð* by Cor. on er. *rihtwisnesse* by Cor. ín pl. of er. *geniht-* from
gemiht-? *-ahauen* by Cor. in pl. of er. 8. *he walt* by Cor. in pl. of er. *ða*
orig.= *ðæ*. *Í gemere* add. by Cor. *-hwyrftes*, fin. let. er.? *eorðe* add. by Cor.
9. *feallað* by Cor. on er. *eorðen*, *n* add. by Cor. 10. *on* er. bef. *iglonde*?
of tarsis add. by Cor.; misplaced but marked to follow *kininges*. *of arabe*
by Cor. in pl. of er. 11. *-biddaþ* by Cor. on er. *of* add. by Cor. 12. *he*
add. by Cor. *friol-*, init. *ge-* er. *Í ricum* add. by Cor. *wedlen*, about two
init. and two fin. lett. er. 13. *wẹdlen*, init. *on-* er.; second *e* from *i*; three
or four fin. lett. er. *hale* orig.= *hæle*. 14. Gloss to *usuris* er.

unrihtwisnesse he scal gefreolsen sæwlæ hiræ 7 byrht
iniquitate   liberabit   animas eorum et preclarum

noma hiræ beforæn him   7 he liofæd 7 bið seælð
nomen eorum coram ipso   15. Et vivet et dabitur

him of golde arabie 7 weorðiað be him simle alne dege
ei de auro arabiae et adorabunt de ipso semper tota die

bletsiæð hine   7 bið trymnes on eorðæn on
benedicent eum   16. Et erit firmamentum in terra in

hyhþo dunæ ɫ munta ofer bið áhauen ofer libanum westm
summis montium super extolletur super libanum fructus

his 7 blosmiæð be ðere ceæstre swæ hieg eorðen
eius et florebunt de civitate sicut faenum terrae

. 7 bið næmæ his gebletsæd on worolde 7 beforæn sunnæn
17. Et erit nomen eius benedictum in secula ante solem

ðurhwunaþ nomæ his 7 beforæn monæn setle his 7 blet-
permanebit nomen eius et ante lunam sedes eius Et bene-

siæþ on him ealla megþæ eorþan eallæ ðioda micliæþ
dicentur in eo omnes tribus terrae omnes gentes magnificabunt

hine   gebletsod dryhten god isræhele se dyð
eum   18. Benedictus dominus deus israel qui facit

wundor micele ænæ   7 gebletsod næmæ megen-
mirabilia magna solus   19. et benedictum nomen maies-

þrymmes his on ecnesse 7 on world æworld 7 gefilled beoð
tatis eius in aeternum et in seculum seculi Et replebitur

megenðrym his eællæ eorðæ sie sie
maiestate eius omnis terra fiat fiat

72.

hwu god god israele þisum ðe rihte sindon heortæn
Quam bonus deus israel his qui recto sunt corde

min soðlice fulneh stired sindon fet fulneh ægotene sindon
2. mei autem paene moti sunt pedes paene effusi sunt

Let. er. bef. *un-* ; *-wis-* add. by Cor. *he scal* add. by Cor. *gefreolsen*, second
e from *i*; *n* add. by Cor. Er. aft. 7. *byrht*, fin. let. (or lett.) er. *noma*, fin.
n er. 15. *he* add. by Cor.; misplaced but marked to precede *liofæd*.
arabie orig. = *æræbie* ? *weorðiað* by Cor. on er. *alns* by Cor. on er. 16. *ɫ*
munta add. by Cor. *áhauen* by Cor. on er. *libanum* by Cor. on er. *westm*,
fin. let. er. ? *hieg*, *i* dotted. 17. *næmæ*, fin. *n* er. 18. *-sod*, let. er.
betw. *s* and *o*; *d* from *ð*. *dyð*, fin. let. er.; *ð* from *d* by Cor. 19. *-sod*, *d*
from *ð*. *-mes* add. by Cor. *beoð* add. by Cor. 72. *hwu god* by Cor. ?
israele add. by Cor. ? *ðe* add. by Cor. ? 2. *soðlice fulneh* by Cor. in pl. of er.

stiepæs mine   Forðæn geelnode on firenfullan sibbe
gressus mei   3. *Quia   zelavi   in peccatoribus pacem*

firenfulræ ł synfullum gesionde   Forðan ne is
peccatorum   videns   4. *Quia   non est*

onhyldnes deæðe hioræ ne   trumnes on wite hioræ
declinatio morti eorum nec firmamentum. in plaga eorum

On gewinnum ł swincum monnæ ne syndon 7 mid
5. *In   laboribus   hominum non sunt et cum*

monnum ne bioð swungene   Forðæn hyold hie
*hominibus non flagellabuntur   6. *Ideo   tenuit eos*

oferhyd hiora oferwrigen sindon of unrihtnesse 7 ærleas-
superbia eorum operti   sunt iniquitate   et impie-

neæssa his   Forðresde swæ swa of fetnisse unrihtwisnesse
*tate sua   7. *Prodiit quasi ex adipe   iniquitas*

hiora hy ferðon on tosetednesse heortæn   hy þohtæn
*eorum transierunt in dispositionem cordis   8. *cogitaverunt*

7 hy sprecen heteniþ unrihtwisnesse on hyhþo hio sprecen
et locuti sunt nequitiam iniquitatem in excelso locuti sunt

hy setton on hefon muð hieræ 7 tunga hiræ foreð
9. *Posuerunt in caelum os suum et lingua eorum transivit*

ofer eorþæn   Forðan cyrreð hider folc min
*super terram   10. *Ideo revertetur huc populus meus*

7 dagas fulle beoð gefundon on him   7 hy cweðon
*et dies pleni invenientur in eis   11. *Et   dixerunt*

hú   wiste god 7 gif is wisdom on heahnesse   Gesieh
*quomodo scivit deus et si est scientia in excelso   12. *Ecce*

hie senfulle 7 genihtsumiende on worolde hafedon ł begeton
ipsi peccatores et abundantes   in seculo   obtinuerunt

---

3. ł *synfullum* add. by Cor.   4. *Forðan, a* orig. = *æ. deæðe, ð* from *d*
by Cor.; fin. *e* prps. by Cor. in pl. of about two (or three) er. lett. *wite, e* by
Cor. on er.   5. ł *swincum* add. by Cor.   6. *hyold* by Cor. on er. *ofer-
worigen* by Cor. on er. *of* add. by Cor.   7. *Forðresde* by Cor. in pl. of er.
swa add. by Cor. *of, f* by Cor. from some other let. *fetnisse* by Cor. in pl.
of er. -*wisnesse* by Cor. in pl. of er. *hy* add. by Cor. *tosetednesse* by Cor.
on er.   8. *hy* add. by Cor. (twice). *sprecen,* fin. *de* er. ; er. aft. this word.
unrihtwisnesse add. by Cor. *hio* add. by Cor. *sprecen,* fin. *de* er. ; er. aft.
this word.   9. *hy* add. by Cor. *foreð,* or *fereð* ; -*eð* on er. prps. by Cor.
10. -*reð* by Cor. on er. *hider* by Cor. in pl. of er. *dagas fulle beoð* by Cor.
on er. -*fundon* by Cor. on er.   11. *hy* add. by Cor. *cweðon, w* from *þ* by
orig. scribe ; *ð* from *d* by Cor. *wiste* by Cor. on er. *gif* by Cor. on er.
heahnesse by Cor. on er.   12. *hie senfulle* by Cor. on er. Er. (gloss to *ab-* ?)
immed. bef. *genihtsumiende* ; -*iende* by Cor. in pl. of er. *hafedon* ł *begeton*
by Cor. in pl. of er.

welæn   7 ic cweð soðlice butan intingæn ic rihtwisode
divicias   **13.** *Et dixi   ergo   sine   causa   iustificavi*

hiorte   mine   7 ic þwoh betweoxen unscyldige handæ mine
cor   meum   et   lavi   inter   innocentes   manus meas

        7 ic wes swungæn æle dege 7 becniend min on uhtlicum
14. *et fui flagellatus tota die et index meus in matu-*

ł degrede   Gif ic cwiðe ic seige swæ efne nu cyðnesse
tino   **15.** *Si dicebam narrabo sic   ecce   natio*

bearna   þinræ   þæm ic gesette   Ic wende   ðæt
filiorum tuorum quibus disposui   **16.** *Existimabam ut*

ic oncnæwæ ðis geswinc is beforæn me   oþþet ic
cognoscerem hoc · labor est ante me   **17.** *donec in-*

ingængæ   on hælignesse godes 7 ic ongete on endas
trem   in sanctuarium dei et intellegam in novissima

hioræ   Soðlice ł þah hweþre fore   sær þu gestigtodest
eorum   **18.**   *Veruntamen   propter dolos   disposuisti*

him yfelu þu æwurpe hie   upahafone weron   hu
eis mala deiecisti   eos dum   allevarentur   **19.** *Quo-*

        gewordene beoð on forletnesse ferlice hie terogoden 7
modo   facti   sunt   in desolationem subito   defecerunt   et

forwurðon   fore   unrihtwisnesse here   swa swa from
perierunt propter iniquitates suas   **20.**   *velut   som-*

slepe arisende drihten on ceæstre þine onlicnesse hiræ to
nio exsurgentes Domine in civitate tua imagines eorum ad

nahte   þu hwirfest   Forðæn gelustfullod is min
nichilum   rediges   **21.** *Quia   delectatum est cor*

heorte 7 eþræn mine æliesde sindon   7 ic to nauhte
meum et renes mei resoluti sunt   **22.** *et ego ad nichilum*

gebeged ł tohworfen ic æm 7 ic ne wiste   Swæ swæ
redactus   sum et   nescivi   **23.**   *Ut*

---

13. ic add. by Cor. cweð, fin. let. er. soðlice by Cor. in pl. of er. ic
rihtwisode by Cor. in pl. of er. *þwoh, -oh* by Cor. in pl. of er. *-oxen unscyldige* by Cor. in pl. of er.   14. *wes* by Cor. in pl. of er. *æle* by Cor. in pl.
of er. *becniend* by Cor. in pl. of er. *ł degrede* add. by Cor.   15. *efne nu*
by Cor. on er. *-nesse, se* add. by Cor.   16. *wende* by Cor. from *gewene* ł
geswinc, s wr. over the line by Cor.; *c* add. by Cor.; orig. = *gewinn.*   17. *ic*
add. by Cor. MS. = *ongængæ, o* dotted, and *i* wr. above the *o* prob. by Cor.;
fin. *n* er. *endas* by Cor. in pl. of er.   18. *ł* prob. add. by Cor. *þah hweþre,
þah-* from *þon* by Cor.; *n* er. after *e*. *-est, ł* add. by Cor. *yfelu, u* add. by
Cor. -e *up-* by Cor. on er. *-ahafone* orig. = *æhæfone.*   19. From *beoð* to
-oden by Cor. in pl. of er. *-wurð-, ð* from *d* by Cor. *-wisnesse* by Cor. on er.
-ere by Cor. on er.   20. *swa swa* by Cor. on er. *-nesse, se* add. by Cor.
nahte þu by Cor.   21. *eþræn, n* add. by Cor.   22. From *ge-* to *æm* by
Cor. on er.; *c* (of *ic*) wr. over the line. 7 on er.

nieten geworden ic eom mid ðæ 7 ic efre ł simle mid þe
iumentum factus sum apud te et ego semper tecum

þu hylde ł name hand swiðran mine 7 on willon
24. *Tenuisti manum dexteram meam et in voluntate*

þinum þu geleddest me 7 mid wuldræ þu genume me
tua deduxisti me et cum gloria adsumpsisti me

hwet soðlice me to lafe stondæt on hefonum 7 from ðe
25. *Quid enim michi restat in caelo et a te*

hwet wolde ic ofer eorðæn   Ateoroðe ł æspræng heorte
quid volui super terram   26.   *Defecit cor*

min 7 flesc min god heorte min 7 diel min god on werolde
meum et caro mea deus cordis mei et pars mea deus in saecula

Forðæn eællenga þæ ðe afeorriað hie from þe forwiorþæþ
27. *Quia ecce qui elongant se a te peribunt*

ðu forspilst eællæ þa ðe forligriað from þe   me
perdes omnes qui fornicantur abs te   28. *Michi*

soðlice togeþeodon gode god is setton on drihten god hyht
autem adherere deo bonum est ponere in domino deo spem

minne þet ic sege ł bodige eællæ lof þine on gatum
meam Ut annuntiem omnes laudes tuas in portis

dohtor ł bearn syon
filiae syon

73.

Towan onweg þu ædrife ł neddest us god on ende yrre
Ut quid reppulisti nos deus in finem iratus

is hatheor[t]nesse ðin ofer sceæp ewedes þines ge-
est furor tuus super oves gregis tui 2. *Me-*

myne gesamnungæ þinre þæ ðu gesceope from frumæn þu
mento congregationis tuae quam creasti ab initio

friolsedest ł alysdest gierde yrfeweærdnesse ðin munt sion on
Liberasti virgam haereditatis tuae mons syon in

---

23. *efre* ł add. by Cor.   24. From *þu* to *mine* by Cor.; *þ* (of *þu*) from *h.*
-est, t add. by Cor. Er. (gloss to *ad-* ?) bef. *genume*.   25. *soðlice me to lafe*
by Cor. on er. *wolde* altered by Cor. from *wile*. *is* add. by Cor.   26. *Ateo-*
rode ł add. by Cor. *diel, i* dotted.   27. *ðe* add. by Cor. (twice). *afeorriað*
hie by Cor. on er. *-st* by Cor. on er. ? *forligriað* add. by Cor.   28. *toge-*
þeodon by Cor. on er. *ł bodige* add. by Cor. *þine, e* add. by Cor. *dohtor ł*
add. by Cor.   73. *onweg* add. by Cor. *ł neddest* add. by Cor. *hatheornesse*
by Cor. in pl. of er.   2. *þu* add. by Cor. *-dest ł alysdest* add. by Cor.
sion by Cor.

þæm þu eærdeast on ꝥ silfum   Upæhefe   hænd   ðine
quo   habitas   in id ipsum   3. *Eleva   manum   tuam*

on oferhyde hiræ on ende hu monega awarigede sio fiond
in superbiam eorum in finem   quanta   malignatus est inimicus

on hælgum þinum   7 wuldrode bioð ðæ þe hatedon
in sanctis   tuis   4. *et gloriati   sunt qui te oderunt*

on midlene cafertunes þines hio setton tæcn here tæcn   7
in medio   atrio   tuo Posuerunt signa sua signa   5. *et*

ne   oncnewon   swæ on wege ofer   heahne   swæ on wudæ
non cognoverunt sicut in via supra summum · quasi in silva

treowæ mid Exum   hy æcurfon duræ   his on þet
lignorum Securibus   6. *exciderunt ianuas eius in id*

selfe mid twibille 7 adese hy æwurpon hy   hy On-
ipsum bipennae et ascia deiecerunt eam   7. *In-*

ęldon ɫ berndon mid fire   hælgunge   þin on eorðæn
cenderunt   igne   sanctuarium tuum in terra

besmiten ɫ befylden eærdung ɫ teld noman ðinum   hy
polluerunt   tabernaculum nominis tui   8.

Cweðon on heortan hiræ kyð ɫ cneoris hira betwiox hie
Dixerunt in   corde   suo   cognatio eorum inter se

cumað forðreccen we eælle dægæs symbel drihten from eorðæn
venite comprimamus omnes dies festos domini   a   terra

   Tacn   ura   ne gesegon we nu   ne is witegæ 7 us
9. *Signa nostra non vidimus iam non est propheta et nos*

ne oncneweð   mæ   hwu lange god edwitæþ
non cognoscet amplius   10. *Usque quo deus inproperabit*

   fiond onlexð bysmrað wiðerwerdæ namæn ðyn on ende
inimicus   irritat adversarius nomen tuum in finem

   Towon gehwirfest þu onsine þine 7 swiðre ðin on
11. *Ut quid   avertis   faciem tuam et dexteram tuam de*

-east, e dotted by Cor.; orig. = -eæst.   Er. (of three lett.?) immed. aft. þ
wh. is from þ by Cor.   3. monega, o from e by orig. scribe. awarigede sio
by Cor. in pl. of er.   4. -ode by Cor. on er. bioð add. by Cor. hatedon by
Cor. on er. hio add. by Cor. here, first e from i; re by Cor. on er. 5. heahne
by Cor. on er. mid by Cor.; misplaced but marked to precede Exum. 6. hy
(1st and 2nd) add. by Cor. adese orig. = adesœ. hy (last), y by Cor. on er.
7. hy add. by Cor. ɫ berndon mid add. by Cor. fire, e add. by Cor.; er. aft.
this word. hæl-, init. ge er.? þin, about two fin. lett. (re?) er. besmiten, fin.
e er. ɫ befylden add. by Cor. ɫ teld add. by Cor.   8. hy add. by Cor.
Cweðon, ð from d by Cor. ɫ cneoris by Cor. in pl. of er. From -ox to we by
Cor. in pl. of er.   9. Tacn orig. = Tæcn. -segon altered by Cor. from something else. we add. by Cor.   10. hwu lange by Cor. on er. onlexð underlined. bysmrað by Cor. wiðerwerdæ, ð from d by Cor.; fin. let. er.   11. To
won, h er. betw. o and w. þu add. by Cor. onsine, e add. by Cor. þine or þinę?

middewærde bearme þine on ende   god soðlice kining
medio   sinu   tuo in finem   12. *Deus autem   rex*

ure ær worlde wrohte   helo on midle eorðæn   þu
noster ante saecula operatus est salutem in medio terrae   13. *Tu*

getrimedest on megene ðinum sæ þu swenctest heafdæ
confirmasti in virtute tua mare tu contribulasti capita

dræcænæ ofer weter   þu gebrece heafod dræcæn
draconum super aquas   14. *Tu confregisti caput draconis*

miceles 7 þu seældest him on mete folce on wędlingum
magni et dedisti eum in escam populo   ethyopum

    ðu   toslite willen 7 rinnellæn ł burnan þu adrigdest
15. *Tu dirrupisti fontes et   torrentes   tu exsiccasti*

flodes ł streæmas of ethæm   þin is dei 7 þin is
    fluvios   etham   16. *Tuus est dies et tua est*

niht þu geworhtes sunnæn 7 monæn   þu worhtes
nox tu fecisti   solem et lunam   17. *tu fecisti*

eælle gemere of eorðe sumer 7 leinten ðu geworhtest þa
omnes terminos terrae estatem et ver tu fecisti   ea

    beo ðu gemindig ðisse gesceafte ðinre fiond   ædwitede
18. *Memor esto huius creaturae tuae inimicus inproperavit*

drihten 7 folc unsnotor gremede ł scunede næmæn ðinne
domino et populus insipiens exacerbavit   nomen tuum

    Ne sele þu wildiorum sawlæ andettende ðe saule
19. *Ne tradas bestiis animam confitentem tibi animas*

ðeærfæne dinræ ne ofergit þu on ende   Lócæ on
pauperum tuorum ne obliviscaris in finem   20. *Respice in*

kiðnesse dinre forðæn gefilde sindon ðæ ðe æðistrode sindon
testamentum tuum quia repleti sunt qui obscurati sunt

eorðe husæ unrihtwisnesse   Ne sie ł bio acerred
terrae domorum iniquitatum 21. *Ne avertatur*

-*dewærde bearme* by Cor. in pl. of er. *þine, e* add. by Cor.   12. *soðlice*
by Cor. on er. *ær* by Cor. on er. *worlde* orig. = *worldæ*. *wrohte* by Cor. on
er.   13. -*dest, t* add. by Cor. *sæ* by Cor. on er. *swenctest* by Cor. on er.
MS. = *dræcænæ heafdæ*, but marked for transpos.   14. -*est, t* add. by Cor.
folce, e add. by Cor.?   15. *willen, n* prob. add. by Cor. *t burnan* add. by
Cor. *adrigdest, a* orig. = *æ* ; *gd* by Cor. from other lett.; *est* by Cor. *flodes*
t add. by Cor. *of* add. by Cor.   17. *of* add. by Cor. *eorðe sumer 7 leinten*
by Cor. on er. -*t þa* by Cor. on er.   18. *beo* by Cor. on er. ł *ædwitede* by
Cor. on er. *gremede* by Cor. on er. *t scunede* add. by Cor. *ðinne* by Cor.
from *ðinum* !   19. *and-* by Cor. on er. *ofergit,* about four fin. lett. er. ; *þu*
by Cor. in pl. of them.   20. *gefilde, d* prob. from *ð. ðe* add. by Cor. -*wis-*
nesse by Cor. on er.   21. -*e t bio acerred* by Cor. in pl. of er.

K

eæðmod geworden gescynd þeærfa 7 wedle herigað nomæn
humilis   factus   confusus pauper et inops laudabunt nomen

þine   Aris   god dem intingæn ðinnæ gemyndig
tuum   **22.** *Exurge deus iudica causam tuam   memor*

beo þu   on edwite   ðinræ   þare ðe fram unsnotre sindon
esto inproperiorum tuorum eorum quae ab insipiente sunt

æle deg   Ne ofergit þu stemfne secende þe ofermodi-
tota die   **23.** *Ne obliviscaris voces querentium te*

nesse 1 oferhyd hiræ ða þe fiogædon æstigæþ simle to þe
superbia   eorum qui te oderunt ascendat semper ad te

74.

we ondetteð þe god we ondettæþ þe 7 we cigæð 1 clypieð
2. *Confitebimur tibi deus confitebimur tibi et   invocabimus*

nomæn ðinne Ic sege 1 cyðe eælle wundor þine   mydþi
nomen tuum   Narrabo   omnia mirabilia tua   3. dum

Ic onfo   tid   ic rihtwisnesse deme   gemolten is
accepero tempus ego iustitiam iudicabo   4. Liquefacta est

eorðe 7 eælle oneardende on hire ic getrimmede swioras
terra et omnes inhabitantes in ea ego confirmavi columnas

hire   Ic cweð to ða unrihtwisum nellen ge unrihte don
eius   **5.** *Dixi   iniquis   nolite   inique agere*

7 ðam agiltendum nelleð ge upahebben horn   Nellen ge
et delinquentibus nolite exaltare cornu   6. Nolite

uphebben on hihþo horn eowerne 7 nellen ge sprecæn togenes
extollere in altum cornu vestrum et nolite   loqui adversus

gode unrihtwisnesse   Forþæn ne of eæstdele ne
deum iniquitatem   7. Quia neque. ab oriente neque

---

eæðmod, fin. let. (e l) er. *gescynd*, a fin. er. made. *þeærfa, a* orig.= æ l;
a fin. let. er. *wedle* by Cor. on er.   **22.** *dem*, fin. let. (e l) er. Er. bef.
gemyndig. beo þu add. by Cor. *þare* by Cor. on er. *ðe* orig.= *ða. fram*
add. by Cor. *æle* by Cor. on er. *deg* altered by Cor. from *dei*.   **23.** Er.
aft. *Ne. þu* by Cor. on er. *þe ofermodinesse l* add. by Cor. *ða, a* by Cor. on
er. l *þe, e* by Cor. on er. l *-don, d* from *ð*; *on* add. by Cor.   **74. 2.** *we
ondetteð* by Cor. *l clypieð* add. by Cor. *l cyðe* add. by Cor.   **3.** *rihtwisnesse* by Cor. on er. Er. bef. *deme*.   **4.** *gemolten* by Cor. on er. *-ende* or
-iende with *i* wr. over the line l *-mede, de* add. by Cor. l *hire* by Cor. on er.
5. *cweð, e* from *i*; fin. let. er. *ða* add. by Cor. l *-wisum nellen ge* by Cor. on
er. *don, d* from *ð*. From *ðam* to *-ben* by Cor. in pl. of er.   **6.** *Nellen ge
uphebben* by Cor. on er. Er. bef. *eowerne. nellen ge* by Cor. on er. *-wis-
nesse* by Cor. on er.   **7.** *ne* (1st and 2nd) by Cor. on er.

of westdele ne from ða westæ dunum   forðæn
ab occidente neque a   desertis montibus **8.** *quoniam*

god demæ is þisne geeæðmedeþ 7 ðisne upæhefð   forðæn
deus iudex est Hunc humiliat et hunc exaltat **9.** *quia*

cælic on hænde drihten wīn hluter ɫ scir ful is gemenged 7
calix in manu domini vini   meri   plenus est mixto Et

onhylde of ðisum on ðis þæh hweðre dresten ɫ drosne his
inclinavit ex hoc in hoc veruntamen   fex   eius

ne is on idelude ɫ amælled drinceð of him eælle ða senfullæɪ
non est   exinanita   Bibent ex eo omnes peccatores

eorðan   ic soðlice on worolde gefio ic singe
terrae   **10.** *ego autem in seucla gaudebo cantabo*

gode · iæcobes   7 eællæ hornæs senfulra ɫ firænfulræ
deo   iacob   **11.** *Et omnia cornua   peccatorum*

ic brice 7 bioð uphæfene hornæs ðas rihtwisas
confringam et exaltabuntur cornua   iusti

75.

Cuð on iudeum god on isræhelæ micel nomæ his
2. *Notus in iudea deus in israel magnum nomen eius*

7 geworðen is on sibbe stow his 7 eærðung his on sion
3. *Et factus   est in pace locus eius et habitatio eius in syon*

ðær he tobrec horn bogæn scild 7 sweord 7 gefioht
4. *Ibi confregit cornua arcuum scutum   gladium et bellum*

Onlihtende þu wundorlice from dunum ɫ muntum ecum
5. *Inluminans tu mirabiliter   a   montibus   aeternis*

gedrefede sindon eællæ unsnotor ɫ unwise heorte hie slepon
6. *turbati sunt omnes insipientes   corde dormierunt*

sleep ɫ swefne hiræ to næht ne funden eælle weres of welenæ
somnum suum et nichil invenerunt omnes viri divitiarum

---

of, f by Cor. from some other let. *-dele* by Cor. in pl. of er. *of, f* by Cor.
prob. from some other let. *ne* by Cor. in pl. of er. *ða* orig.=*ðæ. westæ,*
fin. let. (n?) er.   9. *ɫ scir* add. by Cor. *-ed* (1st), *d* from *ð. onhylde, d*
from *ð. of, f* by Cor. prps. from some other let. From *þæh-* to *his* by Cor.
in pl. of er. *-ude, de* by Cor. in pl. of er. *ɫ amælled* add. by Cor. *drinceð*
by Cor. on er. *of, f* by Cor. from some other let. *ða* orig.=*ðæ* ɫ *sen-* by
Cor. in pl. of er. 10. *soðlice* by Cor. on er. *ic* er. bef. *gefio* ɫ *iæcobes, s* add.
by Cor. 11. *senfulra ɫ* add. by Cor. *ic* by Cor. *brice,* init. *ge-* er. ɫ *ðas*
rihtwisas by Cor. in pl. of er.   75. 2. *Cuð* by Cor. 3. *geworðen, ð*
from *d* by Cor. 4. *he tobrec* by Cor. in pl. of er. 5. *dunum, d* from *ð.*
ɫ muntum ecum add. by Cor. 6. *ɫ unwise* add. by Cor. *sleep,* first *e* from *i*
by Cor. and also dotted by Cor. *ɫ swefne* add. by Cor. *næht,* fin. *e* er. *ne*
funden add. by Cor. *weres of* add. by Cor.

on hændæ hira   From ðræwunge þinra god iæcobes
in manibus suis   7. *Ab increpatione tua deus iacob*

slepon hnappodon ða æstigen hors   ðu egeslic ært
dormitaverunt   qui ascenderunt equos   8. *tu terribilis es*

7 hwilc widstondet þe of ðæm from irræ þinum   Of
et quis resistet tibi extunc ab ira tua   9. *De*

hefonum dom worpod t scotod is eorðæ forhtæþ t biuede 7
caelo iudicium iaculatum   est terra   tremuit   et

stilde t restæt   midðy ðe æriseseþ on dome god þet
quievit   10.   *dum   exurgeret in iudicio deus ut*

hæle he dede ælle stille eorðen   Forðan geðoht
salvos faceret omnes quietos terrae   11. *Quia cogitatio*

monnæ ændettæþ þe 7 lafe   geðohte   deg simbelne
hominis confitebitur tibi et reliquiae cogitationum diem festum

doð þe   Gehataþ 7 gildeþ drihten gode eowere eællæ
agent tibi   12. *Vovete et reddite domino deo vestro omnes*

ðæ þe on ymbgænge his sindon offriað   lac   ðam Egeslican
qui in circuitu eius sunt offertis munera Terribili

7 þam ðe aferreð gæst eældormanna þam egeslicfullan mid
13. *et ei qui aufert spiritum principum   terribili   apud*

kiningæs eorðæn
reges terrae

76.

Mid stefne mīne to drihtne ich cigede t clepode stefne min to
2. *Voce mea ad dominum clamavi   vox mea ad*

dryghtne 7 he beheldeð me   On deg eærfoþnesse mine
deum et intendit michi   3. *In die tribulationis meae*

god ic sohte mid hændum minum on niht beforæn þe 7
deum exquisivi manibus meis nocte coram eo et

---

7. *hnappodon* by Cor. *ða* orig.=*ðæ*. -*en*, *n* add. by Cor.   8. *egeslic*,
fin. let. er. *ært* by Cor. on er. *of*, *f* by Cor. from some other let.   9. *dom*,
d from *ð*. t *scotod* add. by Cor. t *biuede* add. by Cor. *stilde* t by Cor. on
er.   10. *ðe* add. by Cor. *þet*, fin. *te* er. t *hæle*, *e* add. by Cor. *he* add. by
Cor. *dede*, fin. *de* by Cor. (on er. of þ?). *ælle stille eorðen* by Cor. on er.
11. *Forðan* by Cor. on er. *lafe* by Cor. in pl. of er. *geðohte*, fin. *e* add. by
Cor. *deg simbelne doð* by Cor. on er. ; *m* from *b*.   12. -*eþ* orig.= *æþ*. Er.
bef. *eowere* ; fin. *e* add. by Cor. *þe* add. by Cor. *offriað* by Cor. on er. *lac*
orig.= *læc*. *ðam* add. by Cor. -*an* add. by Cor. ? 13. *þam ðe aferreð* by
Cor. on er. -*manna* by Cor. on er. *þam* (2nd) add. by Cor. -*fullan* add. by
Cor.   76. 2. *Mid stefne* by Cor. -*de* t *clepode* add. by Cor. *dryghtne*,
t wr. over the line. *he* add. by Cor. -*eð* add. by Cor.   3. *mid* by Cor. on
er.

ic ne eom beswicen Ic wiðsóc to frefræn saul mine
non sum   deceptus   Negavi   consolari   animam meam

gæmyndig ic wes godæs 7 gelustfullod ic eom bægængen ic eom
4. *memor   fui   dei   et delectatus   sum   Exercitatus   sum*

7 æspræng alythwon gast min forefengen wechen
et defecit   paulisper   spiritus meus   **5.** *anticipaverunt vigilias*

eagan míne gedrefed ic eom 7 ic ne sprech Ic ðohte
oculi   mei   turbatus   sum   et non sum locutus   **6.** *Cogitavi*

dagas ealda 7 geær þa echan on moce ic hebbe 7
dies antiquos et annos   aeternos   in mente   habui   **7.** *Et*

ic gemunde on nichte mid heortæn min ic swanc t bar 7
meditatus sum   nocte   cum   corde   meo   exercitabam   et

windwode on me gast min 7 ic cwið nis þes wæn
ventilabam in me spiritum meum   **8.** *Et dixi   numquid*

on ecnesse forwirpeð god oððe ne toseteð þet wel
in aeternum proiciet deus   aut   non   apponet   ut   bene

gecwemed t licige sie nugit oþþe on ende mildheortnesse
placitum   sit adhuc   **9.** *aut in finem misericordiam*

his he cerfeð from worolde 7 cneorisse t cynrede Is þes wen
suam abscidet   a   seculo et   generatione   **10.** *Numquid*

ofergieteð to mildsian god oþþe hafeð he on yrræ mildheortnes
obliviscetur   misereri   deus aut   continebit in   ira misericordiam

his 7 ic cweþ nu ic ongan ðæs onwendednesse
suam   **11.** *Et dixi   nunc   coepi   haec   inmutatio*

swiðre þas hegan gemindig ic wes weorch drichtnes forðon
dexterae excelsi   **12.** *memor   fui   operum domini   quia*

gemyndig ic beo from frumæn wundræ ðinra 7
memor   ero   ab   initio mirabilium tuorum   **13.** *Et*

smeægende ic eom on eallum weorcum þinum 7 on bihyldnessum
meditatus   sum   in omnibus operibus tuis et in observationibus

---

beswicen by Cor. on er. *Ic* (3rd) add. by Cor. *to* add. by Cor. **4.** *ic wes* by Cor. on er. *alythwon, a* pref. by Cor.; er. aft. this word. *gast* orig. = *gæst*? **5.** *forefengen* by Cor. on er. *ic* (2nd) add. by Cor. *sprech*, fin. let. er.? **6.** *Ic* add. by Cor. *ealda*, fin. let. er. *ic* (2nd), MS. = *io*. *hebbe*, bottom of first *b* and top of second *b* er. **7.** *ic gemunde* by Cor. on er. *ic swanc* by Cor. on er. *t bar* add. by Cor. *-wode* by Cor. on er. **8.** *ic* add. by Cor. *cwið*, fin. let. er. *nis, s* from some other let. Er. aft. *ne*. *-eð, ð* add. by Cor. *þet*, fin. lett. (te?) er. *gecwemed t* add. by Cor. **9.** *oþþe*, fin. let. (t?) er. *-nesse, se* add. by Cor. *he cerfeð* by Cor. on er. *cneorisse t cynrede* by Cor. in pl. of er. **10.** *-eð* (1st), *ð* by Cor. in pl. of two (or three) er. lett. *to* add. by Cor. *-ian* by Cor. in pl. of one er. let. *oþþe*, fin. let. er. *hafeð he* by Cor. on er. **11.** *ic* (1st and 2nd) add. by Cor. *-gan* by Cor. on er. *onwendednesse* by Cor. on er. *þas hegan* by Cor. on er. **12.** *ic beo* add. by Cor.

ðinum me ic begange   god on hælgæn þin weig hwylc god
tuis   me   exercebor   **14.** *Deus in sancto via tua quis deus*

michel swa god ure   ðu eart god þe wyrchest
magnus sicut deus noster   **15.** *tu es   deus qui facis*

wundor ænæ cuþ þu dedest on folche megen þin
mirabilia solus Notam fecisti in populis virtutem tuam

þu lesdest on earma ðinum folc ðin bearn isræhele
16.   *liberasti in brachio tuo populum tuum filios israel*

7 ioseph   Gesægon þe weter god gesæwon þe weter
et ioseph **17.** *Viderunt te aquae deus viderunt te aquae*

7 ˙ondredon 7 gedrefede sindon niowolnesse ł grundes
et timuerunt et   turbatae   sunt   abyssi

monigo sweg wetræ stefne seældon genipe ł wolcne
18. *multitudo sonitus aquarum Vocem dederunt   nubes*

7 soþlice arwen ł strelæ ðine þurhferdon   stefne
et enim   sagittae   tuae pertransierunt **19.** *vox*

of þunorræ þin on hweole Onlihte lihtunge ł blætesunge
tonitrui tui in   rota Inluxerunt   corusca-

ł legræscas þine ymbhwyrf[t] eorþæn gesieg 7 astired is eorðe
tiones   tuae   orbi   terrae vidit et commota est terra

On se wegæs þine 7 stige ł pæðes þine on wetrum miclum
20. *In mari viae tuae et   semitae   tuae in aquis multis*

7 swæðu ł fotlest ðine ne bioð oncnæwene   ðu geleddest
*et   vestigia   tua non cognoscentur   **21.** Deduxisti*

swæ sceæp folc ðinum on hænd moysi 7 ææron
sicut oves populum tuum in manu moysi et aaron

77.

behaldeð ł begymað folc min lage ł ewe ł æ mine onhyldæþ
Attendite   populus meus   legem   meam inclinate

eære eower on word muð min   Ic ontyne ł undo to
*aurem vestram in verba oris mei **2.**   Aperiam   in*

---

15. *eart* orig. ⹀ *eart.* *þe wyrchest* by Cor. on er. *cuþ*, fin. *e* er. *-dest* by
Cor. on er.   16. *þu lesdest* by Cor. in pl. of er.   17. *-gon, g* from *w* by
Cor. *ł grundes* add. by Cor. over the line.   18. *stefne* by Cor. on er.
genipe ł add. by Cor. *wolcne, e* add. by Cor. *arwen ł* add. by Cor. *ðine, e*
add. by Cor.   19. *stefne, e* add. by Cor. *of* add. by Cor. *-orræ*, fin. er.
(ð-ł) made. *on hweole* add. by Cor. *lihtunge ł* add. by Cor. *ł legræscas*
add. by Cor. Let. er. bef. *astired*.   20. *se* by Cor. on er. (orig. ⹀ *siewæ* ł).
ł pæðes add. by Cor. *ł fotlest* add. by Cor.   77. *behaldeð ł begymað*
by Cor. *lage ł* add. by Cor. ; *l* (of *lage*) from *t.* *ł æ* add. by Cor. *word*, fin.
let. er.   2. *ł undo to bispelan* by Cor. on er.

bispelan muð min ic sprice foresetnesse from frumæn world
parabolis   os meum loquar propositiones ab   initio   saeculi

hu monigæ we geherdon 7 we oncnewcn þa 7 federes ure
3. *Quanta   audivimus et cognovimus ea et patres nostri*

hie sedon   us   Ne sindon gedihlede fram beærn
narraverunt nobis   4. Non sunt occultata   a   filiis

monnæ on cneowrisne oþrum Segende 1 cyþende lof drihtes
hominum in generatione altera   Narrantes   laudes domini

7 megen his 7 wundor his ðe he worhte   7 æwehte
et virtutes eius et mirabilia eius quae fecit   5. Et suscitavit

witnesse 1 cyðnesse on iæcobe 7 ewe 1 æ he gesette on isræhele
testimonium   in iacob et legem   posuit   in israel

þæ he bebead fedrum urum þ cuþ bio dydon ðæ beærnum
Quam mandavit patribus nostris ut notam facerent eam filiis

here   þte oncnawa cneowrisne oþer beærn þe bioð acennede
suis   6. ut cognoscat generatio altera Filii qui nascentur

7 arisæþ 7 segeþ 1 cyðað ðæ beærn here   þte hio settæn
et exsurgent et narrabunt eam filiis suis   7. Ut ponant

on gode hyht here 7 ne ofergieten weorc godes here 7
in deo spem suam et non obliviscantur operum dei sui et

bebodæ his secæþ   þ hy ne werðen swæ swa federæs
mandata eius exquirant 8. Ne fiant   sicut patres

hiræ kin þweor 7 þurhbiter kin þet ne gerehte heorte
eorum genus pravum et peramarum genus quod non direxit cor

hiræ 7 ne is gelyfed mid gode gæst his   beærn effrem
suum et non est creditus cum deo spiritus eius 9. Filii effrem

bendende bogæn 7 sendende strelæ 1 arwen his hy gecyrred
intendentes arcum et mittentes sagittas suas conversi

---

3. -her-, e from i by Cor. þa from þu? *federes, es* add. by Cor. *hie, e*
add. by Cor.   4. 1 *cyþende* add. by Cor. *drihtes*, so MS.; *s* from *n* by Cor.
ðe by Cor. on er. *he* add. by Cor.   5. *witnesse 1* by Cor. in pl. of er. *cyð-*,
about two init. lett. (ge ?) er.; *c* from *g*? by Cor. *iæcobe*, fin. *s* er. 1 *æ he*
add. by Cor. *he* (2nd) add. by Cor. *bebead* orig. = *bebeæð*. þ, fin. lett. (te ?)
er. *hio* add. by Cor. *here* by Cor. prob. from *his*   6. *hi* er. bef. *oncnawa*;
first *a* by Cor. on er.; fin. let. (n?) er. Er. bef. *cneow-*. *oþer, -er* by
Cor. on er. (of -re?). *þe* add. by Cor. *acen-, a* prob. pref. by Cor. 1 *cyðað*
add. by Cor. *here, -ere* by Cor. on er.   7. *hio* add. by Cor. *gode, e*
add. by Cor. *here* (1st) by Cor. (from *his* ?). Er. (bioð ?) bef. *ofergieten*;
fin. *ne* er.? *here* (2nd), -*ere* by Cor. on er.   8. *þ hy ne werðen* by Cor.
on er. *swa* add. by Cor. *þweor* by Cor. on er. -*biter* by Cor. on er.
ne add. by Cor. About two lett. er. bef. *gerehte*, in. *e* add. by Cor. *gelyfed*,
d from ð.   9. -*ndende* by Cor. on er. 1 *arwen* add. by Cor. *hy gecyrred*
by Cor. on er.

sindon on deg gefihtes Ne gehioldon hie kiðnesse godes
sunt in die `belli` **10.** *Non custodierunt testamentum dei*

here 7 on ewe ł æ his ne woldon gængæn 7 hy ofergeton
sui et in lege eius noluerunt ambulare **11.** *Et obliti sunt*

weldeda his 7 wundor his ðæ þe he atawode hem
benefactorum eius et mirabilium eius quae ostendit eis

beforæn fedrum hiræ he worhte wundor on eorðæn
12. *coram patribus eorum Fecit mirabilia in terra*

egypti on campo thaneos he toslat þa sæ 7 þurhledde
aeyypti in campo thaneos **13.** *Interrupit mare et perduxit*

hie 7 gesette weter swa swa on cylle ł bytte 7 geledde
eos et statuit aquas quasi `in` *utrem* **14.** *Et eduxit*

hie on wolcne deges 7 eælle niht on lyhtnesse fires
eos in nube diei et tota nocte in inluminatione ignis

 Toslat on westene stan 7 weterode hie swa swa on
15. *Interrupit in heremo petram et adaquavit eos velut in*

neowolnesse ł grunde micle 7 utaledde weter of stane
   abysso multa **16.** *Et eduxit aquam de petra*

7 utgeledde swæ swa flodes ł streamæs weteræ 7
et eduxit tanquam flumina aquas **17.** *Et*

gesetton þagit syngian him on irra hy awehton god
adposuerunt adhuc peccare ei in ira concitaverunt deum

heahne on drignesse 7 hie costodon ł fandedon god
excelsum in siccitate **18.** *Et temptaverunt deum*

on heortæn hiræ þ hie bedon mettæs saulum here 7 yfele
in cordibus suis ut peterent escas animabus suis **19.** *et male*

hie sprecen be gode 7 cwedon Is þies wen miege god
locuti sunt de deo et dixerunt nunquid poterit deus

---

sindon, d from *ð. -es* add. by Cor. 10. *hie* by Cor. ; er. aft. this word.
here altered by Cor. from *his*? *t æ* add. by Cor. 11. *7 hy ofergeton* by
Cor. in pl. of er. *-deda* by Cor. on er. From *þe* to *hem* by Cor. in pl. of er.
12. *he* add. by Cor. 13. *he* add. by Cor. *toslat* orig. = *toslæt*? *þa sæ* by
Cor. in pl. of er. *swa* (2nd) by Cor. on er. *t bytte* add. by Cor. 15. *Toslat* orig. = *Toslæt. stan* orig. = *stæn. weterode* by Cor. in pl. of er. ; *ge* er.
bef. this word. *swa swa* by Cor. on er. *t grunde* add. by Cor. 16. *7
utaledde* by Cor. in pl. of er. *of, f* by Cor. from some other let. *stane* orig. =
stæne. swa flodes t add. by Cor. *weteræ, i* er. betw. *w* and *e.* 17. *þa-* by
Cor. in pl. of er. ; er. aft. *-git. -ian* orig. = *-iæn. hy* add. by Cor. ; misplaced
but marked to follow *irra. awehton* orig. = *awehton. heahne* by Cor. in pl.
of er. *drignesse, e* er. betw. *g* and *n* ; *-esse* prob. add. by Cor. 18. *hie* add.
by Cor. *t fandedon* add. by Cor. *-e b-* on er. *saulum* orig. = *sæulum. here*
by Cor. from *hiræ.* 19. *-e hie* add. by Cor. *sprecen,* fin. *de* er. ? ; word er.
aft. it. *be* by Cor. from *bi.*

geærwigæn misæn on westnesse   Forðan   slóh   stan
parare   mensam in deserto   20. Quoniam percussit petram

7 fleowon węter 7 rinnellæn ł burnen   yðgoden   Is þies wen
et fluxerunt aquae et   torrentes   inundaverunt Numquid

7 hlæf meh he seællæn oþþe geærwiæn misæn folce   his
et panem poterit dare aut parare   mensam populo suo

Forðæn gehierde drihten 7 æriefnede 7 ofersette 7 fir
21. *Ideo   audivit dominus et distulit et superposuit et ignis*

onęled is on iæcobe 7 yrræ astah on isræhele   Forðæn
accensus est in iacob et ira ascendit in israel   22. Quia

ne gelifdon hie on gode here ne gewendon ł hyhton on helo
non crediderunt in deum suum nec   speraverunt   in salutare

his   7 he bebeæd wolcnu bufon 7 duren hefonæs
eius 23. Et mandavit nubibus desuper et ianuas caeli

undyde   7 rinde hem manne ł hefenlich laf to etonne hlæf
aperuit 24. et pluit illis   manna   manducare panem

hefones seælde hem   hlaf englæne   æt   man
caeli dedit eis   25. panem angelorum manducavit homo

hwętes węs[t]mæ he sende hem on genihtsumnesse   7
frumentationem misit eis in habundantiam   26. Et

he æwehte suðenwind of heofonum 7 geledde on megne his
excitavit austrum de caelo et induxit in virtute sua

suðenwestenwind   7 rinde ofer hie swæ   dust   flesc
affricum   27. Et pluit super eos sicut pulverem carnes

7 swæ sand ses fuglæs gefeðerede   7 feollen on
et sicut arenam maris volatilia pennata   28. Et ceciderunt in

midle fiendwice ł cestre hiræ ymbæ eærdunge hiræ
medio   castrorum   eorum circa tabernacula eorum

      7 hie ætan   7 gefillede sindon swiþe 7 willnungæ ł lust
29. *Et manducaverunt et saturati sunt nimis et   desiderium*

---

20. *Forðan*, *a* orig.= *æ*; er. aft. this word. *sta*ⁿ orig.= *stæⁿ*. *ł burnen* add. by Cor.; *on* er. aft. this word? *meh*, fin. *ł* er.? *he* add. by Cor. 21. *astah* orig.= *æstæh*. 22. *hie* add. by Cor. *gode*, *e* add. by Cor. *here* by Cor. from *hiræ*. *ł hyhton* add. by Cor. 23. *duren*, *e* orig.= *æ*; *n* add. by Cor. *undyde* by Cor. on er. 24. *hem*, *e* from *i* by Cor. (twice). *manne* orig.= *mænnæ*. *ł hefenlich laf to* add. by Cor. 25. *englæne*, *ne* add. by Cor. *man* orig.= *mæn*. *he* add. by Cor. *hem*, *e* from *i* by Cor. *-sumnesse* by Cor. on er. 26. *he* add. by Cor. *suðenwind* by Cor. in pl. of er. *suðenwestenwind* by Cor. in pl. of er. 27. *sand* orig.= *sænd*. *ses* by Cor. in pl. of longer er. wh. ended in *e*. *gefeðerede* by Cor. in pl. of er. 28. *feollen* by Cor. on er. *fiendwice ł cestre* by Cor. in pl. of er. 29. *hie ætan* by Cor. in pl. of er. *sindon* by Cor. on er. 7 by Cor. in pl. of er. *ł lust* add. by Cor.

hiræ brohte hem   7 ne sint bescyrede from gewilnungæ
eorum obtulit eis   **30.** *et non sunt fraudati   a   desiderio*

his Nugin mettas hiræ wes on muðe hiræ   7 irræ
suo Adhuc   esca   eorum erat in   ore ipsorum   **31.** *et ira*

godes æstæg ofer hie 7 ofsloh manege of hem 7 gecorene
dei ascendit super eos et occidit plurimos eorum et electos

isræhele he gelette   On eællum ðisum hie sengoden
israel   inpedivit   **32.** *In omnibus   his   peccaverunt*

ðæget 7 ne   gelifdon   on wundrum his   7 ateregoden
adhuc et non crediderunt in mirabilibus eius   **33.** *Et defecerunt*

on idelnesse dægæs hiræ 7 geær hiræ mid   ofeste
in vanitate   dies   eorum et anni eorum cum festinantia

ðanne he ofsloh hie þonne sohton hy hine 7 bioð gecerden
34. *Cum occideret eos tunc inquirebant eum et convertebantur*

beforæn liohtæ 7 cómón to him   7 hy gemundon
ante   lucem et veniebant ad eum   **35.** *Et memorati sunt*

ðet god fultumend hioræ is 7 god se heage friolsend hiræ
quia deus adiutor eorum est et deus excelsus liberator eorum

is   7 hy lufodon hine on muðæ heræ 7 tunga heræ
est   **36.** *Et dilexerunt eum in   ore   suo et lingua sua*

lugen him   heorte soðlice heræ ne wes riht mid
mentiti sunt ei   **37.** *Cor autem eorum non erat rectum cum*

him ne geleafe eærdiendæ is hem on cyðnesse his   he
eo nec fides   habita   est illis in testamento eius   **38.** *Ipse*

soðlice is mildheort 7 milde biþ sinnum heræ 7 ne
autem est misericors et propitius fit peccatis eorum et non

forspilð hie 7 gemonifaldode þet he ácherde wreððe hiræ from
disperdet eos Et multiplicavit ut averteret iram suam ab

hem 7 ne onçlede eæll irræ heræ   7 he gemunde
eis et non accendit omnem iram suam   **39.** *Et memoratus est*

---

brohte by Cor. on er.   hem, e from i by Cor.   30. -nungæ, æ altered from
a by Cor. ↑   31. 7 ofsloh manege of hem add. by Cor.   -ene, fin. e add. by
Cor.   he gelette by Cor. on er.   32. hie sengoden by Cor. on er.   -get by
Cor. in pl. of er. ↑   33. ateregoden by Cor. on er.   34. ðanne he ofsloh
hie by Cor. on er.   sohton hy by Cor.   gecerden, e (2nd) from i by Cor.; n
add. by Cor.   35. hy gemundon ðet by Cor. in pl. of er.   se heage by Cor. in
pl. of er.   36. hy add. by Cor.   heræ, e from i by Cor. (twice).   37. soðlice by Cor. on er.   heræ, e from i by Cor.   geleafe orig. = geleafæ.   hem, e
from i by Cor.   38. soðlice by Cor. on er.   milde by Cor. on er.   heræ, e
from i by Cor.   -spilð altered by Cor. from -spilde.   -ode by Cor. ↑   he
ácherde wreððe by Cor. in pl. of er.   hem, e from i by Cor.   -ede, d from ð;
fin. e add. by Cor.   heræ, e from i by Cor.   39. he add. by Cor.   -unde by
Cor. on er,

ðet hie flesc sindon gast gangende 7 na eftcerrende
quia caro sunt spiritus vadens et non rediens

    hu ofte hie gremedon hine on westene on irræ hy awehton
40. *Quotiens exacerbaverunt eum in deserto in ira concitaverunt*

hine on eorðæn butæn wetre 7 hy gewirfede sindon
eum in terra sine aqua **41.** *Et conversi sunt*

7 costodon gode 7 þane haligne of isræhele hie gremeden
et temptaverunt deum et sanctum israel exacerbaverunt

    hy Ne sindon gemindige hænd his hwylee dege he alysde
42. *Non sunt recordati manuis eius qua die liberavit*

hie of hande swencendes Swæ he settɜ in egipto tacnæ
eos de manu tribulantis **43.** *Sicut posuit in aegypto signa*

his 7 foretacne heræ in campo taneos he acerde on
sua et prodigia sua in campo thaneos **44.** *Convertit in*

    blode flodes ł streæmas heræ 7 regnlice wetræ heræ
sanguine flumina eorum et pluviales aquas eorum

þ hy ne druncen he sende on hem ɟiogæn hundæs 7
ne biberent **45.** *Inmisit in eos muscam caninam et*

    æt hie 7 froxæs 7 he fordyde hie , 7 sealde emele
comedit eos et ranam et exterminavit eos **46.** *Et dedit erugini*

westmæ heræ 7 swinc heræ gershoppan he ofslog
fructus eorum et labores eorum locustae **47.** *Occidit*

on hegle wingeardas heræ 7 byrig heræ on froste
in grandine vineas eorum et moros eorum in pruina

    he selde hegle nytene here 7 ehtæ heræ fyre
48. *Tradidit grandini iumenta eorum et possessiones eorum igni*

    Onsende on him irræ abylgnesse his abilgnesse 7
49. *Inmisit in eos iram indignationis suae indignationem et*

ðet hie by Cor. in pl. of er. gast orig. = gæst. gangende orig. = gængænde. na eft cerrende by Cor. on er. 40. ofte, e add. by Cor. hie by Cor. in pl. of er. hy add. by Cor. awehton orig. = æwehton. 41. 7 hy by Cor. gode, e add. by Cor. þane haligne of by Cor. in pl. of er. hie gremeden by Cor. in pl. of er. 42. hy add. by Cor. hwylce by Cor. on er. he alysde by Cor. in pl. of er. hande orig. = hænde. swencendes by Cor. in pl. of er. 43. his, s by Cor. on er. (of hiræ?). -tacne by Cor. on er. heræ, e from i by Cor. campo orig. = cæmpo. taneos, a orig. = ɟæ. 44. he acerde by Cor. on er. flodes ł add. by Cor. heræ, e from i by Cor. (twice). -gnlice by Cor. in pl. of er. þ hy ne druncen by Cor. 45. he add. by Cor. hem, e from i by Cor. hundæs, s by Cor. he fordyde by Cor. in pl. of er. 46. emele by Cor. on er. heræ, e from i by Cor. swinc add. by Cor. heræ, e from i by Cor. gershoppan by Cor. on er. 47. he ofslog on hegle by Cor. on er. -as prps. orig. = -æs. heræ, e from i by Cor. (twice). byrig by Cor. on er. froste by Cor. on er. 48. From he to here add. by Cor. heræ, e from i by Cor. fyre, e add. by Cor. 49. abylgnesse by Cor. on er. abilgnesse by Cor. on er.

irræ 7 eærfoðnesse   onsandes   þurh englæs yfle   Weig
iram et tribulationem inmissiones per angelos malos   50. *Viam*

he wrohte Stige erres his 7 ne árede from dæðe   saule
   fecit   semitae irae suae et non pepercit a morte animabus

heræ 7 nytene heræ on deæþe he leac   7 he ofslog
eorum et iumenta eorum in morte conclusit   51. *Et percussit*

elcne   frumkinnedne on eorðæn egypti frumsceattas eællæs
omnem primogenitum in   terra aegypti primitias   omnis

gewinnes heræ on eardungæ chæm   7 genæm swa swæ
  laboris eorum in tabernaculis cham 52. *Et abstulit   sicut*

sceæp   folc   his 7 ðurhledde hie swæ swæ ewede   on
 oves populum suum et perduxit eos tanquam gregem   in

westene   7 utledde hie on hihte 7 ne ondredon 7
deserto   53. *Et eduxit eos in spe et non timuerunt et*

fiend   hiræ oferwreah sæ   7 he ledde hie on
inimicos eorum operuit mare   54. *Et   induxit eos in*

dune   hælgungæ   his   dune þisne ðone þe beget
montem sanctificationis suae montem hunc   quem adquisivit

swiðre his 7 aweærp from ansine heræ ðiodæ 7 mid hlyte
dextera eius Et eiecit a   facie eorum gentes et   sorte

he todelede hem eorðæn on   rapæ   todales   7
  divisit   eis terram in funiculo distributionis 55. *et*

eærdæde on geteltungum hiræ megþæ isræhelæ   7
habitavit in tabernaculis eorum tribus   israel   56. *et*

costodon   7 gremedon   god ðane heagan 7 cyðnesse
temptaverunt et exacerbaverunt deum excelsum   et testimonia

his ne hioldon   7 hy acyrdon hy 7 ne hyoldon ł
eius non custodierunt 57. *Et averterunt se et non observa-*

---

begemdon   hwu   gemete   federes   heoræ   gewirfde   sindon   on
verunt   quemadmodum   patres   eorum   conversi   sunt   in

bogæn   On   irræ   hy   æwehton   hine   on   bergum
arcum perversum   **58.** *In   ira   concitaverunt   eum   in collibus*

heræ   7   on agrauene anlicnesse   heræ   onhirgende   sindon   hine
suis   et in   sculptilibus   suis   emulati   sunt   eum

   Geherde   drihten   7   forhogode   7   to nawuhte   gehwarf   swiðe
59. *Audivit   dominus et   sprevit   et ad nichilum   redigit   nimis*

isræhelæ   7   he onweg asceaf teldungæ ł eardunge
israel   **60.** *Et   reppulit   tabernaculum   selem*

ge[t]eldunga   his   on ðæm   ðe   he eærcede   betwioh   monnum
tabernaculum   suum   in   quo   habitarit   inter   homines

   7   seælde   on   heftneðe   megen   heræ   7   fegernesse
61. *Et tradidit   in captivitatem virtutes   eorum   et pulchritudines*

heræ   on   handæ   fiondes   7   beleac   on   sweorde   folc
eorum in   manus inimici   **62.** *Et conclusit in   gladio populum*

his   hirfweærdnesse   his   he forhogede   giongæn   heræ
suum et   haereditatem   suam   sprevit   **63.** *Iuvenes   eorum*

   æt   fyer   7   megdene   heræ   ne   sincon   wopene ł cwiðde
comedit ignis   et   virgines   eorum   non   sunt   lamentate

   Sæcerdos   heræ   on   sweorde   fiollæn   7   widwæn   heræ   ne
64. *Sacerdotes   eorum in   gladio   ceciderunt et   vidue   eorum non*

   wepon   7   æweht   is   swæ   slepende   drihten
ploraverunt   **65.** *Et   excitatus est   tamquam   dormiens   dominus*

swæ   mihti   acworren   of   wine   7   he ofsloh   fiond
quasi potens   crapulatus   a   vino   **66.** *Et   percussit   inimicos*

---

hwu gemete by Cor. in pl. of er.   *federes, es* add. by Cor.   *heoræ, e* from *i* by
Cor.   Gloss to *perversum* er.   58. *hy* add. by Cor.   *bergum* by Cor. on er.
heræ, e from *i* by Cor. (twice).   *on agrauene anlicnesse* by Cor. in pl. of er.
59. *Geherde, e* (2nd) from *i* by Cor. ; *de* by Cor. on er.   *forhogode* by Cor. on
er.   *na-* orig.= *næ-*.   *gehwarf, ge-* pref. by Cor. ; *-arf* by Cor. on er.
60. *he onweg asceaf* by Cor. in pl. of er.   *teld-, d* from *t* by orig. scribe.
ge[t]eldunga, er. where *t* stands ; *e* (2nd) orig.= *æ* ; *a* orig.= *æ* ?   *ðe he* add.
by Cor.   *eærdede* altered by Cor. from *eærdæð*?   61. *-neðe,* first *e* from *i*
prob. by Cor. ; *ð* from *d* by Cor.   *heræ, e* from *i* by Cor. (twice).   *handæ*
orig.= *hændæ.*   *fiondes, es* add. by Cor.   62. *beleac* by Cor. in pl. of er.
his (1st), *s* by Cor. from some other let. and in pl. of about two er. lett.   *his*
(2nd), ditto?   *he forhogede* by Cor. on er.   63. Er. bef. *giongæn.*   *heræ, e*
from *i* by Cor. (twice).   *æt fyer* by Cor. in pl. of er.   *megdene* by Cor. in pl.
of er.   *wopene ł cwiðde* by Cor. on er.   64. *heræ, e* from *i* by Cor. (twice).
fiollæn, init. *ge* er. ?   65. *acworren of wine* by Cor. in pl. of er.   66. *he
of-* by Cor. in pl. of er.

his on efternan ł yterӕn   edwit   ecelic   seӕlde hem
suos in   posteriora   obprobrium sempiternum dedit illis

   7   he aweg asceaf   eardunge   ioseph 7   megð effrem
67. *Et   reppulit   tabernaculum ioseph et tribum effrem*

he ne ceas   ac he ceas megð iudӕn   dun   syon
non elegit   **68.** *sed elegit   tribum iuda   montem syon*

ðӕne he lufodo   7 he timbrede swӕ   ӕnhornӕ
quem   dilexit   **69.** *Et   edificavit   sicut unicornuorum*

halignesse   his   on eorðӕn gestaþolode hie on worolde
sanctificationem suam in   terra   fundavit   eam in saecula

   7 gecӕӕs dӕuid ðeowne his 7 ӕrefnede hine ob ewedum
70. *Et elegit   david servum suum et sustulit eum de gregibus*

sceӕpӕ 7 efter ðam stinkendan onfeng hine   Feden
*ovium   de   postfetantes accepit eum   **71.** Pascere*

iӕcobes   folc   his 7 isrӕhele yrfeweӕrdnesse his.   7
*iacob populum suum et israel   haereditatem suam   **72.** Et*

he fedde hie buton yfelnesse heorte his 7 on sefӕn hӕnde
  pavit   eos sine   malitia   cordis sui et in sensu manuum

hirӕ   geledde hie
suarum deduxit eos

78.

God   comen þioda on yrfeweӕrdnesse ðin   bӕddon
Deus venerunt gentes in   haereditatem   tuam coinquinaverunt

temple   hali   ðin   Setton ierusalem oþþet   ӕpla
templum sanctum tuum Posuerunt ierusalem velut pomorum

gehioldon   gesetton deӕplicnesse þeowa   ðinrӕ
*custodiarum   **2.** posuerunt mortalia servorum tuorum*

mӕtas   fuglas   heuonas flesc   haligra þinra wildordeora
escas volatilibus caeli carnes sanctorum tuorum bestiis

---

his, s by Cor. from some other let. in pl. of about two er. lett.   *efternan ł* by
Cor. in pl. of er.   *hem, e* from *i* by Cor.   67. *he aweg asceaf* by Cor. in pl.
of er.   *eard-* orig. = *eard-*.   *he* add. by Cor.   *ceas* by Cor. in pl. of er.
68. *ac he ceas* add. by Cor.   *ðӕne, ð* from *d* by Cor.; *ne* add. by Cor.   69. 7
he timbrede add. by Cor.   *hal-* orig. = *hӕl-*.   *-lode* by Cor. on er.   70. *ðam*
orig. = *ðӕm*.   *stinkendan* by Cor. on er.   71. *Feden, n* add. by Cor.   *his, s*
from some other let. by Cor. in pl. of about two er. lett.   72. *he fedde* by
Cor. on er.   *yfelnesse* by Cor. on er.   78. With this chapter begins a
fresh hand which ends with the word *earfóðnesse* (Ps. 90, 15). The following
parts are written in a larger (the same ł) hand and in darker ink :—Ps. 78,
from *God* (v. 1) to *blod* (v. 3); Ps. 79, from *Awece* (v. 3) to *us* (1st, v. 7); Ps.
83, from *hu* (v. 2) to *megen* (v. 4); Ps. 84, from 7 *eorðe* (v. 13) to end of Ps.
temple on er.   *Setton*, er. betw. *t* and *t*.   2. Er. bef. *mӕtas.*

on þere eo[r]ðan   guten   blod   hi æ   swæ
   terrae   3. *Effuderunt sanguinem eorum sicut*

wætær on ymbegonge hierusalem 7 ne wes se bebyrgde
aquam   in   circuitu   ierusalem et non erat qui sepeliret

  geworderre we sien on   edwite   neæn urum on hlehtre
4. *Facti   sumus   in obprobrium vicinis nostris   derisu*

7 hyrwnessæ þisum se on ymbegænge   ure   sindon
et contemptu   his   qui in   circuitu   nostro   sunt

  oþþete   dryhten irsæþ on ende biþ onhæled oþþet fir
5. *Usque quo domine irasceris in finem accenditur velut ignis*

ellenwodnes ðin   gegoten irre þin unmiete þu ðe
  zelus   tuus   6. Effunde iram tuam in gentes quae te

ne ne witon 7 on rice ðæ ne geciȝðon namon ðinne
non noverunt et in regna quae non invocaverunt nomen tuum

  Forþan ðe heo heten iæcobes 7 stowe his   tolysdon
7. *Quia   comederunt iacob et locum eius desolaverunt*

  Ne wes þu gemindig unrihtwisnesse ure erðæn þæ hredlice
8. *Ne memineris   iniquitates   nostras antiquas   cito*

us ier onfehþ mildheortnes þin forþan ðearfæn geworþen
nos anticipet misericordia tua quia pauperes facti

ic eom swiþe   gefultome us god hielo   ure 7
sumus nimis   9. Adiuva nos deus salutaris noster et

fore wurþunge nomæn ðine drihten gefriolse us 7 orfest
propter honorem nominis tui domine libera nos et propitius

wes þu sinnæ ure for nomon þinum   þyles
esto peccatis nostris propter nomen tuum   10. Ne quando

cweþæn þiodæ wher is god hiræ 7 on cyþnesse on icyþnessum
dicant gentes ubi est deus eorum et innotescant in nationibus

beforan eagæn urum ywrec blod   þeowræ þinræ þæt
coram oculis nostris Vindica sanguinem servorum tuorum qui

iegoten is   ongeþ on gesihte þinre giomrung liþe-
effusus est   11. intret in conspectu tuo gemitus com-

wacunga Efter   michelnes earmes þinræ ægende bearn
peditorum Secundum magnitudinem brachii tui posside filios

---

3. *ymbegonge*, one let. (b?) er. betw. *m* and *b*.   *hierusalem* on er. (by larger hand?). Er. aft. *ne*.   4. MS. = *geworderre*. *in derisum contemptum*, *in* and fin. *m* (twice) underlined.   5. *on hæ-* in pl. of er. (by larger hand?).   6. *geciȝðon*, about three lett. er. betw. *g* and *ð*.   7. *ðe heo heten* in pl. of er. (by larger hand?). *tolysdon*, *on* in pl. of er.   8. *-wicnesse* on er. *þæ*, the *a* of the *æ* from *e*.   9. Er. bef. 7 (1st).   10. MS. = *wyles*. *wher*, *h* from *w* or *r* by darker ink. Er. bef. 7.

deaþe witnigendræ   gielde neahgeburas urum seofan-
morti   punitorum   12. *Redde.   vicinis   nostris septu-*

faldlich on feþme hiora   on edwite hira ðæt edwitoðon
plum   in sinus eorum improperium eorum quod exprobraverunt

þe drihten -   Us eallenga folc þin 7 scep ewædes
tibi domine   13. *Nos   autem populus tuus et oves gregis*

þines ondettað þe on woroldæ 7 on worold aworold
tui confitebimur tibi in saecula et in saeculum saeculi

we secgaþ lof þin
narrabimus laudem tuam

79.

Se gemearæ ł kynig israhelæs beheald hwilc gelædeþ oþþet
2. *Qui   regis   israel   intende qui deducis velut*

scep iosepes þu sittest ouer cherubin gearwigean   beforan
ovem ioseph Qui sedes super cherubin appare   3. coram

effrem 7 beniamin 7 manassa Awece mihtte þine 7 cum þet
effrem et beniamin et manasse Excita potentiam tuam et veni ut

hælę ðu do us   Drihten god megen gehwyrfe us
salvos facias nos   4. Domine deus virtutum converte nos

7 atæuwa onsyne þinne 7 we gebeoð hihælede   Drihten
et ostende faciem tuam et   salvi erimus   5. Domine

god mægen oðþette yersaþ on gebede þeowes þines
deus virtutum quousque irasceris in orationem servi tui

mettas us hlaf tæra 7 dryng svlest us on tearum
6. *cibabis nos pane lacrimarum et potum dabis nobis in lacrimis*

gemæte þu gesettes us on wiþercwiðolnessæ nean
in mensura 7. Posuisti nos in contradictionem vicinis

urum 7 find urum bismreden us   Drihten god
nostris et inimici nostri deriserunt nos   8. Domine deus

megen gehwyrfe us 7 oniewe onsien þin 7 we bioþ gehelede
virtutum converte nos et ostende faciem tuam et salvi erimus

Wingeard ob egyp æweg aname þu towurpe þeoda 7
9. *Vineam ex aegypto transtulisti eiecisti gentes et*

---

12. Er. bef. *neah-*; *h* from *n* by d. ink. Let. er. immed. aft. *on* (1st).
Er. bef. *ðæt.* 13. *worold,* fin. *a* er. 79. 2. *Se* in the larger hand.
gemearæ, ge and *a* on er. (by larger hand!). *ł kynig* wr. over the line.
israhelæs, fin. *s* in d. ink. *hwilc ge-* wr. on the illuminated let. of the
Latin and in the larger hand; *-lædeþ* also in the larger hand. 3. *manassa,*
or *manassæ*? From *Awece* to *us* (1st, v. 7) in the larger hand. 7. *-nessæ,*
the *a-* part of the *æ* from *e.* 9. *æweg, g* from *i.*

þu awirtwalodes þa   Weg þu worhtes on gesihðe
plantasti   *eam*   **10.** *Viam*   *fecisti*   *in*   *conspectu*

his 7 þu wyrtwalodes wyrtwala his 7 gefilled is eorðe
eius et plantasti   *radices eius et repleta est terra*

Ontynde duna scua his 7 arbusta his cederbeam godes
11. *Operuit montes umbra eius et arbusta eius cedros dei*

Ðu aþenedes folman his oþþette tc sewe 7 oþþette to
12. *Extendisti palmites eius usque ad mare et usque ad*

Streame foreblestinge his   Tohwan þu gesettes
flumen propagines eius   **13.** *Utquid deposuisti*

wah his 7 wingeardas ealla þe þurhferdon węg
maceriam eius et vindemiant eam omnes qui transeunt viam

Abregde hie onforwyrd wúda 7 sinderlice swa whena
14. *Exterminavit eam aper de silva et singularis ferus*

wolberende hie . Drihten god miegen gecirre nu
depastus est eam   **15.** *Domine deus virtutum converte nunc*

loca of hefonum 7 gesioh 7 niosa wingeardas þas 7
respice de caelo et vide et visita vineam istam   **16.** *et*

gereche hie þa gewyrtwelode swiþre þin 7 ofer bearn
dirige eam quam plantavit dextera tua et super filium

manna ða getrimedes þe Anglede fire 7 agotene
hominis quem confirmasti tibi   **17.** *Incensa igni et effossa*

handa from þrawunge ansine þine forwvrdon Sie handa
manu ab increpatione vultus tui peribunt   **18.** *Fiat manus*

þ[i]ne simle wer swiðre þin 7 ofer bearn manna þa
tua super virum dexterae tuae et super filium hominis quem

getrimedes þe 7 ne gewiton from þe Þu gelifiestes
confirmasti tibi   **19.** *et non discedimus a te Vivificabis*

us 7 noman þinne we gecigeað Drihte[n] god
nos et nomen tuum invocabimus   **20.** *Domine deus*

megen gewhyrfe us 7 oþiewe ansiene þine 7 we bioð
virtutum converte nos et ostende faciem tuam et salvi

gehelede
erimus

80.

wynsumiað gode fultumend urvm wynsumiað gode iacob
2. *Exultate deo adiutori nostro iubilate deo iacob*

---

11. MS. = *scura.* MS. = -*bean.*   13. *gesettes,* sec. *t* from *e.*   14. *Abregde,* fin. *n* er. Er. bef. *swa-.*   15. *hefonum,* h from *l.*   16. *of* or *or* (dotted) immed. bef. *ofer.*   18. Er. bef. *þin.*

Nimad sealm 7 sellað swieg salter wynsum
3. *Sumite psalmum et date timpanum psalterium iocundum*

mid hearpan Singoð on frumon monþum byman on
cum cythara 4. *Canite initio mensis tuba in*

dege fyr symbelnesse eowre Forþan þe bebeod
die insignis sollempnitatis vestrae 5. *Quia preceptum*

on israhelum is 7 dom godes iacobes Kiþnesse
in israel est et iudicium deo iacob 6. *Testimonium*

on iosepes gesette hine midþi þe eode on eorðan egypti
in ioseph posuit eum dum exiret de terra aegypti

tungan ðeahþe ne ne wyste gehyrde forðbrohte on
Linguam quam non noverat audivit 7. *divertit ab*

wiorþungum hricg his handa his on spyrtan ðeowigeaþ
oneribus dorsum eius manus eius in cofino servierunt

On earfoðnesse þu geciþes me 7 ic þe gefrielse 7
8. *In tribulatione invocasti me et liberavi te*

ic þe gehirde on gehydnesse hreonnesse costaþ ðe to wætrum
exaudivi te in abscondito tempestatis probavi te ad aquas

wiðwiþorcwiðolnesse gehyre folc min 7 ic sprece
contradictionis 9. *Audi populus meus et loquar*

israhel 7 ic kiþe þe Israhel gif me gehirest ne
israel et testificabor tibi Israel si me audieris 10. *non*

biþ on ðe god irsigende nimþe þu gebidst god fremde
erit in te deus recens neque adorabis deum alienum

Ic soðlice eom drihten god þin se geledde þe on eorþan
11. *Ego enim sum dominus deus tuus qui eduxi te de terra*

egypti gebrede mud þin 7 ic ægefille þęt 7
aegypti Dilata os tuum et ego adimplebo illud 12. *et*

ne gehireð folc min stefn min 7 israhel neals behelt
non audivit populus meus vocem meam et israel non intendit

me 7 forlet hie efter wilnunga heorta
michi 13. *Et dimisi eos secundum desideria cordis*

hioram 7 gangaþ on willan hiora gif folc min
eorum et ibunt in voluntatibus suis 14. *si plebs mea*

gehireþ me israhele gif wegas mine gangaþ to
audisset me israel si vias meas ambulasset 15. *ad*

naþing feond hira ic geeaþmende 7 ofer earfoþige hie
nichilum inimicos eorum humiliassem et super tribulantes eos

80. 6. *Kiþ-* or *ciþ-*? 8. The Latin to 7 (2nd) er. 9. *kiþe* or *ciþe*?
14. *gangaþ*, *þ* in d. ink.

ic onsende hand mine   Fiend drihtenes liogende
mibissem   manum meam   **16.** *Inimici domini   mentiti*

sindon him 7 bið tid hira on ęcnesse   gemetgað
sunt ei et erit tempus eorum in aeternum   **17.** *Cibavit*

hie of fętnesse þes hwietes 7 of stane hunige gefylde hie
eos ex adipe   frumenti   et de petra melle saturavit eos

81.

God stod on gemotstowe be hira on midlene eallenga god
Deus stetit in synagoga deorum in medio   autem deus

astiehþ   Oþ þętte demaþ unrihtnesse 7 doð
discernit   **2.** *Quousque iudicatis iniquitatem et facies*

syngiað genimað   Demaþ stiopcild 7 wieðlan
peccantium sumitis   **3.** *Iudicate pupillo et egeno*

eaþmodan 7 þearfan gesoðfestan   generigan þearfan
humilem et pauperem iustificate   **4.** *Eripite pauperem*

7 wiedlan of handa firenfulra gefriolstð   Nieton
et egenum de manu peccatorum   liberate   **5.** *Nescierunt*

ne ongietaþ on ðe þistron geangað bioþ wænde ealls
neque intellexerunt in tenebris ambulant movebuntur omnia

staþelung eorðan   Ic cwiþe gode ge sindon 7 bearn
fundamenta terrae   **6.** *Ego dixi dii estis et filii*

hyhðo ealle   ge soþlice swa męn sweltoð 7
excelsi omnes   **7.** *Vos autem sicut homines moriemini et*

swa an be ealdormonnan feallaþ   Aris god
sicut unus de principibus cadetis   **8.** *Exsurge deus*

deme eorþan forþan þu hyrfeweardast on eallum þiódum
iudica terram quoniam tu haereditabis in omnibus gentibus

82.

God hwylc gelic biþ þe ne swiga ne emngeniete gode
2. *Deus quis similis erit tibi ne taceas neque compescaris deus*

Forþon gesihþe find þine hieldon 7 to þe fiódon
3. *Quoniam ecce inimici tui sonaverunt et qui te oderunt*

nimað heafod   On filnesse þinre gesettas geþohtas ge-
extulerunt caput   **4.** *In plebem tuam astute cogitaverunt con-*

---

81. 5. *Nieton, i* wr. over the line.   6. MS., hyphen betw. *ge* and
sindon.   82. 3. *hieldon*, init. *i* er.?   4. MS.=*igeþeahtunge*?

þeahtunge 7 ðohton wið healgan his Cwieþon
silium et cogitaverunt adversus sanctos tuos 5. *Dixerunt*

cumað 7 we forspildon hie of ðiode 7 neals gemyndig namon
venite disperdamus eos ex gente et non memorabitur nomen

israhelæ gen ma Forþan ðohton geþeafotunge on
israel amplius 6. *Quoniam cogitaverunt consensum in*

an wið þe gewitnesse gesetton Eardunga
unum adversum te testamentum disposuerunt 7. *Tabernacula*

diobulgild hira 7 þisum maelitum moab 7 aggareni gebal
idumeorum et ismaelitum moab et aggareni 8. *gebal*

7 amon 7 amalech 7 þa fremdon kynren mid geardungum tyrum
et ammon et amalech et alienigene cum habitantibus tyrum

7 soþlice assur somed com mid hiom
9. *Et enim assur simul venit cum illis facti sunt in susceptione*

Mace him swa madian 7 sisare swa iabin
filiis loth 10. *Fac illis sicut madian et sisare sicut iabin*

on rinnellum ácwealde forspildon gewordene
in torrente cison 11. *disperierunt in endor facti*

sint Sete ealdormen hira swa
sunt sicut stercus terrae 12. *Pone principes eorum sicut*

oreb 7 zeb 7 zebe 7 salmana ealle ealdormen hira
oreb et zeb et zebee et salmana omnes principes eorum

ðe ðe cwedon yrfewearðnesse we agon us gehalgunge
13. *qui dixerunt haereditatem possideamus nobis sanctuarium*

godes God min sete hi swa ða hweol 7 swa
dei 14. *Deus meus pone illos ut rotam et sicut*

gedrif biforen ansien windes 7 swa fyr ðe forbierneþ
stipulam ante faciem venti et 15. *sicut ignis qui comburit*

wudas oþþe swa leg oneleð duna Swa þu secsð
silvas velut si flamma incendat montes 16. *Ita persequeris*

hi on hreonesse þinre 7 on irre ðinum gedref hie
eos in tempestate tua et in ira tua conturbabis eos

gefylle onsine hira unwitende 7 secað noman þinne
17. *Imple facies eorum ignominia ut querent nomen tuum*

dryhten Sin gescinde 7 gedrefede on worolde
domine 18. *Confundantur et conturbentur in saeculum*

aworld 7 sin gecirrede 7 forweorðaþ ðet hi oncnawon
saeculi et revereantur et pereant 19. *et cognoscant*

---

8. *fremdon, f* from *r*? *kynren* or *cynren*? 14. *sete*, first *e* from *i*.

forðan   noma   þe   dryhten   þu   ána   ðæs ˙hyhstan   ofer
quia   nomen   tibi dominus   Tu   solus altissimus   super

ealle   eorþan
omnem   terram

83.

hu   lufiende   svnden   erdungæ   þine drythten   megen
2. *Quam amabilia   sunt   tabernacula   tua   domine   virtutum*

gewilnað   7 a pring   saulæ   mine   on akauertune drithten
3. *concupivit   et   defecit   anima   mea   in   atria   domini*

heorte   min   7   fleas   min   hyhtað   on   god   lyuiendne
Cor   meum   et   caro   mea   exultaverunt   in   deum   vivum

7 soðicæ spearwa onuidæþ him   hus   7 turlæ   nestð   þer
4. *et enim   passer   invenit   sibi domum et turtur   nidum ubi*

geseateð   bryddas   hys   Wiebed þin drythten   megen   kyning
reponat   pullos   suos   Altaria tua   domine   virtutum   rex

min 7 god min   Eadige˙ þa eardiað on huse þin
meus et deus meus   5. Beati   qui habitant in domo tua

dryhten   aworold   aworold   hergeað   þe   Eadig wer
domine in saeculum saeculi laudabunt   te   6. Beatus   vir

þęs   is   fultum   from   þe   dryhten   oneled   on heorten
cuius est   auxilium   abs   te   domine   ascensus   in   corde eius

gesette   on denum   teara   on stowe   ðone   þu
disposuit   7. in convalle lacrimarum in   loco   quem dis-

gesettest him   7 eallenga   bletsunga   selleþ   þa   æwe
posuisti eis   8. Et   enim   benedictionem dabit   qui legem

sealde   gangað   be miegne on   miegen   bið gesewen   god
dedit   ambulabunt   de   virtute   in   virtutem   videbitur   deus

goda   on sion   **Dryhten   god   megna   gehyra** benæ˙
deorum in syon   9. Domine   deus virtutum exaudi precem

mine   earum   onfoh   god   iacobes   Scildend   ure
meam   auribus   percipe   deus   iaçob   10. Protector   noster

loca ˙ god 7   loca   on ansine cristes þines   Forþan
aspice deus et respice in faciem christi   tui   11. Quia

selre   is   deig   án   on cafortune þines ofer þusenda geceas
melior est   dies   una   in   atriis   tuis   super   milia   Elegi

frcm aworpenan weran on huse ˙ godes   ma   þeahðe eardion on
abiectus   esse   in domo   dei   magis quam   habitare in

---

83. From *hu* (v. 2), to *megen* (v. 4), exactly one page of the MS., in the larger hand.   3. *fleas*, a fin. er. made?   4. *kyning* or *cyning*?   6. *þęs*, *ę* from *i*.   Let. (h?) er. immed. bef. *is*.   *-ten* (2nd) *tan* or *tœn*?   8. *æwe*, the *a* of the *æ* from *e*?   9. *benœ*, the *a* of the *œ* from *e*?

geteldunga firenfulra   Forþan mildheortnes 7
tabernaculis peccatorum   12. *Quoniam misericordiam et*

soðfestnesse lufað drihten gife 7 wuldor selleð god
veritatem diligit dominus gratiam et gloriam dabit deus

  Dryhten ne wyþerlecað godan gangænde on unsceðenessum
13. *Dominus non privabit bonis ambulantes in innocentia*

dryhten god miegen eadig man se geweneð on þe
domine deus virtutum beatus homo qui sperat in te

84.

  þu gebletsedes dryhten eorðan þine þu ahwyrfdes hieftnied
2. *Be[ne]dixisti domine terram tuam avertisti captivitatem*

iacob   þu forlete unrihtnesse folces þines þu ontyndes
iacob   3. *Remisisti iniquitatem plebis tuae operuisti*

ealle synna hyra   Ðu geþwiærodes eall irre þin
omnia peccata eorum   4. *Mitigasti omnem iram tuam*

þu ahwyrfdes from irre on ebylnesse ðine   , gehwyrfe
avertisti ab ira indignationis tuae   5. *Converte*

us god helo ure 7 ahwyrfe irre þin from us
nos deus salutaris noster et averte iram tuam a nobis

7 neals on ecnesse irsast us Nimðe aðenie irre
6. *ut non in aeternum irascaris nobis Neque extendas iram*

þin from cneowrisne on cneowrisne   god þu gehwyrfe
tuam a progeniae in progeniem   7. *deus tu convertens*

geliffeste us 7 folc þin blissað on þe   Oþiewe
vivificabis nos et plebs tua laetabitur in te   8. *Ostende*

us dryhten mildheortnesse þine 7 helo ðine sele us
nobis domine misericordiam tuam et salutare tuum da nobis

  Ic gehire hwet sprece on me dryhten god forþon
9. *Audiam quid loquatur in me dominus deus quoniam*

sprece sibbe on folce his 7 ofer halga his 7 on him
loquetur pacem in plebem suam et super sanctos suos et in eos

þa gehwyrfað to him silfon   Soþlice ðonne hweðren
qui convertuntur ad ipsum   10. *Verumtamen*

neah is ondriedendum hine hela his ðet oneardigeað
prope timentibus eum salutare ipsius ut inhabitet

wuldor on eorþan úre   Mildheortnes 7 soþfestnes
gloria in terra nostra   11. *Misericordia et veritas*

12. Er. aft. *gife*.   84. 2. -*nied, d* from *t*.   3. *unrihtnesse, t* wr.
over the line.   6. *cneow-* (1st), *e* wr. over the line.

ongean   him   soþfes[t]nesse   7   sib   clippende   sindon   hine
obviaverunt sibi   iustitia   et   pax   complexe   sunt   se

Soþfestnesse of eorþan upcumen is 7 soðfestnes of heofonum
12. *Veritas   de   terra   orta   est et   iustitia   de   caelo*

foreseah   7   soþlice dryhten selleþ   estinesse   7 eorðe
prospexit   13. Et   enim   dominus dabit benignitatem et terra

ure   selð   wæstm   hire   ryhtwisnes beforan hine
nostra dabit fructum suum   14. Iustitia   ante   eum

eode   7   sett on wege steppas his
ambulabit et ponet in   via   gressus suos

85.

Onhield dryhten   eare   ðin   to me 7 gehire me forþan
1. *Inclina   domine   aurem tuam ad me et exaudi me quoniam*

wiedla   7   þearfa   eom   ic   geheald   saula   mine
egenus et   pauper   sum   ego   2. Custodi   animam   meam

forþan   halig   eom   halne   gedo   þew   þinne god   min
quoniam sanctus sum   salvum   fac   servum   tuum deus   meus

gewenende on þe   Miltse   me   dryhten forþan
sperantem   in   te   3. Miserere michi   domine   quoniam

to þe ic clipede elce diege   geblisse saula   þeow ðin
ad te   clamavi tota   die   4. letifica animam servi tui

forþan   þe dryhten uphebbe saula mine   Forðan
quia   ad te domine   levavi animam meam   5. Quoniam

ðu dryhten swete 7 milde is 7 genihtsumnes on mildheortnes
tu domine suavis ac mitis es et   copiosus   in   misericordia

eallum   ic cige   þe   Earum onfoh dryhten gebed
omnibus invocantibus te   6. Auribus percipe domine orationem

min   7 beheald stefne   gebed   min   On deg
meam et intende   voci deprecationis meae   7. In die

earfoþnesse   min ic clipige to þe forþan   þu gehirdes me
tribulationis meae   clamavi ad te quoniam   exaudisti   me

Ne is   gelic   þe on godas dryhten 7 ne is   efter
8. *Non est similis tibi in   diis   domine et non est secundum*

worce þinum   Ealle   þeoda   ða midþy ðe ðu dides
opera   tua   9. Omnes gentes quascumque   fecisti

cumað 7 gebiddaþ beforan þe dryhten 7   wiorþað   noman
venient et adorabunt coram   te domine et honorificabunt nomen

---

13. From 7 (2nd) to end of Psalm in the larger hand.   **85. 4.** þeow,
o from some other let.

þinne   Forþan michel wes þu 7   do   wundor þu
tuum   10. *Quoniam magnus es   tu et faciens mirabilia tu*

eart god ána   geled me dryhten on wéie þinum 7
es deus solus   11. *Deduc me domine in via   tua   et*

ic gange on soþfestnesse þine blissige heorte min þet
ambulabo in   veritate   tua Laetetur   cor   meum ut

he ond[r]ede noman þinne   Ic ondette þe dryhten
    timeat   nomen tuum   12. *confitebor tibi domine*

god min on ealre heorten minre 7   wiorþige   noman þinne
deus meus in toto corde   meo et honorificabo nomen tuum

on ecnesse   Forþan mildheortnesse þin micel is
in aeternum   13. *Quoniam misericordia   tua magna est*

ofer me 7 genere saula mine of helle on þa yteran
super me et eripuisti animam meam ex inferno   inferiori

god þa unsoþfestan   onarisan   on me 7 on gemotstowe
14. *Deus   iniusti   insurrexerunt in me et   synagoga*

miehte   sohton   saula   mine 7 ne forænsetten þe
potentium quesierunt animam meam et non proposuerunt te

beforan   onsine   his   7 þu dryhten god min
ante   conspectum suum   15. *Et tu domine deus meus*

mildsigend 7 mildheort geðyldig 7 micel   mildheort 7 soð
miserator et misericors patiens et multum misericors et verax

Lóca on me 7 mildse me sele mihte cnihte þinum
16. *Respice in me et miserere mei da potestatem puero   tuo*

7 halne do sunu þeowre þinre   Do mid me dryhten
et salvum fac filium ancillae tuae 17. *Fac mecum domine*

tacn on god þet hi geseon ða me fiogað 7 sien gescinde
signum in bono ut videant qui me oderunt et confundantur

Forþan þu dryhten gefultoma me 7 frefrend is me
Quoniam tu domine adiuuisti me et consolatus es me

86.

Staðolas   his on dunum halgum   lufaþ dryhten
Fundamenta eius in montibus sanctis   2. *diligit dominus*

gato syon ofer ealle eardung iacob   þa wuldorfestan
portas syon super omnia tabernacula iacob 3.   *Gloriosa*

---

13. *micel*, *e* from some other let.   14. *forænsetten*, 1st *n* dotted; sec.
e from *o*.   15. Several lett. er. immed. after *micel*; also another er. bef.
mildheort.   17. *geseon*, sec. *e* from *i*.

cweþene sien be ðe ceaster godes   gemyndyg   raab 7
dicta sunt de te civitas dei   **4.** *memor ero raab et*

babilonis witende þe gesihðe þa fremdan 7 tyrus 7 folc
babylonis scientibus te Ecce alienigene et tyrus et populus

ethiopen þa weran on hiræ   Modor sion cwið man
ethyopum hi fuerunt in ea   **5.** *Mater syon dicet homo*

7 man geworden is on hire 7 he staþolað hie se hyhsta
et homo factus est in ea et ipse fundavit eam altissimus

Dryhten siegð on gewrytum   folca   hira 7
6. *Dominus narravit in scripturis populorum suorum et*

ealdordom hira þæ weron on hyra   Swa blissiendra
principum eorum qui fuerunt in ea   **7.** *Sicut laetantium*

ealra urra 7 eardung is on þe
omnium nostrum habitatio est in te

87.

dryhten god helo minre on deige ic cliþige 7 niht beforan ðe
2. *Domine deus salutis meae in die clamavi et nocte coram te*

Ongieð gebed min on gesihþe þinre onhilde eare ðin to
3. *Intret oratio mea in conspectu tuo inclina aurem tuam ad*

bene min dryhten   Forþan gefylled is yfele saul min 7
precem meam domine   **4.** *Quia repleta est malis anima mea et*

lif min on helle. tonealeceð   gewenende ic eom mid
vita mea in inferno appropiabit   **5.** *Estimatus sum cum*

niþerastigendum on seað geworden ic eom swa man butan
descendentibus in lacum factus sum sicut homo sine

fultome betuioh deade friols Swa þa gewundadon
adiutorio   **6.** *inter mortuos liber Sicut vulnerati*

slepende aworpene on byrgnessum. ðara ne wære witende
dormientes proiecti in monumentis quorum non meministi

ma 7 witodlice hie of heanda ðinre cnysede sindon
amplius et quidem ipsi de manu tua expulsi sunt

gesetton me on seaþ on þa yteran on þistrum 7 on scuwan
7. *Posuerunt me in lacu inferiori in tenebris et in umbra*

deaðes On me getrymed is yrre þin 7 ealle upahefnesse
mortis   **8.** *In me confirmata est ira tua et omnes elationes*

---

86. 4. Gloss to *ero* er.?   6. ealdordom, r wr. over the line.   **87.**
2. *deige*, 1st *e* from *i*.   4. on, n cor. by d. ink (wh. was cor. the Latin).
5. *eom* (1st), MS. = eon.   6. witende, *t* from ᵹ.   7. MS. = *scudewan, de*
wr. over the line in d. ink later.

þine ofer me ongeleddes   Fior þu dydes kuþe min from me
tuas super me induxisti   9. *Longe fecisti notos meos a   me*

gesetton me from onwealdendum him geseald ic eom 7 ic ne
posuerunt me in   abominationem sibi traditus sum   et non

gangæ   Eagan mine untrumede sindon forh lewsan
egrediebar   10. *Oculi   mei   infirmati   sunt   pre inopia*

ic clipede to þe dryhten elce deig ic aðenede hande mine to þe
clamavi ad te domine tota die   expandi   manus meas ad te

Is ðes wen deade doende wundor þin oþþet me to cweþenne
11. *Numquid mortuis facies mirabilia   aut   medici*

aweccað 7 ondettað   þe   Is ðes wen siegð elles hu
resuscitabunt et confitebuntur tibi   12. *Numquid enarrabit aliquis*

on byrgenne mildheortnesse þine 7 soðfestnesse þine on forwyrde
in sepulchro misericordiam tuam et   veritatem   tuam in perditione

Is ðęs wen bioþ oncnawenc on þistrum wundor þin oþðe
13. *Numquid   cognoscentur   in tenebris mirabilia tua aut*

soþfestnesse þine on eorðan ofergitende   7 ic to þe
iustitia   tua   in   terra   oblivionis   14. *Et ego ad te*

dryhten ic clipige 7 on morgen gebed min forecymð to þe
domine clamavi et   mane   oratio mea preveniet   te

Tohwen dryhten adrifsð gebed   min þu hwyrfdes onsien
15. *Utquid domine   repellis orationem meam   avertis   faciem*

þin from me   Wędla ic eom ic 7 on gewinnum from
tuam a   me   16. *Egens   sum ego et in laboribus   a*

giogaþhade minum 7 upahafen soðlice geeaþmoded ic eom 7
iuventute   mea   exaltatus autem   humiliatus   sum   et

gescinded   On me þurhfóron irre þin 7 bregnes þinre
confusus   17. *In me pertransierunt irae tuae et terrores tui*

gedrefdon me   Ymbsealdon me swa wæter elce
conturbaverunt me   18. *Circumdederunt me sicut aqua   tota*

dege ymbsealdon me semed   Þu afirdes from me friond
die circundederunt me simul   19. *Elongasti   a me amicum*

7 nihstan 7 cuþe mine from wergunge
et proximum et notos meos a   miseria

88.

Mildheortnesse þine dryhten on ecnesse ic singæ on
2. *Misericordias tuas   domine in aeternum   cantabo in*

---

9. *kuþe* or *cuþe* ? *gesetton*, 1st *t* wr. over the line.   10. *forh*, so MS.
14. morgen, *e* from *o*.   88. 2. *Mildheortnesse*, *t* wr. over the line.

cneowrisne 7 forecneowrisne ic foresecge soþfestnesse þine on
generatione et   progeniae   pronuntiabo   veritatem   tuam in

muðe minum   Forþan þu cwæde on ecnesse mildheortnes
ore   meo   3. *Quoniam   dixisti   in aeternum   misericordia*

biþ getimbred on heofonum gearwiende soþfestnesse þine
aedificabitur in   caelis   preparabitur   veritas   tua

gesette   kyðnesse mine gecorene minum ic swor dauide
4. *Disposui testamentum meum electis   meis   iuravi   david*

þeowe minum   oþþe on ecnesse ic gearwige sed ðin
servo meo   5. *usque in eternum preparabo semen tuum*

7 ic getimbrige on worold aworold setl þin   Bioþ andet-
et aedificabo in saeculum seculi sedem tuam   6. *Confite-*

tende heofonas wundor þin dryhten 7 soðfestnesse þine on
buntur caeli mirabilia tua domine et veritatem tuam in

circan haligra   Forþan hwylc on wolcnu emlice
aecclesia sanctorum 7. *Quoniam quis in nubibus equabitur*

drybtene oþþe hwylc gelic biþ gode betwih bearnum godes
domino aut quis similis erit deo inter filios dei

god sé wuldraþ on geþeahtunge haligra micel 7
8. *Deus qui glorificatur in consilio sanctorum magnus et*

to ondrædonne ofer ealle þa on ymbegonge his sindon
metuendus super omnes qui in circuitu eius sunt

Dryhten god megen hwylc gelic þe mihtig is dryhten
9. *Domine deus virtutum quis similis tiði potens es domine*

7 soþfestnes þin ða on ymbegonge   ðu   wilts
et veritas tua in circuitu tuo 10. *Tu dominaris*

mihte sæwe styrunga eallunga yða his þu geðwerast
potestati maris motum autem fluctuum eius tu mitigas

Ðu geeaðmeddes swa þa gewundedon oferhid 7 on
11. *Tu humiliasti sicut vulneratum superbum et in*

megene earmes þines þu tostenctes find ðine   þine
virtute brachii tui dispersisti inimicos tuos 12. *Tui*

sindon hefonos 7 þin is eorða ymbhwyrf [t] eorþan 7 fylnesse
sunt caeli et tua est terra orbem terrarum et plenitudinem

his þu gegute   Ob eastdele 7 sæwe þu gesceope thabor
eius tu fundasti 13. *Aquilonem et mære tu creasti thabor*

7 hermon on naman þinum hyhtað   þinum earmum
et hermon in nomine tuo exultabunt 14. *tuum brachium*

---

4. *kyð-* or *cyð-* ?   9. *soþfestnes, t* wr. over the line.   12. *fylnesse,* 1st
e from *i.*   14. *þinum, þ* repeated.

mid mihte Biᚦ getrimed hand þin 7 biᚦ uphafen swiᚦre þin
cum potentia   Firmetur   manus tua et   exaltetur   dextera tua

soþfestnes 7   dom   foregearwung setl ᚦin Mildheorte 7
15. *iustitia et iudicium preparatio sedis tuae Misericordia et*

soþfeste foregongaþ beforan onsinæ þinre   eadig folc
veritas   preibunt   ante   faciem tuam   **16.** *beatus populus*

þæt wat on wynsumnesse Dryhten onlihteþ ondwlita þin
qui scit   iubilationem   Domine in lumine vultus   tui

gangaᚦ   7 on naman þinum hyhtaᚦ ealle deg 7 on
ambulabunt   **17.** *et in nomine tuo exultabunt tota die et in*

þinre soþfes[t]nesse gehyhtaᚦ   Forᚦan wuldor megen
tua   iustitia   exaltabuntur **18.** *Quoniam gloria virtutis*

hira þu eart 7 wellicode þine biþ upahafen horn   urne
eorum tu es et in beneplacito tuo   exaltabitur cornu nostrum

Forþon dryhten is onfengnes 7 halig isrhæle kininges
19. *Quoniam domini est assumptio et sancti israel regis*

ures   Đa sprecende is on gesihþe bearn þin 7 þu cwæde
nostri **20.** *Tunc locutus es in aspectu filiis tuis et dixisti*

Sette to fultome ofer mihte 7 upahof gecorene of folce
posui adiutorium super potentem et exaltavi electum de plebe

minum   gemette dauid þeow minne on ele halig minum
mea **21.** *Inveni david servum meum in oleo sancto meo*

smyrede hine   handa soþlice mine bioᚦ fultomiende him
unxi eum **22.** *Manus enim mea   auxiliabitur ei*

7 earm min gestrangaᚦ hine   Noht forᚦswefaᚦ
et brachium meum confortabit eum **23.** *Nichil proficiet*

fiond on him 7 sunu unrihtnessa ne scyᚦeþ him   7
inimicus in eo et filius iniquitatis non nocebit ei   **24.** *Et*

gefeallaþ fiend his from ansiene his 7 fiodon hine on
concidam inimicos eius a facie ipsius et odientes eum in

fleamæ gecirde   7 soᚦfestnes mine 7 mildheortnes min
fugam convertam **25.** *Et veritas mea et misericordia mea*

mid him 7 on noman minum biᚦ uphafen horn his   7
cum ipso et in nomine meo exaltabitur cornu eius **26.** *Et*

sette on siewe hand his 7 on streamum swiᚦran his
ponam in mari manum eius et in fluminibus dexteram eius

---

15. 7 (1st) repeated. *fore-*, e repeated, but sec. er. *beforan*, *a* from *e*.
onsinæ or *onsine*?; fin. *n* er. 16. *gangaᚦ*, init. lett. (two?) cr.; *ga* (1st)
cov. by d. ink. 17. *naman*, 1st *a* prob. from *o*. 18. *-hafen*, *a* from *e*.
19. *kin-* or *cin-*? 23. MS. = *worᚦswefaᚦ*. *unrihtnessa*, *t* wr. over the line.

He gecigdc me feder min wes þu god min 7 onfeng
27. *Ipse invocavit me pater meus es tu deus meus et susceptor*

hælo mine 7 ic frumkennedon ic sette hine on hyhþo
salutis meae 28. *Et ego primogenitum ponam illum excelsum*

fore kiniugas eorþan Ou ecnesse ic healde him
prae regibus terrae 29. *In aeternum servabo illi*

mildheortuesse mine 7 kyðnesse mine geleaffulle him 7
misericordiam meam et testamentum meum fidele ipsi 30. *Et*

ic sette on world aworld setl his 7 ðrymsetl his swa deg
ponam in seculum seculi sedem eius et thronum eius sicut dies

heofona Gif hi forletað bearn bis iewe mine 7 on
caeli 31. *Si derelinquerint filii eius legem meam et in*

domum minum ne gangað Gif mine soþfestnesse
iudiciis meis non ambulaverint 32. *Si iustificationes meas*

forecostigað 7 bebodu mine ne geheoldon Ic niosige
prophanaverint et mandata mea non custodierint 33. *Visitabo*

on girde unrihtnessa hira 7 on swingla sinna hira
in virga iniquitates eorum et in verberibus peccata eorum

Mildheortnessæ eallenga mine ne ic tostence fram him
34. *Misericordiam autem meam non dispergam ab eo*

ne him scyðeð on soþfestnesse mine ne foræcostunga
neque nocebo in veritate mea 35. *neque profanabo*

kyðnesse mine 7 ða forðgað of welerum minum ne
testamentum meum et quae procedunt de labiis meis non

onsien onleccungæ Æne ic swor on halgum minum gif
faciam irrita 36. *Semel iuravi in sancto meo si*

dauid ligað sæd his on ecnesse wunað 7
david mentiar 37. *semen eius in aeternum manebit* 38. *et*

setl his swa sunnæ on gesihþe minre 7 swa mona fulfremed
sedes eius sicut sol in conspectu meo et sicut luna perfecta

on ecnessum 7 gewita on hefonum gelenfful ðu soðlice
in eternum et testis in caelo fidelis 39. *Tu vero*

adrife 7 hyrwdes 7 þu arefdes krist þinne ðu ge-
reppulisti et sprevisti et distulisti christum tuum 40. *aver-*

hwyrfdes kyðnesse þiowes þines forecostunga on eorþan
tisti testamentum servi tui profanasti in terra

---

28. -*ken*- or -*cen*-? *kiningas* or *ciningas*? 29. *ecnesse*, init. *e* repeated,
but repeated let. afterwards er. *kiðnesse* dotted for er. bef. *kyðnesse*; *kyð*- or
cyð-? 33. *niosige*, MS.= *mosige*. 35. *kyð*- or *cyð*-? 38. *setl* repeated
but first dotted for er. 39. *krist* or *crist*? 40. *kyð*- or *cyð*-?

haligdomes his   þu towurpe ealle wagas   his þu gesettes
sanctitatem eius   **41.** *Destruxisti omnes macerias eius posuisti*

wununga   his on   egnesse   todelde   hine ealle
munitiones eius in formidine   **42.** *Diripuerunt eum omnes*

þa ferende węron weg geworden is on   hosp   néan his
    transeuntes   viam   factus   est in obprobrium vicinis suis

þu upahofe swiþre   fionda   his   þu geblissodes ealle
43. *Exaltasti dexteram inimicorum eius   laetificasti   omnes*

find   his   þu ahwyrfdes on fultom sweord his 7 ne
inimicos eius   **44.** *Avertisti adiutorium gladii eius et non*

is fultumend him on gefiohte   þu tolysdes hine fram
es   auxiliatus   ei   in   bello   **45.** *Dissolvisti   eum   ab*

clesnunge   7   setl his on eorþan ðu tolysdes   ðu ge-
emundatione et sedem eius in terram   conlisisti   **46.** *Minor-*

wanodes dagas   tida   his   þurhgute hine on gescindnesse
asti   dies   temporum eius perfudisti eum   confusione

Oð   þte dryhten þu irsað on ende   birnað   swa fyr
47. *Usque quo   domine   irasceris in finem exardescit sicut ignis*

irre þin   Wes gemindig dryhten forþan mine   sped   ne
ira tua   **48.** *Memorare   domine   quae   mea substantia non*

eallenga idle þu gesettes bearn   manna   Hwylc is manna
    enim   vane constituisti filios hominum   **49.** *Quis est homo*

se lifað 7 ne gesihþ   deað oððe hwylc þeowað saule   his
qui vivet et non videbit mortem aut   quis   eruet animam suam

of hande helle   Hwær sindon mildheorte þine   ealde
de manu inferi   **50.** *Ubi   sunt misericordiae tuae antiquae*

dryhten swa swore dauide on ðinre soðfes[t]nesse   Węs ðu
domine sicut iurasti david in   veritate tua   **51.** *Memor*

gemindig hosp   þeowra   þinra   ðæt ic węs hebbende on
esto   obprobrium servorum tuorum quod   continui   in

bosmæ   minum monigra ðeoda   Þęt   edwitodon
sinu   meo   multarum gentium   **52.** *Quod exprobraverunt*

find þine dryhten þæt   edwitodon   stirungæ   kristes
inimici tui domine quod exprobraverunt commutationem christi

þines   gebletsed dryhten on ecnesse   sie sie
tui   **53.** *Benedictus dominus in aeternum fiat fiat*

---

46. *e* (dotted) immed. bef. *on.*   49. Er. bef. *7. gesihþ,* MS. = *geseahþ, ea*
being dotted and *i* wr. above these lett.   51. *on* repeated; Latin *in* also
repeated.   52. *kristes* or *cristes*?

89.

Dryhten gescild gewurden is us from cneowrisne 7 fore-
Domine refugium factus es nobis a generatione et pro-
cneowrisne   Erðan   wæs   duna oððet wes getrymed
  geniae   **2.** *Priusquam fierent montes aut   formaretur*
ymbhwyrft eorðan from world 7 oþþet on   worlda worolde þu
  orbis   terrae   a   saeculo et usque in seculum   tu
eart god   Ne ahwyrfe manna on eaðmodnesse 7 þu cwæde
  es deus   **3.** *Ne avertas hominem in humilitatem et dixisti*
sin gecirde   bearn   monna   Forþan ðusend gearas
convertimini filii   hominum   **4.** *Quoniam mille   anni*
toforan eagan þinum 7 swa dæges of ean ðet forefered 7 swa
ante oculos tuos   sicut dies hesterna quae preteriit Et sicut
gehyldon on nyht   þe fore nawuhte hebbende gear   hira
custodia in nocte   **5.** *quae pro nichilo est habentur anni eorum*
    On morhne   swa   wyrte   feræt on morgen blosmað 7
6.   *Mane   sicut   herba transeat   mane   floreat et*
þurhferet on efen gefeallað aheardað 7 forwisnað   Forþan
pertranseat vespere decidat induret et arescat   **7.** *Quia*
we aspringað on irre þinum 7 on wreðða þinum gedrefede
defecimus   in   ira   tua   et in   furore   tuo   conturbati
we sindon   gesettest þu unrih[t]nesse ure   on gesibþe
  sumus   **8.** *Posuisti   iniquitates nostras in conspectu*
þinre worlde   urum   on   lihtnes   onsin þin
tuo   seculum   nostrum   in   inluminatione   vultus tui
    Forþan ealle dagas ure ateoredon 7 we on irre ðinum
9. *Quoniam omnes dies nostri defecerunt et nos in ira tua*
ateoredon Gear ure swa sand smeagað   dagas
defecimus Anni nostri sicut aranea meditabantur   **10.** *dies*
    geara   ura   on heom hundsiofanti gear gif eallinga on
annorum nostrorum in ipsis septuaginta annis Si autem in
    mihtum hundeahti gearum 7 ge ma hira gewin 7 sar
potentatibus octoginta   anni et plurimum eorum labor et dolor
    Forþan ofercymeð ofer us gedwernes 7 bið gegripene
Quoniam supervenit super nos mansuetudo et corripiemur
    Hwylc cneow mihte irre þine oððet fore ege irre
11. *Quis novit potestatem irae tuae aut pre timore iram*

89. 7. *wreðða*, *e* prob. from *o*.

þin   to rimanne   Swiþre þin dryhten cuþe do   us
tuam   12. *dinumerare Dexteram tuam domine notam fac nobis*

7 getydnesse heorte   on   snytro   gehwyrfe dryhten
et   eruditos   corde   in sapientia   13. *Convertere domine*

elles hu   7   to gebiddenne beo   ofer   þeowas   þine
aliquantulum   et   deprecare   super   servos   tuos

We gefillað on morgen mildheortnes þin 7 uphebbað 7
14. *Repleti sumus   mane   misericordia tua et exultavimus et*

we gelustfulliað on eallum   dagum   urum   Wi sint
delectati sumus   in omnibus diebus   nostris   15. Delectati

gelustfullod for dagum þam us þu geeaðmeddes gearum on
sumus   pro diebus quibus nos   humiliasti   anni   in

þam gesewon yfel   Loca on þeowas þine 7 on weorc
quibus vidimus mala   16. Respice in servos tuos et in opera

ðin   dryhten 7 gerec bearn hira   7 .biþ birhtnes
tua   domine et dirige filios eorum   17. Et sit splendor

dryhtenes godes ures ofer us 7 weorc handan   urra 7
domini dei nostri super nos et opera manuum nostrarum

gerece ofer us
dirige super nos

90.

Se þe eardaþ on fultome þes hyhstan on gescildnesse godes
Qui habitat in adiutorio altissimi in protectione dei

hefonas midwuniendum   kwæð dryhten onfeng min wes 7
caeli commorabitur   2. Dicet domino susceptor meus es et

gescild min god min ic gewene on hine   Forþan he
refugium mea deus meus sperabo in eum   3. Quoniam ipse

gefreolsa me of gegrine huntenda 7 from worde reðe
liberavit me de laqueo venantium et a   verbo aspero

Sculdrum hira ymbscuan þe 7 under fiðrum his þu gewens
4. *Scapulis suis obumbrabit tibi et sub pennis eius sperabis*

Scild ymbscleð þe soðfestnes his þu ne ondredes from
5. *Scuto circumdabit te veritas eius non timebis a*

ege ða nihtlican   From strele fleogænde þurh deg
timore nocturno 6. A sagitta volante per diem a

.13. *gehwyrfe, w* from *þ. to gebiddenne beo,* the Latin is *deprecare, re* being
on er., followed by *esto* wh. has a line drawn through it for er.   90. *Se*
repeated but first er.   2. *kwæð* or *cwæð?* Er. bef. *gescild.*   3. Er. bef.
huntenda.   5. *soðfestnes, t* wr. over the line.

ceapunga ðurhgongende on þistrum from hrýre 7 diobola
negotio   perambulante   in   tenebris   a   ruina   et demonio

on mīdlene   gefeallað of healfe ðine þusend 7 ten ðusenda
meridiano   7. Cadent a latere tuo milïe et decem   milia

of þa swyðran þinra þe eallenga ne   tonealęcð   Soþlice
a   dextris   tuis tibi autem non appropiabit   8. Verum-

ðonne hweðren eagan þine þu sceawast 7 edleanenga   firenfulra
    tamen   oculis tuis considerabis et retributionem peccatorum

þu gesihts   Forþan þu eart dryhten hiht min þes hihstan
  videbis   9. Quoniam tu es domine spes mea altissimum

þu settes gescild þin   Ne ne belimpað to ðe yfel 7
  posuisti refugium tuum   10. Non accedent ad te mala et

swyngla ne genealecęð geteldenga þinre   Forþan
flagella non appropiabunt tabernaculo tuo   11. Quoniam

englum his bebead be ðe ðette gehealdon þe on eallum wegas
angelis suis mandavit de te ut custodiant te in omnibus viis

þine   On handum berað þe þæt nęfre atsporna on
tuis   12. In manibus portabunt te ne umquam offendas ad

stane fot þinum   Ofer neddran 7 beasiliscum
lapidem pedem tuum   13. Super aspidem et basiliscum

gangas þu 7 tredeð leon 7 dracaṁ   Forþan
ambulabis et conculcabis leonem et draconem   14. Quoniam

on me geweneð gefriolsia hine ic gescilde hine forþam oncneow
in me speravit et liberabo eum protegam eum quoniam cognovit

noman min   gecigde me 7 ic gehirde hine mid him
nomen meum   15. Invocabit me et ego exaudiam eum cum ipso

ic eom on earfoðnesse
sum in tribulatione

    Ic hine generie 7 his næmæn swilce
    gewuldrige geond eælle weorðeodæ
    7 him lifdægæs 7 længe sille
    swilce him mine helu holde ætywe

*Eripiam eum et glorificabo eum   16. longitudinem dierum
adimplebo eum et ostendam illi salutare meum*

91.

(1.) [Gód] is ðet mæn drihtne 7 geæræ ændette
    7 neodlice his næmæn æsinge
    þone heæhestæn heleðæ cynnes

7. Er. bef. *healfe*. *eallenga*, fin. *n* er.? *tonealęcð*, one (or two) lett. er.
betw. *o* and *n*. A fresh hand begins with *Ic hine* (ĭ5).

M

2. *Bonum est confiteri domino et psallere nomini tuo altissime*

(**2.**) And þonne on morgenne megenne sege
hu he milde weærð mænnæcynne
7 his soðe sege neæhtes

3. *Ad adnuntiandum mane misericordiam tuam et veritatem tuam per noctem*

(**3.**) þet ic on tin strengum getogen hefde
hu ic ðe on sælterio singæn meæhte
oðð þe mid heærpæn hliste cwemæn
forðon ðu me on ðinum wiorcum wisum lufædest
hihte ic to ðinræ hændæ hælgum dedum

4. *In decachordo psalterio cum cantico et cythara*   **5.** *quia delectasti me domine in factura tua et in operibus manuum tuarum exultabo*

(**4.**) hu micle sint þine megenweorc meæhtig drihten
werun ðine geðæncæs þearle deope

6. *Quam magnificata sunt opera tua domine nimis profunde facte sunt cogitationes tuae*

(**5.**) wonhidig wer ðes wiht ne ceæn
ne þæs ændgyt hæfæd ænig disigræ

7. *Vir insipiens non cognoscet et stultus non intellegit ea*

(**6.**) þonne forðcumæþ firenfulræ ðreæt
heæp sinningræ hige onlic
eælle ðær ætywæð þæ ðe unrihtæs
on weoruld life worhton geornæst
þ hi forwordone weorden siððæn
on worul[d] æworlde 7 to widæn feore

8. *Cum exorientur peccatores sicut foenum et apparuerint omnes qui operantur iniquitatem ut intereant in seculum seculi*

(**7.**) þu on ecnesse æwæ drihten
heæhste bist hefonrices weærd

9. *Tu autem altissimus in aeternum domine*

(**8.**) hi nu ðinre feond fæcne drihten
on eorðwege eælle forweorðæð
7 weorðæþ towrecene wide eælle
ðæ þæ unrihtes eror worhtæn

10. *Quoniam ecce inimici tui domine peribunt et dispergentur omnes qui operantur iniquitatem*

(**9.**) þonne ænhornæ eælræ gelicæst

91. (3.) *meæhte, e* from *i*.   (6.) *þonne,* MS. = *þonnne.*

min horn weorðeð æhæfen swiðe
7 mine yldo beoð æghwer genihtsum

11. *Et exaltabitur sicut unicornis cornu meum et senectus mea in misericordia uberi*

(10.) Ænd eægæ ðin eac sceawade
hwer fynd mine fæcne wæran
7 mine wergend wræðe gehirde
efne ðin ægen eære swilce

12. *Et respexit oculus tuus inimicos meos et insurgentes in me malignantes audivit auris tua*

(11.) Se soðfestæ sæmed anlicæst
beorht on blædum bloweð swæ pælmæ
7 swæ libænes beorh lideð 7 groweð

13. *Iustus ut palma florebit et sicut cedrus libani multiplicabitur*

(12.) Settæþ nu georne on godes huse
þet ge on his wicum wel geblowen

14. *Plantati in domo domini in atriis domus dei nostri florebunt*

(13.) Nu gyt sindæn mænige mænnæ swilcæ
ðe him yldo gebidan ær to genihte
7 þæ mid geðilde þendæn segdæn

15. *Adhuc multiplicabuntur in senecta uberi et bene pacientes erunt*

(14.) Cwedæn þ were soðfest silua drihtæn
7 hine unrihtes æwiht ne heolde

16. *ut annuntient Quoniam iustus est dominus deus noster et non est iniquitas in eo*

92.

(1.) drihten ricsode wlite he scyrdde   (2.) scrydde drihten
1. *Dominus regnavit decorem   induit*   *Induit   dominus*

st[r]angnesse 7 he begirde hine of megene
fortitudinem et precinxit   se   virtute

(3.) 7 þæ ymbhwirft eorðæn getrimede
swæ folde stod festæ siððæn

Et enim firmavit orbem terre qui non commovebitur

(4.) Geæru is ðin setl 7 ðu ece god
er worulde frumæn wunæst butan ende

(11.) *anlicæst, a* from *o.*   (13.) *gebidan, a* from *o.*   **92.** (1.) This v. by Cor. in pl. of er.   (2.) This v. (except drihten) by Cor. in pl. of er.

2. *Parata sedes tua deus ex tunc a saeculo tu es*

(5.) hofæn hioræ stefne streæmæs drihtæn
hofæn 7 hlynsædæn hludæn reordæ
fræm weter stefnum widræ mænigræ

3. *Elevaverunt flumina domini elevaverunt flumina voces suas*

4. *a vocibus aquarum multarum*

(6.) Wreclice syndæn wege ægængæs
.þonne sǽstreæmæs swiðust .flowæð
swæ is wundorlic weældend usser
hælig drihten on heænessum
Mirabiles elationes maris mirabilis in excelsis dominus

(7.) þin gewitnes is drihten weorcum geleæfsum
.　7 mid soðe is swiðe getrewæþ

5. *Testimonia tua domine credibilia facta sunt nimis*

(8.) huse þinum hælig gedæfenæþ
drihten usser 7 dægæs længæ
Domum tuam decent sancta domine in longitudine dierum

93.

(1.) God wrecenæ god 7 ðu me æhwrecæn
swilce æna gefreogan ægh[w]ylcne mæn

1. *Deus ultionum dominus deus ultionum libere egit*

(2) Ahef ðe on hellen eorðæn demæ
gild oferhidegum swæ hi er græmæ worhton

2. *Exaltare qui iudicas terram redde retributionem superbis*

(3.) hu længe fyrenwyrhtæn foldæn wcældaþ
oððe manwyrhtæn morðra gylpað

3. *Usque quo peccatores domine usque quo peccatores gloria-buntur*

(4.) hi oftust sprecæþ unnyt secgað
7 woh meldiað wyrceæþ unriht

4. *Pronuntiabunt et loquentur iniquitatem loquentur omnes qui operantur iniustitiam*

(5.) Folc hi þin drihten fæcne gehindæn
7 yrfæ ðin eæll forcomæn

---

93. (1.) *God* prob. by Cor.　　(4.) *wyrceæþ*; before this word is *wrecæþ* with a line drawn through for er.

5. *Populum tuum domine humiliaverunt et hereditatem tuam vexaverunt*

(6.) Eallðeodige men eærmæ widwæn
stiopcildæ feæla stundum acwealdan

6. *Viduam et advenam interfecerunt et pupillos occiderunt*

(7.) Segdæn 7 cweðæn þ ge ne sæwe
drihten æfre dyde swæ he wolde
ne ðet iacobes god ongitan cuðe

7. *Et dixerunt non videbit dominus nec intelliget deus iacob*

(8.) Onfindæn ðeð 7 ongeoton þe on folce nu
unwiseste eælre sindon
disige hwethwygu deope þet oncnæwæn

8. *Intelligite nunc qui insipientes estis in populo et stulti aliquando sapite*

(9.) Se ðe erest ealdum earan worhte
hu se oferhleoður æfre wurde
7 him eægana gesihð eallum sealde
7 he scarpe ne mæge gesceawiau
7 se ðe ege healdað eallum ðeodum
7 his ðrea ne sio þa for awiht
se ðe men læreð micelne wisdom

9. *Qui plantavit aurem non audiet aut qui finxit oculum non considerat* 10. *qui corripit gentes non arguet qui docet hominem scientiam*

(10.) God eælle can guman geðancas
eorðbuendræ forðon hi ydle sind

11. *Dominus novit cogitationes hominum quoniam vane sunt*

(11.) þæt bið eædig mæn ðe ðu hine ece god
on þinre soðre æ sylfa getihtest
7 hine þeodscipe þinne lerest
7 him yfele dagas eulla gebeorgest
oð ðet bið fræcne seæð þæm fyrænfullæn
deop adolfen deorc 7 ðistre

12. *Beatus homo quem tu erudieris domine et de lege tua docueris eum* 13. *ut mitiges eum a diebus malis donec fodiatur peccatori fovea* .

(12.) hefre wiðdrifeð drihten ure
his ægen folc ne his yrfe ðon ma
on ealdre wile hefre forletæn

14. *Quia non repellet dominus plebem suam et haereditatem suam non derelinquet*

(8.) *eælre, r* from *l.*

(13.) hwilc ðonne gena gewerfeþ bið
    þ he on unriht eft ne oncyrre
    oððe wilc nimeð me þet ic man fleo
    7 mid rihtheortum redes ðence

15. *Quoad usque iustitia convertatur in iudicium et qui tenent eam omnes qui recto sunt corde*

(14.) hwylc ariseð mid me þ ic riht fremme
    7 wið awirgdum winne 7 stænde
    ðe unrihtes eælle wirceæð

16. *Quis exsurget michi adversus malignantes aut quis stabit mecum adversus operantes iniquitatem*

(15.) Nimðe me drihten demæ usser
    gefultumed fegere æt þeærfe
    weninga min saul sohte ·helle

17. *Nisi quia dominus adiuvasset me paulominus habitaverat in inferno anima mea*

(16.) Gif ic ðet segde þ min silfes fot
    ful sarlice asliden nerc
    þæ me mildheortnes mihtigan drihtnes
    gefultumede þ ic feorh ahte

18. *Si dicebam motus est pes meus misericordia tua domine adiuvabit me*

(17.) Æfter ðere mænigeo minræ saræ
    ðe me ær æn ferhðe feste gestodæn
    þæ me þine frofre fegere drihten
    gesibbedæn sawule mine

19. *Secundum multitudinem dolorum meorum in corde meo consolationes tuae domine laetificaverunt animam meam*

(18.) Ne etfligeð þe æhwer facen ne unriht
    þu gefestnæst eæc facen sares
    hi soðfeste sniome geheftæþ
    7 hioræ sawle ofslean ðenceað
    blod soðfestræ bitere agcotan

20. *Nunquid adheret tibi sedes iniquitatis qui fingis dolorem in precepto*   **21.** *captabunt in animam iusti et sanguinem innocentem condempnabunt*

(19.) Forðon me is geworden wealdend drihten
    to friðstole fest 7 gestæþcled
    is me fultum his fest on drihtne

(13.) *gewerfeþ, w* from *f.* MS. = *urriht.*   (15.) *weninga, ga* on er.

22. *Et factus est michi dominus in refugium et deus meus in auxilium spei meae*

(20.) þoune him gyldeþ god elmihtig
    ealla þa unriht þe hi gearnedæn
    7 on hiora facne feste todrifeð
    drihten elmihtig dema soðfæst

23. *Et reddet illis dominus iniquitates ipsorum et in malitias eorum disperdet illos dominus deus noster*

94.

(1.) Cumeð nu to gedremene uten cweman gode
    winnum drihten wealdind herigean
    urum helende hildo gebeodan

1. *Venite exultemus domino iubilemus deo salutari nostro*

(2.) wutun ansine arest seceæn
    þ we andettæn ure fyrene
    7 we sealmas him singæn mid winne

2. *Preoccupemus faciem eius in confessione et in psalmis iubilemus ei*

(3.) Forðon is se micla. god [mihtig drihten
    and se micla] kining ofer eall manne godu

3. *Quoniam deus magnus dominus et rex magnus super omnes deos*

(4.) Forðon ne wiðdrifeð drihten usser
    his agen folc æfre æð ðeærfe
    he þæs heahbeorgæs healdeð swilce

Quoniam non repellet dominus plebem suam   4. quia in manu eius sunt omnes fines terrae et altitudines montium ipse conspicit

(5.) Eæc he seæs wealdeð 7 he sette ðone
    worhte his folme eæc foldæn drige

5. *Quoniam ipsius est mare et ipse fecit illud et aridam manus eius fundaverunt*

(6.) Cumæð him fore 7 cneow bigeað
    on ansine ures drihtnes
    7 him wepan fore ðe us worhte ær

6. *Venite adoremus et procidamus ante deum ploremus coram domino qui fecit nos*

(20.) *ealla* = orig. *eælla* ?   **94. (1.)** *Cumeð* prob. by Cor. *-mene* add. by Cor. ?   **(4.)** *-drifeð, i* wr. over the line.

(7.) Forðon he is drihten god dema usser
     werum we his fele folc 7 his fægere sceæp
     þæ þe on his edisce ær æfedde

7. *Quia ipse est dominus deus noster nos autem populus eius et*
oves pascue eius

(8.) Gif ge to dege drihtnes stefne
     holde gehiran nefre ge heortan geðanc
     deorce forhirdan drihtnes willan

8. *Hodie si vocem eius audieritis nolite obdurare corda vestra*

(9.) Swæ on grimnesse fyrngeræ dydan
     on ðam wraðan dege 7 on westenne
     þer min ðurh facen federas eowre
     þisse cneowrisse cunnedan. georne
     þer hi cunnedon cuð ongeaton
     7 min silfes weorc geseawon mid eægum

9. *Sicut in exacerbatione secundum diem temptationis in deserto*
ubi temptaverunt me patres vestri probaverunt et viderunt opera mea

(10.) Nu ic feowertig folce ðyssum .
     wintra rimes wunedæ neah
     áñ 7 simble cweð 7 eæc 7 swa oncneow
     þet hi on heortan hige disegan

10. *Quadraginta annis proximus fui generationi huic et dixi*
semper hi errant corde

(11.) hi wegæs mine wihte ne oncneowan
     ꝥ ic er on yrre æðe benemde
     gif hi on mine reste ricenedon eodon

11. *Ipsi vero non cognoverunt vias meas quibus iuravi in ira mea*
si introibunt in requiem meam

95.

(1.) Singað nu drihtne sangæs niowe
     singe ðeos eorðe eæll eceum drihtne

Cantate domino canticum novum cantate domino omnis terra

(2.) Singæð nu drihtne 7 his soðne næmæn

2. *Cantate domino et benedicite nomen*

his   welsecgað   of dege on dege   helo   his   Kweðað
eius bene nuntiate de die in diem salutare eius   3. *Adnuntiate*

(7.) *æfedde,* sec. *d* from *e.*   95. (1.) *Singað* prob. by Cor.   (2.) With
his welsecgað begins a fresh hand (the same wh. immed. precedes the 'poetry'
hand.   3. *Kweðað* or *cweðað?*; a mark (false?) before the *k* (or = *Ikweðað?*).

betwioh þioda wuldor his on eallum fclc wunder his
inter gentes gloriam eius in omnibus populis mirabilia eius

Forðan micel dryh[t]ues 7 hergendlic swyðe egeslic is
4. *Quoniam magnus dominus et laudabilis nimis terribilis est*

ofer ealle goda   Forðan ealle goca þioda diofla
super omnes deos **5.** *Quoniam omnes dii gentium demonia*

dryhten soþlice heofona worhte   andetnes 7 fegernes on
dominus autem caelos fecit **6.** *Confessio et pulchritudo in*

gesihte his haligdom 7 micelnesso on gehalgunge his
conspectu eius sanctitas et magnificentia in sanctificatione eius

Tobrengað dryhtene ęðles þioda tobrengað dryhtene wuldor
7. *Afferte domino patriae gentium afferte domino gloriam*

7 wiorðnyng   tobryngað dryhtene wuldor noman his
et honorem **8.** *afferte domino gloriam nomini eius*

Ontynað dura 7 ingangað on cafortune his   gebiddaþ
Tollite hostias et introite in atria eius **9.** *adorate*

dryhten on ricedome halig his Bið onstyred of onsiene his
dominum in aula sancta eius Commoveatur a facie eius

eall eorþæ   secgað on kyþnessene dryhten rixað of
universa terra **10.** *dicite in nationibus dominus regnavit a*

treow 7 soðlice gegryp ymbhwyrft eorðan se ne bið anwended
ligno et enim correxit orbem terrae qui non commovebitur

demað folce on emlicnesse 7 þioda on irre his
Iudicabit populos in aequitate et gentes in ira sua

        blissiað heofonas 7 wynsumað eorþa onstyrað sæ 7
11. *Laetentur caeli et exultet terra moveatur mare et*

fylnes his   gefioð feldas 7 ealle þa on him
plenitudo eius **12.** *Gaudebunt campi et omnia quae in eis*

sindon ðonne hyhtað ealle treow wuda   beforan sine
sunt tunc exultabunt omnia ligna silvarum **13.** *ante faciem*

dryhtenes forþan kymð forþan kymð dema eorðan demco
domini quoniam venit quoniam venit iudicare terram Iudicabit

ymbhwyrft eorða on emlicnesse 7 folc on soþfestnesse hira
orbem terrae in aequitate et populos in veritate sua

96.

Dryhten rixað hyhteð eorða blissað eglondum monegum
Dominus regnavit exultet terra laetentur insulae multae

wuldor, MS. = *fuldor*.   8. Er. bef. *Ontynað*.   *cafortune*, MS. = *eafortune*.
10. *kyþ-* or *cyþ-*?   13. *beforan sine*, so MS.   *kymð* or *cymð*? (twice).
ymbhwyrft, false let. er. betw. *b* and *h*.

wolcn 7 þysternes on ymbegonge his soðfestnesse 7   dom
2. *Nubes et   caligo   in   circuitu eius   iustitia   et iudicium*
gerecnes setl his   Fyr biforan him gearwað 7   onligeð
correctio sedis eius   **3.** *Ignis ante   eum   preibit et inflammabit*
on ymbehwyrfte   fiend   his   Onlihton þunreslege his
in   circuitu   inimicos eius   **4.** *Inluxerunt fulgora   eius*
ymbhwyrft eorðe gesihð 7 onstyred is eordæ   duna
   orbi   terrae vidit et commota est terra   **5.** *Montes*
swa   weacx toflowað from ansiene dryhtenes from ansiene
sicut   cera   fluxerunt   a   facie   domini   a   facie
dryhtenes forhtaþ   eall   eorða   Siedon   hefonas
domini   tremuit   omnis   terra   **6.** *Adnuntiaverunt   caeli*
soðfestnesse his 7 gesioð   eall   folc   wuldor his   Sin
iustitiam eius et viderunt omnes populi gloriam eius   **7.** *Con-*
gescinde ealle þa ðe gebiddað þa sliðan 7 þa wuldriað on
fundantur omnes qui   adorant sculptilia et qui gloriantur in
diofolgildum hira gebiddaþ hine ealle englas his   gehirde 7
simulachris suis Adorate eum omnes angeli eius   **8.** *audivit et*
blissiende is sion 7 wynsumiað bearn iude fore   domas þine
 letata   est syon et exultaverunt filiae iude propter iudicia tua
dryhten   Forðan þu eart dryhten þes hyhstan ofer
domine   **9.** *Quoniam tu es dominus altissimus super*
ealle eorðan swiðe upahefon eart ofer ealle godas
omnem terram nimis exaltatus es super omnes deos
      ða þe lufigeað dryhten fiogað yfel   gehet   dryhten
10. *Qui diligitis dominum odite malum custodit dominus*
saule þiowra   hira   of handa fyrenfulra gefriolsæð hie
animas servorum suorum de manu peccatorum liberabit eos
      Upcumæn is soþfeste rihteheortæn blyssæ   blis-
11. *Lux   orta   est iusto et rectis corde laetitia*   **12.** *lae-*
siæþ þæ soþfestæn on drihtne 7 ondettæþ gemind hæligdom-
tamini   iusti   in domino et confitemini memoriae sancti-
nesse his
tatis eius

97.

Singað dryhten sæng niwne forðon wundor worhte dryhten
Cantate domino canticum novum quia mirabilia fecit dominus

---

96. 4. *þunreslege his* by Cor. on er.; the Latin to it is also by Cor. on er.
5. *from* (1st), *r* in pl. of er. let. (o?).   **9.** *upahefon*, *o* from *e* (or vice versa?).
10. *dryhten* (2nd), MS. = *dryþten*.   With *gefriolsæð* begins a fresh hand,
ending with '*drihten*' (142. 11).   **97.** *Singað* prob. by Cor.

Gehele hiene þæ swyþræn his 7 hæærm hælige his
Salvabit sibi dextera eius et brachium sanctum eius

Cuþ dyde drihten helo his beforæn gesihþe
2. *Notum fecit dominus salutare suum ante conspectum*

ðiodæ onwrihð soðfestnesse his   gemyndig wes þu
gentium revelavit iustitiam suam   **3.** *Memor fuit*

mildheortnes þinre iæcob 7 soðfestnes his hus isræhele
misericordiae suae iacob et veritatis suae domui israel

Gesioþ eælle ende eorðæn helo godes ures wyn-
Viderunt omnes fines terrae salutare dei nostri **4.** *iubi-*

sumiæþ gode eæll eorðe singæþ 7 hyhtæð 7 singað
late deo omnis terra cantate et exultate et psallite

Singæþ gode ure on hearpæn on heærpæn 7 stefne
5. *Psallite deo nostro in cythara in cythara et voce*

psealmæ   on bymæn geleddon 7 stefne byme horn
psalmi   **6.** *in tulis ductilibus et voce tube cornee*

wynsumiaþ on gesihþe kynges   Onwendæþ
iubilate in conspectu regis domino **7.** *Moveatur*

siewe 7 fylnes his ymbwyrft eorðenæ 7 eællæ ðæ
mare et plenitudo eius orbis terrarum et universi qui

eærdiæþ on hire   Streæmæs heofræþ hændum on þet
habitant in ea **8.** *Flumina plaudent manibus in id*

sylfe dunæ hyhtæþ   beforæn onsine drihtnes
ipsum montes exultaverunt **9.** *ante faciem domini*

forðon kymþ forðæn kymð to demanne eorðæn demæð
quoniam venit quoniam venit iudicare terram iudicabit

ymbwyrft eorðæn on soþfestnesse 7 folc on emlicnesse
orbem terrae in iustitia et populos in aequitate

98.

Drihten rixæþ yrsæþ folc se ðe siteþ ofer cherubin
Dominus regnavit irascantur populi qui sedes super cherubin

bið onstyred eorðe   Drihten on syon micel 7 on hihþo
moveatur terra **2.** *Dominus in syon magnus et excelsus*

ofer eæll folc   anddettæþ nomæn þinum mycel
super omnes populos **3.** *Confiteantur nomini tuo magno*

---

3. *gemyndig*, first *g* nearly rubbed out.   98. *Drihten* prob. by Cor.

7 egeslic forðæn   hælig is   7 wior[ð]mynd kyninges
et terribili quoniam sanctum est   **4.** *et   honor   regis*,

   dom   lufæþ þu geærwodes emlicnesse   dom   7 soþfest-
iudicium diligit Tu   parasti   aequitatem iudicium et iusti-

nesse on iacobe ðu worhtes   Wynsumiæþ drihten god
tiam in iacob tu   fecisti   **5.** *Exaltate dominum deum*

urne 7 gebiddæþ scæmol   fet his forþæn hælig is
nostrum et adorate scabellum pedum eius quoniam sanctum est

   Moyses 7 ææron on sæcerdhæd his 7 sæmuhel betwih hie
6. *Moyses et aaron in sacerdotibus eius et samuel   inter   eos*

þæ gecygæþ nomæn is Gecigæþ   drihten 7 he gehiræþ
qui invocant nomen eius Invocabant dominum et ipse exaudiebat

hie   on swiorum wolcn sprecon to him Gehyldon
eos   **7.** *in columna nubis loquebatur ad eos Custodiebant*

kyþnesse his 7 bebodæ his se sælde him   Drihten
testimonia eius et precepta eius quae dederat illis   **8.** *Domine*

god ure ðu gehirest hie god þu ærfest were him 7
deus noster tu exaudiebas eos deus tu propitius fuisti illis et

wrece on eællum tilenge hiræ   hihtæþ drihten
vindicans in omnia studia eorum   **9.** *Exaltate dominum*

god urne 7 gebidæþ on dune hælig his forðæn
deum nostrum et adorate in monte sancto eius quoniam

hælig is drihten god ure
sanctus est dominus deus noster

99.

   Dremeð gode eælle corðæ ðeowiæþ drihtne on blyssæ
2. *Iubilate deo omnis terra servite domino in laetitia*

Ongængæþ on gesihþe his on hihte   witæð ge
Intrate in conspectu eius in exultatione   **3.** *scitote*

þet drihten he is god he dyde us 7 ne he us Us
quod dominus ipse est deus ipse fecit nos et non ipsi nos Nos

soðlice folc his 7 sceæp leswæ his   ongæn gæþ
autem populus eius et oves pascue eius   **4.** *intrate*

gætu his anddetnesse cafortun his on ymenum and-
portas eius in confessione atria eius in ymnis con-

detnesse hergæþ nomæ his   forðæn swete is
fessionum Laudate nomen eius   **5.** *quoniam suavis est*

6. Er. bef. *gecygæþ.*   99. 2. *Dremeð* prob. by Cor.

drihten on ecnesse mildheortnes his 7 oððet on world
dominus in aeternum misericordia eius et usque in saeculum

æworld soþfestnes his
saeculi veritas eius

100.

Mildheor[t]nesse 7 dom ic singe þe drihten ic singe
Misericordiam et iudicium cantabo tibi domine psallam

7 ic ongite on wege unwemmæ þonne kymþ to me þurh-
2. *et intellegam in via inmaculata quando venies ad me Peram-*

gænge unscyþnesse heorte min on myddæn hus þine
bulabam in innocentia cordis mei in medio domus tuae

Ncæles foregesette beforæn eægæn mine wyse yfel doende
3. *Non proponebam ante oculos meos rem malam facientes*

foreliornesse fionge 7 ne ietfylgþ me heorte geærwe
preva[ri]c[at]iones odivi et non adhesit michi 4. *cor pravum*

Onhildinge from me ne ic ne ongite tionde
Declinantes a me malignos non agnoscebam 5. *detrahentem*

wyþ nixtæn his diglice þisne ic fylge Oferhyd
adversus proximum suum occulte hunc persequebar Superbo

eægæn 7 on mine unæsecgenlic heortæn myd þisum ic
oculo et insatiabili corde cum hoc simul non

ne etc Eægæn mine ofer geleæful eorþe þet he sitte
edebam 6. *Oculi mei super fideles terrae ut sedeant*

þes mid me gonge on wegæ unwemme þes me ðeniæþ
hi mecum ambulans in via inmaculata hic michi ministrabat

Ne eærdæþ on middæn hus min se deþ oferhid
7. *Non habitabit in medio domus meae qui facit superbiam*

se sprecende on unriht ne gerecþ or gesihþe eægænæ
qui loquitur iniqua non dirigetur in conspectu oculorum

minræ On uhtlicum ic acweælde eælle þæ fyrænfullæn
meorum 8. *In matutinis interficiebam omnes peccatores*

eorþæn þet ic forspilde on ceæstre drihten eælle þæ þe
terrae ut disperdam de civitate domini omnes qui

wyrcæþ unrihtnesse
operantur iniquitatem

101.

Drihten gehire gebed min 7 cierm min to þe
2. *Domine exaudi orationem meam et clamor meus ad te*

---

100. *Mildheornesse* prob. by Cor.   2. *þurhgænge*, MS. *= þurþgænge*.
101. 2. *Drihten* prob. by Cor.

kymeþ   Ne æwyrfe onsien þin from me On swæ
perveniat   3. *Ne avertas faciem tuam a me in qua-*

hwilcum dege sie geeærfodoþ Onhyld to me eære ðin On
cumque die tribulor inclina ad me aurem tuam In

swæ hwylcum dege ic þe gecige hredlice gehire me
quacumque die invocavero te velociter exaudi me

Forðæn æsprungæn swæ smyc dei mine 7 bæn mine swæ
4. *Quia defecerunt sicut fumus dies mei et ossa mea sicut*

on gebrecnesse gebrocene syndon   þurhslegen ic eom
in frixorio confrixa sunt   5. *Percussus sum*

swæ hi 7 forwysnæþ heorte min forþæn ofergitende eom
sicut foenum et aruit cor meum quia oblitus sum

to ettænne hlæf minne   from stemne giomrunge min
manducare panem meum   6. *a voce gemitus mei*

etfiolæp bæn mine flęsc min   Gelic geworden
adheserunt ossa mea carni meae   7. *Similis factus*

ic eom felle hundes on licnesse geworden eom swæ nihthrefn
sum pellicano in solitudine factus sum sicut nocticorax

on husehere   toweccæn 7 geworden ic eom swæ
in domicilio   8. *vigilavi et factus sum sicut*

speræ æn on getimbernesse   Elce dęge etwitodon
passer unicus in aedificio   9. *Tota die exprobrabant*

me fiend min 7 þæ me hergæþ wiþ me swæriæþ
me inimici mei et qui me laudabant adversum me iurabant

. swæ æxe swæ læf ic et 7 drinc min myd
10. *Quia cinerem sicut panem manducabam et potum meum cum*

wope Gemetliece   From onsiene yrre on ebilgæn
fletu temperabam   11. *A facie ire indignationis*

þinum forðæn upæhebbende upæhof me   dægæs mine
tuae quia elevans elisisti me   12. *Dies mei*

swæ scuwæ onhildon 7 ic swæ hei forwisnæþ
sicut umbra declinaverunt et ego sicut foenum arui

þu soþlice drihten on ecnesse þurhwunæþ 7 gemyndbliþe
13. *Tu autem domine in aeternum permanes et memoriale*

þine on worlð æworlde   þu ærise drihten þu bist
tuum in seculum saeculi   14. *Tu exurgens domine mise-*

miltsiend syon forðæn kymþ tid tomildsiend him   Forðæn
reberis syon quia venit tempus miserendi eius   15. *Quia*

---

4. *smyc*, MS. = *smyt*?   12. *scuwœ*, MS. = *scwutœ*.   15. Part of a false
let. bef. *eorþe* not er.

wellicungæ   hebbende   þiowæs   þine   stænæs   his   7   eorþe   his
beneplacitum   habuerunt   servi   tui   lapides   eius   et   terrae   eius

miltsiende   7   ondredon   ᵭiodæ   nomæ   þine   drihten
miserebuntur   16. *Et   timebunt   gentes   nomen   tuum   domine*

7   eælle   kyninges   eorᵭæn   wuldor   þine   Forᵭæn
et   omnes   reges   terrae   gloriam   tuam   17. *Quoniam*

getimbreþ   drihten   syon   7   gesioþ   on   megenþrimme   his
aedificavit   dominus   syon   et   videbitur   in   maiestate   sua

7   forelocæþ   on   gebede   þeærfænæ   7   ne   hyrweþ   bebod
18. *Et   respexit   in   orationes   pauperum   et   non   sprevit   preces*

hioræ   Writæþ   ᵭæs   on   cneowrisne   oᵭer   7   folc
eorum   19. *Scribantur   haec   in   generatione   altera   et   populus*

se   gescop   hergæþ   drihten   Forᵭæn   forelocæþ   of
qui   creabitur   laudabit   dominum   20. *Quoniam   prospexit   de*

hihþo   hælig   his   drihten   of   hefonum   on   eorᵭæn   forelocæþ
excelso   sancto   suo   dominus   de   caelo   in   terram   prospexit

þette   gehireþ   giomrung   þæræ   gebuncenæ   7   ælise   beærn
21. *Ut   audiret   gemitus   vinculatorum   et   solveret   filios*

on   hiræ   forwirþe   ᵭette   si   gecyþeᵭ   on   syon   næmæ
interemptorum   22. *Ut   adnuntietur   in   syon   nomen*

drihtnes   7   lof   his   on   ierusælem   On   to   gemetænne
domini   et   laus   eius   in   ierusalem   23. *In   conveniendo*

folc   o[n]   æn   7   kyninges   ᵭet   hi   þiowien   drihtne   *and-*
populos   in   unum   et   regna   ut   serviant   domino 24. *Re-*

swerode   him   on   weige   megen   his   feæwum   dægæ   hiræ
spondit   ei   in   via   virtutis   suae   paucitatem   dierum   meorum

onsiege   me   7   tolies   þere   wisen   stefne   me   on
enuntia   michi   et   25.   *ne   revoces   me   in*

middæn   dægæ   minræ   on   world   æworld   geær   ᵭines
dimidio   dierum   meorum   in   saeculum   saeculi   anni   tui

On   frumæn   eorþæn   þu   gestæþlodes   drihten   7   wiorc   hændæ
26. *Initio   terram   tu   fundasti   domine   et   opera   manuum*

ᵭiuræ   sindon   hefonæs   ·   hi   forwiorᵭæþ   þu   soþlice
tuarum   sunt   caeli   27. *Ipsi   peribunt   tu   autem*

þurhwunæþ   7   eælle   swæ   hriegl   eældigæþ   7   swæ   þæ
permanes   et   omnia   sicut   vestimentum   veterescent   et   sicut   oper-

wircendum   wenst   þæ   7   biᵭ   æwend   þu   soþlice
torium   mutabis   ea   et   mutabuntur   · 28. *Tu   autem*

---

19. *se, e* from *c*? 20. *Forᵭæn*, false let. er. aft. *r.* 23. *kyninges, es*
nearly er. 25. *tolies, i* wr. over the line. 27. *þurh-*, the long stroke of
the *h* is extended much below the line.

þ selfe he is 7 geær þine ne ætiorde   beærn þiowæ
idem ipse es et anni tui non deficient   29. *Filii servorum*

þinræ onherdiæþ þer 7 sied hiræ on worlde world
tuorum inhabitabunt ibi et semen eorum in seculum seculi

beoð geraht
dirigetur

102.

gebletse sæwle mine drihten 7 eælle on þæ yteræn mine næmæ
Benedic anima mea domino et omnia interiora mea nomen

hælig his   Gebletsæ sæwlæ mine drihten 7 ne ceæræ
sanctum eius   2. *Benedic anima mea dominum et noli*

þe ofergitende eælle edleænunge his   þæ ærfest bið
oblivisci omnes retributiones eius   3. *Qui propitius fit*

eællum on unrihtnessum þinum se geheleð eælle untrume þine
omnibus iniquitatibus tuis qui sanat omnes languores tuos

Se þe æliseþ of forwyrde lif þin   se gefillæþ
4. *Qui redemit de interitu vitam tuam*   5. *qui satiat*

on god wyllæn þinæ Se þe gecist þe on yrmðe 7
in bonis desiderium tuum Qui coronat te in miseratione et

mildheortnesse bioþ geedniwode swæ eærn giogæþe ðinræ
misericordia renovabitur sicut aquilae iuventus tua

doende mildheortnes drihten 7 dom eællum ontionæn
6. *Faciens misericordias dominus et iudicium omnibus iniuriam*

geþyld   kuþe dide wegæs his moysi beærn isræhele
pacientibus   7. *Notas fecit vias suas moysi filiis israel*

willæn hiræ   Mildheort 7 miltsiend drihten geþyldig
voluntates suas   8. *Misericors et miserator dominus paciens*

7 mycel myldheortnes   Ne on ende yrsæþ ne on
et multum misericors   9. *Non in finem irascetur neque in*

ecnesse onebilgæn   Neæles efter synnæ ure
aeternum indignabitur   10. *Non secundum peccata nostra*

wuorhte us ne efter unrihtnessæ uræ eædleænunge
fecit nobis neque secundum iniquitates nostras retribuit

us   Forþæn efter hyhþo hefonæs 7 eorþæ
nobis   11. *Quia secundum altitudinem caeli a terra*

getrymeþ drihten myldheortnes his ofer ondredende hine
confirmavit dominus misericordiam suam super timentes eum

---

29. *-e world beoð geraht* by Cor. in pl. of er.   102. *gebletse* prob.
by Cor.   3. *ærfest, e* in pl. of er. let.

hu monigæ gestihtode upcumende from firstmeærce æfiorrodæ
12. *Quantum   distat   oriens   ab   occasu   elongavit*

from us unrihtnessæ uræ   Swæ mildsiende feder
a   nobis iniquitates nostras 13. *Sicut miseretur pater*

beærn swæ miltsiend is drihten ondredende hine   forðæn
filiis ita misertus est dominus timentibus se   14. *quia*

he wæt sliþe mod ure   Geminde drihten þet dust myl
ipse scit figmentum nostrum Memento domine quod pulvis

ic eom   mon swæ hei dægæs his 7 swæ blosmæ
sumus 15. *homo sicut foenum dies eius et sicut flos*

lændes swæ blosmæþ   Forðæn gæst þurhferet from
agri ita florebit 16. *Quia spiritus pertransibit ab*

him 7 ne bið 7 ne oncneweþ mæ stowe his   Mild-
eo et non erit et non cognoscet amplius locum suum 17. *Mise-*

heortnes soþlice drihtnes from worlde 7 oþ þ on world
ricordia autem domini a saeculo est et usque in saeculum

æworlde ofer ondredende hine 7 soþfestnesse his ofer beærn
seculi super timentes eum Et iustitia eius super filios

beærnæ   heældendum kyþnesse his 7 gemynd
filiorum 18. *custodientibus testamentum eius et memoria*

wyþhebbendum bebodo his þet hi don þæ   drihten
retinentibus mandata eius ut faciant ea 19. *Dominus*

on hefonum geærwæþ setle his 7 rice his eælles biþ
in caelo paravit sedem suam et regnum eius omnium do-

weældend   bletsiæþ drihten eælle englæs his mihte
minabitur 20. *Benedicite dominum omnes angeli eius potentes*

megen se þæ deð word his to gehirænne stefne word
virtute qui facitis verbum eius ad audiendam vocem sermonum

his   bletsiæþ drihten eællæ megen his 7 þeinæs
eius 21. *Benedicite dominum omnes virtutes eius ministri*

his ge þe doþ willæn his   Bletsiæþ drihten
eius qui faciti voluntatem eius 22. *Benedicite dominum*

eælle wiorc his on eællum stowum biþ weældend, his geblet-
omnia opera eius in omni loco dominationis eius bene-

sige sæwle mine drihten
dic anima mea dominum

-

16. *from*, MS. = *fron*.   21. Er. aft. *megen*. Er. bef. *his* (2nd).

N

103.

gebletsige   sæwle   mine   drihten   drihten   god   min   micel
Benedic   anima   mea   dominum   domine   deus   meus   magnificatus

is   swiþe   anddetnesse 7 wlite ðu gegiredes   æn-
es vehementer Confessionem et decorem   induisti   2.

forleten lioht   swæ   hrægl Apeniende hefon swæ   fell
amictus lumine sicut vestimento Extendens caelum sicut pellem

   se bewrih on wetrum þæ uplecæn his Se þe setæþ wolcn
3. *qui tegis   in   aquis   superiora eius Qui ponit   nubem*

æstignesse his   se   gieþ   ofer fiðræs windæ   Se
ascensum suum qui ambulat super pennas ventorum   4. Qui

geworhte englæs his   gæst 7 þægnæs his fyre biernende
facit   angelos suos spiritus et ministros suos ignem urentem

   Se gestæþolode eorþæn ofer gestaðolung his ne bið onhylt
5. *Qui fundavit terram super stabilitatem eius non inclinabitur*

on worold æworlde   Niowolnes swæ   ryft   forleten
in saeculum seculi   6. Abyssus sicut pallium amictus

his 7 ofer dunæ stændæþ weter   From cydunge
eius   super montes stabunt aquae   7. Ab increpatione

þinre flioþ from stefne þunerræd þinre onegeæþ   Asti-
tua fugient   a   voce tonitrui tui formidabunt 8. Ascen-

gæð. dunæ 7 æstigæþ feldæn on stowe þæm gestæþolædes
dunt montes et descendunt campi in locum quem   fundasti

him   gemære þu gesettes him þonne neælles liorende
eis   9. terminum posuisti eis quem   non   trans-

gongende þyles sin gecirde to ontynænne eorþæn   Se
gredientur neque convertentur   operire   terram   10. Qui

sendeþ wyllæs betwioh   denum   on mydlene dunæ þurh-
emittit fontes   in   convallibus inter medium montium per-

feræþ   weter   druncon þæ eælle wildioræ wudæ
transibunt aquae   11. Potabunt ea omnes bestiae silvarum

onbidæþ on ðæm londum on þurstæ hiræ   ofer þæ
expectabunt   onagri   in sitim suam   12. super ea

fuglæs hefonæs heærdiæþ on midlene stænæ   sellæþ stefne
volucres caeli habitabunt de medio petrarum dabunt voces

his   Leccende dunæ be ðæm yferum his ob westme
uas   13. Rigans montes de superioribus suis de fructu

---

103. *gebletsige* prob. by Cor.   12. *fuglæs, g* from a false let.

weorcæ þinræ biþ gefylled eorþe   Forþgongende hih
operum tuorum satiabitur terra   **14.** *Producens foenum*

nietenæ 7 wirtæ þiowdom monnæ þette geledet hlæf of
iumentis et herbam servituti hominum Ut educat panem de

eorðæn   7 win geblissæþ heor*æn mænnæ ðette
terra   **15.** *et vinum laetificat cor hominis Ut*

bredlice ic do on ele 7 hlæf . heorte mænne getrimeþ
exhilaret faciaem in oleo et panis cor hominis confirmet

bioþ gefyllede eælle triowæ wudæ 7 cedorbeæm libæni
16. *Satiabuntur omnia ligna silvarum et cedros libani*

ðæ gewirtwælodes   ðer speræn nistliæþ Twiogendlice
quas plantasti   **17.** *illic passeres nidificabunt Fulice*

hus lætiow is hiræ   dunæ of hyhðo heort stæn
domus dux est eorum   **18.** *montes excelsi cervis petra*

gescild ilæs   worhte monæn on ðæ tide sunnæn
refugium herinaciis   **19.** *Fecit lunam in tempore sol*

oncneow fyrstmearc his   þu settes ðiostræ 7 geworden
cognovit occasum suum   **20.** *Posuisti tenebras et facta*

is niht on him ðurhferæþ eælle wilddioræ wudæ
est nox in ipsa pertransibunt omnes bestiae silvarum

hwelpæs leonæ grymitiende 7 gegripæþ 7 secæþ from
21. *Catuli leonum rugientes ut rapiant et querant a*

gode mete him   Upcumæn is sunne 7 gesomnede
deo escam sibi   **22.** *Ortus est sol et congregati*

sindon 7 on bedcliofæn hiræ hine stæðoliæþ   Geð
sunt et in cubilibus suis se collocabunt   **23.** *Exiet*

mæn to wiorce his 7 to wircendum his oððet to efenne
homo ad opus suum et ad operationem suam usque ad vesperum

hu monigæ sind wiorc þine drihten eælle on
24. *Quam magnificata sunt opera tua domine omnia in*

snytro ðu dydest gefylled is eorþe gesceft ðinre   þis
sapientia fecisti repleta est terra creatura tua   **25.** *Hoc*

siæ micel 7 fyrst þer gripende
mare magnum et spaciosum illic reptilia quorum non est numerus

7 midmicele 7 micele   ðer scip þurhferæþ
animalia pusilla et magna   **26.** *illic naves pertransibunt*

dræco dæs þone ðu gehiwodes 7 to bismerenne him   eælle
Draco iste quem formasti ad inludendum ei   **27.** *omnia*

---

14. *monnæ*, MS. = *monnnæ*.   21. *from*, MS. = *fron*.

N 2

from þe onbidæþ drihten þ selle him mete on ðæ tide
a te expectant domine ut des illis escam in tempore

   Sellende him gesomniaþ ontinæþ de hænde ðine eælle
28. *Dante te illis colligent aperiente te manum tuam omnia*

bioþ gefillede briostberende   Æwirfe þe eællengæ ðe
replebuntur ubertate   **29.** *Avertente autem te*

onsine ðine bioð gedrefede afirre gæst hiræ 7 æspringæþ
faciem tuam turbabuntur auferes spiritum eorum et deficient

7 on duste his sien gecirrede   Onsende gæst
et in pulverem suum revertentur   **30.** *Emitte spiritum*

þinne 7 gesceope 7 geedniwodes onsine eorðæn   Sie
tuum et creabuntur et renovabis faciem terrae   **31.** *Sit*

wuldor drihtnes on world æworld blissiæþ drihten on
gloria domini in saeculum saeculi laetabitur dominus in

wiorcum his   Se þe locæþ on eorðæn 7 deþ ðæ
operibus suis   **32.** *Qui respicit in terram et facit eam*

forhtiæþ se onhryn dunæ 7 meþgiæþ   Ic singe
tremere qui tangit montes et fumigabunt   **33.** *Cantabo*

drihtne on liue mine ic singe gode minum swæ l[o]nge swæ
domino in vita mea psallam deo meo quamdiu

ic bio   Winsum sie him hernes mine ic soðlice lust-
ero   **34.** *Suavis sit ei laudatio mea ego vero de-*

fullige on drihten   Æspringæþ fyrenfullæ from eorðæn
lectabor in domino   **35.** *Deficiant peccatores a terra*

7 unriht þet ne sie gebletsæ sæwle mine drihten
et iniqui ita ut non sint benedic anima mea dominum

104.

   Andetteð drihtne 7 gecigæþ nomæn his tosecgæð betwioh
1. *Confitemini domino et invocate nomen eius adnuntiate inter*

þiodæ wiorc his   Singæþ him 7 singaþ 7 segcæþ
gentes opera eius   **2.** *Cantate ei et psallite et narrate*

eælle wuldor his   hergæþ on nomæn hæligæn
omnia mirabilia eius   **3.** *Laudamini in nomine sancto*

his blissiæþ heorte secende drihten   secæþ drihten
eius Laetetur cor querentium dominum   **4.** *Querite dominum*

7 getrimmæþ secæþ ænsine his simle   gemynæd ge
et confirmamini querite faciem eius semper   **5.** *Mementote*

---

34. *lustfullige, g* from *e.*   104. 1. *Andetteð* prob. by Cor.

wundor   his   þæ   he worhte forebeæcn 7   dom   muþ his·
mirabilium eius quae   fecit   prodigia et iudicia oris eius

  Sied Æbræhæmes ðeow his beærn iæcobes gecorene· his
6. *Semen   abraham   servi eius filii   iacob   electi   eius*

  he drihten god ure on eællre eorðæn dom his
7. *Ipse dominus deus noster in universa terra iudicia eius*

  gemindig wese on worolde kyþnessə his word oððet
8. *Memor   fuit   in seculum testamenti sui verbi quod*

bebeæd on þusende kynrene   þet gesettes to.
mandavit in   mille   generationes 9. *Quod disposuit ad*

æbræhæmes 7 æþswyrde his   ysææc   7 gesette.
abraham   et iuramenti sui ad ysaac 10. *et statuit*

þet iæcobe on bebod 7 isræhele on kyþnessum on ecnes-
illud iacob in preceptum et israel in testamentum aeter-

sum   Cwedon ðe selle ic eorþæn on chænǽǽn
num 11. *Dicens tibi dabo terram chanaan*

ræpægewælc yrfeweærdnes ure   Midþi weron on
funiculum haereditatis vestrae 12. *Cum essent in*

rieme scortlice feaulicum 7 on bigonge on him   7
numero brevi paucissimi et incole in ea   13. *et*

þurhferdon of þiode on ðiodæ 7 be ˙.rice to folce
pertransierunt de gente in gentem et de regno ad populum

oðre   Ne foreleteþ monnum scyððæn him 7 gegripæþ
alterum 14. *Non permisit. hominem nocere eis et corripuit*

for him kyninges   Ne ceæro eow hrinon cristes
pro eis reges   15. *Nolite   tangere christos*

min 7 on witgæn mine ne ceæro eow þæm minnæn   7
meos et in prophetis meis nolite   malignari   16. *Et*

gecigde hunger ober eordæn 7 eælle trymnessæ hlæfes ge-,
vocavit famem super terram et omne firmamentum panis con-

eærfogoþæþ   Sende beforæn hie wer on þiowdom
trivit   17. *Misit   ante   eos virum in   servum*

atersellende wes iosepe   geeæðmeddon on fotgemetum
venundatus est ioseph   18. *humiliaverunt in compedibus*

fot his swæ hwenæ ðurhferæð sæwle his   oððet
pedes eius ferrum pertransivit animam eius   19. *donec*

kymeþ word his gesprec drihtnes 7 onligð hine   Sende
veniret verbum eius eloquium domini inflammavit eum 20. *Misit*

kyning 7 list hie eældormæn folcæ 7 forliet hie
rex   et solvit eum princeps populorum et dimisit eum

7 gesette hie drihten hus his 7 eældormæn eælle
21. *Et constituit eum dominum domus suae et principem omnis*

ehtæ   his   þette getyde eældormæn his swæ
possessionis suae   **22.** *Ut erudiret principes suos sicut*

silfum him 7 hyldræn his   snitro   lierde   7
se ipsum et seniores suos prudentiam doceret   **23.** *Et*

ongiedo isræhele on   egypto 7 iæcobes eærdodon on eorðæn
intravit israel in aegyptum et iacob habitavit in   terra

chænææn   7 gedyrstlecte   folc   his swiþe 7
chanaan   **24.** *Et   auxit   populum suum nimis et*

getrimede hine ofer   fiend his   Gecyrde heorte
confirmavit eum super inimicos eius   **25.** *Convertit   cor*

hiræ þette fiodon   folc his 7   sær dydon on þiowum
eorum ut   odirent populum eius et dolum facerent in   servos

his   Sende moysen ðyow his 7   ææron ðone
eius   **26.** *Misit   moysen servum suum et aaron   quem*

geceæs he self   gesette on him word   tæcn   hiræ
elegit   ipsum   **27.** *Posuit in eis verba signorum suorum*

7 forebeæcne   hiræ   on eorþæn cænææn   Sende
et prodigiorum suorum in   terra chanaan   **28.** *Misit*

þystro 7 æþystrode hie forðæn þæ   beedon   word his
tenebras et obscuravit eos   quia   exacerbaverunt sermones eius

Gehwyrfde weter hiræ on   blod   7 æcweælde fyxæs
29. *Convertit aquas eorum in sanguinem et   occidit   pisces*

hiræ   Sende on eorðæn hiræ froxæs 7 ou hiræ bed-
eorum   **30.** *Misit in terram eorum ranas et in   cubi-*

clefum rice   hiræ   Cweþ 7 kymþ mycgæs 7 gnettas
libus regum ipsorum   **31.** *Dixit et venit cynomia et scinifes*

o[n] eællum gemere hiræ   Sette renæs hiræ on
in omnibus finibus eorum   **32.** *Posuit pluvias eorum in*

hegle   fyrnæn   birnende   on eorþæn hire   7
grandinem ignem comburentem in   terra ipsorum   **33.** *Et*

þurhsloh wingeærdæs hiræ 7 forðswebung   7 geeær-
percussit vineas   eorum et ficulneas   eorum et con-

fogoþæþ eælle triow wingeærd hiræ   Cweþ 7 kymð
trivit omne lignum finium eorum   **34.** *Dixit et venit*

---

28. *þystro*, fin. *de* er.

gersstæpæ 7 grimenæ þus   ne wes   rim   7 eteþ
locusta et bruchus cuius non erat numerus   35. et comedit

eælle   eorðæn hiræ   7 þurhsloh eælne þæ
omnem fructum terre   eorum   36. Et percussit omne pri-

frumkynnedon on eorþæ egypti þæ frumæn eælle gewinn hiræ
mogenitum   in terra egypti primitias omnis laboris eorum

      7 geledde hie on siolfro 7 golde 7 ne wes on miegþum
37. Et eduxit eos in argento et auro et non erat in tribubus

hiræ untrum   blissiende is egyptus on gedefum
eorum infirmus   38. Letata   est aegyptus in prefectione

      forþæn gefioll ege hiræ   ofer hie   Aþenede
eorum quia cecidit timor eorum super eos   39. Expandit

wolcn on ge[s]cilde hiræ 7 fyr þette lihteð him þurh
nubem in protectionem eorum et ignem ut luceret eis   per

niht   biddæþ flesces 7 kymþ ðæ nihtlecæn 7
noctem   40. Petierunt carnes et venit eis coturnix   et

hlæf hefonæs gefylleþ hie   Toslitæþ stæn 7 flowæþ
pane caeli saturavit eos   41. Disrupit petram et fluxerunt

weter 7 gængæþ on drigæn streæmæ   Forðæn gemindi
aquae et abierunt in sicco flumina   42. Quia   memor

wes word hælig his þet sprecende is to Abræhæme cnihte
fuit verbi sancti sui quod locutus est ad abraham puerum

his   7 geledde folc   his on hihte   7
suum   43. Et eduxit populum suum in exultatione et

þæ gecorenen his on blysse   7 seælde him rice
electos   suos in letitia   44. Et dedit eis regiones

ðiodæ 7 gewinn folcæ   agon   On-
gentium et labores populorum possederunt   45. Ut cus-

geheældæð soðfestnesse his 7 æwe his secæþ
todiant iustificationes eius et legem eius exquirant

105.

      Andetteð dribten forðæn god forðæn on ecnesse
1. *Confitemini domino quoniam bonus quoniam in seculum*

mildheortnesse his   wilc sprecæþ mihte drihtnes
misericordia   eius   2. Quis loquetur potentias domini

---

38. *hie*, a let. (s?) er. betw. *i* and *e*.   105. 1. *Andetteð* prob. by
Cor. -*nesse* (2nd) in p. ink.   2. *wilc* on er.

gehirnessæ deð eæll lof his   Eædige ðæ ðe geheældæþ
auditas faciet omnes laudes eius   3. *Beati   qui   custodiunt*

domæs 7 doþ soðfes[t]nesse on eælle tide   gemine
iudicium et faciunt   iustitias   in omni tempore   4. *Memento*

ure drihten on wellicunge folces þines 7 niosæ us on
nostri domine in beneplacito populi tui   visita nos in

helo þine   To gesionne on godnesse gecorenræ þinræ
salutari tuo   5. *Ad videndum in bonitate electorum tuorum*

to blissienne on blisse þiodæ þine ðet ðu lofæst mid
ad letandum in letitia gentis tuae ut   lauderis   cum

yrfeweærdnesse ðinre   we gefyrenodon mid feder urum
hæreditate   tua   6. *Peccavimus   cum patribus nostris*

ðæ unrihtæn we doð unrihtnesse we doð   Feder ure
iniuste   egimus iniquitatem fecimus   7. *Patres nostri*

on egypto ne ongeton wundor þin 7 ne weron gemindige
in aegypto non intellexerunt mirabilia tua et non fuerunt memores

monigo mildheortnesse þine 7 onlehton   astigende
multitudinis misericordiae tuae Et irritaverunt eum ascendentes

on reædre sewe   7 gefriolsie hie forðæn nomæn his ðet
in rubrum mare   8. *et liberavit eos propter nomen suum ut*

cuðe dyde mihte his   7 ofercidde sie ðæ readæn
notam faceret potentiam suam   9. *Et increpavit mare rubrum*

7 ædrugod wes 7 geliedde hie on weter micel swæ on westene
et siccatum est et eduxit eos in aquis multis sicut in deserto

7 gefriolsede hie of hænde fiondræ 7 ælisde hie of hændæ
10. *Et liberavit eos de manu odientium et redemit eos de manu*

fiondæ   7 worhte weter eærfogoðiende hie æn of him
inimicorum   11. *et operuit aqua tribulantes eos unus ex eis*

ne wunode   7 gelyfdon on wordum his 7 sungon
non remansit   12. *Et crediderunt in verbis eius et cantaverunt*

lof his   hredlice dydon 7 ofergitende sindon wiorc
laudes eius   13. *cito defecerunt et obliti sunt operum*

his 7 ne arefnodon geðeæht his   7 gewilnedon
eius et non sustinuerunt consilium eius   14. *Et concupierunt*

gewilnungæ on westene 7 costodon god on drinesse
concupiscentias in deserto et temptaverunt deum in siccitate

7 selæð him benæ hiræ 7 sende fylnesse on sæulum
15. *Et dedit eis petitiones eorum et misit saturitatem in animas*

hiræ   7 onlyhton moysen on herewicum 7 ææron
eorum   16. *Et irritaverunt moysen in castris et aaron*

hælige drihtnes   geoponod is eorþe 7 forswylhð dætæn
sanctum domini   **17.** *Aperta est terra et deglutivit dathan*

7 ontynde ofer gesæmnunge æbyron   birned fyre on
et operuit super synagoga   abyron   **18.** *Exarsit ignis in*

gemotstowe hiræ 7 leg   onberneð fyrenfullæ   7
synagoga eorum et flamma conbussit peccatores   **19.** *Et*

worhton sceælf on choreb 7 gebedon ðæ sliðelecæn   7
fecerunt vitulum in choreb et adoraverunt sculptile   **20.** *et*

onwendon wuldor his on gelicnesse sceælfes hetende
mutaverunt gloriam suam in similitudinem vituli manducantis

heg   7 obergitende sindon god se gefriolseð hie se
foenum   **21.** *Et obliti sunt deum qui liberavit eos qui*

worhte þæ minnæn on egyptum   wundor on eorðæn
fecit magnalia in aegypto   **22.** *mirabilia in terra*

chænæan egeslic on sie redre   7 cwið þette forspilde
chanaan terribilia in mari rubro   **23.** *Et dixit ut disperderet*

hie gif   moyses gecorene his gesette on gebrecnesse on gesihþe
eos si non moyses electus eius stetisset in confractione in conspectu

his þette æcyrde yrre from his ne forspildo hie   7 for
eius ut averteret iram ab eis ne disperderet eos   **24.** *Et pro.*

næhte habbæþ eorðæn wilnungæ 7 ne gelifdon on
nichilo habuerunt terram desiderabilem et non crediderunt in

wordum his   7   gnornodon on geteldunge his no
verbis eius   **25.** *et murmuraverunt in tabernaculis suis nec*

gehirdon stefne drihtnes   7 upahof hænd his ober
exaudierunt vocem domini   **26.** *Et elevavit manum suam super*

hie þette foreastrehte hie on westene   7 þette towurpe
eos ut prosterneret eos in deserto   **27.** *et ut deiceret*

sęd hiræ on gekiðnessum 7 þette hi tostencte on hiræ londum
semen eorum in nationibus et dispergeret eos in regionibus

7 gediglede sindon oþþæ swæ hwenæ 7   eton
28. *Et consecrati sunt beelphegor et manducaverunt*

7 onsegdnessæ deædræ   7˙ onlehton hine on tielengum
sacrificia mortuorum   **29.** *Et irritaverunt eum in studiis*

hiræ 7 gemonigfældod is on him hryre   Stent ende 7
suis et multiplicata est in eis ruina   **30.** *Stetit finees et*

gebidd 7 ablinnæþ ðæ gefyllæþ   7 geteæld is him to
exoravit et cessavit quassatio   **31.** *et reputatum est illi ad*

---

18. *birned*, the stroke of the *r* below the line er. *fyre*, top part of the
f er.

soðfestnes from cneowrisne on   cneowrisn   oððet on world
iustitiam   a   generatione in generationem usque in saeculum

         7 onlehton hine to wetrum   wiðwiþorcwidolnesse 7
32. *Et irritaverunt eum ad   aquas   contradictionis   et*

geswenceð is moyses fore hie   forðæn þæ   beeodon
vexatus est moyses propter eos   **33.**   *quia   exacerbaverunt*

gæst   his 7 gestihtode   on welerum his   Ne
spiritum eius et distinxit   in labiis   suis   **34.** *Non*

forspildon ðiodæ   ðæ sedæ drehten him   7
disperdiderunt gentes quas dixerat dominus illis   **35.** *et*

gemengede sindon betwih þiodum 7 geleornodon wiorc h[i]ræ
commixti sunt   inter gentes et didicerunt opera eorum

        7 þiowdon sliðnesse hiræ 7 geworden is him on
36. *et servierunt sculptilibus eorum et factum est illis in*

geswece   7   onsedon beærn hiræ 7 beorn hiræ
scandalum **37.** *Et immolaverunt filios suos et filias suas*

dioflæ   7 æguton blod   unscyððende blod
demoniis **38.** *et effuderunt sanguinem innocentem sanguinem*

beærnæ   hiræ 7 beærnæ ðæ   onsedon   ðæ sliððæn
filiorum suorum et filiarum quas sacrificaverunt sculptilibus

chænææn 7 betwioh acweældon is eorðe on   blodum
chanaan Et   interfecta   est terra in sanguinibus

        7 onsecgende is on wiorcum hiræ 7 efehylsiende sindon
39. *et contaminata est in operibus eorum Et fornicati sunt*

on gehilnessum his   7 irre is sæwl drihten on
in observationibus suis **40.** *et iratus est animo dominus in*

folce   his 7 fræm weældendæ is irfeweærdnesse his
populum suum et abominatus   est haereditatem suam

        7 seælde hie on hændæ ðiodæ 7 weældende sindon hiræ
41. *Et tradidit eos in manus gentium et dominati sunt eorum.*

þæ fiodon hic   7 eærfogoþodæn hic fiend hiræ 7
qui oderunt eos **42.** *Et tribulaverunt   eos inimici eorum et*

geeæðmedde sindon under hændum hiræ   gelomlice
humiliati sunt   sub manibus eorum   **43.**   *sepe*

gefriolsode hie hii eællengæ becodon   hine on geþeahte hiræ
liberavit eos Ipsi autem exacerbaverunt eum in consilio suo

7 geeæðmedde sindon on hira unrihtnessum   7 forelocode
et humiliati   sunt   in suis iniquitatibus   **44.** *Et respexit*

---

33. MS. soðfestn-s *gestihtode* in pl. of er. word. 34. *for-,* stroke of the *r*
elow the line er.   43. *hira, r* prob. from *s.*

hie midti geeærfoþgodo weron midti gehireþ gebed hiræ
eos cum tribularentur cum exaudiret orationes eorum

7 gemindi wes kiþnesse his 7 neælęcte him efter
45. *Et memor fuit testamenti sui et paenituit eum secundum*

micelnesse mildheortnesse his 7 seælde hie on
multitudinem misericordiae suae **46.** *Et dedit eos in*

mildheortnesse on gesiłþe ealræ þæ hie onfengon
misericordiam in conspectu omnium qui eos ceperunt

hale us dó drihten god ure 7 gesomno us be
47. *Salvos nos fac domine deus noster et congrega nos de*

kennessum *and*gedettæþ nomen halige þinum 7 wuldrien on
nationibus ut confiteamur nomini sancto tuo et gloriemur in

lof ðinum Gebletsige drihten god isræhel from worlde
laude tua **48.** *Benedictus dominus deus israel a seculo*

7 oððet on worlde 7 cweþæþ eællæ folc sie sie
et usque in seculum et dicat omnis populus fiat fiat

106.

Andetteð drihtne forðæn he is god forðæn on worold
1. *Confitemini domino quoniam bonus quoniam in seculum*

mildheortnes his Cweðæþ nu þæ ælisede sindon from
misericordia eius **2.** *Dicant nunc qui redempti sunt a*

drihtne þæ ælisde of hændæ fiondæ of lændum 7 gesomnæþ
domino quos redemit de manu inimici de regionibus congregavit

hie From sunnæn upkyme firsmerc from eæstdæle 7
eos **3.** *A solis ortu et occasu ab aquilone et*

sie dwolodon on þicnesse on drignesse wei ceastre
mari **4.** *erraverunt in solitudine in siccitate viam civitatis*

eærdunge ne metton hingriende 7 þirstende sæwlæ
habitationis non invenerunt **5.** *Esurientes et sitientes anima*

hiræ on him asprungon 7 clipiæþ to drihtne midti
eorum in ipsis defecit **6.** *Et clamaverunt ad dominum cum*

geeærfod 7 be niedþeærfum hiræ gefriolsæþ hie 7
tribularentur et de necessitatibus eorum liberavit eos **7.** *Et*

geledde hie on weg rihtne þette fereþ on ceæstre eærdungæ
eduxit eos in viam rectam ut irent in civitatem habitationis

---

44. ·foþ-, þ·wr. over the line. **106.** 1. *Andetteð* prob. by Cor. 3. *-dæle,*
æ from e.

Ondettæþ drihtne mildheortnesse his 7 wuldor   his beærn
8. *Confiteantur domino misericordiae eius et mirabilia eius filiis*,

mænnæ   Forðæn gefilde sæwle on ydelnesse 7 sæwle
hominum **9.** *Quia satiavit animam   inanem   et animam*

hingriende gefielde god   Sittæþ on ðystrum 7 deæþes
esurientem satiavit bonis   **10.** *Sedentes in tenebris et umbra*

scuæn   7 bendæ gebundene on leæsingum 7 swæ hweno
mortis et vinculis   ligatos in mendicitate et   ferro

    Forðæn beeodon   gesprec godes 7 geþeæht þes hihstæn
11. *Quia exacerbaverunt eloquium domini et consilium altissimi*

  onlihton   7 geeæðmeddon is on gewinnum heorte hioræ
irritaverunt   **12.** *Et humiliatum est in laboribus   cor   eorum*

7 untrume sindon ne wes se gefultomæþ   7 clipodon
infirmati sunt nec fuit qui adiuvaret   **13.** *Et clamaverunt*

to   drihten   mydþi geeærfogode weron 7 be niedðeærfnessum
ad dominum   cum   tribularentur   et de   necessitatibus

hiræ gefriolsode hie   7 geledde hie of ðistrum 7 for
eorum liberavit eos   **14.** *Et eduxit eos de tenebris et de*

deæðes s[c]uæn 7 bendæs hiræ toslæt   anddettæþ
umbra mortis et vincula eorum disrupit **15.** *Confiteantur*

drihtne mildheortnes his 7 wundor his beærn mænnæ
domino misericordiae eius et mirabilia eius filiis hominum

    Forðæn tobricð gætu ęrene 7 gewordene ysene gebricð
16. *Quia   contrivit portas ereas et   vectes   ferreos confregit*

Onfeghð hie be wege unrihtnesse hiræ forðæn on soðfestnesse
17. *Suscepit eos de via   iniquitatis eorum propter iniustitias*

soðlice hire geeædmedde sindon   Eælle mete from
enim suas   humiliati sunt   **18.** *Omnem escam ab-*

weældende is sæwlæ hiræ 7   neælecton oððet to gætum
hominata est anima eorum et adpropiaverunt usque ad portas

deæþes   7 clipodon to drihten midþy geeærfogode
mortis **19.** *Et clamaverunt ad dominum cum   tribularentur*

7 be niedðeærfum hira gefriolseð hie   Sende word
et de necessitatibus eorum liberavit eos   **20.** *Misit verbum*

his 7 gehelde hie 7 generede hie be onforwyrde hiræ
suum et sanavit eos et eripuit eos de interitu eorum

    Ondettæð drihtne mildheortnes his 7 wundor his beærn
21. *Confiteantur domino misericordiae eius et mirabilia eius filiis*

---

17. *be* repeated. *soðlice*, MS. = *soðrce*.   18. Two lett. (oð ?) er. bef.
oððet.   20. *his*, stroke of the *h* above the line er.

monnæ   ðette hie sedon [o]nsegdnesse lof þette
hominum   **22.** *Ut sacrificent sacrificium laudis et*

hie kyðen wiorc his on winsumnesse   þæ æstigæþ
adnuntient opera eius in exultatione ·   **23.** *Qui descendunt*

sie on scipum doende wircende on wetrum mongum
mare in navibus facientes operationes in aquis multis

   hii gesæwon wiorc drihtnes 7 wur.dor his on dypon
24. *Ipsi viderunt opera domini et mirabilia eius in profundo*

   Cwęð 7 stod gæst forhswebung 7 hyhtende sindon yðæ
25. *Dixit et stetit spiritus procellae et exaltati sunt fluctus*

his   Astigæð oððet to hefonum 7 misstigæþ oððet
eius   **26.** *Ascendunt usque ad caelos et descendunt usque*

to niwolnessum sæwlæ hiræ on yfel onegæn   gedrefede
ad abyssos anima eorum in malis tabescebat   **27.** *Turbati*

sindon 7 onstyrede sindon swæ druncne 7 eælle snitro hiræ
sunt et moti sunt sicut ebrius et omnis sapientia eorum

b[e]swolgen is   7 clipodon to drihtne midþy
deglutita est   **28.** *Et clamaverunt ad dominum cum* ·

geeærfoðo 7 be niedþeærfnesse hiræ gefriolsede hie   7
tribularentur et de necessitatibus eorum liberavit eos   **29.** *Et*

gesette forðswebung on golde 7 ætswidon yðæ his   7
statuit procellam in auram et siluerunt fluctus eius   **30.** *et*

blissiende sindon þet hie swiðon 7 geledde hie on gætum
laetati sunt quod siluerunt Et eduxit eos in portum

willæn hiræ 7 be niedþeærfum hiræ gefriolseð hie
voluntatis eorum et de necessitatibus eorum liberavit eos

   anddettæþ drihtne mildheortnes his 7 wundor his beærn
31. *Confiteantur domino misericordiae eius et mirabilia eius filiis*

mænnæ   7 uphebbæþ hine on circæn folc 7 on setle
hominum   **32.** *Et exaltent eum in ecclesia plebis et in cathedra*

yldrenæ hergæþ hine   Forðæn gesette stræm
seniorum laudent eum   **33.** *Quia posuit flumina*

on westene 7 utgæng wætræ on ðurste   Eorðæn
in desertum et exitus aquarum in sitim   **34.** *Terram*

westmberende on ðæm sliþendum heteniþ oneærdigæþ
fructiferam in salsilaginem a malitia inhabitantium

on him gesette westen on tine weter 7 eorðe butæn
in ea   **35.** *Posuit desertum in stagnum aquae et terram sine*

---

22. onsegd-, the o wholly and the n part. er.   24. Er. aft. on.   30. þet,
MS. = þet.   34. sliþendum, n part. er.

wætræ   on   hutgænge wætræ   7 gestaþolode ðer
aqua   in   exitus aquarum   **36.** *Et   collocavit illic*

hingriende 7   gesette   ceæstræ heærdigæd   7
esurientes et constituerunt civitatem habitationis   **37.** *Et*

sêwon   lond 7 wyrtwælodon wingeærdes 7 worhton
seminaverunt agros et plantaverunt   vineas   et   fecerunt

westmæs gebirde   7 gebletsode hie 7 gemonigfælde
fructum nativitatis   **38.** *Et benedixit eos et   multiplicati*

sindon swiðe 7 nietenu hiræ ne sindon gewænode   feæ
sunt nimis et iumenta eorum non sunt minorata   **39.** *Pauci*

gewordene sindon 7 geswencede sindon fræm eærfoþnesse
facti   sunt et   vexati   sunt   a   tribulatione

yfelæ 7   sær   Agoten is geflit ofer
malorum et dolorum **40.** *Et   effusa est contentio super*

eældermæn hiræ 7 hine geledde hie on wege 7 no on weg
principes eorum et seduxerunt eos in invio et non in via

     7 gefultomæþ þeærfæn be wedlungæ 7 gesette swæ sceæp
41. *Et adiuvit   pauperem de inopia   et posuit sicut   oves*

hiredes   gesæwon rihte 7 blissæþ 7 eælle unrihtnes
familias   **42.** *Videbunt recti et laetabuntur et omnis iniquitas*

ne geoponode muþ his   Forðæn snytro 7 gehylt þæs 7
oppilavit   os suum   **43.** *Quis sapiens et custodiet haec et*

ðæ onget mildheortnes drihten
tunc intelleget misericordias domini

107.

    geare heorte min god geæro heorte min ic singe 7
2. *Paratum cor meum deus paratum cor meum cantabo et*

singe ic cwiðe drihtne   Aris wuldor min ærise
psalmum dicam domino   **3.** *Exurge gloria mea exurge*

sæltere 7 heærpæn ic arise on morgen   Ic ondette
psalterium et cythara exurgam diluculo   **4.** *Confitebor*

þe on folce drihten seælm ic cwiðe þe betwioh þiodum
tibi in populis domine psalmum dicam tibi inter   gentes

   Forðæn gemicelod ís oððet to hefonum mildheortnes þin
5. *Quoniam magnificata est usque ad caelos misericordia tua*

---

42. *ne* add. by Cor.   107. 2. *geare* prob. by Cor.

7　oððet　to　wolcnum　soðfestnes　þin　　　　　Upæhebbæn
et　usque　ad　nubes　veritas　tua　　　　**6.**　*Exaltare*

ofer　hefonæs　god　7　ofer　eælle　eorðæn　wuldor　þin
super　caelos　deus　et　super　omnem　terram　gloria　tua

　　þet　sin　gefrilsede　gecorene　þine　hælne　me　dô　swiðre
7.　*ut　liberentur　electi　tui　Salvum　me　fac　dextera*

þin　7　gehire　me　　　　god　sprecende　is　on　hælge　his
tua　et　exaudi　me　　**8.** *deus　locutus　est　in　sancto　suo*

blissæ　7　todele　þæ　drigæn　7　denæ　geteælde　on-
letabor　et　dividam　sicimam　et　convallem　tabernaculorum　me-

segdnesse　　　　　　Min　is　helm　7　min　is　wuniende　7
　tibor　　　　　**9.** *Meus　est　galaad　et　meus　est　manasses　et*

effrem　stren[g]þo　heæfdes　mines　Iudæ　kyning　min　　　　moæb
effrem　fortitudo　capitis　mei　Iuda　rex　meus　　**10.** *moab*

ollæ　hiht　min　on　ilcum　minum　aþene　gescy　min
olla　spei　mee　in　idumeam　extendam　calciamentum　meum

me　olæphili　underþiedde　sindon　　　　hwilc　geledeð　me
michi　allophyli　subditi　sunt　　**11.** *Quis　deducet　me*

on　ceæstre　monegum　oþþet　hwilc　geledeð　me　oððet　on　ilcæn
in　civitatem　munitam　aut　quis　deducet　me　usque　in　idu-

minum　　　　Ne　eælles　þu　god　þu　ædrife　us　7
meam　　**12.** *Nonne　tu　deus　qui　reppulisti　nos　et*

ne　ælles　gængende　god　on　megnum　urum　　　　Sele　us
　non　egredieris　deus　in　virtutibus　nostris　　**13.** *Da　nobis*

fultum　of　eærfoðnessum　7　idle　helo　mænnæ　　　　On
auxilium　de　tribulatione　et　vana　salus　hominis　　**14.** *In*

gode　doþ　megen　7　he　to　næhte　geledeð　eærfoþ-
deo　faciemus　virtutem　et　ipse　ad　nichilum　deducet　tribu-

igæn　us
lantes　nos

108.

God　lof　min　ne　swigæ　forðæn　muð　firenfulle　7
2. *Deus　laudem　meam　ne　tacueris　quia　os　peccatoris　et*

inwid　ofer　me　ontineþ　is　　　　Sprecende　sindon　　　wið
dolosi　super　me　apertum　est　　**3.** *Locuti　sunt　adversum*

me　tungæ　7　inwid　7　wordum　fiodon　ymbseældon　me　7
me　lingua　dolosa　et　sermonibus　odii　circundederunt　me　et

---

8. *onsegdnesse*, g from some other let.　　108. 2. *God* prob. by Cor.

fuhton   me swiþe   Foreðæn þitte   lufodon   me
expugnaverunt me gratis   4. *Pro eo   ut   diligerent me*

wiþtugon   me   ic   eællengæ gebiddæþ   Setton
detrahebant michi ego   autem   orabam   5. *Posuerunt*

wið   me   yfel fore gode 7 fiong fore   lufon
adversum me mala pro bonis et odium pro dilectione mea

gesette   ofer him ðæ firænfullæn 7 diobol   stit on
6. *Constitue super eum   peccatorem   et diabolus stet a*

ðæ swiþræn his   Midþy demæþ he utgange geniðrad
dextris   eius   7. *Cum iudicatur exeat   condemnatus*

7 bed his syo on synne   sy eardungstow his westa 7
et oratio eius fiat in peccatum Fiat   habitatio   eius deserta et

ne syo þe eardige on hire   Sie dægæs his feæwæ
non sit qui habitet in ea   8. *Fiant dies eius pauci*

7 biscopum his onfoh oþer   Sie beærn his
et episcopatum eius accipiat alter   9. *Fiant   filii eius*

stiopcyld 7 wif his wiodwe   wendnes bioð onstirede
orfani et uxor eius vidua   10. *Commoti   amoveantur*

beærn his 7 liogæþ bioþ aworpene be   eærdungæ his
filii eius et mendicent   eiciantur   de habitationibus suis

Smeægende wiorðigende eælle   spede   his 7 ne gene-
11. *Scrutetur   fenerator omnem substantiam eius et   diri-*

rigæþ þæ fremdæn eæll gewin his   Ne sie him
piant alieni   omnes labores eius   12. *Non sit illi*

fultum ne sie se mildsigend stiopcyld his   Sie
adiutor nec sit qui misereatur pupillis eius   13. *Fiant*

gebyrd his on forwirþ on an   cneowrisn sie adilgode nomæ
nati eius in interitu in una generatione deleatur   nomen

his   On geminde efthwirfe unrihtnes fedræ his
eius   14. *In memoriam redeat iniquitas patrum eius*

on gesihþe drihten 7 synne moder his ne adilgode
in conspectu domini et peccatum matris eius non deleatur

Sie wið drihten simle 7 forspilde of eorðæn gemynd
15. *Fiant contra dominum semper et dispereat de terra memoria*

hiræ   Forðæn þet ne is gemindig don mildheort-
eorum   16. *Pro eo quod non est recordatus facere miseri-*

nesse   7 ehtende is monnæ 7 ðeærfc 7
cordiam   17. *et persecutus est hominem   pauperem et*

---

7. From *he* to *hire* by Cor. in p. ink on er.; also Latin equivalent ditto.
12. *him, m* on er.

liæsungæ 7 onbridnesse heorte deæde ȝeælde   7
mendicum et conpunctum corde morti tradidit   **18.** *Et*

lufode wirgcwidolnesse 7 kymþ him 7 nolde bletsunge
dilexit maledictionem et veniet ei et noluit benedictionem et

                from him 7 gierwæþ hine wirigcwidolnesse swæ
prolongabitur ab eo Et induit se maledictione sicut

hriegl 7 ongeð swæ weter on ðæm yteræn his 7 swæ
vestimentum et intravit sicut aqua in interiora eius et sicut

ele on bænum his   Sie him swæ hriegl þio
oleum in ossibus eius   **19.** *Fiat ei sicut vestimentum quo*

bið ontiened 7 swæ sweg ðy symble begierded   þis
operitur et sicut zona qua semper precingitur   **20.** *Hoc*

wiorc hiræ ðæ betioþ me mid gode 7 þæ sprecæþ
opus eorum qui detrahunt michi apud dominum et qui loquuntur

yfel wið sæwle mine   7 þu drihten
mala adversus animam meam   **21.** *Et tu domine domine*

dó mid me mildheortnes fore nomæn þinum forðæn winsum
fac mecum misericordiam propter nomen tuum quia suavis

is mildheortnesse þin gefriolsæ me   forðan wædle
est misericordia tua Libera me   **22.** *quoniam egenus*

7 ðarfe ic am heorte min gedrefed is on me
et pauper sum ego et cor meum conturbatum est in me

          Swæ scuæ mydþy onhildeþ tobroht ic eom 7 onscæcens
23. *Sicut umbra cum declinat ablatus sum et excussus*

ic eom swæ   Mine cneowu geuntrumo sindon
sum sicut locusta   **24.** *Genua mea infirmata sunt*

fore festene 7 flesc min onwend is fore ele   7
pre ieiunio et caro mea inmutata est propter oleum   **25.** *et*

ic geworden eom edwid him gesæwon 7 wendon
ego factus sum obprobrium illis Viderunt me et moverunt

heæfdæ hiræ   gefultumæ me drihten god min 7
capita sua   **26.** *adiuva me domine deus meus*

hælne me do fore mildheortnesse þinre   þette
salvum me fac propter misericordiam tuam   **27.** *Ut*

witon forðæn hændæ þine þis is 7 þu drihten ðu didest þæ
sciant quia manus tua haec est et tu domine fecisti eam

---

18. Er. aft. *-nesse* (2nd).   22. From *forðan* to *am* by Cor. in p. ink on er. ;
also Latin ditto (from *me* (2nd) v. 21 to *et* (2nd) v. 22).   23. *eom* (1st),
MS. = *eon*.

Yfelkweðæþ hii 7 þu gebletsæst þæ   onariseseþ on me
28. *Maledicent illi et tu   benedices qui   insurgunt in   me*
sin ge[s]cinde þiow soþlice þin blissæþ   bioð ge-
*confundantur servus autem tuus letabitur   **29.** Indu-*
gierede ðæ wiðtioþ   me wið drihten cirrendræ 7 sin wyrcende
antur qui detrahunt michi   reverentia et operiantur
swæ betwion gescindnesse hiræ   Ic andette drihtne
*sicut diploide confusione   sua   **30.** Confitebor domino*
swiðe on muþe minum 7 'on midlene monigræ ic herie hine
nimis in   ore   meo   et in   medio   multorum laudabo eum

Forðæn stændeþ to swiþræn þearfænæ þette hæle   deþ
81. *Quia   adstitit ad   dextris pauperis ut   salvam faceret*
from   ehtendom   sæwle   mine
a   persequentibus animam meam

109.

cweð drihten to drihtne minum site on þæ swiþræn minre
Dixit dominus   domino   meo   sede a   dextris   meis
Oððette ic gesette fiond   þine   scæmol   fot   þinre
Donec   ponam   inimicos tuos scabellum pedum tuorum

Gierd megnes ðines utæsendeð drihten ob sion 7 weæl-
2. *Virgam virtutis tuae   emittet   dominus ex syon et domi-*
dendum on middæn   fiondæ   þinræ   Mid þe eældordom
*naberis in medio inimicorum tuorum   **3.** Tecum principium*
on dege megen þines biorhtnessum hæligræ on innoþe
in die   virtutis tuae in splendoribus sanctorum ex utero
beforæn liohte swæ hwenæ ic þe kende   Swor
*ante   luciferum   genui te   **4.** Iuravit*
drihten 7 ne hreowsode hine þu eært sæcerd on ecnesse
dominus et non paenitebit eum tu es sacerdos in aeternum
efter endebirdnesse melchisedech   drihten þere
*secundum ordinem   melchisedech   **5.** Dominus a dex-*
swiþræn þin gebriceþ on deig yrres his kyninges   demæþ
*tris   tuis confregit in die ire suae reges   **6.** Iudicabit*
on kyþnessum gefillæþ hryræs gebrietæþ heafdo monega on
in nationibus implebit ruinas conquassabit capita multa in

---

28. *-ariseseþ*, so MS.   29. The Latin to *wið drihten* (*apud dīm*) has a
line drawn through it for er.   109. *cweð* prob. by Cor. *site*, MS. =
sete with first *e* dotted and *i* wr. above it.

eorðæn genihtsume   Ob rinnellæn on weige   forðæn
terra   copiosa   7. *De torrente in via bibit propterea*
uphæhifd heæfod
exaltabit caput

110.

Ic andette ðe drihten on eælre heortæn minre on geþeæhte
1. *Confitebor tibi domine in toto corde meo in consilio*

soðfest 7 gesomnunge   micle wiorc drihtnes Bege-
iustorum et congregatione   2. *magna opera domini Exqui-*

tende on eælle willæn his   anddetnes 7 micelnes
sita in omnes voluntates eius   3. *confessio et magnificentia*

wiorc his 7 soðfestnes his wunæþ on worlde aworlde
opus eius et iustitia eius manet in seculum seculi

gemynd dyde wunder hira mildheort 7 miltsiend
4. *Memoriam fecit mirabilium suorum misericors et miserator*

drihten mete seælde ondredende hine gemindig bið
dominus 5. *escam dedit timentibus se Memor erit*

on worlde kyþnesse his megen wiorc hiræ
in seculum testamenti sui 6. *virtutem operum suorum*

onsegþ folc his þette seleþ him yrfeweærdnesse
annuntiabit populo suo 7. *ut dei illis haereditatem*

ðiodæ wiorc hændæ his soðfestnes 7 dom ge-
gentium Opera manuum eius veritas et iudicium 8. *fide-*

leæffullæ eællæ bebodu his getrimed on worold æworlde
lia omnia mandata eius confirmata in saeculum saeculi

geworden on soðfestnesse 7 emlicnesse Ælisnesse sende
facta in veritate et aequitate 9. *Redemptionem misit*

folce his bebeæd on ecnesse cyþnesse his halig 7
populo suo mandavit in aeternam testamentum suum sanctum et

egeslic nomæ his On frumæþ snytro ege drihten on
terribile nomen eius 10. *Initium sapientiae timor domini in-*

andgitte god eællum dondum ðane hernes his wunæþ
tellectus bonus omnibus facientibus eam Laudatio eius manet

on worlde æworlde
in seculum seculi

111.

Ædig wer se ondredeþ drihten on bebode his wilnæþ
1. *Beatus vir qui timet dominum in mandatis eius cupit*

10 9. *cyþnesse*, y from *i*.   *nomæ*, fin. let. (n ?) er.

swiðæ   Myhtig on eorðæn bið sęd his cneowrisn
nimis   2. *Potens* *in* *terra* *erit* *semen* *eius* *generatio*

rihtræ gebletsie   wuldor 7 welæ on huse his 7
rectorum benedicetur   3. *Gloria et divitiae in domo eius et*

soðfestnes his wunæþ on worlde æworolde   Upcumen
iustitia eius manet in seculum   seculi   4. *Exortum*

is on ðystrum lioht rihte heorte mildheortnes 7 miltsiend 7
est in tenebris lumen rectis corde   misericors   et miserator et

soðfest drihten   • wynsum mæn se mildsæþ 7
iustus dominus   5. *Iocundus homo qui miseretur   et*

gemetlecæþ geseteð word his on domo   forðæn
commodat disponet sermones suos in iudicio   . 6. *quia*

on ecnesse ne bið onwendeþ   On gemynde on ecæn
in aeternum non commovebitur   7. *In memoria aeterna*

biþ soðfest from gehirnessum yfle ne ondred Geæro is
erit iustus ab   auditu   malo non timebit Paratum est

heorte his gewenæþ on drihten   .   getrymed is heorte
cor eius sperare in domino   8. *confirmatum est cor*

his ne bið onwendeþ oððet gesiehð fiend his   To-.
eius non commovebitur donec videat inimicos suos   9. *Dis-*

stenceþ seælde þeærfæn 7 soðfestnes his wunæþ on worlde.
perdit   dedit pauperibus   iustitia eius manet in seculum

æworlde horn his biþ upæhæfen on wuldor   Sinngiend
seculi cornu eius exaltabitur in gloria   10. *Peccator*

gesihþ 7 yrsæþ toþum his grymetæþ 7 onegið on wyllæn
videbit et irascetur dentibus suis fremebit et tabescet desiderium

fyrenfulræ forwiorðæþ
peccatorum   peribit

112.

Herigæd cnihtes drihten herigæþ nomæn drihten   sie
1. *Laudate pueri dominum laudate nomen domini*   2. *Sit*

nomæ drihtnes gebletsod ob þisum nu 7 oððet on worlde
nomen domini benedictum ex hoc   nunc et usque in seculum

From sunnæn upkyme oððet fyrstmeærc herigæþ nomæn
3. *A   solis   ortu usque ad occasum laudate nomen*

drihten   heæh ofer eælle ðiodæ drihten   ofer
domini   4. *Excelsus super omnes gentes dominus et super*

111. 3. Er. bef. *wunæþ*.   5. *winsum*, MS.=*.w.sum*.   10. *forwiorðaþ*,
MS.=*forwiorðæþ*.

hefonæs wuldor his
caelos gloria eius

se on hiehþum eærdæþ
qui in altis habitat

hefonum 7 on eorðæn
caelo et in terra

7 to rædrum heorte reæcende þeærfæn
et de stercore erigens pauperem

hine mid eældordome mid eældordome folc his
eum cum principibus cum principibus populi sui

to eærdienne worhte berende on hus
habitare facit sterilem in domo

Wilc swæ drihten god ure
5. *Quis sicut dominus deus noster*

7 geeædmeððe forelocæþ on
6. *et humilia respicit in*

æweccende from eorðæn
7. *Suscitans a terra inopem*

þte gestæþolige
8. *Ut collocet*

þær
9. *Qui*

modcr beærnæ blissiende
matrem filiorum laetantem

113.

On utgonge israele of egypte   hus iacob of folc bærbæron
1. *In exitu israel de aegypto domus iacob de populo barbaro*

geworden is iudæ gehælgung his israele myht his
2. *Facta est iudea sanctificatio eius israel potestas eius*

israele rixæþ on him
israel regnavit in ea

gehwirfð is on becling
conversus est retrorsum

weðeræs 7 hyllæ oððet lomb sceæpæ
arietes et colles velut agni ovium

ðet þu fluge 7 þu iordænis forwæn gehwirfed is on beclung
quod fugisti et tu iordanis quare conversus es retrorsum

dunæ forwæn gehihtæþ ðet weðeræs 7 hillæ oððet lomb
6. *Montes quare exaltastis ut arietes et colles velut agni*

sceæpæ
ovium

Sie gesihþ 7 wes iordænis
3. *Mare vidit et fugit iordanis*

dunæ hihtæþ ðet
4. *Montes exultaverunt ut*

hwet is sie
5. *Quid est mare*

from onsine drihtnes onwend is eorðe from
7. *A facie domini commota est terra a*

onsine godes iæcob
facie dei iacob

Se gehwyrfeð on ænnesse stæn
8. *Qui convertit solidam petram*

on tine wetres 7 rinnende on wyllæn wætræ
in stagnum aquae et rupem in fontes aquarum

Ne
1.

ælles us drihten ne eælles us æh nomæ þin sele wuldor
Non nobis domine non nobis sed nomini tuo da gloriam

---

113. 2. *him*, MS. = *hin*.   5. *beclung*, c from a false let.

Ofer   mildheortnesse þine 7 soðfestnesse þine   ðylies
2. *Super   misericordiam tuam et   veritatem   tuam nequando*
cweðæþ ðiodæ hwer is god hiræ   god eællengæ ure
dicant gentes ubi est deus eorum   **3.** *Deus   autem noster*
on hefonum up on hefonum 7 on eorðæn eællæ swæ mitteðe
in celo sursum in caelo et in terra omnia quaecumque
wyle deð   diobolgield ðiode sylfren   7 gylden
voluit fecit   **4.** *Simulachra gentium argentum et aurum*
wiorc hændæ   mænnæ   Muð hæbbeþ 7 ne sprecæþ
opera manuum hominum   **5.** *Os habent et non loquentur*
egæn hæbbæþ 7 ne   gesioð   Eæræn hæbbæþ 7 ne
oculos habent et non videbunt   **6.** *Aures habent et non*
gehiræþ nosæ hæbbæþ 7 ne gebiddæþ   hændæ hæbbæþ
audient nares habent et non odorabunt   **7.** *Manus habent*
7 ne græpiæð fet hæbbæþ 7 ne   gængæð   Ne
et non palpabunt pedes habent et non ambulabunt   Non
cigæð on ciolon hiræ ne   soðlice is gæst on muþe
clamabunt in gutture suo neque enim est spiritus in ore
hiræ   Gelic him bioð ðæ ðe doþ ðæ 7 eælle
ipsorum   **8.** *Similes illis fiant qui faciunt ea et omnes*
ðæ getriewæþ on him   hus isræele gewenæþ on
qui confidunt in eis   **9.** *Domus israel   speravit in*
drihten fultumend hiræ 7 scyldend hiræ is   hus
domino adiutor   eorum et protector eorum est   **10.** *Domus*
æærones geweneþ on drihten fultumend hiræ 7 scildend hiræ
aaron speravit in domino adiutor eorum et protector eorum
is   Se ondredeð drihten gewenæþ on drihten fultu-
est   **11.** *Qui timent dominum sperent in domino adiu-*
mend hiræ 7 scildend hiræ is   drihten gemyndig
tor eorum et protector eorum est   **12.** *Dominus memor*
wesc ure 7 gebletsæ us gebletsæ   hus isræele bletsæ
fuit nostri et benedixit nos benedixit domum israel benedixit
hus ææron   gebletsæ eælle ondredende hine drihten
domum aaron   **13.** *benedixit omnes timentes se dominus*
medmicel mid tionum   Togeþicdeþ drihten ofer
pusillis cum maioribus   **14.** *Adiciat   dominus super*
eow ofer eow 7 ofer beærn eowre   gebletsige eow
vos super vos et super filios vestros   **15.** *Benedicti vos*

15. -*sige*, *g* from *e*.

from drihtne se worhte hefon 7 eorðæn   hefon
a domino qui fecit caelum et terram   16. *caelum*

hefones drihten eorðæn witoðlice seælde beærn monnæ
caeli domino terram autem dedit filiis hominum

    Neælles þæ dedæn herigæð ðe drihten ne eælle ðæ
17. *Non mortui laudabunt te domine neque omnes qui*

æstigæþ on helle   Ah us ðæ þe libbæþ
descendunt in infernum 18. *Sed nos qui vivimus*

bletsie drihten of þisum nu 7 oððet on worolde
benedicimus dominum ex hoc nunc et usque in saeculum

114.

    Ic lufude forðæn gehireð drihtæn stefne gebed min
1. *Dilexi quoniam exaudivit dominus vocem orationis meae*

    Forðæn onhilt eære hiræ me 7 on dægum minum
2. *Quia inclinavit aurem suam michi et in diebus meis*

ic cige hine Ymbseældon me sær deæþes freæcnesse
invocabo eum 3. *Circumdederunt me dolores mortis pericula*

on helle onmetton me Eærfoþnesse 7 sær ic. mette
inferni invenerunt me Tribulationem et dolorem inveni

    7 næmæ drihtnes ic cige Eowlæ drihten gefrilse sæwle
4. *et nomen domini invocabo O domine libera animam*

mine   mildheortnes drihten 7 soðfest 7 god ure
meam   5. *misericors dominus et iustus et deus noster*

miltsigend   heældiend cild drihten geeæþmedeð
miserebitur   6. *Custodiens parvulos dominus humiliatus*

eom 7 gefrilse me   gewirfe sæwle mine on rieste
sum et liberavit me   7. *Convertere anima mea in requiem*

þine forðæn drihten wel deþ me   Forðæn genereþ
tuam quia dominus benefecit michi   8. *Quia eripuit*

sæwle mine o[f] deæþe egæn mine from teærum fot
animam meam de morte oculos meos a lacrimis pedes

mine from sinde   licige· drihtne on londe
meos a lapsu   9. *placebo domino in regione*

lifiendræ
vivorum

114. 1. *Ic lufude* by Cor.?   2. *cige, g* from *e.*

115.

Ic lefde forðæn   þet   sprecende eom   ic   eællengæ geæþme-
10. *Credidi propter quod   locutus   sum ego   autem humilia-*
deð eom swiðe   Ic   cwiþe on ymbgonge mod   mine
tus sum nimis   11. Ego dixi   in   excessu   mentis   meae
7 eælle mæn   leæse   þet   edleænige drihten   for
omnis homo mendax   12. Quid   retribuam   domino   pro
eællum   ðæ   edleænæþ   me   Cælic   helo   ic
omnibus quae retribuit michi   13. Calicem salutaris acci-
onfo 7 næmæ drihtnes on ic gecige   diorwiorðæ   is
piam et nomen domini   invocabo   15. Preciosa   est
on gesihþe drihten deæþ   hæligræ   his   Eowlæ
in conspectu domini mors sanctorum   eius   16. O
drihten ic   þeow ðin ic   þiow ðin   7 beærn þeowne   ðinre
domine ego servus tuus ego servus tuus et filius ancillae tuae
þu toslite bendæ mine   ðe   ic æsecge   tyber   lof
Dirupisti vincula mea   17. tibi sacrificabo hostiam laudis
gehæt min drihtne ic gilde   on cofortone   hus
18. *Vota mea domino reddam   19. in   atriis   domus*
drihten on gesihþe eæll   folc   his   on midlene þines
domini in conspectu omnis populi eius   in   medio   tui
hierusælem
ierusalem

116.

heriað   drihten cælle ðiodæ 7 emnhergæþ   eælle folc
1. *Laudate dominum omnes gentes et conlaudate eum omnes populi*
Forðæn   getrimed   is   ofer   us   mildheortnes   his   7
2. *Quoniam confirmata est   super   nos   misericordia   eius   et*
soðfestnes drihtnes wunæþ on ecnesse
veritas   domini   manet in aeternum

117.

Andetteð drihten forðæn   god   forðæn   on   worold
1. *Confitemini domino quoniam bonus quoniam in   seculum*

---

115. 10. *Ic lefde* by Cor.?   18. *gilde, g* from *c.*   19. *eall,* fin. *e* er.
116. 1. *heriað* by Cor.?   **117.** 1. *Andetteð* prob. by Cor.

mildheortnes his   kweþe nu   isræhel forðæn god
miseriordia eius   **2.** *Dicat nunc   ierael quoniam bonus*

forðæn on worold mildheortnes his   kweþe nu .
quoniam in seculum misericordia eius   **3.** *Dicat nunc*

hus ææron forðæn god forðæn on worlde mildheortnes
domus aaron quoniam bonus quoniam in   seculum misericordia

his   kueþe   nu   eælle   ðæ   ondredeþ drihten
eius   **4.** *Dicant nunc omnes qui   timent   dominum*

forðæn god forðæn on worlde mildheortnes his   On
quoniam bonus quoniam in seculum misericordia eius   **5.** *In*

eærfoðnesse on ic gecige drihten 7 gehireþ me on   bredo
tribulatione   invocavi dominum et exaudivit me in latitudine

drihten me fultumend is ne ic ondrede hwet deþ   me
6. *Dominus michi adiutor est non   timebo   quid faciat michi*

mon   drihten me fultum is 7 ic gesio   fiend
homo   **7.** *Dominus michi adiutor est et ego videbo inimicos*

mine   god   is to getriwenne on drihten þeæhþe
meos   **8.** *Bonum est   confidere   in domino   quam*

to getriwenne on   mæn   god is to gewenænne on
confidere   in hominem   **9.** *Bonum est   sperare   in*

drihten þeæhþe gewene on eældordom   Eælle ðiodæ
domino   quam   sperare in principibus   **10.** *Omnes gentes*

ymbseældon me 7 on næmæn drihten ofer   þ on him
circumdederunt me et in nomine domini ultus sum in eos

Ymbseældon   ymseældon   me 7 on næmæn drihtnes ofer
11. *Circumdantes circumdederunt me et in nomine domini ultus*

þ   on him   Ymseældon me swæ   7
sum in eos   **12.** *Circumdederunt me sicut apes   et*

onburnæn swæ fyr on þornum 7 on nomæn drihtnes
exarserunt sicut ignis in spinis et in nomine domini

oferswiðeð on him   Oncnyseþ drohtiende eom þete
.vindicabor in eis   **13.** *Inpulsus versatus   sum ut*

gefeællen 7 drihten onfeng me   Strengþo mine 7
caderem et dominus suscepit me   **14.** *Fortitudo mea et*

herenes min drihten 7 geworden is me on   helo
laudatio mea dominus et   factus   est michi in salutem

Stef blisse 7 helo on geteldungum soðfestræ   Swiðre
15. *Vox letitiae et salutis in tabernaculis iustorum* **16.** *Dextera*

---

4. *mildheortnes*, MS. = *mildheort̄.*   7. ic repeated.

drihtnes worhte megen swiðre drihtnes uphæbefþ me   Ne
domini   fecit   virtutem dextera domini   exaltavit me   17. Non

swilte æh libbe 7 ic sexge wiorc drihtnes   Clensiende
moriar sed vivam et narrabo opera domini   18. Castigans

geclensæþ me drihten 7 deæþ ne seælde me   Ontynæþ
castigavit me dominus et morti non tradidit me   19. Aperite

me gætu soðfestnesse 7 ongænge on him   Ic anddette
michi portas iustitiae   et ingressus in eas   confitebor

þe drihten   þæs gætu drihtnes soðfeste ongæþ þurh
domino   20. haec porta domini iusti intrabunt per

hine   Ic ændette þe drihten forðæn gehirdon me
eam   21. Confitebor tibi domine quoniam exaudisti me

7 geworden is me on helum   Stæn þone
et factus es michi in salutem   22. Lapidem quem

hie costodon tymbrodon þes geworden is on heæfod on whæmme
reprobaverunt aedificantes hic factus est in caput   anguli

from drihtne geworden is 7 is wundor on eægæn urum
23.   *a   domino factus est et est mirabile in oculis nostris*

þis is deg ðone worhte drihten hihten we 7 blissien we
24. *Haec dies quam fecit dominus exultemus et laetemur*

on hine   From drihtne hælne me do from drihtne wel
in ea   25. O domine salvum me fac o domine bene

to forswebienne   gebletsæ se ðe com on nomæn drihtnes
prosperare   26. Benedictus qui venit in nomine domini

gebletsie eow of huse drihtnes   god drihten 7
benediximus vobis de domo domini   27. deus dominus et

onliehte us gesette ðone [s]ymbeldeig on gebignessum
illuxit nobis Constitui te diem sollemnem in confrequentationibus

oððet to horn wihodes   god min wes þu 7 ic ændette
usque ad cornu altaris   28. Deus meus es tu et confitebor

þe god min wes þu 7 ic þe upæhebbe Ic ændette þe
tibi deus meus es tu et exaltabo te   Confitebor tibi

drihten forðæn gehire me 7 geworden is me on helo
domine quoniam exaudisti me et factus es michi in salutem

anddettaþ drihtne forðæn god forðæn on worlde
29. *Confitemini domino quoniam bonus quoniam in seculum*

mildheortnes his
misericordia eius

---

17. *sexge,* so MS.   24. *is,* an er. in the Latin under this word.

· 118.

א

þæ unwemmæn on wege   gongæþ on gewe drihtnes
1. *Beati inmaculati   in via qui ambulant in lege domini*

Eædige ðæ þe smeægæþ gewitnesse his on eælre heortæn
2. *Beati   qui scrutantur testimonia eius in toto   corde*

secæþ hine   Neælles soðlice ðæ ðe wircæþ
exquirunt eum   3. Non   enim   qui operantur

unrihtnesse on wegum his   gongæþ   þu bebude
iniquitatem in   viis eius ambulaverunt 4. Tu mandasti

bebodu þine drihten to gehældenne swiðe   witoþlice
mandata tua domine   custodiri nimis   5. Utinam

sien gerehte wegæs mine to gehældenne soþfestnesse þine
diriyantur viae meae ad custodiendas iustificationes tuas

þonne ne bío gescinded midþy ic locige on eælle bebodu
6. *Tunc non confundar dum   respicio in omnia mandata*

þine   Ic anddette þe drihten on gerecenesse heortæn
tua   7. Confitebor tibi domine in directione cordis

on him þ ic geleornede domæs soðfestnesse þine
in eo quod didici   iudicia iustitiae tuae

Soþfestnesse þine ic gehælde ne   forlet þu me
8. *Iustificationes tuas   custodiam ncn me derelinquas*

lenge swiþor
usquequaque

ב

ðæm gerecþ giongræ wegas his on to gehældenne
9. *In quo corrigit iunior viam suam in custodiendo*

word þine   On eælre heortæn minre ic þe sohte þe ne
sermones tuos 10. In toto corde meo exquisivi te ne

ædrif þu me from bebodum þ[i]num   On heortæn minre
repellas me a mandatis tuis   11. In corde meo

ic gehidde gesprecæ þine þ ic ne gefyrenode þe   Gebletsod
abscondi eloquia tua ut non peccem tibi 12. Benedictus

ðu eært drihten lere me soðfestnesse þine   On welerum
es domine doce me iustificationes tuas 13. In labiis

minum foresiegð eælle domæs muþæs þines   On wege
meis pronuntiavi omnia iudicia oris tui 14. In via

118. 1. *qui*, gloss to this word (ðæ?) er.

kyðnesse þinræ gelustfullod ic eom swæ on eællum
testimoniorum tuorum delectatus sum sicut in omnibus

welum   On bebodum þinum me ic begonge 7 gesceæwige
divitiis   15. *In mandatis tuis me exercebo et considerabo*

wegæs þinæs   On þinum soðfestnessum smeægæþ ne
vias tuas   16. *In tuis iustificationibus meditabor non*

bio ofergietende   word   þine
  obliviscar   sermones tuos

ɔ

                    þeowe ðinum weg 7 ic geheælde word þine
17. *Retribue   servo   tuo   vivam et   custodiam sermones tuos*

Onwreoh eægæn mîne 7 ic gescæwige wundor be þinre æwe
18. *Revela   oculos meos et considerabo mirabilia de lege tua*

Elðiedi ic eom on eorðæn ne hide ðu fræm me bebodu
19. *Incola ego sum in terra non abscondas a me mandata*

þine   Gewilnæþ sæwle mine to wilnienne soðfestnesse
tua   20. *Concupivit anima mea desiderare iustificationes*

þine on eælle tyde   þu oferciddes ðæ oferhidigæn 7
tuas in omni tempore   21. *Increpasti   superbos*

þæ wirgcwidlon þæ þe becierdon from þinum bebodum
  maledicti   qui declinant a mandatis tuis

Æfirre from me edwit 7 hirwnesse ðæ forðæn kyðnesse
22. *Aufer a me obprobrium et contemptum quia testimonia*

þine ic sohte   7 soðlice sieton eældormæn 7 wid
tua exquisivi   23. *Et enim sederunt principes et adversum*

me sprecon ðeow soðlice þin ic begonge on þinum
me loquebantur servus autem tuus exercebatur in tuis

soðfestnessum   kuþlice 7 gewitnesse þine smeægungum
iustificationibus   24. *Nam et testimonia tua meditatio*

min is 7 frofor min soðfestnesse þine
mea est et consolatio mea iustificationes tuae

٦

Tocleofode fylghþ firhto sæwlæ mine geliffeste me efter
25.   *Adhesit pavimento anima mea vivifica me secundum*

---

14. *welum*, MS. has a stroke over the *u* (*ū*).   21. *wirg-*, *g* from *c*.
25. *Tocleofode* prob. by Cor.

worde þinum   Wegæs mine ic secge ðe 7 þu gehierdes
verbum tuum   **26.** *Vias meas enuntiavi tibi et   exaudisti*

me lere me soðfestnesse þine   Weig soðfestræ
me doce me iustificationes tuas   **27.** *Viam iustificationum*

þinræ on tæcnæ   7 ic begænge on wundrum þinum
tuarum insinua michi et exercebor in mirabilibus tuis

    Slepþ sæwle mine for unluste getrime me on wordum
28. *Dormitavit anima mea pre tedio confirma me in verbis*

þinum   Weg unrihtnessæ æwend from me 7 be æwe
tuis   **29.** *Viam iniquitatis amove a me et de lege*

þinre miltsæ me   Weg soðfestræ ic geceæs domæs
tua miserere mei   **30.** *Viam veritatis elegi iudicia*

domæs þine ic ne eom ofergitend   Etfylhþ kyþnessæ
tua non sum oblitus   **31.** *Adhesi testimoniis*

drihten þine ne ceæro me gescyndæn   Weg bebode
tuis domine noli me confundere   **32.** *Viam mandatorum*

þinre ic yrne mydþy þu gebriedest heorte min
tuorum cucurri dum dilatasti cor meum

ה

    Læge ł æ sete me drihten weg soðfestræ þinræ
33. *Legem pone michi domine viam iustificationum tuarum*

7 ic sece hie simle   Sele me andget 7 ic smeæge
et exquiram eam semper   **34.** *Da michi intellectum et scrutabor*

ewe þine 7 ic geheælde hie on eælræ heortæn minre
legem tuam et custodiam illam in toto corde meo

    Gelied me on stige bebodæ þinræ forðæn hine
35. *Deduc me in semita mandatorum tuorum quia ipsam*

ic wille   Onhild heort min on gewitnesse þine 7
volui   **36.** *Inclina cor meum in testimonia tua et*

ne eælles on epegitsungæ   Æhyrfe eægæn mine ne
non in avariciam   **37.** *Averte oculos meos ne*

gesioþ ydelnesse on wege þinum geliffeste me   Gesete
videant vanitatem in via tua vivifica me   **38.** *Statue*

ðeowe þinum gesprec þin on ege þinum   Onweg æcieorf
servo tuo eloquium tuum in timore tuo   **39.** *Amputa*

edwid min þet ic eom gewenende domes soðlice
obprobrium meum quod suspicatus sum iudicia enim

---

29. *miltsæ, t* from a false let. (s?).

þines   Eællengæ ic wilnige bebodæ þine on
  tua   iocunda   40.   *Ecce   concupivi   mandata   tua   in*
emlicnesse þine geliffeste me
  aequitate   tua   vivifica   me

                                    ꝺ

    And cume ofer me mildheortnes þin drihten helo þine
41.   *Et   veniat super me   misericordia tua domine salutare tuum*
efter   gesprec þin   7 ic andswerige edwitiendum
  secundum eloquium tuum   42.   *Et   respondebo   exprobrantibus*
me   word forðæn ic gewene on wordum þinum   7
  michi verbum   quia   speravi   in sermonibus   tuis   43. *Et*
ne æfyrre þu of muðe min   word   soðfestnesse lenge swiðor
  ne   auferas   de   ore   meo verbum   veritatis   usquequaque
forðæn on   domo   ðine ic gewenc   7   ic geheældæ
  quia   in   iudiciis tuis   speravi   44. *Et   custodiam*
ecwe þine simle on ecnesse 7 on world æworlde   7
  legem tuam semper in aeternum et in seculum seculi   45. *Et*
    ic gonge on   bredo forðæn bebodu þine ic sohte   7
  ambulabam in latitudine quia   mandata tua exquisivi   46. *Et*
ic sprece be gewitnessum þinum on   gesihþe kyningæ 7 ne
  loquebar de   testimoniis   tuis   in conspectu regum   et non
bio gescinded   7 ic smeæge on bebodum þinum þæ
  confundebar   47. *Et   meditabor in   mandatis   tuis   quae*
ic lufige swiðe   7 ic upæhebbe hænde minum to   bebod
  dilexi   nimis   48. *Et   levavi   manus   meas ad   mandata*
þin   ðæ ic lufie   swiþe   7 ic begonge on þinum   sodfest-
  tua   quae   dilexi vehementer et   exercebor   in   tuis   iustifica-
nessum
  tionibus

                                    ꝺ

    Gemyne   wordes þines þeow þin drihten on ðæm   me
49.   *Memor esto   verbi   tui   servo tuo domine in   quo michi*
hieht þu seældes   ðeos me frefrende is on eædmodnesse
  spem   dedisti   50.   *Haec me consolata est in   humilitate*
minre forðæn gesp[r]ec þin   geliffeste me   oferhydige
  mea   quia   eloquium tuum vivificavit me   51.   *Superbi*
unriht   dyde   lenge swiðor ic gescœæs eællenge þine neælles
  iniquae agebant usquequaque   a lege   autem   tua   non

oncyrde   gemyndi ic wes   doɲæ   þinɽæ   from
declinavi   **52.** *Memor   fui   iudiciorum   tuorum   a*

worolde drihtnes 7 ic wes frefrende   Æspringnes mod
seculo   domine   et   consolatus sum   **53.** *Defectio   animi*

min hiefþ me fore fyrenfullæn   forletendum   ewe   þin
tenuit me   pro   peccatoribus   derelinquentibus   legem   tuam

          Sængæs   me   bioð soðfestnesse þiɲc on stowe
54. *Cantabiles michi   erant iustificationes tuae in   loco   incolatus*

min   Gemindy ic wes o[n] niht nomæn ðines drihten
mei   **55.** *Memor   fui   in   nocte nominis tui   domine*

7 ic geheold ewe þine   þios me geworden is forðæn
et custodivi legem tuam   **56.** *Haec michi   facta   est   quia*

soðfestnesse þine ic sohte
iustificationes tuas exquisivi

ᴨ

          Del min drihten ic cwiðe to gehældenne   ewe   þine
57. *Portio mea   domine   dixi   custodire   legem tuam*

          Ic wes biddende ænsine þine on eælre heortæn minre
58. *Deprecatus sum   faciem tuam   in   toto   corde   meo*

miltsæ me   efter   gesprece þinne   Forðæn ic ðohte
miserere mei secundum eloquium tuum   **59.** *Quia   cogitavi*

wegæs þine 7 gewyrfe fet   mine on kydnesse ðinre
vias   tuas   et   converti pedes meos in   testimonia   tua

          Geæro ic eom 7 ne eom gedrefed þet ic gehælde bebodu
60. *Paratus sum   et non sum turbatus ut custodiam mandata*

þine   Ræpæs fyrenfulræ ymbwundon sindon me 7 ewe
tua   **61.** *Funes peccatorum circumplexi   sunt   me et legem*

þin   ne eom ic ofergitend   Middel nihtum ic ærise
tuam non   sum   oblitus   **62.** *Media   nocte   surgebam*

to anddettenne þe ofer domæs soðfestnesse þine   Ic
ad confitendum tibi super iudicia   iustitiae   tuae **63.** *Par-*

eom dielnimende eæll ondredende þe 7 gehældendræ bebodu
ticeps sum ego omnium timentium te et custodientium mandata

þine   Mildheortnes þin drihten gefylled is heorðe
tua   **64.** *Misericordia tua domine plena est terra*

soðfestnesse þines lere me
iustificationes tuas doce me

ʊ

On Godnesse ðu dydes myd þeow þin drihten   efter
65. *Bonitatem   fecisti   cum   servo   tuo   domine   secundum*

word   þine   godnesse 7 ðiodscype 7 wisdom
verbum tuum **66.** *Bonitatem   et   disciplinam   et   scientiam*

gelere me forðæn on bebodum þinum ic gelifde   Erðæm
doce me   quia   in mandatis tuis   credidi   **67.** *Priusquam*

sie geeæðmedeþ   ic   forlete   forðæn   gesprecæ   þine   ic
humiliarer   ego   deliqui   propterea   eloquium   tuum   ego

geheælde   god   wes ðu drihten 7 on godnesse þine
custodivi   **68.** *Bonus   es   tu domine et in   bonitate   tua*

lere me rihtwisnesse þine   Gemonifaldod is ofer me
doce me iustificationes tuas   **69.** *Multiplicata   est super me*

on unriht oferhydigræ ic   eællengæ on eælre heortæn min
iniquitas   superborum ego   autem   in   toto   corde   meo

ic smeæge bebodu þine   Gerunnen is swæ meolc
scrutabor   mandata tua   **70.** *Coagolatum est sicut   lac*

heorte heræ ic   soðlice   ewe þin biom smeægende
cor   eorum ego   vero   legem tuam   meditatus sum

God   me   deð þu geeædmeddes me ðet ic geliornige
71. *Bonum michi quod   humiliasti   me   ut   discerem*

soðfestnesse þine   god   me iewe muð þin ofer
·iustificationes tuas   **72.** *Bonum michi lex   oris tui super*

þusendæ goldes 7 seolfres
milia   auri et argenti

＼

ho[n]dan þine drihten dydon ł wrohton me 7 gewlitegodon
73. *Manus tuae   fecerunt   me et plasmaverunt*

me Sele me   andgiet þet ic leornige bebod þine
me da   michi intellectum   ut   discam   mandata tua

þæ þe ondredæþ ðe gesioð me 7   blissiæð forðæn on
74. *Qui   timent   te videbunt me et laetabuntur quia   in*

worde þinum ic gewene   Ic oncneow drihten forðæn
verbum tuum   speravi   **75.** *Cognovi   domine quia*

emlicnes dom þine 7 on soþfestnesse ðinre geeædmeddes me
aequitas iudicia tua et in   veritate   tua   humiliasti   me

---

65. *On* by Cor.   70. *is* nearly er.   73. *hodan* by Cor. The Latin to
drihten dotted for er.

Sie   nu   mildheortnes ðine drihten 7 · frefrende me
76. *Fiat nunc misericordia tua   domine ut consoletur me*

efter   gesprece þine þ[e]ow þin   Cume   me
secundum eloquium tuum   servo tuo   77. *Veniant michi*

mildsæ   ðine 7 ic libbe forþæn ewe þine smeægende min is
miserationes tuae et vivam quia lex tua meditatio mea est

Sien gesciende þæ oferhydgæn forðæn on unriht unrihtnesse
78. *Confundantur superbi quia iniuste iniquitatem*

fidydon on me ic soðlice 7 ic bio gængen on bebodum þinum
fecerunt in me ego autem exercebor in mandatis tuis

Sien gescirrede to me 7 þæ ðe ondredæþ þe 7 ðæ þe ne
79. *Convertantur ad me qui timent te et qui*

witon   kyþnesse þine   Sie heorte min unwemme
noverunt testimonia tua 80. *Fiat cor meum inmaculatum*

on þinum soþfestnesse þette ne sie gesciended
in tuis iustificationibus ut non confundar

 כ

Aspræng on   helo þine sæwl min 7 on worde þin
81. *Defecit in salutari tuo anima mea et in verbum tuum*

ic wene   Æsprungon eægæn miɼe on gesprece þine
speravi   82. *Defecerunt oculi mei in eloquio tuo*

cweþende hwonne ðu bisð frefrende me   Forðæn
dicentes quando consolaberis me   83. *Quia*

geworden ic eom swæ bytte on hrime soðfestnesse þine ne
factus sum sicut uter in pruina iustificationes tuas non

eom ic ofergitende   hu moniga sindon dægæs þiow
sum oblitus   84. *Quot sunt dies servi*

þine hwonne dest be me ehtendum   dom   Se-
tui quando facies de persequentibus me iudicium 85. *Narra-*

don me unriht gesprecæ æc nes swæ þet ie ðin drihten
verunt michi iniqui fabulationes sed non ita ut lex tua domine

Eællæ bebod ðin soðfestnes unriht ehtende sindon me
86. *Omnia mandata tua veritas iniqui persecuti sunt me*

gefultome me   hwene lies geendodon me on
adiuva me   87. *Paulo minus consummaverunt me in*

---

79. *gescirrede*, so MS.   82. *bisð*, so MS.   83. *bytte*, MS.=orig. *kylle*
altered to *bytte* by cor.   85. *ie*, so MS. orig.; the *e* connected later with
the *i* by two strokes (to make it into *æ*?).

eorðæ ic soðlice ne forlet þu bebodu þine   efter
terra ego vero non dereliqui mandata tua   88. Secundum

mildheortnes þin geliffeste me þet ic geheælde gewitnesse
misericordiam tuam vivifica me ut custodiam testimonia

muð þin
oris tui

ל

ecnesse drihten þurhwunæþ word þin on hefonum
89. *In aeternum domine permanet verbum tuum in caelo*

7 On worold æworlde soðfestnes þin þu gestæðolodes
90. *Et in seculum seculi veritas tua Fundasti*

eorðæn 7 þurhwunæþ   endebyrdnes þin forwurdon
terram et permanet   91. *ordinatione tua perseverat*

dægæs forðæn eælle þeowigæþ ðe   Nimðe ðet ewe
dies quoniam omnia serviunt tibi   92. *Nisi quod lex*

þin smeung min is þonne is þes wen ic forwiorðe on
tua meditatio mea est tunc forsitan perissem in

eædmodnesse minre   On ecnesse ne bio ofergitende
humilitate mea   93. *In aeternum non obliviscar .*

soðfestnesse þine forðæn on him geliffeste me   ðin
iustificationes tuas quia in ipsis vivificasti me   94. *Tuus*

eom ic hælne me do forðæn soðfestnes þine ic sohte
sum ego salvum me fac quia iustificationes tuas exquisivi

Me onbydon þæ fierenfullæn þette forspilden me kyþ-
95. *Me expectaverunt peccatores ut perderent me testi-*

nesse þine ic ongiet   Eælre geendunge gesioh
monia tua intellexi   96. *Omni consummationi vidi*

ende bredæ bebod þin swiþe
finem latum mandatum tuum nimis

מ

þu lufodes æwe þine drihten eælne deg smeæ-
97. *Quomodo dilexi legem tuam domine tota die medi-*

gung min is   Ofer fiend min snytro me
tatio mea est   98. *Super inimicos meos prudentem me*

ðu dydest bebod ðin forðæn on ecnesse me is   Ofer
fecisti mandato tuo quia in aeternum michi est   99. *Super*

88. *þet*, MS. *=ðet*.   90. *On*, MS. *= Ond*.

eælle lierende me ondgiet forðæn gewitnesse þine smeægung
omnes docentes me intellexi quia testimonia tua meditatio

min is   Ofer yldræn ongiet forðæ[n] bebod þine
mea est   100. *Super seniores intellexi quia mandata tua*

ic sohte   From eælum wegæs yfele ic bewererede
exquisivi   101. *Ab omni via mala prohibui*

fet mine þet ic gehælde word þin   From dome
pedes meos ut custodiam verba tua   102. *A iudiciis*

þinum ne behylde forðæn þu æwe gesettes   hu
tuis non declinavi quia tu legem posuisti michi   103. *Quam*

swetæ gomum minum gesprecæ þin drihten ofer huni 7 biebred
dulcia faucibus meis eloquia tua domine super mel et favum

muð min   from bebodum þinum ongiet forþæn
ori meo   104. *A mandatis tuis intellexi propterea*

fioung hebbe eælne weg unrihtnesse forðæn þu ewe
odio habui omnem viam iniquitatis quoniam tu legem

gesettes me
posuisti michi

ꝺ

fotum minum word þin drihten 7 lioht
105. *Lucerna pedibus meis verbum tuum domine et lumen*

stigæ minum   Ic swor 7 ic gesette to gehældenne
semitis meis   106. *Iuravi et statui custodire*

dom sodfestnesse ðine   geeædmedded ic eom lenge
iudicia - iustitiae tuae   107. *Humiliatus sum usque*

swiðor drihten geliffeste me efter word þin   Wil-
quaque domine vivifica me secundum verbum tuum   108. *Vo-*

sumlice muð min wylnungæ do drihten 7 dom ðin liere
luntaria oris mei beneplacita fac domine et iudicia tua doce

me   sæwlæ mine on hændæ þinum simle 7 ewe
me   109. *Anima mea in manibus tuis semper et legem*

þine ic ne eom ofergitend   Gesetton þæ fyrænfullæn
tuam non sum oblitus   110. *Posuerunt peccatores*

gegrine me 7 from gebodum þinum ne gedwolode   yrfe-
laqueos michi et a mandatis tuis non erravi   111. *Hae-*

weærdnesse to ic sohte kyðnesse ðine on ecnesse forðæn
reditate adquisivi testimonia tua in eternum quia

101. *bewererede*, so MS.

P 2

winsumnesse heorte min sindon   Onhylde heorte mine
  exultatio   cordis mei   sunt   **112.** *Inclinavi   cor   meum*
to   donne   soðfestnesse þine on ecnesse forðæn edleænunge
ad faciendas iustificationes tuas in aeternum propter retributionem

ð

    Vnrichtwise fioung hefð 7 ewe þine ic lufode   To
113. *Iniquos   odio habui et legem tuam   dilexi*   **114.** *Ad-*
fultome 7 onfeng min wes þu 7 on worde þinum ic gewene
  iutor   et susceptor meus   es   tu et in verbum tuum   speravi

    Onhyldæþ from me þæ wirhdæn 7 smeægen bebodu godes
115. *Declinate   a   me   maligni   et scrutabor mandata dei*
mines   Onfoh   me   efter   gesprec þin 7 libbe
  mei   **116.** *Suscipe me secundum eloquium tuum et vivam*
7 ne gescynde me from gesihþe minre   gefultumæ
et ne confundas me ab expectatione mea   **117.** *Adiuva*
me 7 hæl ic biom 7 ic smeæge on ðinum   soðfestnesse sinble
me et salvus   ero   et meditabor in tuis iustificationibus semper

    ðu hyrwdes · eælle niðerstigende from soþfestnesse þinum
118. *Sprevisti omnes   discedentes   a   iustificationibus tuis*
forþæn þæ unsoðfestæn geþoht hieræ is   Oferliorende
   quia   iniusta   cogitatio eorum est   **119.** *Prevaricantes*
geteælde eælle fyrenfulle eorþe forðæn þu lufodes kiðnesse
  reputavi omnes peccatores terrae ideo   dilexi   testimonia
þine   gefestnæ ege þinne flesc minum from
  tua   **120.** *Infige timore tuo carnes meas   a*
domum soðlice þinum ondriet
iudiciis enim tuis timui

y

    Ic dyde   dom   7 soðfestnesse ne sele þu me from me
121. *Feci iudicium et iustitiam   ne tradas me   perse-*
ehtendum   Ic gesceæs þiow þinne on god þte
quentibus me   **122.** *Elige   servum tuum in bonum ut*
ne sien heærmcweþende me oferhydige   Eægœn
non   calumnientur   michi superbi   **123.** *Oculi*
mine æsprungon on helo þine 7 on gesprecum soðfestnesse
mei   defecerunt in salutari tuo et in   eloquio   iustitiae

ðine   dó myd þeowe þinum   efter   mildheortnes
tuae   124. Fac cum servo tuo secundum misericordiam

þine 7   soðfestnesse ðine liere me   þiow ðin eom
tuam et iustificationes tuas doce me   125. Servus tuus sum

ic sele me   andgiet ðet ic wite kyðnesse þine   Tyde
ego da michi intellectum ut sciam testimonia tua 126. Tempus

doende drihten tostencton unriht ewe ðine   Forðæn
faciendi domine dissipaverunt iniqui legem tuam 127. Ideo

þu lufodes bebod þin ofer gold 7 seærogim   Fore-
    dilexi   mandata tua super aurum et topazion 128. Prop-

þæn 7 eælle bebodo þine ic recce æghwylcne weg unriht
terea ad omnia mandata tua dirigebar onnem viam iniquam

fiounge hiefde
odio habui

ꝺ

Wunderlice   kyðnesse þine drihten forðæn smeægende is
129. *Mirabilia   testimonia tua domine ideo scrutata est*

sæwl min   .   byrhtnes wordæ þinræ onliehte
ea anima mea   130. Declaratio sermonum tuorum inluminat

me 7 ongiet seleð litlengum   Muþ min ontiene 7
me et intellectum dat parvulis 131. Os meum aperui et

wiðteæh gæst forðan bebod þin ic willnige   locæ
adtraxi spiritum quia mandata tua desiderabam 132. Aspice

on me 7 miltsæ me   efter   lufiendræ dom 7 nomæn
in me et miserere mei secundum iudicium diligentium   nomen

þinre   Steæpæs mine gerece efter   gesprec þin
tuum   133. Gressus meos dirige secundum eloquium tuum

þet ne sie wældend min eælle on unrihtwisnesse   Ælise
ut non dominetur mei omnis   iniustitia   134. Redime

me heærmcwidolnesse mænno þet ic gehælde bebod þin
me a   calumniis   hominum ut custodiam mandata tua

Onsien þin onlihte ofer þiow ðinne 7 liere me
135. *Faciem tuam inlumina super servum tuum et doce me*

soðfestnesse þine   Utgæð wætræ ferdon eægæn
iustificationes tuas   136. Exitus aquarum transierunt oculi

min forðæn ne geheldon ewe þine
mei quia non custodierunt legem tuam

Ʒ

Rihtwis is drihten 7 rihtwis   dom   þinne   behodu
137. *Iustus es domine et rectum iudicium tuum*   **138.** *Mandasti*

soðfestnesse   kyðnesse   þine   7   soðfestnesse   þine   swiðe
iustitiam   testimonia   tua   et   veritatem   tuam   nimis

    Onegæn   me dyde ellenwodnes / hus   þin forðæn ofergiten
139. *Tabescere me fecit   zelus (domus tuae quia   obliti*

sindon word þine   fiend   mine   gesprecæ
sunt verba tua inimici   mei   **140.** *Ignitum eloquium*

þin ·   swiðe   7 þeow þin lufode þet   Mín
tuum vehementer et servus tuus dilexit illud   **141.** *Adoles-*

ungleæwnes ic   eom   7 hirwnessæ   soðfestnesse   þine   ne
centior   ego sum et contemptus iustificationes tuas non

eom ic ofergitend   Soþfestnes þine drihten soðfestnesse
sum   oblitus   **142.** *Iustitia   tua   domine   iustitia*

on   ecnesse   7 ewe þine sodfestnes   Eærfoþnes 7
in   aeternum et lex tua   veritas   **143.** *Tribulatio et*

neærones gemetton me bebodæ soþlice þin smeæung min is
angustia invenerunt me mandata autem tua meditatio mea est

    Emlicnes gewitnesse þin on   ecnesse   7 ondgiet sele
144. *Equitas   testimonia   tua in   aeternum et intellectum da*

me 7 ic libbe
michi et vivam

ꝼ

    Ic clepode on eælre heortæn mín gehire me drihten
145. *Clamavi   in   toto   corde   meo   exaudi me domine*

soðfestnesse þines ic sece   Ic clipie to þe hælne
iustificationes tuas requiram   **146.** *Clamavi ad te salvum*

me do þet ic geheælde bebodu þine   Forecom   on
me fac ut custodiam mandata tua   **147.** *Preveni   in*

hredlicnesse 7 ic clipige 7 on   worde   þinum ic gewene
maturitate   et clamavi   et in verbum   tuum   speravi

    Forecomon eægæn min to þe on mergen þet hie smeægen
148. *Prevenerunt oculi mei ad te   diluculo ut   meditarer*

gespreco ðine   Stefne mine gehire drihten   efter
eloquia tua   **149.** *Vocem meam exaudi domine secundum*

mildheortnesse ðine 7   efter   dom   þin geliffeste me
misericordiam tuam et secundum iudicium tuum vivifica   me

Toneæleæcton   ehtende   me   unriht from ewe   soþlice
150. *Appropiaverunt persequentes me iniqui   a   lege   autem*

þine   fiorr gewordenne sindon   Neæh is þu drihten
tua   longe   facti   sunt   151. *Prope es tu domine*

7 eælre   bebod þin soþfestnesse   On frumæn ic oncneow
et omnia mandata tua   veritas   52. *Initio   cognovi*

be kyþnesse þinum forðæn on ecnesse gestæþole þæ
de testimoniis tuis   quia   in eternum fundasti ea

ꝛ

gesioh eæþmodnesse   mine 7 genere me forðæn   ewe þine
153. *Vide humilitatem meam et eripe me   quia   legem tuam*

ne   eom ic ofergitend   deme 7   dom   minne 7
non   sum   oblitus   154. *Iudica   iudicium meum et*

ælise me   fore   gesprecum þinum geliffeste me   Fiorr
redime me propter eloquium   tuum vivificc me   155. *Longe*

is fræm þæm fyrenfullæn helo forðæn soðfestnesse ðine ne
est a   peccatoribus   salus quia iustificationes tuas non

sohton   Miltsæ   ðine monige swiþe drihten
exquisierunt   156. *Miserationes tuae multe nimis domine*

efter   dome   þinne geliffeste me   Monigæ
secundum iudicium tuum   vivifica   me   157. *Multi*

ehtende   me 7 eærfoþiende me from kyþnessum þinum ne
persequentes me et tribulantes me a testimoniis tuis non

onhyld   gesioþ ne eælles wero 7   onege
declinavi   158. *Vidi non servantes pactum et tabescebam*

forðæn gesprec þin ne   gehælden   gesioh forðæn
quia eloquia tua non custodierunt   159. *Vide quia*

bebod þin ic lufode drihten on þin mildheortnes geliffeste
mandata tua   dilexi   domine in tua misericordia vivifica

me   Eældordom wordæ   ðinræ soðfestnes on
me   160. *Principium verborum tuorum veritas in*

ecnesse eællræ domæs soþfestnesse þine
eternum omnia iudicia iustitiae tuae

ש

ehtende sindon me swiþe 7 from wordum þinum
161. *Principes persecuti sunt me gratis et a verbis tuis*

154. *deme*, first *e* prob. from *o*.

onegæn heorte min   blissige ic ofer gesprecæ
formidavit cor meum   **162.** *Letabor ego super eloquia*

þine swæ ðæ cymeþ reæflæc micel   Unrihtnesse
tua sicut qui invenit spolia multa   **163.** *Iniquitatem*

fiongæ ic hebbe 7 fræm ðæm weældendum ewe soþlice þine
odio habui et abominatus sum legem autem tuam

ic lufode   Seofæn siþum on deg   lof ic cwiþe þe
dilexi   **164.** *Septies in die laudem dixi tibi*

ofer dom soþfestnesse þine   Sib micel lufigende
super iudicia iustitiae tuae   **165.** *Pax multa diligentibus*

ewe þin drihten 7 ne is on him geswic   Ic onbide
legem tuam domine et non est in illis scandalum   **166.** *Expectabam*

helo ðine drihten 7 bebod þin ic lufode   gehylt
salutare tuum domine et mandata tua dilexi   **167.** *Custodivit*

sæwl min kyþnesse þine 7 lufode ðæ swiðe   Ic gehiold
anima mea testimonia tua et dilexit ea vehementer   **168.** *Servavi*

bebodu þine 7 kyþnesse þine forðæn eælle wegas mine on
mandata tua et testimonia tua quia omnes viae meae in

gesihþe þine drihten
conspectu tuo domine

ꞁ

gebed min on gesiehþe þinre drihten
169. *Appropinquet oratio mea in conspectu tuo domine*

efter gesprecæn þinræ sele me ondgiet   Ongonge
secundum eloquium tuum da michi intellectum   **170.** *Intret*

gebed min on gesihþe þine drihtne efter gesprecæ
postulatio mea in conspectu tuo domine secundum eloquium

þinum genere me   Uproccæntæð wcleræs mine ymen
tuum eripe me   **171.** *Eructuabunt labia mea ymnum*

ðone þu lierest me soþfestnes ðine   Forekyðæþ
dum docueris me iustificationes tuas   **172.** *Pronuntiabit*

tungæ min gesprecæ þine forðæn eælle bebodu þin emlicnes
lingua mea eloquia tua quia omnia mandata tua aequitas

Sie hændæ þinæ ðctte hælne me gedo forðæn bebodu
173. *Fiat manus tua ut salvum me facias quia mandata*

ðine ic gesceæs   wilnæþ helo þine drihten 7 ewe
tua elegi   **174.** *Concupivi salutare tuum domine et lex*

þine smeæung min is   lifæþ sæwl min 7 ic herige
tua meditatio mea est   **175.** *Vivet anima mea et laudabit*

---

170. *Ongonge, e* from *o*?   173. *gesceæs,* so MS.

þe 7 domæs ðine tofultomien me   Gedwolode swæ
te et iudicia tua adiuvabunt me   **176.** *Erravi sicut*

sceæp þæ forwiorðæþ ic sece diow þinne drihten forðæn
ovis quae perierat require servum tuum domine quia

bebodu ðine neom ofergiten
mandata tua non sum oblitus

119.

drihtne   ic bio geeærfogædoð ic clipie 7 gehiere me
Ad dominum dum   tribularer   clamavi et exaudivit me

drihten gefrilsæ sæwlæ mine from welerum unrihtum 7
2. *Domine libera animam meam a labiis iniquis et*

from tungæn inwidre   ðet bid sellende þe oððet hwet
a lingua dolosa **3.** *Quid detur tibi aut quid*

to bið geseteþ ðe 7 from tungæn inwidre   Strelæ mihtæ
adponatur tibi a lingua dolosa **4.** *Sagitte potentis*

sceærpe mid gledum   Eow me forðæn
acute cum carbonibus desolatoriis **5.** *Heu me quod*

onwrecscipes mines forebredeþ is eærdunge mid eærdigendum
incolatus meus prolongatus est habitavi cum habitantibus

cedron micel On elðiodgum wes sæwl min   Mid
cedar **6.** *multum incola fuit anima mea* **7.** *Cum*

þisum ðæ fiogæþ sibbe ic bio gesibsum midðie ic sprece him
his qui oderunt pacem eram pacificus dum loquebar illis

onfuhton me swiðe
inpugnabant me gratis

120.

eægæn mine to dunum hwænon cume fultum
1. *Levavi oculos meos ad montes unde veniat auxilium*

me   Fultum minne from drihtne se worhte hefon 7
michi **2.** *Auxilium meum a domino qui fecit caelum et*

eorþæn   Ne seleþ onwendnesse fotum þinum nemne
terram **3.** *Non det in commotionem pedem tuum neque*

slepeþ þæ gehielt ðe   Eællengæ ne slæpæþ ðælies
obdormiet qui custodit te **4.** *Ecce non dormitabit neque*

slæpæþ þæ gehelt isræhel   drihten gehylt þe drihten
obdormiet qui custodit israel **5.** *Dominus custodit te dominus*

175. *me* repeated.   176. *sece*, final *e* from *g*.   120. 4. *gehelt*, second *e* from *i*.

forescyldnes ðin ofer hænd swiðre ðin   þurh deg
protectio tua super manum dexteram tuam   **6.** *Per diem*

sunne ne bierneþ þe ðylïes monæ ðurh niht   drihten
sol non uret te neque luna per noctem   **7.** *Dominus*

gehielt ðe from eællum yfel gehcælde sæwle þine drihten
custodit te ab omni malo custodiat animam tuam dominus

   drihten geheælde on ingonge þinum 7 utgonge þinum ob
8. *Dominus custodiat introitum tuum et exitum tuum ex*

þisum nu 7 oððet on worold
hoc nunc et usque in seculum

121.

Ic blitsige   on þysum þæ gecweðene syndon to me on
Letatus sum in his quae dicta sunt michi in

huse drihtnes we gað   Stondende bioð fiet ure on
domum domini ibimus   **2.** *Stantes erant pedes nostri in*

cæfortunum þinum ierusælem   hierusælem sio is getymbred
atriis tuis ierusalem   **3.** *Ierusalem quae aedificatur*

þet þæ ceæstre þies delnimende his on ðet selfe   ðeræ
ut civitas cuius participatio eius in id ipsum   **4.** *Illuc*

soðlice æstigon mægþo mægþo drihten kyþuessæ on
enim ascenderunt tribus tribus domini testimonium in

isræhelum to anddettenne nomon ðinum   Forðæn þier
israel ad confitendum nomini tuo   **5.** *Quia illic*

sieton setl on dome setle ofer hus dæuides biddæð
sederunt sedes in iudicio sedes super domum david   **6.** *Rogate*

ðæ to sibbe sindon on ierusælem 7 genihtsumnesse lufigende
quae ad pacem sunt in ierusalem et abundantia diligentibus

þe   Sie sib on meigne þine 7 genihtsumnes on torrum
te   **7.** *Fiat pax in virtute tua et habundantia in turribus*

þinum   Forðæn broþor min 7 þæ nixtæn mine 7 ic sprece
tuis   **8.** *Propter fratres meos et proximos meos loquebar*

sibbe be þe   Forðæn hus drihtnes godes ure
pacem de te   **9.** *Propter domum domini dei nostri*

forðæn him god ðe
quesivi bona tibi

---

121. After *blitsige* is *ic eom on him* underlined for er., *him* having an
additional line drawn through it. *we gað* in pl. of er.   **3.** *þies*, cf. note
to *ic* (118: 85).   **6.** *geniht-*, MS. = *gemiht.*

122.

To þe ic uphebbe eægæn mine ðu eærdæst ou heofonum
1. *Ad te levavi oculos meos qui habitas in caelo*

Eællengæ swæ eægæn deowæ on hændum weældendræ
2. *Ecce sicut oculi servorum in manibus dominorum*

hiræ swæ eægæn ðiowenne on hændum drihten hieræ swæ
suorum Et sicut oculi ancille in manibus domine suae ita

eægæn uræ to drihten gode urum oððet miltsiend us
oculi nostri ad dominum deum nostrum donec misereatur nobis

Miltsie us drihten miltsige us forðæn micelice gefillede
3. *Miserere nobis domine miserere nobis quia multum repleti*

we sindon 7 hirwnesseum 7 micelice gefilled is sæwl
sumus contemptione 4. Et multum repleta est anima

uræ edwid genihtsumnes 7 forsiewen ðæ oferhidgæn
nostra obprobrium abundantibus et despectio superbis

123.

Nimðe ðet drihten wes on us cweðæþ nu isræhele
1. *nisi quod dominus erat in nobis dicat nunc israel*

nimþe forðæn drihten wes on us Midti æriseþ
2. *nisi quia dominus erat in nobis Dum insurgerent*

men on us ic ðies wen lifiende to beswelgenne æh
homines in nos 3. forsitan vivos deglutissent

næ us Midti bið irsiendæ sæwlæ hiræ wið us
nos Dum irasceretur animus eorum adversum nos

ic ðies wen oððet weter wiðset æhnæ us Rinnelle
4. *forsitan velut aqua obsorbuissent nos 5. Torrentem*

ðurhferð sæwl ure ic ðies wien þurhferæþ sæwle ure
pertransivit anima nostra forsitan pertransisset anima nostra

weter unæriefnedlic gebletsie drihten ðæ seleþ
aquam intolerabilem 6. Benedictus dominus qui non dedit

us hieftniede toðum hiræ Sæwlæ ure swæ
nos in captionem dentibus eorum 7. Anima nostra sicut

speræwæ gegripen is be grine atriendum gegrino getirged is
passer erepta est de laqueo venantium Laqueus contritus est

7 us gefriolsede we sindon to fultome urum on nomæn
et nos liberati sumus 8. adiutorium nostrum in nomine

drihtnes se worhte hefon 7 eorðæn
domini qui fecit celum et terram

124.

getriewæþ on drihten swæ dun syon ne bið onwendeþ
Qui confidunt in domino sicut mons syon non commovebitur

on ecnesse se eærdæþ   on hierusælem dunæ on
in aeternum qui habitat   2. *in ierusalem Montes in*

ymbegonge his 7 drihten on ymbegonge folces his ob þisum
circuitu eius et dominus in circuitu populi sui ex hoc

nu 7 oððet on world   Forðæn ne forleteþ drihten
nunc et usque in seculum   3. *Quia non derelinquet dominus*

gierde firenfulræ ofer hlyt soðfestræ ðet ne æðenigæþ
virgam peccatorum super sortem iustorum ut non extendant

soðfeste to unrihtnesse hændæ his   wel do drihten god
iusti ad iniquitatem manus suas   4. *bene fac domine bonis*

7 rihte heortæn   Onhildende soðlice to ofergitnesse
et rectis corde   5. *Declinantes autem ad obligationem*

togeledeþ drihten myd wyrcendum unrihtnes sibb ofer
adducet dominus cum operantibus iniquitatem pax super

isræhele
israel

125.

cyrrende drihten hieftnied syon gewordene sindon swæ
In convertendo dominus captivitatem syon facti sumus sicut

efnfrefrende ðonne gefylled is gefeæn muð ure 7
consolati 2. *Tunc repletum est gaudio os nostrum et*

tungæ ure on winsumiæþ ðonne cweðæþ betwioh þiodæ mi-
lingua nostra in exultatione Tunc dicent inter gentes mag-

clæþ drihten don mid him miclæþ drihten
nificavit dominus facere cum illis 3. *magnificavit dominus*

don us mid gewordenne we sindon blissiendc Gecirre
facere nobiscum facti sumus letantes · 4. *Converte*

drihten hæftnied uræ swæ rinnellæ on rodre ðæ ðæ
domine captivitatem nostram sicut torrens in austro 5. *Qui*

sæwæþ on teærum on gefcæn ripæþ utgongende 7
seminant in lacrimis in gaudio metent 6. *euntes ibant et*

wepæþ sendende sed hiræ Cumende soðlice cumæþ on
flebant mittentes semina sua Venientes autem venient in

hyhte berendc his deðæ
exultatione portantes manipulos suos

126.

drihten   tymbreþ   hus   on ydelnesse winnæþ   ðæ tym-
Nisi dominus edificaverit domum in   vanum   laborant   qui aedi-

bræð   ðæ Nimme drihten   gehylt   ceæstre on ydelnesse
ficant eam   Nisi   dominus   custodierit civitatem in   vanum

wæciæþ ðæ gehældæþ ðæ   On ydelnesse is eow beforæn
vigilant qui custodiunt eam   2. In   vanum   est vobis   ante

liohte   ærison   ærisoþ   efterðæm te   sittæð   ðæ   etæþ
lucem   surgere   surgite   postquam   sederitis qui manducatis

blæf   særes Midti þe seleþ ðæm liofastæn his   slep   þios
panem doloris Cum dederit   dilectis   suis somnum 3. haec

is   yrfeweærd drihtnes beærn egnwirhtæ westmæ inuoðes
est   haereditas   domini   filii   mercis   fructus ventris

swæ strielæ on hændæ mihtig swæ   beærn onscuniendræ
4. *Sicut sagitte in manu potentis ita et filii   excussorum*

Eædige wer se gefylleþ willæþ   his   on him   ne
5. *Beatus   vir   qui   implebit desiderium suum ex ipsis non*

bið gescynded mid ic sprece fiond   his   on gætæ
confundetur dum loquetur inimicis suis   in porta

127.

eælle   ðæ ðe   ondredæð   drihten   ðæ   gongæþ   on
Beati omnes   qui   timent   dominum qui   ambulant   in

wegum his   Gewin wes[t]m ðinræ   þu etaþ Eædig
viis   eius   2. Labores fructum tuorum manducabis beatus

ðu biist 7 wel þe bið   [Wi]f ðin swæ lif geniht-
es   et bene tibi erit   3. Uxor tua sicut vitis abun-

sumnes on heælfum hus   ðin beærn þin swæ niwræ elebergennæ
dans in lateribus domus tuae Filii tui sicut novella   olivarum

on ymbegonnge gemetes þines   Gesihþe swæ sie gebletsod
in   circuitu   mense tuae   4. Ecce   sic   benedicetur

eælle mon þe ondret drihten   Gebletsige þe drihten
omnis homo qui timet dominum   5. Benedicat te dominus

ob syon 7 gesioð ðæ godæ sindon oꞃ hierusælem eællum
ex syon et videas quae bona   sunt in   ierusalem omnibus

---

126. 3. *egn-, g* from some other let.   127. 3. [*Wi*]*f*, two lett. er. where
indicated. *elebergennæ* in pl. of er.   5. *bona* repeated, first with line drawn
through it and second dotted.

dægum lif ðin   7 gesihst beærn beærnæ þinre
diebus vitae tuae   6. *Et videas filios filiorum tuorum*

sib ofer isræhele
pax super israel

128.

gefuhton me from gigoþe minre cweðæþ nu
Sepe expugnaverunt me a iuventute mea dicat nunc

isræhel   gelomlice   fuhton   me from giogoþe
israel   2.   *sepe expugnaverunt me a iuventute*

minre 7 soðlice ne miehton me   Ofer hrycg
mea etenim non potuerunt michi   3. *Supra dorsum*

minne tymbrodon firenfullæ forelengnesse unrihtnesse his
meum fabricaverunt peccatores prolongaverunt iniquitates suas

drihten soðfest æciorfe swioræn firenfulræ   sien
4. *Dominus iustus concidet cervices peccatorum*   5. *con-*

gescinde 7 gewirfede eælle ðæ ðe fiogæþ sion   wese
fundantur et revereantur omnes qui oderunt syon   6. *Fiant*

swæ heg getymbriendræ þet ærðæm utæluceþ forwisneþ
sicut foenum edificiorum quod priusquam evellatur arescit

be ðæm ne gefilleþ hændæ his sæ þæ ripþ ne
7. *De quo non implebit manum suam qui metit nec sinum*

his ðæ minnæn gesomnæð   Ond ne cwedon ðæ þurh-
suum qui manipulos colliget   8. *Et non dixerunt qui pre-*

ferdon bletsung drihtnes ofer eow we bletsiæþ eow on
teribant benedictio domini super vos benediximus vobis in

nomæ drihtnes
nomine domini

129.

ic clipige to þ[e] drihten   drihten
De profundis clamavi ad te domine   2. *domine*

gehire gebed min Sien eærc ðin beheældenne on gebede
exaudi orationem meam Fiant aures tuae intendentes in orationem

ðeow ðin   Gif unrihtnes ðu gehielts drihten
servi tui   3. *Si iniquitates observaveris domine domine*

se ærefneð   Forðæn se mid ðe ærfull is 7
quis sustinebit   4. *Quia apud te propitiatio est et*

foreðæn ewe ðine ærefneþ ðe drihten ærefnede sæwlæ min
propter legem tuam sustinui te domine Sustinuit anima mea

129. 4. *propter*, MS. = *proplem.*

on worde ðinum   geweneþ sæwl min on drihten
in verbum tuum   5. *speravit anima mea in domino*

   From gehealdenum þæm uhtlican oððet to   niht geweneþ
6. *A   custodia   matutina   usque ad noctem speret*

isræhel on drihten   forðæn mid drihten mildheortnes
israel in domino   7. *Quia apud dominum misericordia*

is 7 genihtsum mid him ælysnes   7 he ælisnes
est et copiosa   apud eum redemptio   8. *Et ipse redimet*

isræhele ob eællum unrihtnessum his
israel ex omnibus iniquitatibus eius

130.

Drihten ne   is upæhæfæn heorte min nimðe gebredde sindon
Domine non est exaltatum   cor   meum neque elati sunt

eægæn mine Nimðe ic gonge on miclum nimþe on wundrum
oculi   mei Neque ambulavi in magnis neque in mirabilibus

ofer   me   Gif ne geeæðmeċeþ geðæfotungæ æh
super   me   2. *Si non   humiliter   sentiebam   sed*

upæhefe sæwle   mine swæ blissiende   ofer modor his
exaltavi animam meam Sicut ablactatus est super matrem suam

swæ geeædleænæst on sæwle mine   geweneþ isræhele
ita   retribues   in animam meam   3. *Speret   israel*

on drihten ob þisum nu 7 oððe on worold
in domino ex hoc   nunc et usque in seculum

131.

gemyne drihten dæuides 7 eælle geðwærnessæ his   Swæ
Memento domine david et omnis mansuetudinis eius   2. *Sicut*

swor drihten gehæt gehet gode iæcobes   Gif ic gonge
iuravi domino votum vovit deo iacob   3. *Si introiero*

on eærdunge   hus min gif ic æstige on bedde s[t]rewene
in tabernaculum domus meae si ascendero in lectum stratus

minum   Gif ic selle slep eægæn minum oððe
mei   4. *Si dedero somnum oculis meis   aut*

briewum minum hneæppungæ   oððe rieste on tidum
palpebris meis dormitationem   5. *aut requiem temporibus*

minum Oððette gemette stowe drihtnes eærdungæ gode
meis Donec inveniam locum domino tabernaculum deo

iæcobes   Eællengæ gehiræþ þæ on eufræten onge-
iacob   6. *Ecce   audivimus ea in effrata   inve-*

metton þæ   on   feldæ   þes wides   On ingonge
nimus   ea   in   campis   silve   **7.** *Introibimus*

on geteldungæ   his we gebiddæþ on stowe hwer stodon
in tabernaculum eius adoravimus   in   loco   ubi   steterunt

fet his   Ærise drihten on   reste   ðine ðu 7
pedes eius   **8.** *Exurge domine in requiem tuam tu et*

bogæ   gehælgungæ   ðine   Sæcerdos þine gegirede
archa sanctificationis tuae   **9.** *Sacerdotes tui induantur*

soðfestnessæ 7 hælige þine blissiende   Fore   dæuiþ
iustitia et sancti tui laetentur   **10.** *Propter david*

ðiow þinne ne æh hwirfe onsine cristes þines   swor
servum tuum non avertas faciem christi tui   **11.** *Iuravit*

drihten dæuiþ soðfestnesse 7 ne   gebrec   þæ be westme
dominus david   veritatem et non frustrabitur eum De fructu

innoðes ðines ic sette ofer setl min   gif geheæl-
ventris tui   ponam super sedem meam   **12.** *si custo-*

dæþ beærn þin gewitnessæ   min 7 kiþnessæ mine ðæs
dierint filii tui testamentum meum et testimonia mea haec

ic liere hie 7 beærn hiræ oððet on worolde seton
quae docebo eos Et filii eorum usque in seculum sedebunt

ofer setl þin   Forðæn gesceæs drihten sion
super sedem   meam   **13.** *Quoniam elegit dominus syon*

foregesceæs hie on eærdungæ him   ðios   rest
preelegit eam in habitationem sibi   **14.** *Haec requies*

min on worold æworolde her eærdig[e] forðæn foregesceæs
mea in seculum   saeculi   hic habitabo quoniam preelegi

him   Wuduwe his gebletsie bletsiæ þeærfæn his
eam   **15.** *Viduam eius benedicens benedicam pauperes eius*

ic gefylle hlæf   Sæcerd his ongirge hielo 7
saturabo panibus   **16.** *Sacerdotes eius induam salutare et*

ðæ hælgæn his   hihte   hihte   ðer forðgelede
sancti eius exultatione exultabunt   **17.** *Illuc producam*

horn dæuides geærwæþ blicerno   xpo minum   Fiend
cornu david   paravi lucernam christo meo   **18.** *Inimicos*

his on gerelæn anddetnes ofer hine soðlice blosmæþ gehæl-
eius induam confusione super ipsum autem florebit sancti-

gungæ mine
ficatio mea

131. 12. *þin,* Latin to this word er. and *meam* (unglossed) wr. aft.‡ the er.
13. *gesceæs,* top part of first *s* er.   14. *eardig[e],* a fin. let. (e or o?) indistinct.
forðæn, bottom part of *r* rubbed out.

132.

hu   god   7   hu   winsum   eærdigæn   broðre   on
Ecce quam bonum et quam iocundum   habitare   fratres   in

ænum   Swæ   smirnessæ   on heæfde þet   æstæh   on
unum   **2.** *Sicut unguentum in capite quod descendit in*

bærbæm bærbæm ææron ðet   æstæh   on muþe hre[g]l his
barbam barbam aaron Quod descendit in hora vestimenti eius

swæ   dreærung hermon   ðet æstæh   on   dune   sion
3. *sicut   ros   hermon   qui descendit in   montem   syon*

Forðæn hredlice bebeæd   drihten   bletsunge 7   lif
Quoniam illic   mandavit dominus benedictionem et vitam

oðð on world
usque in seculum

133.

Efne   nu   gebletsige drihten   eælle   ðiow drihten hwilc
Ecce   nunc   benedicite dominum omnes   servi domini   Qui

stondeþ on   huse   drihtnes on cæfortune hus   godes ures
statis   in   domo   domini   in atriis   domus   dei   nostri

On nihtum nimæþ hændæ eowre on hælgum 7 gebletsæ
2. *In noctibus extollite manus vestras in sancta et benedicite*

drihten   Gebletsa   drihten ob sion se worhte
dominum   **3.** *Benedicat te dominus ex syon qui fecit*

hefon 7 eorðæn
caelum et terram

134.

heriað nomæn drihtnes hergæþ þio[w] drihten   ðæ
Laudate nomen domini   laudate servi dominum   **2.** *Qui*

stondæð on huse drihtnes on cæfortune hus godes ures
statis   in   domo   domini   in   atriis   domus dei   nostri

herigæþ drihten forðæn   estig   is singæþ nomæn his
3. *Laudate dominum quoniam benignus est psallite nomini eius*

forðæn winsum is   Forðæn iæcob gesceæs him
quoniam suavis est   **4.** *Quoniam iacob elegit sibi*

drihten isræhele on gesetnesse him   Forðæn ic oncniew
dominus israel   in possessionem sibi   **5.** *Quia ego cognovi*

ðet   micel is drihten 7 god ure fore eællum dægum
quod magnus est dominus et deus noster pre omnibus diis

---

132. 2. *hora, h* pref. later.   133. 3. *Gebletsa, t* wr. over the line.

Q

Eællæ swæ wylcne wolde drihten worhte on hefenum 7 on
6. *Omnia quecumque voluit dominus fecit in caelo et in*
eorðæ on sie 7 on niowelnessum   7 geledeþ wolcn
terra in mari et in   abyssis   7. *Et educens nubes*
from   eorðæn leghtu ou rene worhte Se forðliedeþ
ab extremo terrae fulgura in pluviam fecit Qui producit
wind be goldhordum his   se þurhsliht formæ kinn
ventos de thesauris suis   8. *qui percussit primogenita*
egypti from monnum oððet to nietenæ   Sende tacnæ
aegypti ab homine usque ad pecus   9. *Misit signa*
7 forebeæcn on middæn   egyptum on phæræonem 7 on
et prodigia in medio tui aegypte in pharaonem et in
eællum þiowæs his   Se ðurhslihþ ðiodæ monigæ 7
omnes servos eius   10. *Qui percussit gentes multas et*
æcweleþ cininges stronge   Sion kining lufu hiræ
occidit reges fortes   11. *Seon regem amorreorum et*
          7 eælle rice chænææa ofsloh   7
og regem basan et omnia regna chanaan occidit   12. *Et*
seælde eorðæn hiræ yrfeweærð yrfeweærð isræhelum folc
dedit terram eorum haereditatem hereditatem israel populo
his   drihten nomæn þinne on ecnesse drihten
suo 13. *Domine nomen tuum in aeternum domine*
gemindbliðe   on world world   Forðæn demæþ
memoriale tuum in seculum seculi   14. *Quia iudicabit*
drihten folc his 7 on þiowum his bið frefrende
dominus populum suum et in servis suis consolabitur
diobulgild ðiodæ siolfor 7 gold wiorc hændæ
15. *Simulachra gentium argentum et aurum opera manuum*
monnæ   Muð hæbbæþ 7 ne sprecæþ eægæn hæbbæþ
hominum 16. *Os habent et non loquentur oculos habent*
7 ne gesioð   Eæræn hæbbæð 7 ne geheræþ
et non videbunt 17. *Aures habent et non audient*
nosæ hæbbæþ 7 ne gebiddæþ hændæ hæbbæþ 7 ne græpiæþ
nares habent et non odorabunt Manus habent et non palpabunt
fiet hæbbæþ 7 ne gongað Ne clipiæð on cilæn his
pedes habent et non ambulabunt Non clamabunt in gutture suo
nimþe soðlice is gæst on muþe hiræ   Gelic
neque enim est spiritus in ore ipsorum   18. *Similes*

134. 8. *nietenæ*, MS. = *metenæ*.   17. *is*, *s* from *c*.

him sien ðæ ðe doþ   7 eælle ðæ getriwæþ on his
illis fiant qui faciunt ea et omnes qui confidunt in eis

   hus gebletsige drihten huʒ æ æron bletsie
19. *Domus israel benedicite dominum domus aaron benedicite*

drihten   hus ðenæs bletsiæ drihten dæ
dominum   **20.** *domus levi benedicite dominum Qui*

ondredæþ drihten bletsige drihten   gebletsige
timetis dominum benedicite dominum   **21.** *benedictus*

drihten ob syon se eærðæð on hierusælem
dominus ex syon qui habitat in ierusalem

135.

Andętteð drihten forðæn god forðæn on world mild-
Confitemini domino quoniam bonus quoniam in seculum miseri-

heortnes his   Ondettæþ godə godæ forð
cordia eius   **2.** *Confitemini deo deorum quoniam*

  Ondettæþ drihten weældendra forþ   Se worhte
3. *Confitemini domino dominorum quoniam*   **4.** *Qui fecit*

wundor micel ænæ forþ   Se worhte wundor on
mirabilia magna solus quoniam   **5.** *Qui fecit caelos in*

andgiete   Se gestæþolode eorðæn ofer
intellectu quoniam   **6.** *Qui fundavit terram super*

wet'   Se geworhte lioht micel ænæ
aquas quoniam   **7.** *Qui fecit luminaria magna solus*

   Sunne on mihte dægæs   Monæ
quoniam   **8.** *Solem in potestatem diei quoniam*   **9.** *Lunam*

7 steorræn on mihte nihtæ   Se þurh-
et stellas in potestatem noctis quoniam   **10.** *Qui per-*

slihþ egyptum mid eældormon hiræ   7
cussit aegyptum cum primitivis eorum quoniam   **11.** *Et*

geledde ob midlene hiræ   On hændæ
eduxit israel de medio eius quoniam   **12.** *In manu*

strængæ 7 eærm hihþo   Se todieleþ on sie reædre
forti et brachio excelso   **13.** *Qui divisit mare rubrum*

on todelnes   7 geledeþ þurh midlum
in divisiones quoniam   **14.** *Et eduxit israel per medium*

his   7 wered his'
eius quoniam   **15.** *Et excussit pharaonem et exercitum eius*

135. *Andętted* by Cor.?   6. MS. = *wet'*.   8. *Sunne*, S (capital) er. twice
bef. this word.

on sie riedre Se þurhledde folc
in mari rubro quoniam 16. *Qui transduxit populum*

h[i]ræ þurh westæn Se geledde wetere ob
suum per desertum quoniam 17. *Qui eduxit aquam de*

stæne rupis Se þurhsloh kiningæs micele
petra rupis quoniam Qui percussit reges magnos quoniam

7 æcweælde kiningæ wundor Seon
18. *Et occidit reges mirabiles quoniam* 19. *Seon*

kining lufu hiræ 7 þet ewed bæson
regem amorreorum quoniam 20. *Et og regem basan*

7 seælde eorðæn hiræ yrfeweærð
quoniam 21. *Et dedit terram eorum haereditatem quoniam*

Yrfeweærd isræbele þiow his Forðæn
22. *Haereditatem israel servo suo quoniam* 23. *Quia*

on eæþmedum urum gemindig wes þu uræ drihten
in humilitate nostra memor fuit nostri dominus quoniam

7 æliese us ob hændum fiondæ urræ
24. *Et redemit nos de manu inimicorum nostrorum quoniam*

Se seleþ mete egwylcum fliesce and-
25. *Qui dat escam omni carni quoniam* 26. *Con-*

dettæþ gode heofonæs anddettæþ drihtne weældende
fitemini deo celi quoniam Confitemini domino dominorum

forðon on worold mildheortnesse his
quoniam in seculum misericordia eius

136.

Ofer streæmæs bæbilonis þer we seton 7 wepon mid gemin-
1. *Super flumina babylonis illic sedimus et flevimus dum recor-*

dige þin sion On singendum on middæn his
daremur tui syon 2. *In sallicibus in medio eius*

we hengon swegas ure Forðæn þer æxodon
suspendimus organa nostra 3. *Quia illic interrogaverunt*

us ðæ heftniþ eow geleddon us word singendræ 7 ðæ
nos qui captivos duxerunt nos verba cantionum et qui

geleddon us Ymen singæþ us be þæm cwidum syon
abduxerunt nos Ymnum cantate nobis de canticis syon

---

20. Aft. *quoniam* is ' *Et omnia regna chanāān occidit quoniam* ' (all dotted);
7 *eællæ* glosses *Et omnia,* but is not dotted. 23. *uræ,* MS. looks like
urie, prps. on account of top part of *a* being rubbed out.

hu　we siugæþ　singæþ　drihtne　on eorðæn　ðæ fremdæn
4. *quomodo cantabimus canticum domini in terra aliena*

Gif ofergietend ic bio þines　　　　ofergietend me swidre
5. *Si oblitus fuero tui ierusalem obliviscatur me dextera*

me　　7 ic ætbio tunge min gomum minum gif ic ne bio
mea　**6.** *adhereat lingua mea faucibus meis si non*

gemindi þine Gif ic fore ne gesette　　　on frumæn
meminero tui Si non proposuero ierusalem in principio

blis min　　gemynde drihten beærnæ edom on deig
laetitiae meo　**7.** *Memento domine filiorum edom in diem*

ierusælem ðæ cw[e]ðæþ ob ænnesse ob ænnesse oððet　to
ierusalem qui dicunt exinanite exinanite quo usque ad

stoþolungæ on him　　beærn bæbylonis mildsiend eædig
fundamentum in ea　**8.** *Filia babylonis misera beatus*

se geedlcænæþ þe edleænungæ þeæh þu edleænodes us
qui retribuet tibi retributionem quam tu retribuisti nobis

Eædig bið se ðe hefþ 7 tobroht litlingæs his to stæne
9. *Beatus qui tenebit et allidet parvulos suos ad petram*

137.

ic andette ðe drihten on eælre heortæn minre forðæn
Confitebor tibi domine in toto corde meo quoniam

gehire eælle word muð mines 7 on gesihþe englæ
exaudisti omnia verba oris mei et in conspectu angelorum

ic singæ þe　　To þe ic gebidce to þinum hælgum
psallam tibi　**2.**　*Adorabo ad templum sanc-*

temple 7 ic ondette nomon þinum Ofer mildheortnes þin
tum tuum et confitebor nomini tuo Super misericordiam tuam

7 soðfestnes þine forðæn micelodes ofer us nomæ
et veritatem tuam quoniam magnificasti super nos nomen

hælig ðin　　On swæ wilcum dæge ic gecige þe
sanctum tuum　**3.** *In quacumque die invocavero te*

gehire me gemonigfeældæst on sæwle min megen þin
exaudi me multiplicabis in anima mea virtutem tuam

Ondeddæþ ðe drihten eælle kiningæs eorðæn forðæn
4. *Confiteantur tibi domine omnes reges terrae quoniam*

---

136. 4. *fremdæn*, MS. = *frendæn*.　5. *þines*, þ repeated.　137. *ic andette* by Cor.?

gehirdon eælle word muð ðin   7 singæþ on songum
audierunt omnia verba oris tui   5. *et cantent in canticis*

drihtne Forðæn micel is wuldor drihtnes   forðæn
domino Quoniam magna est gloria domini   6. *quoniam*

hihþo drihten 7 eæþmod gelocæ 7 hihþo fiorr oncniweþ
excelsus dominus et humilia respicit et alta a longe agnoscit

  Gif ic gonge on midlene eærfoþnes geliffeste me 7
7. *Si ambulavero in medio tribulationis vivificabis me et*

ofer fiondæ minræ þu æþenedæst hændæ þine 7
super iram inimicorum meorum extendisti manum tuam et

hælne me dide swiðre þine   drihten geeædleænæ for
salvum me fecit dextera tua   8. *Domine retribue pro*

me drihten mildheortnes ðin on worlde 7 wiorc hændæ
me domine misericordia tua in seculum et opera manuum

þinræ ne forsioh
tuarum ne despicias

138.

Drihten þu costodes me 7 oncnewe me   7 þu oncniewe
Domine probasti me et cognovisti me   2. *tu cognovisti*

obsetnesse mine 7 ærise minne   þu ongeæte
sessionem meam et resurrectionem meam   3. *Intellexisti*

geþohtæs mine fiorr stigæ mine 7 gerecnesse mine
cogitationes meas a longe semitam meam et directionem meam

þu geswæþodes   7 eælle wegæs mine forsæwe forðæn
  investigasti   4. *et omnes vias meas praevidisti quia*

ne is sær on tungæn minre   Gesihþe ðu drihten
non est dolus in lingua mea   5. *Ecce tu domine*

oncniewe eællæ us þæ nixtæn 7 ðæ eældæn þu gehiwodes me 7
cognovisti omnia novissima et antiqua tu formasti me et

þu settes ofer me hændæ þine   Wundor geworden
posuisti super me manum tuam   6. *Mirabilis facta*

is wisdom þin ob me gestrængod is ic ne mihte to him
est scientia tua ex me confortata est nec potero ad eam

  ðy ic gonge from gæstæ þinum 7 from onsine þine þy
7. *Quo ibo a spiritu tuo et a facie tua quo*

ic flioge   Gif ic æstige on hefonum þu þer is gif
fugiam   8. *Si ascendero in caelum tu illic es si*

---

138. *Drihten* by Cor. ?   4. *forsæwe*, MS. = *forsære.*   7. *from* (2nd),
MS. = *fron.*

ic æstige   on   helle   to him   Gif   ic nime   feðeræ
descendero in   infernum   ades   **9.** *Si   sumpsero   pennas*

mine   beforæn   liohte   7   ic eærdige   on   þet   uteron   sie
meas   ante   lucem   et   habitavero   in   postremo   maris

   7 soþlice   ðer   hænd   þine geliedeþ me 7   hefþ   me swiðre
10. *Etenim   illuc manus   tua   deducet   me et   tenebit   me dextera*

ðin   7 cwiðe is ðies wien ðistro   7
tua   **11.** *Et dixi   forsitan   tenebre conculcabunt   me et*

niht   onlihtnes   min   Forðon þystro
nox   inluminatio   mea   in deliciis meis   **12.** *Quia   tenebre*

ne   byd   æþistrode from þe 7 niht swæ deg bið onlihteð
non   obscurabuntur   abs   te et   nox sicut   dies   inluminabitur

swæ þystro his swæ 7 lioht his   forðæn þu drihten
Sicut tenebre eius ita et lumen eius   **13.** *quia   tu domine*

ægende æðræ minæ þu onfenge me ob innoðe modor minre
possedisti renes meos   suscepisti   me de   utero matris meae

   Ic anddette þe   drihten   forðon   egeslic   wundriende
14. *Confitebor   tibi   domine   quoniam   terribiliter   mirificatus*

is wundor wiorc   7 sæwlæ min wæt swiþe   Ne
es   mira   opera tua et anima mea novit nimis   **15.** *Non*

is   bedigled   muð   min   from þe ðet þu dydes on diglæn 7
est occultatum os   meum   abs   te quod   fecisti   in occulto et

spedæ   min on þæm yterum eorðæn   On fulfremed-
substantia mea in   inferioribus   terrae   **16.** *Inper-*

nessum minum gesæwon eægæn þine 7 on bocum þinum eælle
fectum meum   viderunt oculi tui et in libro   tuo   omnes

bioð writone dægæs getriemende 7   on him   me
scribentur Dies firmabuntur et nemo in eis   **17.** *michi*

sodlice swiþe wiorðionde sindon fiend þine god swiðe gestrængod
autem nimis honorificati sunt amici tui deus nimis confortatus

is   cældordom hiræ   be þæm ic ærime hie 7 ofer
est   principatus eorum   **18.** *Dinumerabo   eos et super*

sond   gemonigfældodc   ærist   7   nu   mid þe ic bio
arenam   multiplicabuntur resurrexi et adhuc   tecum   sum

   gif ic ofsleæ god ðæ firænfullæn weræs   blod   behildæþ
19. *si occidas deus peccatores Viri sanguinum declinate*

from me   forðæn cweðæþ on geþohtum eowrum
a me   **20.** *quia   dicitis in cogitationibus vestris*

---

16. After *dægæs þeod* (or *þeod* ?) is wr. over the line.   19. *ofsleæ*, *s* from *l*.

onfengon on ydelnesse ceæster his   Ne eælles se ðe
accipient in vanitate civitates suas   **21.** *Nonne qui te*

fiodon god fiodon hie 7 ofer fiend þine ic onege
oderunt deus oderam illos et super inimicos tuos tabescebam

   þurhfulfremede fioung ic fioung hie fiend geworhte
22. *Perfecto odio oderam illos inimici facti*

sindon me   Costæ me god 7 wite heorte min
sunt michi   **23.** *Proba me deus et scito cor meum*

  æxæ me 7 oncnæw stigæ minæ   7 gesioh
interroga me et cognosce semitas meas   **24.** *Et vide*

him unriht on me is 7 gelied me on weg ecnæ
si via iniquitatis in me est et deduc me in via eterna

139.

  genere ł alys me drihten from men yfel from yrre
2. *Eripe me domine ab homine malo a viro*

on unriht gefriolsæ me   ðæ þohton heteniþ on
iniquo libera me   **3.** *Qui cogitaverunt malitias in*

beortæn elce deg gesetton gefioht æscirpton tungæn
corde tota die constituebant proelia   **4.** *Acuerunt linguas*

hiræ swæ niedræn ætrenum nedrenæ under welerum hiræ
suas sicut serpentes venenum aspidum sub labiis eorum

  gehæl me drihten ob hændæ firenfulræ from mænnum
5. *Custodi me domine de manu peccatoris ab hominibus*

unrihtum gefrilsæ me ðæ ðohton underwirtwæloden stepæs
iniquis libera me Qui cogitaverunt subplantare gressus

mine behyddon oferhydig gesprecu me 7 ræpæs
meos   **6.** *absconderunt superbi laqueos michi et funes*

æðenedon on grino fotum minum ncæh siðfæt geswic
extenderunt in laqueo pedibus meis iuxta iter scandalum

gesetton me   Ic cwiðe drihten god min is þu
posuerunt michi   **7.** *Dixi domino deus meus es tu*

gehire drihten stefne gebed min   drihten drihten
exaudi domine vocem orationis meae   **8.** *Domine domine*

megen helo mine ymscuwæþ hæfod min on deig gefiohtes
virtus salutis meae obumbra caput meum in die belli

  Ne sele me on wyllæn minne firenfulle ðohton
9. *Ne tradas me a desiderio meo peccatores cogitaverunt*

wið   me ne   forlet   me   ðielies efre   bið uphæfen
adversum me ne derelinquas me   ne umquam   exaltentur

    heæfod ymbgong hiræ   gewin gewinnæ   ætiewde
10. *Caput circuitus eorum labor labiorum ipsorum operiet*

hie   Gefeælleþ ofer he gliedæ   fier   on firre
eos   11. *Cadent   super eos carbones ignis in ignem*

æwirpeþ hie on yrmþum ne understondet   ðæ ærfes-
deicies eos in miseriis non   subsistent   12. *Vir lin-*

tæn weræs ne bið gereht ofer eorðæn   wer   þæ unsoðfestæn
quosus. non dirigetur super terram virum.   iniustum

yfel nimæþ on forwirð   Oncnæwe forðæn dyde
mala capient in interitum   13. *Cognovi quoniam faciet*

drihten dom   on hlewesæ 7 wrece   þeærfenæ   soð-
dominus iudicium inopum et vindictam pauperum   14. *Ve-*

lice þonne hweðere soðfeste anddettaþ   noman   þinum 7
runtamen   iusti confitebuntur nomini   tuo   et

eærdigæd riehte mid ondwlitæn þinum
habitabunt recti cum vultu   tuo

140.

Drihten ic clipie to þe gehire me behald steafne gebed
Domine   clamavi ad   te exaudi me intende   voci   orationis

min midti ic clipie   to þe   Sie gereht gebed min
meae dum clamavero ad te   2. *Dirigatur oratio mea*

swæ onsegdnessum on gesihþe þinre upæhæfennes hændæ
sicut   incensum   in conspectu tuo   Elevatio   manuum

minræ onsægdnessum þæ æfenlicum   Sete drihten
mearum   sacrificium   vespertinum   3. *Pone domine*

geheæld muþ minne 7 to duræ ymbstondende weleræs mine
custodiam ori meo et ostium circumstantiae labiis   meis

ðet ne hilde heorte min on wordum yfel to onsceæ-
4. *Ut non declines cor meum in verbum malum ad excu-*

cænnæ ob sceæcnessum on sinnum Mid monnum wircendum
sandas excusationes in peccatis Cum hominibus operantibus

unriht 7 ic ne wende mid gecorenum hiræ   Ge-
iniquitatem et non combinabor cum electis   eorum   5. *Cor-*

---

14. *noman*, a from some other let.   140. *Drihten* by Cor.?   2. *onsegd-*,
g from *i*.

gripe me soðfest on mildheortnesse 7 ofercideþ me ele
ripiet me iustus in misericordia et increpabit me oleum
soðlice firenfulle ne gedipeð heæfod min Forðæn nu gio
autem peccatoris non inpinguet caput meum Quoniam adhuc
is gebed min on hiræ wellicungum hiræ hleotende
est oratio mea in beneplacitis eorum 6. absorti
sindon niieh stænæs domæs hiræ gehirdon word min forðæn
sunt iuxta petram iudices eorum audient verba mea quoniam
mihton swæ gemildre eorðæn utroccende ofer
potuerunt 7. Sicut crassitudo terrae eructuat super
eorðæn 7 tostenscede sindon bæn uræ neæh helle
terram dissipata sunt ossa nostra secus infernum
Forðon to þe drihten drihten eægæn mine on þe ic wene ne
8. *Quia ad te domine domine oculi mei in te speravi ne*
æfirre sæwle mine Geheæld me from gegrine þone
auferas animam meam 9. Custodi me a laqueo quem
gesetton me 7 beswice wyrcende unrihtnesse Ge-
statuerunt michi et ab scandalis operantibus iniquitatem 10. Ca-
feællæþ on netteægæn his firenfulræ sinderlice eom ic oððet
dent in reciaculo eius peccatores singulariter sum ego donec
fereþ
transeam

141.

Mid stefne mine to drihten ic clipie stefne mine to gode
2. *Voce mea ad dominum clamavi voce mea ad dominum*
biddende eom Ic ægite on gesihþe his gebed
deprecatus sum 3. Effundam in conspectu eius orationem
min 7 cærfoðnessæ mine beforæn him forekyþe
meam et tribulationem meam ante ipsum pronuntio 4. In
Unæspringedo on me gæst min 7 þu oncnewe stigæ
deficiendo in me spiritum meum et tu cognovisti semitas
mine On wege from þæm ic gonge behiddon þæ oferhidgæn
meas In via hac qua ambulabam absconderunt superbi
gegrino me gesccæwige to þæ swiðræn 7 ic gesio
laqueos michi 5. considerabam ad dexteram et videbam
7 ne bið se ongiteþ me Forewirþ flionde from me 7 ne
et non erat qui agnosceret me Periit fuga a me et non

is se ðe secet   sæwl   mine   ic clipie to þe drihten
est qui requirat animam meam   6. *clamavi ad te domine*

ic cwiðe þu eært hyht min gæto mine on eorðæn lifgendræ
dixi   tu es spes mea portio mea in   terra viventium

beheæld on   gebede   mine forðæn geeæþmeded ic eom
7. *Intende in orationem meam quia humiliatus sum*

swiþe gefriolse me from ehtendum   me forðæn gestrongode
nimis Libera me a   persequentibus me quoniam confortati

sindon ofer me   Geleæd ob ceærcern sæwle mine
sunt super me   8. *Educ de carcere animam meam*

7 ic ondette nomæn þinum Me onbidæþ soðfeste oððet
ad confitendum nomini tuo Me expectant iusti donec

geedleænæst me
retribuas michi

142.

Drihten gehire gebed min eærum onfoh   benæ
Domine exaudi orationem meam auribus percipe obsecrationem

mine on soðfestnesse þine gehire me on þine soðfestnessæ
meam in veritate tua exaudi me in tua   iustitia

7 ic ne gonge on domæs mid þiowe þine forðæn næ
2. *Et non intres in iudicium cum servo tuo quia non*

bið gesoðfest on gesihþe ðinre eællæ lifigende   Forðæn
iustificabitur in conspectu tuo omnis vivens   3. *Quia*

ehtende is fiond. sæwl mine geeædmedeð on eorðæn
persecutus est inimicus animam meam humiliavit in terra

lif min Gestæþolæð me on ðisternessum swæ deæde
vitam meam Collocavit me in obscuris sicut mortuos

worold   7 geniered on me gæst min on me
seculi 4. *et anxiatus est in me spiritus meus in me*

gedrefed is heort min   Gemindig ic wes dægæ
turbatum est cor meum 5. *Memor fui dierum*

eældenæ 7 smeægende ic eom on eællum wiorcum ðinum 7
antiquorum et meditatus sum in omnibus operibus tuis et

on dedum hændæ þinræ smeægende   æþenede
in factis manuum tuarum meditabor 6. *Expandi*

hændæ mine to þe sæule mine swæ eorðe buton weteræ þe
manus meas ad te anima mea sicut terra sine aqua tibi

hredlice gehire me drihten æspræng gæst min 7 ne
7. *velociter exaudi me Domine defecit spiritus meus ne*

æwyrfe onsiene þine from me 7 ic bio gelic   æstigendum on
avertas faciem tuam   a me et ero similis descendentibus in

seæþ   Gehiræð   me   do on morgen mildheortnesse
lacum   **8.** *Auditam michi fac   mane   misericordiam*

þine forðæn on þæ ic gewene drihten   Cuð   me   do
tuam quia in te speravi domine Notam michi fac

on margan mildh[e]ortnesse forðæn to þe drihten upæhof
viam in qua ambulem   quia ad te domine levavi

sæwle mine   Genere me of fiondum minum drihten
animam meam   **9.** *Eripe me de inimicis meis domine*

to ðe flioh   lære me don   willæn ðinne
ad te confugi   **10.** *doce me facere voluntatem tuam*

forðæn þu eært god min   gæst þin god gelied me on
quia tu es deus meus Spiritus tuus bonus deducet me in

weg rihtne   forðæn nomæn þine drihten geliffeste me
via recta   **11.** *propter nomen tuum domine vivificabis me*

on emlicnesse þinra 7 geled of earfoðnesse saule mine
in aequitate tua Et educes de tribulatione animam meam

     7 on mildheortnesse þinre forspilde fiend mine 7
12. *et in misericordia tua disperdes inimicos meos Et*

forspilde ealle ða earfoðiað saule mine forþan þeow
perdes omnes qui tribulant animam meam quoniam servus

ðin ic eom
tuus ego sum

143.

gebletsed dryhten god min se liereð hande mine to gefioht
Benedictus dominus deus meus qui docet manus meas ad proelium

7 fingras mine to gefioht   Mildheortnes min 7 gescild
et digitos meos ad bellum   **2.** *Misericordia mea et refugium*

min onfeng min 7 friolsend min Gescild min 7 on him
meum susceptor meus et liberator meus Protector meus et in ipso

ic gewene underwiorpende folc under me   dryhten
speravi subiciens populos sub me   **3.** *Domine*

hwæt is mon þet ðu gecirdes him oððe bearn monna
quid est homo quid innotuisti ei aut filius hominis

forþan geteles hine   Mon idel gelic geworden
quoniam reputas eum   **4.** *Homo vanitati similis factus*

---

142. 8. *on margan mildhortnesse* add. by Cor.; the Latin variant wh. it
glosses is wr. by the same Cor.   9. *Genere*, G on er.   11. With the
word *gcliffeste* begins a fresh hand ending with the last word of Ps. 148.
143. 2. Er. aft. *Gescild*.

is deg his swa sceadu forwiorþað   dryhten onhield
est dies eius sicut umbra pretereunt   **5.** *Domine inclina*

hefonas þine 7 astig ahrine duna 7 hi smokiað
caelos tuos et descende tange montes et fumigabunt

blatesung blatesunga ðina 7 tostente hie onsende strela
6. *Corusca coruscationes tuas et dissipabis eos emitte sagittas*

þine 7 gedrefde hie   Onsende handa þine of hihþo
tuas et conturbabis eos   **7.** *Emitte manum tuam de alto*

genere me 7 gefriolsa me of wetrum miclum 7 be handa
eripe me et libera me de aquis multis et de manu

bearna fremdra   ðara muþ sprecendæ is idelnesse
filiorum alienorum   **8.** *Quorum os locutum est vanitatem*

7 swiðre hira swiþre unrihtnes   god sang
et dextera eorum dextera iniquitatis   **9.** *Deus canticum*

niwne ic singe þe on saltre tien strengan ic singe
novum cantabo tibi in psalterio decem chordarum psallam

þe   ða þu sillest hielo kyningen þu gefriolsast
tibi   **10.** *Qui das salutem regibus qui liberas*

dauid þiow þin of sweorde þa minnan   genere me
david servum tuum de gladio maligno   **11.** *Eripe me*

7 gefriolsa me of wetrum miclum 7 of handa bearna . fremde
et libera me de aquis multis et de manu filiorum alienorum

þara muþ sprecende is idelnesse 7 swiþre hira swiþre
Quorum os locutum est vanitatem et dextera eorum dextera

unrihtnes   þara bearn swa niwe wyrtwalunge
iniquitatis   **12.** *Quorum filii sicut novelle plantationes*

staþolfestlice from giogoþa his bearn hira geseted ymb-
stabiliti a iuventute sua Filie eorum composite cir-

fretwed swa gelicnesse þes temples   ða fuslecan
cumornate ut similitudo templi   **13.** *Promptuaria*

hira fulle utroccettaþ of þysum on þæt Sceap hira feðer-
eorum plena eructuantia ex hoc in illud Oves eorum fe-

fete genihtsumiað on siðfute his   oxa hira fętte
tose habundantes in itineribus suis   **14.** *boves eorum crassi*

Ne is hriere wealles ne forliorende ne ceapung on
Non est ruina macerie neque transitus neque clamor in

---

5. *astig, s* er. bef. this word. *smokiað* or *smociað* ?   6. *þine* in pl. of er.
8. *idelnesse,* MS. = *idelnesnesse.*   10. *kyningen* œ *cyningen* ? *þu gefriolsast*
on er.   11. *swiþre* (2nd), *r* er. betw. *þ* and *r.*   13. *fuslecan,* two lett. er.
betw. *e* and *c.*   14. *wealles* on er.

worðigum hira   Eadige   cweðað   folc   þan þas
plateis   eorum   15. *Beatum dixerunt populum cui haec*
sindon eadige   folc   ðes is dryhten god   hira
sunt   beatus populus cuius est dominus deus eorum

144.

Ic uphebbe þe god min   kyning min   7   gebletsie noman
Exaltabo   te deus meus   rex   meus et benedicam nomen

þinne on   ecnesse   7   on   worolde   worolde   ðurh
tuum   in   aeternum et in   seculum   seculi   2. *Per*

sindrige   dagas   ic bletsige   þe 7   ic herige   noman þinne on
singulos   dies   benedicam   te et   laudabo   nomen tuum   in

ecnesse   7   on   worolda worold   micel   dryhten 7
aeternum et in   seculum   seculi   3. *Magnus dominus et*

hergendlic swiþe 7   michelnes   his ne is ende   kneow-
laudabilis nimis et magnitudinis eius non est finis   4. *Gene-*

risn 7   kneowrisn   hergeað   worc þin 7   mihte   ðine fore-
ratio et generatio laudabunt opera tua et potentiam tuam pro-

ciðaþ   Micelnes   meigenþrim   ðinne   7
nuntiabunt   5. *Magnificentiam   maiestatis   tuae   et*

haligdom   þinne bioþ sprecende 7   wundor   ðin   secgað
sanctitatem tuam   loquentur   et mirabilia tua   narrabunt

    Megen   egeslicra   ðinra   cweþað 7   micelnesse   þine
6. *Virtutem terribiliorum tuorum   dicent et   magnitudinem tuam*

secgað   gemynd   genihtsum   swetnesse þine
narrabunt   7. *Memoriam   habundantiae   suavitatis   tuae*

utroccettað 7   soþfestnesse þinne wynsumiað   Mildheort
eructuabunt et   iustitiam   tuam   exaltabunt   8. *Misericors*

7 mildsigend dryhten geþyld 7   michel milðheort   Wynsum
et miserator dominus patiens et multum misericors   9. *Suavis*

dryhten   ealle   7   mildsa   his   ofer   ealle weorc his
dominus universis et miserationes eius super omnia opera eius

     Ondettað   þe dryhten ealle   weorc þine 7   halige þine
10. *Confiteantur tibi domine omnia opera tua et sancti tui*

bledsiað   þe   Wuldor rices þines cweðað 7   mihtc
benedicent te   11. *Gloriam regni tui   dicent et potentiam*

---

144. *meus* (bef. *rex*) dotted; Eng. *min* not dotted. *kyning* or *cyning*?
4. *kneow-* or *cneow-*? (twice).

þine sprecende   þet cuð dyde bearn manna
tuam loquentur   **12.** *Ut notam faciant filiis hominum*

mihte þine 7 wuldor micelnesse rices þines   Rice
potentiam tuam et gloriam magnificentiae regni tui   **13.** *Regnum*

þin dryhten rice ealra world 7 gewealdes þines
tuum domine regnum omnium seculorum et dominatio tua

on eallum cneowrisnum 7 forecneowrisn geleafful dryhten on
in omni generatione et progeniae Fidelis dominus in

wordum his 7 halig on eallum wiorcum his   Upa-
verbis suis et sanctus in omnibus operibus suis   **14.** *Alle-*

hefð dryhten ealle þæ adunfeallað 7 gereceð ealle afylledan
vat dominus omnes qui ruunt et erigit omnes elisos

Eagan ealra on ðe hopiað dryhten 7 þu sellest mete
15. *Oculi omnium in te sperant domine et tu das escam*

him on tide gehyðlic ðu untyns hand þine 7
illis in tempore oportuno   **16.** *Aperis tu manum tuam et*

gefylst ealle nietenu blitsunge   Soðfest dryhten on
imples omne animal benedictione   **17.** *Iustus dominus in*

eallum wegum his 7 halig on eallum worcum his
omnibus viis suis et sanctus in omnibus operibus suis

Neah is dryhten eallum gecigendum hine on soþfes[t]nesse
18. *Prope est dominus omnibus invocantibus eum in , veritate*

Willende ondriedende hine deð 7 gebed hira
19. *voluntatem timentium se faciet et orationes eorum*

gehireð 7 hale deð hie gehylt dryhten ealle
exaudiet et salvos faciet eos   **20.** *Custodit dominus omnes*

lufigenda hiue 7 ealle firenfulle forspilð   Lof
diligentes se et omnes peccatores disperdet   **21.** *Laudem*

dryhtenes sprecað muþ min 7 gebletsað eghwylcne licomon
domini loquetur os meum et benedicat omnis caro

noman halig his on ęcnesse 7 on worlda 7 world
nomen sanctum eius in aeternum et in seculum seculi

145.

Here saule mine dryhten ic herige dryhten on life
2. *Lauda anima mea dominum laudabo dominum in vita*

---

14. *ruunt*, MS. = *corruunt*, *cor* having a line drawn through it for er.
15. *gehyðlic*, fin. *e* er. 16. *blitsunge*, *s* er. betw. *i* and *t*. 19. Er. aft.
deð (1st). 145. 2. *saule* repeated but second er.

minum ic singe gode minum swa longe swa ic libbe Ne cearo ðe
mea psallam deo meo quamdiu ero Nolite

getrywan on ealdormannum ne on bearnum monna
confidere in principibus 3. *neque in filiis hominum*

on þam ne is helo Utgieð gast his 7 bið
in quibus non est salus 4. *Exiet spiritus eius et rever-*

gecirred on eorþan his on þam dege forwiorþað ealle
tetur in terram suam in illa die peribunt omnes

geþancas hiera Eadig þæs god iacob tofultomiend
cogitationes eorum 5. *Beatus cuius deus iacob adiutor*

his 7 hiht his on dryhten god his Se geworhte
eius et spes eius in domino deo ipsius 6. *Qui fecit*

heofona 7 eorðan sæ 7 ealle þa on him siendon
celum et terram mare et omnia quae in eis sunt

Se gehealdaþ soðfestnesse on worlde deð dom
7. *Qui custodit veritatem in seculum facit iudicium*

ontionan geðyldiendum selleð mete hingriendum Dryhten
iniuriam pacientibus dat escam esurientibus Dominus

gerecaþ aspornena dryhten alisde efenemne dryhten
erigit elisos dominus solvit compeditos 8. *dominus*

onliehtað blinda dryhten lufað soþfeste dryhten
illuminat cecos dominus dirigit iustos 9. *Dominus*

gehyld unkuþan stiopcild 7 wuduwan onfehð 7 weg firen-
custodit advenam pupillum et viduam suscipiet et viam pecca-

fulra abregeð Rixað dryhten on ecnesse
torum exterminabit 10. *Regnabit dominus in aeternum*

god þin sion on world aworld
deus tuus syon in seculum seculi

146.

Hergeað dryhten forþan god is sealm gode urum
Laudate dominum quoniam bonus est psalmus deo nostro

wynsum sie herenes getymbrede hierusalem dryhten 7
iocunda sit laudatio 2. *Edificans ierusalem dominus et*

tostengnesse israhcle gesamnode Se hieleð gestirgide
dispersiones israel congregans 3. *Qui sanat contritos*

3. *is*, let. (i?) er. bef. this word.   7. *ontionan*, fin. *n* orig. = *m*.   9. *un-*
kuþan or *uncuþan*? *abregeð*, a er. bef. this word.   146. 3. *hieleð*, fin. *e* er.

heortan 7 gebindað þa unrettan hira   Se rimæd
corde et alligat contritiones eorum   **4.** *Qui numerat*

mienigo stiorrana 7 eallum his noman cigeað   Micel
multitudinem stellarum et omnes eis nomina vocans   **5.** *Magnus*

dryhten ure 7 micel miegen his 7 snytro his ne is
dominus noster et magna virtus eius et sapientiae eius non est

hrim   Onfonde geþwiernesse dryhten geeaðmodaþ
numerus   **6.** *Suscipiens mansuetos dominus humiliat*

soðlice þa firenfulran oððe to eorþan   Onginnað dryhtene
autem peccatores usque ad terram   **7.** *Incipite domino*

on andetnesse singað gode ure on hearpan   Se worhte
in confessione psallite deo nostro in cythara   **8.** *Qui operit*

heofon wolcnum 7 gearwað eorþan ren   Se forþlæd on
caelum nubibus et parat terrae pluviam Qui producit in

dunum hieg 7 wyrta ðiowdomes monna   Se
montibus foenam et herbam servituti hominum   **9.** *Qui*

selleð nietenum mete hira 7 briddas crawan oncigende
dat iumentis escam ipsorum et pullis corvorum invocantibus

hine   Nealles on   horses willan hæfþ ne
eum   **10.** *Non in viribus equi voluntatem habebit neque*

on geteldungum weres wellicunga is him   Wellicunga
in tabernaculis viri beneplacitum est ei   **11.** *Beneplacitum*

is dryhtene ofer ondriedende hine 7 on him þa wenað on
est domino super timentes eum et in eis qui sperant in

mildheor([t]nesse) his
misericordia eius

147.

Hereð ierusalem dryhten hera god þinne sion
12. *Lauda ierusalem dominum lauda deum tuum syon*

Forþan gestrangað sweoras gato ðinra gebletsað
13. *Quoniam confortavit seras portarum tuarum benedixit*

bearn þine on þe   Se gesette ende þine sibbe 7
filios tuos in te   **14.** *Qui posuit fines tuos pacem et*

mid gefetnesse hwętes gefyllað þe   Se þe sendeð
adipe frumenti satians te   **15.** *Qui emittit*

---

8. *wolcnum* on er. *forþlæd*, a fin. er. (eþ?) made.   10. *viribus*, gloss to
this word (*werum*) er. but still visible. *hæfþ*, *f* from *w*.   11. *dryhtene*, fin.
s er. *ondried-*, *n* er. betw. *e* and *d*. *mildheor*, fin. -*nesse* er.   147. 13. Er.
aft. *Forþan*.   15. Er. aft. *Se*.

R

gespreca his eorþe hredlice irneð word his Se
eloquium suum terrae velociter currit sermo eius 16. *Qui*

selleð snáw swa wullæ mist oððe axæ astreweð
· *dat nivem sicut lanam nebulam velut cinerem spargit*

Sendeð cristalla his swa gehrino hlaf beforan onsiene
17. *Mittit cristallum suum sicut frusta panis ante faciem*

chiles his se aræfneð Sendeð word his 7
frigoris eius quis subsistet 18. *Mittit verbum suum et*

meltende gedeþ ða bleowæð gast his 7 floweð wæter
liquefaciet ea flavit spiritus eius et fluent aquae

Foresecgende word his iacobes soþfestnesse 7 dom his
19. *Pronuntians verbum suum iacob iustitias et iudicia sua*

israhele Ne deþ ðyllico eallunga 7 dom his
israel 20. *Non fecit taliter omni nationi et iudicia sua*

ne gekyððæþ him
non manifestavit eis

148.

Hergeað dryhten of hefonum hergeað hine on hyhþo
Laudate dominum de caelis laudate eum in excelsis

Hergeað hine ealle englas his hergeað hine ealle mægen
. 2. *Laudate eum omnes angeli eius laudate eum omnes virtutes*

his Hergeað hine sunne 7 mona hergeað hine ealle
eius 3. *Laudate eum sol et luna laudate eum omnes*

stiorran 7 lioht Hergeaþ hine hefona hefona 7 weter
stelle et lumen 4. *Laudate eum caeli caelorum et aque*

þa ofer hefonas sint hergen nomon dryhtenes Forðan
quae super caelos sunt 5. *laudent nomen domini Quia*

he cwęð 7 gewordene sindon he bebead 7 gesceapene
ipse dixit et facta sunt ipse mandavit et creata

sindon gesette ða on ecnesse 7 on worolde world
sunt 6. *Statuit ea in eternum et in seculum seculi*

bebode gesette 7 ne forliorde hergeað dryhten
preceptum posuit et non preteribit 7. *Laudate dominum*

of eorðan dracon 7 ealle niowolnesse Fyr hagol
de terra dracones et omnes abyssi · 8. *Ignis grando*

snaw ís gast forspebicndra se doþ word his
nix glacies spiritus procellarum quae faciunt verbum eius

20. *gekgððæþ* or *yecyððæþ* ?

Duna 7 ealle hilla triow wæstmberendæ 7 ealle cedorbeam
9. *Montes et omnes colles ligna   fructifera   et omnes   cedri*

wildeora 7   ealle   nietenu niedran 7 fuglas gefiþerede
10. *Bestie et universa   pecora   serpentes et volucres   pennate*

kyningas eorþan 7 ealle folc ealdormen 7 ealle   dom
11. *Reges   terrae et omnes populi principes et omnes iudices*

eorðan   gionga 7 femnan þa yldran mid giongum
terrae   12. *Iuvenes et virgines seniores cum iunioribus*

hergeaþ noman dryhtnes   Forðan uphafen is noman
laudent nomen domini   13. *Quia   exaltatum est nomen*

his ana   andetnes his ofer hefon 7 eorðan 7
eius solius   14. *confessio eius super caelum et terram Et*

upahefð horn folces his ymen eallum halig his bearn
exaltavit cornu populi sui ymnum omnibus sanctis eius filiis

israele folc tonealecende him
israel populo appropianti sibi

149.

Singæþ drihtne   sæng   niwne herenes his on circæn
Cantate domino canticum novum laudatio eius in aecclesia

haligræ   Blissiæþ isræhele on him se deð him 7
sanctorum   2. *Letetur israhel in eo qui fecit ipsum et*

beærn syon hihtæþ ofer kiningæs   Hergæð nomæn
filie syon exultent super regem suum   3. *Laudent nomen*

his on þrete on swege 7 sælteræ singæþ him   Forðan
eius in choro in tympano et psalterio psallant ei   4. *Quia*

wellicung is drihtne on folce his 7 wynsumiæþ geðwere
beneplacitum est domino in populo suo et   exaltavit   mansuetos

on helum   hihtæð hælige on wuldre blissæþ on
in salutem   5. *Exultabunt sancti in gloria letabuntur in*

bedcliofum his   Wynsumnessæ godes on gomum hiræ
cubilibus suis   6. *Exultationes dei in faucibus eorum*

7 swiord nimende on hændæ hiræ   To donne
et gladii ancipites in manibus eorum   7. *Ad faciendam*

wrece on kyðnessum ofercidungæ on folce   To
vindictam in nationibus increpationes in populis   8. *Ad*

<hr>

148. 11. *kyningas* or *cyningas*?   149. A fresh hand begins here, ending with *stondende* (Cant. Moysi, v. 4). *his* repeated. 4. *geðwere, geð* on er.

gebinddenne kiningas hiræ on gesettnessum 7 eþelum hiræ on
alligandos   reges   eorum in compedibus   et nobiles eorum in

bendum isenum   ðette ðeð on him dom   emnwriten
vinculis ferreis   9. Ut faciant in eis iudicium conscriptum

wuldor ðis is eællum hælgum his
gloria haec est omnibus sanctis eius

150.

hergæþ god on hælige   his hergæþ hine on trimnesse
Laudate deum in sanctis eius laudate eum in firmamento

megnes his   hergæþ hiene on   meigne   his hergæð
virtutis eius   2. Laudate eum in potentatibus eius laudate

hine efter   micelnes   micelnessæ his   herigæð
eum secundum multitudinem magnitudinis eius   3. Laudate

hine on swege bymæn hergæþ hine on psæltere   7   herpe
eum in sono   tube   laudate eum in psalter[i]o et cythara

    hergæð hine on hylsongæ 7 ðreæt hergæð hine on heortan
4. Laudate eum in tympano et choro laudate eum in cordis

7 orgænum   hergæð hine on cymbalum wel   cwegendum
et organo   5. Laudate eum in cymbalis bene   sonantibus

hergæd hine on cymbalum wynsumnesse   eælle   gæst
laudate eum in cymbalis iubilationis   6. omnis spiritus

hergæd drihten
laudet dominum

. ðeð, so MS.   150. *on* (1st), MS. = *ond*. *in* (2nd) of Latin repeated.

CANTICLES.

1.

Ic andete ðe drihten forða[n] yrre is me gecyrred
1. *Confitebor tibi domine quoniam iratus es michi conversus*

is hatheortnes þin 7 þu frefrendest is me   Eællengæ god
est furor tuus et consolatus es me 2. *Ecce deus*

helend min getreowlice ic doo 7 ic ne ondredo forðan
salvator meus fiducialiter agam et non timebo Quia

strengþo mine 7 hernes min drihten 7 geworden is me on
fortitudo mea et laudatio mea dominus et factus est michi in

helo   hlædæð weter on gefean be wyllæn helendes
salutem 3. *Haurietis aquas in gaudio de fontibus salvatoris*

7 cweðæð on ðæm dege ondettæð drihtne 7 gecigæþ
4. *et dicetis in illa die confitemini domino et invocate*

nomæn his Cuð doð on folce 7 on gemetnesse his
nomen eius Notas facite in populis et inventionis eius

gemynde ðe forðan heæh is noma his   Singæð
mementote quoniam excelsum est nomen eius 5. *Cantate*

drihten forðæn micel dide seigað ðis on eælre
domino quoniam magnifice fecit annunticte hoc in universa

eorðæn   Wynsumæ 7 here eærdunge syon forðan micel
terra 6. *Exulta et lauda habitatio syon quia magnus*

on midle þines hælig isræhele
in medio tui sanctus israhel

2.

Ic cwiðe on midlene dægæ minræ ic gonge to gætum
10. *Ego dixi in dimedio dierum meorum vadam ad portas*

ðæm yterum Ic sohte gesetnesse geæræ minræ ic cwiðe
inferi Quesivi residuum annorum meorum 11. *dixi*

1. 1. From *gecyrred* to *þu* by Cor. on er. -*st* wr. above the line.

ne ic geseo drihten god on eorðæn lifigendæ Ne locigen
non videbo dominum deum in terra viventium Non aspiciam

men ofer ðet 7 eærdunge se gerest cneowrisn
hominem ultra et habitatorem quievit 12. *generatio*

min tobroht is 7 onwylwed is from me swæ seo geteldung
mea ablata est. et convoluta est a me quasi tabernaculum

hirdæ Biddende is oððed from þe obðe lif min midti
pastorum Precisa est velut · a texentae vita mea dum

þægiet endebyrdnes æcweælde me From morgne oððet
adhuc ordirer succidit me De mane usque

to efen ende me from efenne oððe to morgen
ad vesperam fines me 13. *a vespere usque ad mane*

swæ seo leo swæ geearfegæþ eællæ bæn mine From morgne
quasi leo sic contrivit omnia ossa mea De mane

oððe to efene ende mines swæ briddæs swealue
usque ad vesperam fines me 14. *sicut pullus yrundinis*

swæ ic · fræ Anumenne sint eagan mine
sic clamabo meditabor ut columba Attenuati sunt oculi mei

locigende on heænessum drihten þeæh drowige onswere fore
suspicientes in excelso Domine vim patior responde pro

me hwet ic cwiðe oððe hwet onswærige me ðiet
me 15. *quid dicam aut quid respondebit michi quod*

he ic doo Ic ðence eælle geær mine on biternesse
ipse fecerim Recogitavi omnes annos meos in amaritudine

sawle minre drihten gif swæ lifigende oððe on ðylcum
animae meae 16. *Domine si sic vivitur aut in talibus*

lif gæst min gegrip me 7 geliffeste me Eællenga
vita spiritus mei corripies me et vivificabis me 17. *Ecce*

on sibbe biterlic min biterlice ðu cællenge genere
in pace amaritudo meo amarissima tu autem eruisti

sawle mine ðiet ne forweorðe 7 ðu æwurpe ðæ uteron
animam meam ut non perirem et proiecisti postergum

ðine eælle sinnæ minæ forðon neælles on helle
tuum omnia peccata mea 18. *quia non infernus*

ic ondctte ðe ne deæþ hereþ ðe Neeæles onbidon
confitebitur tibi neque mors laudabit te Non expectabunt

ðæ æstigaþ on seæþ soðfestnesse þinre lifigende
qui descendunt in lacum veritatem tuam 19. *vivens*

---

2. 12. oððet, MS. ðððet.   14. Er. betw. ic and -fræ.

lifigende he biÐ ondettende Ðe swæ 7 ic to dege Feder
vivens ipse confitebitur tibi sicut et ego hodie Pater

beærn kuÐ deÐ soÐfestnesse þine   drihten hæle us
filiis notam faciet veritatem tuam 20. *domine salvos nos*

Ðeþ 7 hæle ure singæþ eallum dægum lif ure on
fac et psalmos nostras cantabimus cunctis diebus vitae nostrae in

huse drihtnes
domo domini

3.

CANTICUM ANNE MATRIS SAMUELIS (1 SAM. 2. 1).

heorte min on drihten 7 upæhæfen is horn min
1. *Gaudebat cor meum in domino et exultatum est cornu meum*

on god min Gebred is muÐ min ofer fiend nine
in deo meo Dilatatum est os meum super inimicos meos

forÐæn blissigende ic eom on helo Ðine   Neæles is
quia letata sum in salutari tuo 2. *Non est*

hælig þet is drihten nimÐe soÐlice is oÐer butæn þe 7 ne
sanctus ut est dominus neque enim est alius extra te et non

is stræng swæ god ure   Ne ceæro eow monigfeældigæn
est fortis sicut deus noster 3. *Nolite multiplicare*

sprece under wundriende gewitæþ eældæn of muÐe owrum
loqui sublimia glorificantes recedant vetera de ore vestro

forÐæn god wisdomæ drihten is 7 he geærwigende geÐohtæs
Quia deus scientiarum dominus est et ipsi preparantes cogitationes

Bogæ stræng oferigende is 7 untrume begirÐe sindon
4. *Arcus fortium superatus est et infirmi accincti sunt*

strengÐo   Gefillede er fore hlæfum 7 hine gestæÐolode
robore 5. *Repleti prius pro panibus se locaverunt*

7 his lice gefilde sindon OÐÐe berendum kinde monigæ 7 dæ
et famelici saturati sunt Donec sterilis peperit plurimos et que

monigæ hefÐ beærn untrumod is   drihten deædberende
multos habebat filios infirmata est 6. *Dominus mortificat*

7 liffesteÐ geledeþ 7 to nietenum 7 geledeþ   Drihten
et vivificat deducit et inferos et reducit 7. *Dominus*

Ðeærfæ deÐ 7 gedendeÐ geeæÐmeÐeþ 7 underÐeoÐeþ
pauperem facit et ditat humiliat et sublimat

Æweæhte ob mille Ðone wedlæn 7 of fulnesse upnimende
8. *Suscitans de pulvere egenum et de stercore erigens*

3. 1. *Gaudebat* al. *Exultavit*. 6. -teÐ, Ð on er.?

ðeærfan   7   þ iesette mit eældormænnum 7 ænum   wuldor
pauperem   Ut sedeat cum   principibus   et solium   glorie

hiefð ðrihtnes sodlice sindon   eorðe 7 gesette ofer hie
teneat Domini   enim   sunt   cardines terrae et posuit super eos

ymbwyrft   Fot   hæligræ   hiræ   gehilt 7 eærleæsæ
orbem   9. Pedes sanctorum suorum servabit et   impii

on   ðystrum   on unsongum Forðæn   ne   on   strengþo   his
in   tenebris   conticiscent   Quia   non   in   fortitudine   sua

bið gestrongod wer   drihten   oneigeð   þæ wiðerweærdæn
roborabitur   vir   10. dominum formidabunt   adversarii

his 7 ofer   his   on hefone onthunað Drihten   demæþ   ende
eius et super ipsis in caelis   tonabit   Dominus iudicabit fines

eorðe 7 seleþ ærleæsæ recedom his 7 underþeodeþ horn
terre et dabit imperium   regi   suo et   sublimabit   cornu

cristes his
christi   sui

4.

         drihtne wuldor soðlice   gewurðod   is Emlice 7
1. *Cantemus domino gloriosae enim honorificatus est Equum et*

æstigende æweorpeð on   sie   fultumend 7 scildend geworden
ascensorem proiecit in mare   2. Adiutor et protector   factus

is me on helum her god min 7 ic weorðige hine god fieder
est michi in salutem Hic deus meus et   honorabo   eum deus patris

min 7 ic uphebbe hine   Drihten brecende gefioht
mei et   exaltabo   eum   3. Dominus conterens   bella

drihten nomæn is him   Ryne phæræonis 7 weredes
dominus nomen est ei   4. Currus pharaonis et exercitum

his æweærp on siewe Gecorene upstigende þriræ stondende
eius proiecit in mare Electus ascensores   terni   stratores

he besencte on   þere readan sea   widsea oferwreah
demersit   in   rubro   mare   5. Pelago   cooperuit

hy becomon on   grund   swa swa stan   þeo swiþre
eos devenerunt in profundum tanquam lapis   6.   Dextera

ðin laueord gewuldrud is on meagne swidre   hand   ðin
tua domine glorificata est in   virtute   dextera   manus tua

laueord forbreac   fynd   7 þurh   menege   megen
domine confregit inimicos   7. Et per   multitudinem maiestatis

---

10. *-hunað* in p. ink in pl. of er.   4. 1. MS. = *gewurðdððod.*   4. With
he begins a fresh hand.

þin　þu forbrittest　wiþerlingas　þu asendest　yrre　þin　7
tuae　contrivisti　adversarios　Misisti　iram　tuam　et

hit æt hi swa swa erbleadd　7 þurh　gast　eorsunge
comedit eos tanquam stipulam　8. et per spiritum iracundiae

þinre todeled is weter gefruron　swa swa　weallas weteru
tuae　divisa　est　aqua Gelaverunt tanquam　murus　aquae

gefruron　yþa　on middele seas　cwæð　feond　ehtende
gelaverunt fluctus in medio maris　9. Dixit inimicus persequens

ic gegripe　ic dæle　herereaf　ic geþylle　saule　mine
comprehendam　partibor　spolia　replebo　animam　meam

ic cwelle　sweord min bið weældend hænde mine　þu sendes
interficiam gladio meo dominabitur manus mea　10. Misisti

gæst　ðinne　7　bewreæh hie　sie　besencte　swæ swæ
spiritum　tuum　et　cooperuit　eos　mare merserunt　tamquam

leæd　on weter swiðæð　hwilc gelic þe on
plumbum in aqua validissimo　11. Quis similis tibi in

his dægum drihten hwylc gelic　ðe wuldorfest on hælgum
diis　domine　quis　similis　tibi　gloriosus　in　sanctis

wundrum on megenðrimimu doende forebeacc　ðu æþenedes
mirabilis in maiestatibus faciens prodigia　12. Extendisti

swiðræn ðine 7 forsweælg hie eorðe　gifernes soðfestnesse
dexteram tuam et devoravit eos terra　13. gubernasti iusticia

þine folc　þin ðisne þonc gefrilsodes Upcumen is on meigne
tua populum tuum hunc quem liberasti Exortatus es in virtute

ðinum 7 on gescildnesse halige ðine　gehiræþ ðiodæ
tua et in refectione sancta tua　14. Audierunt gentes

7 yrsiende sindon sær　gegripon　on eærdunge philistim
et iratae sunt dolores conprehenderunt inhabitantes philistiim

þonne efstende weron læteow edom 7 eældormon
15. Tunc festinaverunt duces edom et principes Moabi-

7 gegræp heo fyrhto Onegæn eælle oneærdigende
tarum adprehendit eos tremor Tabuerunt omnes inhabitantes

chænææn　gefeællæþ ofer hie eige 7 fyrhto micelnes
chanaan　16. decidant super eos timor et tremor magnitudinis

eærmes þines Sic swæ swæ stæn occðet leored folc
brachii tui Fiant tanquam lapis donec transeat populus

þin drihten oððet midti þurhfereþ folc ðin ðisne
tuus domine usque dum pertranseat populus tuus hunc domine

---

8. *þurh*, u from some other let.　*weteru*, MS. = *wetereu* with third *e* dotted.
9. With *sweord* begins a fresh hand.　11. *megenðrimimu*, so MS.

þone tobegeate   Ongeliedde wyrtwælæs hie on   dune
quem adquisisti   **17.** *Inducens   plantas   eos   in   montem*

yrfeweærdnesse   ðine on gerwungum   heærdungæ   ðine   ðet
hereditatis   tue   in   preparato   habitaculo   tuo   quod

ðu gearwodes   drihten   Gehælgunge   ðine   drihten   ðiet
preparasti   domine   Sanctimonium   tuum   domine   quod

geærwodon   handa   þine   drihten   se   rixæþ   on
*preparaverunt   manus   tue   **18.** domine   qui   regnas   in*

ecnessum 7 on worolde 7 nugean   Forðæn ingeð
*eternum et in seculum et adhuc   **19.** Quia   introivit*

emlicnesse phæræonis mid feðerfealdum   stigendum on sie
equitatus pharaonis cum   quadrigis   et ascensoribus in mare

7 ongeledde ofer hie drihten weter sewe beærn eællengæ
et   induxit   super eos dominus aquas maris Filii   autem

isræhele   eodon   þurh drige þurh midde sie
israhel ambulaverunt per   siccum   per   medium mare

5.

CANTICUM ABBACUC (HAB. 3).

        ic gehire gehirnesse ðine 7 ic ondred Ic sceæwige
2. *Domine   audivi   auditum tuum et   timui   Consideravi*

weorc ðin 7 forhtaþ On midlene tweiæ   nietenæ   on
opera tua et expavi In   medio   duorum   animalium in-

kiðnesse Midti toneælecton geæres oncnæwnesse midti
notesceris Dum   adpropiaverint   anni   cognosceris   dum

he tokymeð   tid   æteowð On him   midti bið gedr[e]fed
advenerit   tempus ostenderis In   eo   dum   conturbata

bið   sæwle mine on yrræ mildheortnes gemindig   God
fuerit anima mea in ira misericordiae memor eris **3.** *Deus*

from ðæm fremdon cumæþ 7 hælig of   dune   ymbscuæn
a   libano   veniet et sanctus de   monte   umbroso

7 ðicnes Ontynæþ hefon megenðrim him 7   lof   his
et condempso Operuit celos   maiestas   eius et   laude   eius

full is eorðe   birhtnes his swæ lioht bioð horn
plena est terra   **4.** *Splendor eius sicut lumen erit cornua*

sindon on hændæ his ðer getrimeþ is megen wuldor
sunt in manibus eius Ibi confirmata est virtus gloriae

---

5. 2. *tweiæ?* Probably orig.=*twegæ* (with bottom part of *g* er. and what
is left touched with darker ink to make it into *i*?)

his 7 gesette birhtnesse trimnes strengðo his 　　Beforæn
eius et posuit claritatem firmam fortitudinis sue 　5.　*Ante*

onsine his eode word 7 utgieð on feldon fet his
faciem eius ibit verbum et exibit in campis pedes eius

　stodon 7 æwend is eordæ forelocede 7 tofleowæn
6. *steterunt et mota est terra Aspexit et defluxerunt*

ðeodæ gebrocene sindon dunæ swiþe 7 utfleowen hyllæ
gentes confracti sunt montes vehementer et defluxerunt colles

ecelecæn siðfiet ecnessum his 　　fore gewinnum weræ
aeternales itinera eternitatis eius 　　7. *prae laboribus viri*

　　　　eærdungæ eorðe mædiæn
Tabernacula ethiopum expavescent tabernacula terrae madian

　Nimðe on streæme yrre ðin drihten oððe on streæme
8. *Numquid in fluminibus ira tua domine aut in fluminibus*

wylm ðin oððe on se onblest þin Forðæn æstigende
furor tuus aut in mare inpetus tuus Quoniam ascendens

æstigende ofer hors þin 7 emlicnessæ þine helæ 　beheæld-
ascendes super equos tuos et equitatus tuus sanitas · 9. *Tend-*

ende 7 æðene bogæn ðinne ofer þæ rihtæn cweð drihten
ens extendes arcum tuum super sceptra dicit dominus

streæmum bið tosliten eordæ 　　gesioþ 7 særgiæð
Fluminibus scindetur terram 　　10. *videbunt te et dolebunt*

folc Æstrewigende weter on soðfatum his seælde on
populi Aspaergens aquas in itineribus suis dedit

onewolnesse stefne his ob heænnessum fulluhtes his
abyssus vocem suam ab altitudine phantasiae suae

Upæhæfæn is 　　　sunne 7 monæ stod on endebyrdnesse
Elevatus est 　11. *sol et luna stetit in ordine* :

his On liehte scotunge þine gongende on byrhtnesse ligetu
suo In lumine iacula tua ibunt in splendore fulgoris

wepnæ ðinræ 　　On wendunge þinræ gelitlunge eorþæn
armorum tuorum 12. *In cominatione tua minorabis terram*

7 on wylme þinum wiðtihst þeodæ 　　þu were on hielum
et in furore tuo detrahes gentes 　13. *Existi in salutem*

folce ðinum 7 hale ðu dest criste þinum þu sende on
populi tui ut salvos facias christos tuos Misisti in

heæfde ðone unrihton deæþ 7 æweæhtes bendæ oð
capita iniquorum mortem excitasti vincula usque ad

---

5. 6. *his*, MS. = *hæs*. 　10. *-fatum*, *a* from some other let. 　13. A let.
(*d*) bef. *sweoræ*, with prps. something er. bef. it.

sweoræ   ðu æwurpe on ðæ frendon heæfdæ   mihte
cervices   14. *Precidisti in alienatione capita potentium*

onwende   on him ðeoðæ from ontynende tid hiræ   swæ
movebuntur in ea gentes Ad aperient ora sua sicut

ðeærfæ etende on diglæn   ðu sendes on sie hors þin
pauper edens in occulto   15. *Misisti in mare equos tuos*

gedrefende weter monige   Gehilt 7 onegð innoþ
turbantes aquas multas   16. *Custodivit et expavit venter*

min from stemfne gebed gewinnæ winræ 7 ineode
meus a voce orationis labiorum meorum Et introivit

fyrhto on bæn mine 7 beneoþæn me gedrefed is innoþmegen
tremor in ossa mea et subtus me turbata est virtus

min Ic reste on deg eærfoðnessæ mine þet ic æstige to
mea Requiescam in die tribulationis meae ut ascendam ad

folce ferende leorende min   Forðæn ne fordswebed
populum transmigrationis meae   17. *Quoniam ficus non*

forðbringþ westm 7 neæles biþ cneowrisn on ende Liogende
afferet fructum et non erit generatio in vineis Mentietur

wiorc elebergæn 7 feld ne deþ mete Æspringon from
opus olive et campi non facient escas Defecerunt ab

metæ sceæpæ 7 na beoð on binne oxan   Ic soðlice
esca oves et non erunt in praesepio boves 18. *Ego autem*

on drithne ic wuldrige ic gefagenie on gode hælende minum
in domino gloriabor gaudebo in deo ihesu meo

Drihten god megen min gesette fet mine on geend-
19. *Domine deus virtus mea constitue pedes meos in consum-*

unge 7 ofer on hyhðo gesette me þet oferswiðe on
matione et super excelsa statuit me ut vincam ·in

birhtnesse his
claritate ipsius

6.

CANTICUM MOYSI (DEUT. 32. 1).

hefon 7 sprece 7 geh[i]ræþ eorðe word of muþe
1. *Audite caelum et loquar et audiat terra verba ex ore*

minum Onbideþ swæ ren gesprec min 7 æstige
meo 2. *Exspectetur sicut pluvia eloquium meum et discendant*

---

17. From *na* to *minum* (of next verse) by Cor.   19. *his, s* on er. of about
two lett.   6. 1. *geh*[i]*ræþ*, MS.=*geÿræþ.*

swæ deæw word min Swæ scur ofer hegel 7 swæ snæw
sicut ros verba mea Sicut ymber super gramen et sicut nix

ofer heg forðæn nomæn drihtnes ic cige Sellæþ
super fenum 3. *quia nomen domini invocabo Date*

micelnesse gode urum soðlice weorc his 7 eælle wegas
magnitudinem deo nostro 4. *vera opera eius et omnes viae*

his domas God 7 ne is unrihtnes on him soðfest 7
eius iudicia Deus fidelis et non est iniquitas in eo iustus et

halig drihten Gefirenedon neæles him beærn unwemme
sanctus dominus 5. *Peccaverunt non ei filii inmaculati*

cyðnessæ gerwæ 7 þurh ðæm isleæcæn ðis drihten
natio prava et perversa 6. *hec domino*

ðu foregulde Gif folc disig 7 neæles snotor neæles þeos he
retribuisti Si plebs fatua et non sapiens nonne hic ipse

þin feder ægende þe worhte ðe 7 gesceop ðæ On
tuus pater possedit te fecit te et creavit te 7. *In*

gemynde hæbbæþ dægæs worlde on andgite gear gecynnesse
mente habete dies seculi intelligite annos nationis

gecynda axa feder ðinne 7 he bodaþ ðe yldran
nationum [i]*nterroga patrem tuum et annunciabit tibi seniores*

ðine 7 hi secgað þe ða þa todælde se meara þeoda
tuos et dicent tibi 8. *Cum diviserit excelsus gentes*

swa swa he todælde bearn adames he gesette gemæro
quemadmodum dispersit filios adae Statuit terminos

ðeoda efter gerime engle godes geworden is
gentium secundum numerum angelorum dei 9. *Et facta est*

dæl drihtnes folc his iacob rap hyrfeweardnesse his
pars domini populus eius iacob funiculus hereditatis eius

israel genihðsumiend hine he dyde him on westene on
israhel 10. *Sufficientem eum fecit sibi in heremo in*

ðurst hæte þær na wes wæter he ymbledde hine 7 he lærde
sitim caloris ubi non erat aqua Circunduxit eum et erudivit

hine 7 he geheold hine swa swa seon eagæs Swa swa
eum et custodivit eum sicut pupillam oculi 11. *Sicut*

earn wrihð nest his 7 ofer briddas his sit t sæt
aquila tegit nidum suum et super pullos suos considet

he aðenede fiþeru his 7 he anfeng hy 7 he underfeng hy ofer
Expandit alas suas et accepit eos et suscepit eos super

---

5. *perversa.* Compare gloss to same word, 6. 20.　　7. With *gear* begins
a fresh hand.　　11. *t* er. bef. *sit*; *sit t* in d. ink prob. add. by Cor.

sculdras his   Drihten · æn lierde hie 7 ne bioþ mid
scapulas suas   **12.** *Dominus solus docebat eos et non erat cum*

him god fremdæn   7 togeledde hie on strengþo eorþæn
eis deus alienus   **13.**   *Adduxit eos in fortitudine terre* .

gemetgode hie ðæ kennedæn londæ   feddon hunigæ of stane
cibavit eos   nascentias agrorum Suxerunt mel   de petra

7 ele be ðæm trumæn stæne   Buture oxnæ 7 meolc
et oleum de   firma   petra   **14.** *Butyrum bovum et lac*

sceæpæ mid fetnesse londæ 7 weðeræ beærnæ feærræ 7
ovium cum   adipe agnorum et arietum filiorum taurorum et

buccænæ mid fetnesse eþeræ hwetes 7   blod   Drincþ
hyrcorum cum   adipe renium tritici et sanguinem uvae Bibit

win 7   et   iæcob   7 gefilled is 7 sporetungæ
vinum et manducavit iacob   **15.** *et saciatus est et   recalci-*

wiðtiehþ lustful   fæt geworden is 7 on fetnesse   gebreden
travit dilectus Pinguis factus est et incrassavit et dilatatus

is 7   forelet   hine se worhte hine 7 gewæt fræm gode helo
est et dereliquit deum qui fecit eum et recessit a   deo salutari

his   Beeodon   me on fremdum 7 fræm weældendum
suo   **16.** *Exacerbaverunt me in alienis   in abominationibus*

his   æwehton   me   Er onsiedon dioblum 7 neæles
suis concitaverunt me   **17.** *Sacrificaverunt demoniis et   non*

godæ godæs þæ   ne   witon recedomæs   comon   to him
deo   deos   quos non   noverunt novi recentes venerunt

ða ne wiston fieder hiræ   God se ðe kende ðu forlete
quos nesciebant patres eorum   **18.** *Deum qui te genuit dereliquisti*

7 tobroht wes god þæ fremdæn   Geseæh drihten 7
et oblitus est deum   alentem   te   **19.** *Vidit dominus et*

ellenwod   7 begongende wes   for   yrre beærnæ hiræ   7
zelatus est et exacerbatus est propter iram filiorum suorum et

dohtræ   7 cweð ic ærwyrfe onsiene mine from him 7
filiarum   **20.** *Et dixit avertam   faciem meam ab eis et*

ic etiewe þet bið his   forðæn cneowrisn wyðerweærd 7
ostendam quid erit eis in novissimo Quia generatio   prava   et

þurh mislice beærn on þæm   ne is geleæfæ on him   him
perversa   filii   in quibus non est fides   in ipsis   **21.** *Ipsi*

---

12. With *Drihten* begins a fresh hand.   13. *stane*, *a* from *o*.   14. 7
(1st) part. er.   *feærræ* repeated in MS., the Latin to the first er.   15. *spore-*,
MS. = *swore?*   17. *ða* on er.   19. Er. (*hiræ?*) aft. *dohtræ*; Latin to this
also er.

ellenwodnes   todrifon   7 neæles on gode on irræ
in   zelo   conpulerunt me et non in deo in ira

æwehton me on diobolgild his 7 Ic on ellenwodnes ic adrife
concitaverunt me in   idolis suis Et ego in   zelo   expellam

hie 7 ne on ðeode on ðeode on unsnitro ic lece hie
eos et non in gentem in gentem insipientem irritabo eos

Forðæn fyr bernþ from yrræ nimum 7 bernþ oððet
22. *Quia ignis exarsit ab   ira   mea et ardebit usque ad*

yteræn niþer Fretæþ eorðe kennessæ hiræ 7 gemylte
inferos deorsum Comedit terram nascentias eorum et concremavit

stæðolæs   dunæ   ˌ Ic biere on him yfel 7 strelæ
*fundamenta montium   * **23.** *Congeram in ipsis mala et sagittas*

mine ic geendige on him   Oneægæn hungre 7 mete
*meas consummabo in eis   * **24.** *Tabescentes fame et esca*

sceæpæ 7 et gewene niþen on wedendum Teþ wyldeoræ
erunt avium et   extentio dorsi insanabilis Dentes bestiarum

onsende on him mid wylme teondræ ofer eorðæn
inmittam in eis cum furore trahentium super terram

From uton butæn beærn   hio sweord 7 on   fusnesse
25. *A foris sine filiis privabit eos gladium et in promptuariis*

muð ege Geonge mid femnon fedende mid stæþlunge eældes
timor Iuvenis cum virgine lactans cum stabilito sene

Cwið Ic tostence hie ic gearwige soðlice ob mannunum
26. *Dixit dispergam eos   privabo   autem ex hominibus*

˙ gemind hiræ   Nimþe for irre yrre feondæ on
*memoriam eorum   * **27.** *Misi propter iram inimicorum ne*

longræ tide sien ofer eorðæn Ne me geþæfetæþ ðæ wyðer-
longo tempore sint super terram Ne   consensciant adver-

weærdæn 7 cweðæþ hændæ uræ ob hihþo 7 neæles god worhte
sarii et dicant manus nostra excelsa et non deus faecit

þis eællæ   forðæn þeod ferspild geþeæhtung is 7 ne
*haec omnia   * **28.** *Quia gens perdito consilio est et non*

is on him æneþæn   Neæles wisdom ongitende ðæs 7
*est in eis disciplina   * **29.** *Non sapuerunt intellegere haec*

to onfonne on ðæ towerdæn tide   hu   fylgende
*percipient in futuro   tempore   * **30.** *Quomodo persequitur*

æn þusend 7 twæm leorende æstyred tien þusendæ Nimþe
unus mille et duo transmovebunt dena milia Nisi

---

24. *niþen*, sec. *n* from *r*.   26. *mannunum*, so MS.   27. *irre yrre*, so MS.
29. Latin to 7 er.

forðæn drihten underfeælde hie 7 god seælle hie   forðæn
quia dominus subdidit   eos et deus tradidit illos   **31.** *Quia*

ne is god ure swæ godæ hiræ   fiend soðlice urum on sefæn
non est deus noster sicut dii illorum inimici autem nostri insensati

      Ob wyngeærdum hiræ   on sodomorum   lif   hiræ 7
32. *Ex   vinea   enim   sodomorum   vitis   eorum et*

for hieþenscipe ob gomorræ Songæs hiræ songæs geællenæ 7
propago eorum ex gomorra Uva   eorum uva   fellis et

gehweðres biternesse on him   Wylm dræcenæ wyn
  botrus   amaritudinis ipsis   **33.** *Furor draconum vinum*

hiræ 7 wylm niedrenæ on wedendum   Neæles þæs
eorum et furor aspidum   insanabilis   **34.** *Nonne haec*

gesomnede sindon mid me 7 tæcn   on go[l]dhordum minum
congregata sunt   aput me et signata in   thesaaris   meis

    on deg ofer þet ic gielde him on tide se slide bið
35. *In die ultionis reddam illis in tempore quo lapsus fuerit*

fotum hiræ Forðæn neæh is dægæs forwirde hiræ 7 þæs
pes eorum Quia   prope est dies perditionis eorum et haec

sindon gegeærwod eow   Forðæn dend   drihten folce
sunt   parata vobis   **36.** *Quia iudicabit dominus populum*

his 7 on þeowum his bið frefrende gesigþ soðlice   geswencende
suum et in servis suis consolabitur Vidit enim eos fatigatos

        on utlednesse 7 toliesede   7 cweð wer sindon
et defectos in abduxione et dissolutos   **37.** *Et dixit ubi sunt*

godæ hiræ   on þæm getriewæþ on him   ðæræ
dii illorum in quibus confidebatis in ipsis   **38.** *Quorum*

fetnesse onsegdnessæ   eton 7 druncon wyn fræcedon hiræ
adipem sacrificiorum edebatis et bibebatis vinum libationis eorum

  ærisæ   nu   tofultumæþ eow 7 sien   eow   scildend
Exurgant nunc et   adiuvent   vos et fiant vobis   protectores

  Gesioþ gesioþ forðæn ic eom god 7 ne is oþer buton me
39. *Vidẹte videte quoniam ego sum deus et non est alius preter me*

Ic æcwelle 7 to libbenne ic do þurhsleæ 7 ic helo 7 ne
Ego occidam et vivere faciam percutiam et ego sanabo et non

is se generæð of hændum minum   Forðæn ic nime on
est qui eripiat de manibus meis   **40.** *Quia   tollam in*

hefen hændæ minum 7 ic swerige þurh   7 cwiðe
celum manum meam et iurabo   per dexteram meam et dicam

---

36. *dend,* so MS.

lifige ic on ecnesse   forðæn ob wetere oðꝺet ligetunc
vivo ego in eternum   **41.** *Quia   exacuam   velut   fulgur*

sweord min 7   dom   hændæ mine 7 ic gilde   dom
gladium meum et aget iudicium manus mea Et retribuam iudicium

fiondum 7 ðæ ðe fiogæþ me ic gilde   strelæ
inimicis et his qui oderunt me reddam   **42.** *Inhebriabo sagittas*

mine on   blod   7 sweord   min   eꝫæþ   flesc   from
meas in sanguine et gladius meus manducabit carnes   A

blode   wungendra 7 hæftnyde fram heafde ealdra ɫ fromra
sanguine vulneratorum et captivitate a   capite   principium

feonda   blissiað heofnas somod mid ꞕim 7 gebiddaþ hine
inimicorum Letamini   celi   simul cum eo et   adorent   eum

ealle   engles godes   blissiad þeoda mid folce   his 7
omnes angeli dei   **43.** *Letamini gentes cum populo eius et*

getrimmen hine ealle bearn godes forðan blod   bearna   his
confirment eum omnes filii   dei   Quia sanguis filiorum eius

bið gescild 7 he gescildeþ 7 he agildeþ   dom   feondum 7 þam
defendetur et   defendet   et retribuet   iudicium inimicis et iis

þe hatedon hine he agildeþ 7 geclensade crihten eorðan folces
qui oderunt eum   reddet   Et emundabit dominus terram populi

his
sui

7.

Bletsige   ealle wiorc drihtnes drihten herigæð 7 ofer
57. *Benedicite omnia opera domini domino laudate et super-*

him on worold   bletsie englæs drihtnes drihten
exaltate eum in secula   **58.** *Benedicite angeli domini domino*

bletsige hefonæs drihten   Bletsige weter eælle
59. *benedicite caeli   domino*   **60.** *Benedicite aque omnes*

ðæ   ofer hefonæs sindon drihten   bletsige   eæll
quae super caelos sunt domino   **61.** *benedicite omnes*

mægen drihtnes drihten   Bletsige sunne 7 monæ drihten
virtutes domini domino   **62.** *Benedicite sol et luna domino*

bletsige stiorræn hefonæs drihten   Bletsige scuræ
63. *benedicite stelle caeli domino*   **64.** *Benedicite ymber*

---

42. With *wungendra* begins a fresh hand.   43. On the margin marked
to follow *gentes*, is *simul*, which is glossed by *somod*.   *hi* er. bef. *hatedon*.
7. 57. With *Bletsige* begins a fresh hand.

7 deæwung drihten   bletsige eælle gæstæs
et   *ros*   *domino*   **65.** *benedicite omnis spiritus dei domino*

     7 heto drihten   bletsige ciele 7
66. *Benedicite ignis et estus domino*   **67.** *benedicite frigus et*

hetæ drihten   Bletsige   7 hrim drihten
estas domino   **68.** *Benedicite*   *rores*   *et pruina domino*

bletsige   7 ciele drihten   bletsige
69. *benedicite gelu et frigus domino*   **70.** *Benedicite glacies et*

snæw drihten   bletsige nihtæ 7 dægæs drihten   blet-
nives domino   **71.** *benedicite noctes et dies domino*   **72.** *Bene-*

sige   7 þiestro drihten   bletsige ligetu 7 wolcn
dicite lux et tenebrae domino   **73.** *benedicite fulgura et nubes*

drihten   eorðæ drihten heræþ 7 ofer
domino   **74.** *Benedicat terra dominum laudet et superexaltet*

him on world   Bletsige muntes 7 hillæ drihten
eum in secula   **75.** *Benedicite montes et colles domino*

bletsige ealle upspringende on eorðæ drihten   Blet-
76. *benedicite universa germinantia in terra domino*   **77.** *Bene-*

sige wyllæn drihten   bletsige se 7 streæmæs drihten
dicite fontes domino   **78.** *benedicite maria et flumina domino*

Bletsige hwelæs 7 eælle ðæ beoð weonde on wetere
79. *Benedicite caete et omnia quae moventur in aquis*

drihten   bletsige eælle fuglæs hefonæs drihten
domino   **80.** *benedicite omnes volucres caeli domino*

Bletsiæ eælle wildeoræ 7 eælle nietenæ drihten   blet-
81. *Benedicite omnes bestiae et pecora domino*   **82.** *bene-*

sige beærn mænnæ drihten   bletsige isræhel drihten
dicite filii hominum domino   **83.** *Benedicat israel dominum*

herigæþ 7 ofer   him on world   bletsie æwe-
laudet et superexaltet eum in secula   **84.** *Benedicite sacer-*

weærdæs drihtnes drihten   bletsige þeow drihtnes drihten
dotes domini domino   **85.** *benedicite servi domini domino*

Bletsige gæstæs 7 sæwules soðfeste drihten   blet-
86. *Benedicite spiritus et animae iustorum domino*   **87.** *bene-*

sige hælige 7 eæþmode heortæn drihtæn   bletsige
dicite sancti et humiles corde domino   **88.** *Benedicite*

rænæniæs æzæriæs misæhel drihten herigæþ 7 ofer
anania azaria misael domino laudate et superexaltate

---

81. *nietenæ, i* wr. above the line.

hine on world   bletsige   fæder 7 sunu mid hælig gæst
eum in secula Benedicamus patrem et filium cum sancto spiritu
þe herigæþ 7   ofer we uphebbæþ hine on world gebletsod is
laudemus et superexaltemus eum in secula Benedictus es
drihten on trimnesse hefonæs 7 herigæþ 7 wuldorfest 7 ofer
domine in firmamento caeli et laudabilis et gloriosus et super-
upæhæfæn on worold
exaltatus in secula

8.

[TE DEUM LAUDAMUS.]

þe God we heriað þe drihten we andetteð   þe
1. *Te deum laudamus te dominum confit.mur*   2. *Te*

ecne fæder eal eorðe wurðað   þe ealle engles
aeternum patrem omnis terra veneratur 3. *Tibi omnes angeli*

þe heofenas 7 ealle anwealdu   þe
tibi caeli et universae potestates 4. *Tibi cherubin et seraphin*

unablinnendlicere stefne clypeð   halig halig
incessabili voce proclamant 5. *Sanctus Sanctus*

halig drihten god Sabaot   fulle beoð heofenas 7
Sanctus dominus deus sabaoth 6. *Pleni sunt caeli et*

eorðe mægenþrymmes wuldres þines   þe wulderfull
terra maiestatis gloriae tuae 7. *Te gloriosus*

erendracen wered þe witegena hergendlic getel
apostolorum chorus 8. *Te prophetarum laudabilis numerus*

þe cyþra iwitad herað here   þe
9. *Te martyrum candidatus laudat exercitus* 10. *Te per*

embhwyrft eorþene halig undet gesomnung   fader
orbem terrarum sancta confitetur aeecclesia 11. *Patrem*

ormetes mægenþ[r]immes   arwurðne þinne soðne 7
inmense maiestatis 12. *Venerandum tuum verum et*

anlicne sune haligne witodlice frefrigende gast
unicum filium 13. *Sanctum quoque paraclytum spiritum*

þu king wuldres crist þu fæderes ece
14. *Tu rex gloriae christe* 15. *Tu patris sempiternus*

þu eart sune þu to alysenne þu anfenge man
es filius 16. *Tu ad liberandum suscepturus hominem*

8. 1. With *þe* (1st) begins a fresh hand.   4. *-ere*, first *e* dotted.

þu ne ascunedest femnen　innoð　　　　þu　oferswiðedum
non horruisti　virginis　uterum　　**17.** *Tu　　devicto*

deaþes ángan þu antendest gelyfedum　rice　heofena　　　　þu
mortis aculeo　aperuisti　credentibus　regna caelorum　**18.** *Tu*

on ða swiðran　godes settle on　wuldre fæderes　　　Deme
ad　dexteram　dei　sedes　in　gloria　patriç　**19.** *Iudex*

þu eart gelyfed wesen　toward　　　þe eornostlice we halsiað
crederis　esse　venturus　**20.** *Te　ergo　　quesumus*

　　　þinum þeowum gehelp þa of deorwyrðum blode þu alysdest
　tuis　famulis subveni quos　precioso　sanguine redemisti

　　　ece　do　mid　halgum þine　wuldor　beon forgefen
21. *Eterna fac　cum　sanctis　tuis　gloria　munerari*

　　　hal　do　folc　þin drihten 7 bletsa yrfeweardnysse
22. *Salvum fac populum tuum domine et benedic　hereditati*

þine　　　　7 gerece hy 7 upahef hy oððe on ecnesse
tuae　　**23.** *Et　rege　eos et extolle illos usque in aeternum*

　　　þurh syndrige dages we bletsiað þe　　　7 we heriað
24. *Per singulos dies benedicimus te*　　**25.** *Et laudamus*

namen þinne on worulde 7　awor[l]d　　　gemedeme
nomen tuum in seculum et in seculum seculi　**26.** *Dignare*

drihten dage þisum buten synne us gehealdan　　　gemiltse
domine die　isto　sine peccato nos custodire　**27.** *Miserere*

　　us drihten gemiltsa　us　　　　beo mildheortnysse þin
nostri domine miserere nostri　　**28.** *Fiat　misericordia tua*

drihten ofer　us　swa swa　we hyhtað on þe　　　on þe
domine super nos quemadmodum speravimus in te　**29.** *In te*

drihten ic hihte　ne　beo ic gescynd on ecnysse
domine speravi non　confundar　in aeternum

9.

PROPHETIA ZACHARIE (LUKE 1. 68).

　　　gebletsod béo　drihten　god　getreowra forðan　　he
　68. *Benedictus dominus deus　israhel　quia　visitavit*

7 dyde gelysednesse folces his　　　　7 he arerde horn
et fecit redemptionem plebis suae　　**69.** *Et　erexit　cornu*

hæle　us on huse dauiðes cnihtes his　　　　swa swa
salutis nobis in domo david　pueri sui　　**70.** *Sicut*

---

23. *upahef*, MS. = *aipahef* (or *u* from *a* ?).　24. A leaf misplaced in MS.
aft. *singulos*.　　**9.** 68. *gebletsod*, *t* from *l*.

he spræc þurh muð haligra forðan woruldo beoð witegena
locutus est per os sanctorum quia seculo sunt prophetarum
his   hele of feondum ure 7 of hande ælre
eius **71.** *Salutem ex inimicis nostris et de manu omnium*
ðe hatedon us   to donne mildheortnysse mid
qui oderunt nos **72.** *Ad faciendum misericordiam cum*
fæderum urum 7 gemunen cyðnysse his haligre ap-
patribus nostris et memorari testamenti sui sancti **73.** *Ius-*
swering þane he swor to habrahame fæder urum to gefene
jurandum quod iuravit ad abraham patrem nostrum daturum
hine selfne us   þeð butan ege of handen fionda
se nobis **74.** *Ut sine timore de manu inimicorum*
uræ alysede we þewien him   On halignesse 7
nostrorum liberati serviamus illi **75.** *In sanctitate et*
rihtwisnesse beforan him ealle dagum urum   7
iusticia coram ipso omnibus diebus nostris **76.** *Et*
þu cnapa witege þæs hehstan þu beost gecliped þu foregest
tu puer propheta altissimi vocaberis preibis
soðlice beforan ansyne drihtnes gearwien wegas his to
enim ante faciem domini parare vias eius **77.** *Ad*
gefene ingehid hele folce his on alysednysse synne
dandam scientiam salutis plebi eius in remissionem peccatorum
heora þurh innoðes mildheortnesse godes ure on ðas
eorum **78.** *Per viscera misericordiae dei nostri in quibus*
he neosode us upspringende of ufene   Onlihtan þa
visitavit nos oriens ex alto **79.** *Illuminare his*
þe on þiostrum 7 on scade deaðes sittað to gerechenne
qui in tenebris et in umbra mortis sedent ad dirigendos
fet ure on weg sibbe
pedes nostros in viam pacis

10.

CANTICUM SANCTE MARIE (LUKE 1. 46).

gemiclað sauwl min drihten   7 gefægenode
46. *Magnificat anima mea dominum* **47.** *Et exultavit*

70. From *woruldo* to *his* wr. on the illustration; part of the border of the
illustration er. to make room for this English and the corresponding French
of the other gloss. 79. Er. aft. *Onlihtan.* 10. 46. With *gemiclað*
begins a fresh hand; *Magnificat* is also glossed by *Magnifieð.*

gast   min   on gode   hælo   minre   for   he geseah
spiritus   meus   in   deo   salutari   meo   **48.** *Quia   respexit*

eadmodnesse   þinene   his   efne   soþlice   heononforð   eadige
humilitatem   ancillae   suae   ecce   enim   ex hoc   beatam

me seagað ealle   cneoressa   forðan þe dyde   me
me   dicent   omnes generationes   **49.**   *Quia   fecit michi*

miclan seo þe mehtig is 7 halig   name his   7
magna   qui   potens   est et sanctum   nomen eius   **50.** *Et*

mildheortnesse   his   fram   kynne   to   kynne   ondredende
misericordia   eius   a   progenie   in   progenies   timentibus

hine   he dyde   mihte   on earme his he tosteincte
eum   **51.** *Fecit   potentiam   in brachio suo   dispersit*

ofermode of mode heortan his   he asette rice 1 wlance
superbos   mente   cordis   sui   **52.** *Deposuit   potentes*

of setle 7 he upahof eaðmode   hingriende he gefylde
de sede et   exaltavit   humiles   **53.** *Esurientes   implevit*

of godum 7 welige he forlet idele 1 ælæte   he anfæng
bonis   et divites   dimisit   inanes   **54.** *Suscepit*

israel cnapen   his   geþancol mildheor[t]nesse his   swa
israel puerum suum recordatus   misericordiae   suae   **55.** *Si-*

swa   he sprec to fædrum   urum   abraham 7   sædsworne his
cut   locutus est ad patres   nostros   abraham et   semini   eius

on woruld 1 awuorld
in   secula

11.

CANTICUM SIMEONIS (LUKE 2. 29).

Nu   forlet   þeow   þinne drihten   æfter   word   þine
29. *Nunc dimittis servum tuum domine secundum verbum tuum*

on sibbe   forðan   gesegen   eagen mine   hela   ðine
in pace   **30.** *Quia   viderunt   oculi   mei   salutare tuum*

þet   ðu garewodest   beforan   ansyne   ælles   folkes
31. *Quod   parasti   ante   faciem omnium populorum*

leoht   to   awrigennesse   þeoda 7 wuldor folkes   ðines
32. *Lumen ad   revelationem gentium et gloriam plebis   tuae*

ISRAEL
israel

---

49. With *forðan* begins a fresh hand.   51. With *mihte* begins a fresh
hand.   55. *awuorld, l* wr. above the line.   11. 29. With *Nu* begins
a fresh hand.   31. From *þet* to *ansyne* wr. on the border of the illustration.

12.

[GLORIA IN EXCELSIS.]

wulder on heahnesse gode   7 on eorðan sib   manne
1. *Gloria in   excelsis   deo*   2. *Et in   terra   pax hominibus*

gódes   willun   We heriað þe   We bletsiað þe
bone   voluntatis   3. *Laudamus te*   4. *Benedicimus te*

    we   We wuldrieð þe   þankes we doð
5. *Adoramus te*   6. *Glorificamus te*   7. *Gracias agimus*

þe fore wuldre þine miclum   drihten godd kining
tibi propter gloriam tuam magnam   8. *Domine deus   rex*

heofonlic   God fæder ælmihtig   drihten sunu
caelestis   9. *Deus pater omnipotens*   10. *Domine fili*

ankenned helende crist   drihten god lamb godes sune
unigenite   iesu   christe   11. *Domine deus agnus dei filius*

fæderes   þu þe   synna middaneardes gemiltsa us
patris   12. *Qui tollis peccata   mundi   miserere nobis*

    þu þe   synna middeneardes onfoh beɔe ɪ halsunga ure
13. *Qui tollis peccata   mundi   suscipe deprecationem nostram*

    þu ðe sitest on þa swiþran healfe fæderes gemiltsa us
14. *Qui   sedes ad   dexteram   patris miserere nobis*

forðan þu ana halig   þu ana drihten   þu
15. *Quoniam tu solus sanctus*   16. *Tu solus dominus*   17. *Tu*

ana se hegesta helende crist   Mid haligum gaste on
solus altissimus iesu   criste   18. *Cum   sancto spiritu in*

wuldre godes fadres gealage ɪ sy swa
gloria   dei   patris   Amen

13.

[PATER NOSTER.]

fæder ure   þe ært on hefone sy gebletsod name ðin
1. *Pater noster qui es in caelis sanctificetur nomen tuum*

    cume rice þin   gewurðe willæ þin swa swa
2. *Adveniat regnum tuum*   3. *Fiat voluntas tua   sicut*

on heofone 7 on eorþan   breod ɪ hlaf ure degwamlich
in   caelo et in terra   4. *Panem nostrum cotidianum*

12. 11. From *god* to end of v. wr. on the illustration.

geof us to dæg   7 forgeof us ageltes ura swa swa
da nobis hodie   5. *Et dimitte nobis debita nostra sicut   et*

we forgeofen agiltenden urum   7 ne led us   on
nos dimittimus debitoribus nostris   6. *Et ne nos inducas in*

costunge   Ac alys us fram yfele swa beo hit
temptationem   7. *Sed libera nos a   malo   Amen*

14.

[CREDO.]

Ic gelefe on gode fædera ælwealdend ł ealmihtig sceppend
1. *Credo   in deum patrem   omnipotentem   creatorem*

heofones 7 eorðan 7 on helende   crist   suna his anlich
 caeli   et terrae et in iesum christum filium eius unicum

drihten   ure   Syo þe akynned is of ðam halig gaste
dominum nostrum   2. *Qui conceptus est de   spiritu sancto*

boran of M   pilate 7
natus ex maria virgine   3. *Passus sub pontio pilato*

on rode ahangen   dead   7 beberiged   he adun astæh to
  crucifixus   mortuus et sepultus   4.   *Descendit   ad*

hellæ ðriddan degge he aras fram deaþa   he astah
inferna tercia   die   resurrexit a   mortuis   5. *Ascendit*

to heofone sit on swi[ð]ran healfe godes fæderes   ealmihtig
ad caelos sedet ad   dexteram   dei   patris ` omnipotentis

þanen   he is to cumene 7 to demenna quiche 7   deade
inde   venturus   iudicare   vivos   et mortuos

Ic gelefe on halig   gast 7 on halig   gesomnunge
6. *Credo   in spiritum sanctum   sanctam   aecclesiam*

fulfremede halegan   himennesse   forgyfenysse   synna
catholicam sanctorum communionem remissionem peccatorum

flecsces uparisnesse   lif   eche   beo hit swa
carnis resurrectionem vitam aeternam   Amen

15.

[QUICUMQUE VULT.]

Swa hwa swa wile hal beon beforan ealle ðinge þearf
1. *Quicumque vult salvus esse   ante   omnia   opus*

14. 2. What is wanting aft. *M-* is cut out, somebody having stolen the tail of an illuminated capital *Q.*

is ꝥ he healde þane fulfremedon geleafan þane bute
est ut teneat catholicam fidem 2. *Quam nisi*

hwilc halne 7 unwemne gehealde buton tweon on ecnesse
quisque integram inviolatamque servaverit absque dubio in aeternum

he forwyrð Geleafe soðliche fulfremed þis is ꝥ enne
peribit 3. *Fides autem catholica haec est ut unum*

gode on þrynnysse 7 þrynnysse on annesse we arwurðien
deum in trinitate et trinitatem in unitate veneremur

7 na gemyngende hades 7 na spede syndriende
4. *Neque confundentes personas neque substantiam separantes*

Sum is soðliche had fæderes sum sunes sum hali
5. *Alia est enim persona patris alia filii alia spiritus*

gastes Ac fæderes 7 sunes 7 gastes haliges an is
sancti 6. *Sed patris et filii et spiritus sancti una est*

godcundnesse gelic wuldor efeneche swylc
divinitas equalis gloria coaeterna maiestas 7. *Qualis*

fæder swylc is sune swylc is se hali gast Vngesceapen
pater talis filius talis spiritus sanctus 8. *Increatus*

fader ungesceapen sune ungesceapen gast halig Un-
pater increatus filius increatus spiritus sanctus 9. *Im-*

ametenlic fæder unametenlic sune unametenlic gast halig
mensus pater immensus filius immensus spiritus sanctus

ece fæder ece sune ece gast halig
10. *Eternus pater aeternus filius aeternus spiritus sanctus*

7 þah na þrie ece ac an ece Swa swa
11. *Et tamen non tres aeterni sed unus aeternus* 12. *Sicut*

na þry ungesceapene ne þry unametegude ac an un-
non tres increati nec tres immensi sed unus in-

gesceapen 7 an unametegod gelic ælmihtig fæder
creatus et unus immensus 13. *Similiter omnipotens pater*

ælmihtig sunu ælmigti gast halig and þaeh
omnipotens filius omnipotens spiritus sanctus 14. *Et tamen*

na þryo ælmihtige ac an ælmihtig swa god
non tres omnipotentes sed unus omnipotens 15. *Ita deus*

fader god sune god gast halig And þeah na
pater deus filius deus spiritus sanctus 16. *Et tamen non*

þryo godas ac an is god Swa drihten fæder
tres dii sed unus est deus 17. *Ita dominus pater*

---

15. 1. *healde* on er. *geleafan* on er. ? 3. Let. er. aft. *we.* 12. Let.
er. bef. *ungesceapene.*

drihten sune drihten   gast   halig   And þeah na
dominus filius dominus spiritus sanctus   18. *Et   tamen non*

þryo drihtnes ac an is drihten   Forðan swa swa
tres domini sed unus est dominus   19. *Quia   sicut*

synderliche anne gehwylcne   had   gode oððe drihten
singillatim unam quamque   personam deum aut dominum

andetten cristenre soðfestnesse we beoð genyd   Swa þrio
confiteri christiana veritate   compellimur   20. *Ita tres*

godes oððe drihtnes cweþan of cyriclicre æfestnesse we beoð
deos aut dominos dicere catholica religione   prohi-

forboden   Fader of nanum is geworðen ne gesceapen
bemur   21. *Pater a nullo est factus nec creatus*

ne gecenned   Sune of fæder anum is ne geworðen
nec genitus   22. *Filius a patre solo est non factus*

na gesceapen ac akenned   Gast   halig
nec creatus sed genitus   23. *Spiritus sanctus*

fram fæder 7 sune na geworðen ne gesceapen ne
a   patre et filio non factus nec creatus nec

akenned ac forðgewitende   An eornostlice fader na
genitus sed procedens   24. *Unus ergo   pater non*

þryo faderes an sune nawith ðreo sunes an hali gast
tres patres unus filius non tres filii unus spiritus sanctus

nawith ðreo halie gastes   7 on þissan þrinnesse
non   tres spiritus sancti   25. *Et in hac   trinitate*

nan þing hærest oððe læter nan þing mare oððe leasse
nichil prius aut posterius nichil maius aut minus

    Ac ealle þrio hades   euenece him beoð 7 euenlice
26. *Sed tote tres persone coaeternae sibi sunt et coequales*

    swa þ þurh ealle swa swa nu ió bufen gecweðen is 7
27. *Ita ut per omnia sicut iam supra dictum est et*

þrynnesse on annysse 7 annysse on þrynnesse to arwurðienne sy
trinitas in unitate et unitas in trinitate   veneranda   sit

    se þe wile eornostlice hal beon swa be þare þrynnesse
28. *Qui. vult ergo   salvus esse ita de   trinitate*

angite   Ac neodbehefe is to þere ecen hele þeð
sentiat   29. *Sed necessarium ad aeternam salutem ut*

<hr>

18. *drihtnes, t* wr. above the line.   19. *drihten,* MS.=*drihtnen,* with first
n dotted.   24. With *sune* begins a fresh hand.   26. With *Ac* begins a
fresh hand.

he flescnesse witodlice drihtnes ures helendes cristes getrywlice
incarnationem quoque domini nostri iesu christi fideliter

gelefe Is eornostlice geleafe riht þeð we gelefen 7
credut 30. *Est ergo fides recta ut credamus et*

andetten þeð drihten ure helend crist godes sune god 7
confiteamur quia dominus noster iesus christus dei filius deus et

man is God is of spede fæderes ær woruld acenned
homo est 31. *Deus est ex substantia patris ante secula genitus*

7 mann is of spede modor on wurulde acenned Fulfremed
et homo est ex substantia matris in seculo natus 32. *Perfectus*

god fulfremed man of saule gesceadwisre 7 menniscum flesce
deus perfectus homo ex anima rationali et humana carne

wuniende efenlic fæder æfter godcundnysse læsse
subsistens 33. *Equalis patri secundum divinitatem minor*

þam fæder æfter menniscnesse Syo þeac he byo god
patre secundum humanitatem 34. *Qui licet deus sit*

7 man na twu þæh hweðere ac an is crist An
et homo non duo tamen sed unus est christus 35. *Unus*

soðlice na of gecyrrednysse godcundnysse on flesce ac
autem non conversione divinitatis in carnem sed

of afangennysse mennisclicnysse on gode An eallunge
assumptione humanitatis in deum 36. *Unus omnino*

na of gemenge spede ac of annesse hades Witodlice
non confusione substantiae sed unitate persone 37. *Nam*

swa swa saul 'gesceadwislic 7 fles an is mann swa god 7
sicut anima rationalis et caro unus est homo ita deus et

man an is crist Sye þeolade pine for healðe hure
homo unus est christus 38. *Qui passus est pro salute nostra*

lithte into helle 7 on ðan þriddan deige aras off deaðe
descendit ad inferos tercia die resurrexit a mortuis

Asteh to heouenan sitt on þes feaderes godes swiððran hond
39. *Ascendit ad caelos sedet ad dextram dei patris*

almithtin 7 þeonan is to cumane 7 deman quican 7 deadan
omnipotentis inde venturus est iudicare vivos et mortuos

7 to whæs tocuman alle menn sculen arisan mid
40. *Ad cuius adventum omnes homines resurgere habent cum*

---

30. *andetten*, MS.=*andentten*, with second *n* dotted. 32. *wuniende, i* in
pl. of *er*. 36. *gemenge*, fin. let. *er*. 38. With *Sye* begins a fresh hand
(to end of MS.).

heore lichoman 7 geouan antsweare off heore ahgen wercan
corporibus suis et reddituri sunt de factis propriis

mid sceadwisnesse 7 ða god duden sculen fearan to
rationem **41.** *Et qui bona egerunt ibunt in*

hechan liue 7 to seoðan ða ðe huuel duden into hechan fure
vitam aeternam qui vero mala in ignem aeternum

þis his ðe hilæua himeane ðe hwilc mann ne hileaueð
42. *Haec est fides catholica quam nisi quisque fideliter*

festlice 7 treowlice ne meagen heo hiborhgen beon
firmiterque crediderit salvus esse non poterit

16.

[HIC PSALMUS PROPRIE SCRIBTUS DAVID EXTRA NUMERUM CUM
PUGNAVIT CUM GOLIA.]

þes ilca psalm is iwriten bi seoluan dauide 7 is wiðutan
Hic psalmus proprie scribitur david et extra

ðere tale of dan hundrede 7 fifti psalman 7 ðeosne ilcan he
numerum

machede ða he feath wið goliam þes psalm nis nawiht on
cum pugnavit cum goliath hic psalmus in ebreis

hebreisse bocan hach ða hundseouenti bigueðeres othðe
codicibus non habetur sed nec a septuaginta inquit inter-

latimeres hine habbað idon to þan heoðran 7 forþi he is to
pretibus additus est et iccirco repu-

ascunianne Ic wes lest imo[n]g mine broððran 7 alra
diandus **1.** *Pusillus eram inter fratres meos et ad-*

gugest in mines feader huse ic wes sceapheorda mines feader
olescentior in domo patris mei pascebam oves patris mei

Heo[n]dan mine warhten organan 7 fingras mine gearcaden
2. *Manus meae fecerunt organum et digiti mei aptaverunt*

psalterium 7 wha talde mine lauerde off me
psalterium **3.** *Et quis annuntiavit domino meo de me*

Himseolf þe lauerd himseolf off allan hiheret Himseolf
4. *Ipse dominus ipse omnium exauditor* **5.** *Ipse*

---

16. Title taken from Vespas. Psalter. From *þes ilca* to *ða he* wr. on the
border of the illumination; the Latin from *Hic psalmus* to *repudiandus* wr. in
red. *hebreisse*, fin. *e* nearly er.

ansente   his engel 7 nom me from mines feader sceapan 7
misit angelum suum et tulit me   de   ovibus patris mei   et

smirædæ me on þere miltse his smiræleuse   Mine broꝺꝺre
unxit me in misericordia unctionis suae   6. Fratres mei

gode 7 michelæ 7 ne wes on heom godwillendæ þe lauerd
boni et   magni et non fuit beneplacitum in eis   domino

   Ic heodæ   ongean anan uncuꝺꝺan 7 he me cursadæ on his
7. *Exivi   obviam   alienigene   et maledixit michi in sim-*

godes anlicnesse   Ic soꝺliches atæh from him his hagen
  ulacris suis   8. Ego autem evaginato ab eo   ipsius

sweord 7 achearf his heauod off 7 binom   þet ædwit off
gladio   amputavi caput eius et abstuli opprobrium a

israheles sunan
filiis israel

     7. *anlicnesse*, MS. = *anlitnesse*.

www.ingramcontent.com/pod-product-compliance
Lightning Source LLC
Chambersburg PA
CBHW021100030726
47496CB00006B/1921